WAVE-TOUCHED

DAUGHTER OF VANRIS
BOOK TWO

NIKKI McCORMACK

ISBN: 979-8-9903922-9-8
First Edition 2025

Published by
Elysium Books
Bellevue, WA

Written by Nikki McCormack
(https://nikkimccormack.com/)
Cover Design by Robert Crescenzio
(https://robertcrescenzio.artstation.com/)
Map Design by Melissa Nash
Typesetting and Design by Brian C. Short
Editing by Alexander Lockwood

•

To all the authors, artists, and other creators who courageously share their authentic selves with the world. Keep making magic.

•

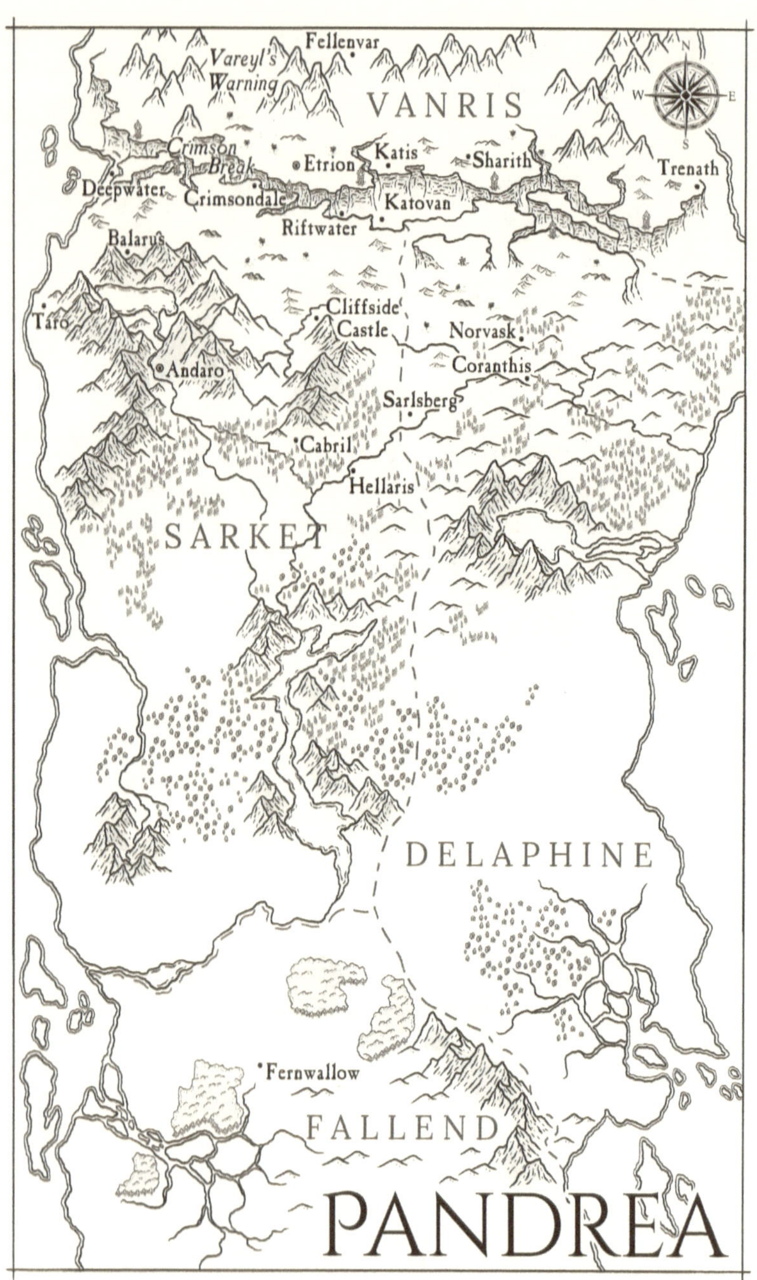

VANRIS
Fellenvar
Vareyl's Warning
Crimson Break
Etrion
Katis
Sharith
Trenath
Deepwater
Crimsondale
Katovan
Riftwater
Balarus
Taro
Cliffside Castle
Norvask
Coranthis
Andaro
Sarlsberg
Cabril
Hellaris
SARKET
DELAPHINE
Fernwallow
FALLEND
PANDREA
N
S
E
W

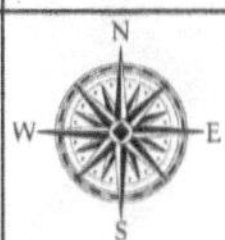

THAELIS ISLANDS

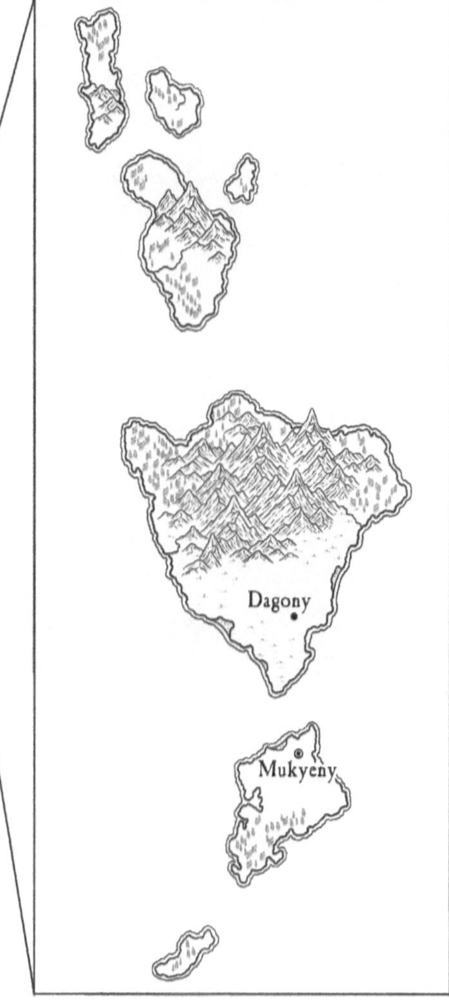

The fort overlooking the ocean at the south-western corner of Vanris was built of the same black stone used in the border watchtowers and much of the city of Etrion. It was odd how just the sight of that stone made Veyl homesick for the black city even while she dreaded leaving the ocean behind. Weary after the voyage from Thaelis and heartsick from losing Lorek in the Sarketi attack on their ship, she followed her grandfather, Dhomvalen Arhk, through the grounds and into the fort's main keep. The two Thaelian officers, Jinau and Nalika, accompanied them, along with Arhk's trio of elite personal guards.

Lorek's death hung heavy over a brief reunion inside the entrance with Gannon and Ahrin's father, Darro, and his sharp-tempered tehnaak, Kince. Despite the sorrow weighing on them all, their warm welcomes eased some of the feeling she had of no longer belonging in her own homeland, brought on at least in part by the role she had assumed as an ambassador for Thaelis. These people, members of her father's tehsheyn—his bonded spirit family—were as much her family in a way as her grandfather. Still, the Thaelian uniform she wore forced a distance between them, so she took her comfort from an unexpected source. Whenever they passed an open window, the rumble of the nearby ocean reassured her, provided she didn't dwell too deeply on her connection to those untamable waters.

Ahrin, Gannon, and Iyvalin disappeared into a private room where they could grieve. Tath, the twins' mother, and Nerith, both healers who had firsthand experience losing a tehnaak, followed them inside, bringing food, drink, and an abundance of empathy. Veyl watched them shut the door with an ache of longing. Her new role didn't afford her the opportunity to join them as they mourned.

Instead, she followed Arhk to a meeting room where some attendants were also delivering food and drink. Kince, Darro, and the officer in charge of the fort joined them. At Veyl's insistence, Jinau and Nalika also took seats at the table. She hoped to set a precedent for both sides by including them in proceedings from the start. Arhk's elite guards stood along the wall behind him, their intimidating stares locked on the two Thaelians.

Arhk eyed her new companions. "What discipline of mind-crafters are you?"

"Charmer," Jinau stated in his concise, less-than-charming way, his amber eyes taking in their company and the stark, utilitarian surroundings.

Veyl caught the faintest hint of a smirk on Arhk's lips before he schooled it away and shifted his expectant gaze to Nalika.

"I am an Evoker, Dhomvalen."

Arhk's expression hardened, and he gestured to one of his guards. "Ahnvaris Zafyr is an Evoker as well. She will know if you use your ability here. Be warned that we will consider doing so a hostile act. I strongly advise against it."

Nalika's lips pressed into a tight line. The look she gave Zafyr when she nodded her understanding was far from friendly, but she didn't seem foolish enough to believe she had a choice now that she was among the minority. Seeing the woman forced to rein in her temper wasn't nearly as satisfying as Veyl would have liked it to be.

Arhk's icy regard came to rest on her. "Let me see this agreement, Ahninveth."

She had an instant yearning to be anywhere else. How would he react to the demands the Thaelian council made in those pages? What would he think of the terms she had agreed to, such as returning to Thaelis when this was over or maintaining the zenyal bond with Jinau? Would he consider her a fool for having signed it? He might be her grandfather, but he would always be Dhomvalen, the military leader of Vanris, first. That was just his nature.

Drawing a shallow breath to brace herself, she reached into the satchel and pulled out the papers, handing them to him. After neatly unfolding them and smoothing them out on the table, he inclined his head to read, some of his long, white-blond hair falling forward, conveniently masking his reactions from the Thaelians sitting off to that side. Veyl followed his progress from across the table, remembering every line from the hours she had spent studying their contents. The others took advantage of the opportunity to drink and partake of the fruit and bread. Hungry though she might be, Veyl's roiling stomach and dancing nerves aggressively rejected that distraction.

Arhk's expression remained diplomatically neutral until the exact moment she expected it to change, then darkness crept in at the edges of his eyes and pressure increased in the room. A ripple of tension moved through the group, most of them fully aware of how his Frightener ability manifested. Though his ability couldn't manifest her fears because she was now a Frightener too, Veyl had somehow become more attuned to its other effects. Was that normal? It didn't seem like the right time to ask.

Arhk's gaze rose to Jinau, his voice dangerously calm. "You have the audacity to assume such control over a khesran of Vanris?"

The other three Vanrians at the table looked between Arhk and Jinau now, unspoken questions on their lips, though none of them appeared willing to step in front of Arhk's anger and ask.

Jinau didn't flinch before the dhomvalen's fury or shrink from the darkening of his pale, gray-green eyes. "The Thaelian council ordered me to hold this bond solely as a method of protecting our people from her uncontrolled Frightener ability. I intend Ahninveth Veyl no harm, nor do I desire to demean her."

Trying to ignore how disconcerting it was to hear Jinau use her title and actual name for once, Veyl said, "I agreed to leave it this way." She had consented to those terms under duress because she believed she had little choice if she wanted to convince them to send her home, but the circumstances didn't matter now. She needed to keep the situation from falling apart before negotiations got underway, or her role as ambassador would become meaningless. They hadn't even reached Etrion yet. "Please, Dhomvalen, Ahndhomen Jinau suffered injuries shielding me from the explosion when Sarket's ships attacked ours. I believe you can take him at his word when he says he means me no harm."

Arhk's nostrils flared as he drew a breath, and he clenched his jaw, the black slowly retreating from his eyes.

"Pardon, Dhomvalen Arhk, but to what control are you referring?" Kince asked, absently brushing some of his long blond hair away from his face, exposing the symbols of the dark blue ke'hanoath tattoo on that cheek.

"They have tethered her to this man using a zenyal bond."

The three still looked lost.

"It is a type of nonreciprocal bond that allows the dominant half of the pairing the ability to, among other things, inflict debilitating mental pain on the submissive one." Arhk's voice was thick with disgust as he explained it. "A method of control that was outlawed soon after the first Vanrians set foot on Pandrea."

Arhk turned his attention back to the agreement and resumed reading. It was the thoughtfulness that had stolen over Jinau in response to his words that intrigued Veyl now. Intense calculations were working behind his amber eyes, and she itched for insight into what they were.

Arhk folded the document and handed it back to her. "You signed your name to these pages. For now, it seems, you must abide by the commitment you made to Thaelis. We can revisit that, and the other terms discussed therein, once we reach Etrion."

He turned his attention to Darro and the officer in charge of the fort, apparently not bothered by the scowls the implications behind his words drew from Nalika and Jinau. "Sarket's attack on any ship in Vanrian waters is a breach of their fealty agreement. Not that it is the first such infraction they have committed in recent months, but it was the most public and one that will necessitate a response sooner than we might have preferred."

"Is Jaysen here?" Veyl asked before either man could respond.

Arhk's gaze returned to her. "The crown prince has gone into hiding in Etrion for now. Sarket is not yet aware that he lives."

"And he did not vouch for the Thaelians who brought him here?" She had asked him on the beach, but frustration compelled her to ask again, hoping that he might at least elaborate on his earlier answer.

Arhk shook his head, confusion furrowing his brow.

"As I said before, he did not. In fact, he encouraged us to imprison them and use them as leverage against their country. Why would he have defended his captors?"

Jaysen had not merely ignored her request, he had done the exact opposite of what she wanted of him. Granted, she was never able to explain the entire situation to him in Dagony, but she had asked him to work with Kyril. The Feral ahnkreth must have discussed his intentions with Jaysen on the voyage over. What convinced him to turn against them? Not that the Thaelian attack on Deepwater and their abduction wasn't reason enough for him to want to. Jaysen hadn't gotten to know people in Dagony the way she did. They never wanted him in Thaelis to begin with. But she had dared to hope the bond they had shared would be enough to get him to trust her. She was unlikely to understand why he chose not to until she talked to him.

"It doesn't matter right now. We need to continue to Etrion. We can straighten all of this out there. There are negotiations to be held, and I wish to see the rest of my family." She stood. "We've wasted enough time."

Arhk rose, gesturing for the others to remain seated. "I would like to speak to my granddaughter alone for a moment. Stay and refresh yourselves."

Nalika shifted as if she meant to follow, but Jinau caught her arm and shook his head. When she settled, he met Veyl's eyes, and she nodded, offering him a look of gratitude. He answered with a slight nod of his own. She would grant him her trust, but she expected the same in return, and it appeared as though he would give it, for now.

Veyl followed Arhk through a door and up a narrow flight of stairs to a private study on the second floor. He strode to a window at the back of the room, looking over the outer fort wall toward the ocean. Walking up beside him, she gazed out at the water and the ships moving beyond the shore. The mighty expanse beckoned, and the prospect of leaving it behind sharpened the sorrow she was trying to keep buried.

"We have a Bondmaker here, Veyl."

She was silent for a moment, considering his words. He was offering to remove the zenyal bond, but it would mean breaking the agreement with Thaelis before negotiations had even gotten underway. Not the most promising place to start from. "No. I will stand by the pages I signed as long doing so doesn't bring more harm to my people."

Arhk turned to consider her. "Why? The Thaelians cannot touch you here."

She faced him, a flush of determination warming her. "Because I want to protect the Vanrians who are still on Thaelis. And because the people of Thaelis are good people, even if their leaders leave something to be desired. I refuse to see any of them harmed by this conflict if I can prevent it. Besides, I know Ahndhomen Jinau will not abuse the power of the bond. Seh'hali ne Kunua means Daughter of the Ocean. The natives on Thaelis, the Qwilki, believe I am blessed by their ocean gods. He is, as best I can tell, more Qwilki at heart than Thaelian. He would not harm me unless he felt he had no other choice."

"He had best not," Arhk stated flatly. "It will not end well for him if he does."

Veyl removed the edge from his words with a fond smile. "I missed you."

He looked her over, his gaze taking in her garments and the decorations in her hair. "It is unsettling to see you in their uniform, wearing their trinkets on your Vanrian braids."

She touched the spiral shell, hearing the echo of Jinau's remark in her head, noting how the one Kyril had given her was always the one she reached for.

"These tokens are a Qwilki tradition. As is the hair stain many of the Thaelian crew members use. There is much I could tell you about why I want to protect them, but perhaps it makes more sense to save all that for when my mother and father are also present."

Arhk drew a breath, sorrow pinching his brows as he considered her. "You are not the same young woman who left for Balarus with her parents. You have clearly grown and learned a great deal in a relatively short time. I hate to imagine what you must have suffered for the experience to have changed you this much."

Veyl looked out at the ocean again. Memories flashed through her mind. Of the attack in Deepwater and the severing of her renewed tehnaak bond with Jaysen, of the voyage to Thaelis and her struggles with Kyril and her ability, and that moment of despair when she had tried to kill herself. And of when she lashed out at Gannon with her power and shattered the trust of her dearest friends, one of whom she would never have the chance to make it up to.

But it wasn't all pain and misery. There was her newly discovered affinity for the ocean and the way Ceris had expressed a fondness for her from the start that left her feeling a little less alone. Many people in Thaelis had welcomed her warmly enough that she had felt compelled to protect them from the Ukhen'kya and to save Nagi from the kel'inuk. Through it all wove the thread of that strange and unexpected connection she had developed with the man who had taken her from her home. Her cheeks flushed at the memory of his touch, his kiss, of everything she had given him.

"It feels like years since I left here," she murmured.

"I am skeptical of your support for these people," Arhk said, drawing her attention to him. "I will not pretend otherwise, and I do not envy you the task of convincing your parents to negotiate with them after what they did to you and so many others. You have grown stronger out of necessity, I fear. But I will stand by you so long as I believe you are the one behind your convictions, and they are not the product of some outside influence."

She looked deep into those eyes that matched her own. The one person who could truly understand the challenges she faced with her ability. "Thank you."

He stepped close to place a kiss on her forehead, then gestured toward the door. "Let us rejoin the others. We have a few days of travel still ahead to return you to where you belong, and I am curious to see what your vision of the future regarding our relations with these people looks like."

Veyl glanced out the window once more. She was finally back in Vanris, ready to negotiate with her own parents on behalf of those who had taken her from them. She had no intention of letting the Thaelian council come out on top, but she hoped to find a way the people of both countries might avoid more suffering. Whether that was possible didn't matter. She intended to try.

The sun blazed down on the desert, making a mirage of the massive black city of Etrion on the horizon for several miles before its edges became more distinct. Veyl could see the towering spires of the palace and a few other structures coming into focus around the time they slowed, letting the horses walk for a bit to rest.

The ride to Etrion from the coast took a little less than three days. Veyl traveled with Arhk, his trio of elite guards, and Jinau. The modest size of their group allowed them to travel at greater speed. They had run into a transportation problem when the time came to leave the fort. There were no horses on the islands of Thaelis, nor much need for mounts of any kind. Most locations were reasonably accessible either on foot or by boat. The bigger islands had a few small herds of large deer called kednu that people used as pack animals and occasional mounts. Jinau professed to having ridden them in races against other children on his island growing up. His quick competence when they put him on a horse supported that tale and made it possible for him to travel with their group.

Nalika, like Kyril, grew up sailing and had no experience handling a mount of any kind. Gannon, Ahrin, and Iyvalin were heading to Etrion as well, but they were traveling along with a wagon carrying Lorek's body. Darro, Kince, Nerith, and Tath stayed back to ride with them and with Nalika, who would make use of the seat on the wagon. Veyl got the impression that the separation of the two Thaelians pleased Arhk, in that it would give the two Vanrian parties a chance to assess them individually. Nalika had grumbled about it, but Jinau appeared entirely unconcerned.

Arhk kept a demanding pace, allowing five hours of rest at night and a few brief breaks during the day, more for the sake of the horses than their riders. They changed out mounts at each of the watchtowers between the coast and Etrion to avoid injuring the animals with the speed they maintained. With the city and her family so close now, it was all Veyl could do not to push her horse to run ahead, but she stayed with the others, giving the animals a much-needed respite.

Jinau rode alongside her, behind Arhk and his guards. The Thaelian ahndhomen had seemed troubled by the massive black watchtowers along Vanris's southern border. He appeared even more so now, gazing upon the looming black walls of a city designed using aggressive angles deliberately evocative of bladed weapons.

"Are all your cities like this one?"

Veyl welcomed the distraction of his question. "No. Etrion was just being built when war broke out with the southern kingdoms. The architect's goal, once that happened, was to make it so intimidating that no one would dare to attack it. He took his design inspiration from Vareyl's Warning, the black crag formation to the north of us."

His eyes followed the line of her finger to the enormous spires of black rock jutting from the landscape on the horizon. "What began the war?"

Veyl cracked a smile. "Would you believe it started with a Charmer looking to impress a girl?"

He responded with a humorless chuckle. "I would."

"Our southern neighbors decided they didn't want us here once they discovered some of us had abilities that could manipulate minds." She considered him for a moment; the harsh angles of his features made more severe by his ever-stern expression. A hint of danger, of threat, hung about him, reinforced by the way his eyes seemed to take in everything in a glance and the casual ease with which he carried himself. "You don't strike me as a Charmer. Most of the Charmers I have known are more…"

"Engaging? Charismatic?" He offered. "Charmers are notorious for causing mischief, particularly the younger ones, but do not doubt that power. It can be as disturbing and dangerous in the right hands as your Frightener ability."

Arhk slowed his mount to fall back alongside her, casting a look full of dark suspicion at Jinau. "What exactly do you do in Thaelis, Ahndhomen?"

Jinau met his eyes, his expression as guarded as the dhomvalen's. "I solve problems."

Arhk nodded, his mouth setting in a grim line.

"Not…" Veyl looked between them, then settled her gaze on Jinau. "Like an assassin?"

"It isn't always about killing, but for simplicity's sake, that's close enough."

A chill swept through her, that darkness he had spoken of on their journey over becoming more literal. "What *problems* have you solved?"

Arhk gave her a hard look. "I believe the horses have gotten enough rest if you are ready to bring this journey to an end."

If his goal was to divert her from the subject, he had chosen the perfect way to go about it. She wanted nothing in the world more than to see the rest of her family and Jaysen. All the challenges that awaited her in the days to come would be worth it just for that. A reunion

Lorek and his family would never have.

That thought subdued her excitement as they broke into a fast trot, and she focused her energy on managing her weight in the saddle to make it easier on her weary horse. When they reached the main entrance, the black gates with dark metal spikes on their fronts stood open. Two guards on the ground spotted Arhk and hailed him. They noticed her in the next moment, both individuals she had worked with around the city.

"Khesran Veyl!" one exclaimed, grinning excitedly as the other shouted, "You're back!"

"I knew Dhomvalen Arhk would be the one to find you," the first declared.

The smug look he gave his companion told her they probably had a wager going, and he had just won. She wasn't sure whether she should be amused or offended by that.

"Open the side passage," Arhk ordered before she could respond.

They continued through the gates and Jinau's eyes widened a fraction as he got his first glimpse of the great city. Etrion boasted within its walls multiple barracks with training grounds, two vast academies, extensive neighborhoods, taverns, markets, beast habitats, and the grand palace with its highest spires towering over it all.

"Welcome to Etrion, the southern capital of Vanris." Veyl struggled to hold her mount back beside him, the animal prancing in response to the flutter of excited energy coming from her.

Jinau's brows rose a fraction. "You have more than one capital?"

"Yes. Our original capital, now the northern capital, is Doran, several days' travel beyond Vareyl's Warning. Etrion is home to the largest kanodrak and tethdrak populations in Vanris now. It was strictly a military city before the war ended."

"The councilors are fools," Jinau muttered.

She nudged her mount closer. "Why do you say that?"

He kept his voice low. "They arrogantly believed any new Vanrian civilization could not be greater than Thaelis, at least as we were before the Devastation. When our ancestors from the district of Thaelis left the original homeland, the larger population that remained was working to amass enough ships to bring more beasts and medicinal plants with them. The Thaelian leaders believed those who lingered would not have time to accomplish their goals before being forced to flee and that they would suffer much greater losses because of it. It appears they not only succeeded in what they set out to do but have since thrived here."

"To be fair, they did lose hundreds of people because they stayed as long as they did, but on Pandrea, they recovered and came back stronger in time."

Jinau nodded. "That I can see. I can also see that this land must be rich in resources. By its isolated nature as an island nation, Thaelis is less so."

"Did you wish to return home or merely loiter at the city gates?" Arhk asked her, turning his shrewd gaze on them.

The doors to the large, enclosed passage that followed the inside of the city wall around to the palace stood open, waiting for them. The last stretch before she could finally step foot within the walls of the palace again. They urged their horses toward the entrance, stopping abruptly when a familiar voice shouted her name, drawing their attention back to the gate.

Veyl turned to see her father galloping up on Niskenya. The massive, vaguely feline predator, her silvery-gray scaled hide picking up a satiny sheen in the bright sunlight, skidded to a stop behind them. The lack of reaction from the horses that would normally be her prey made it clear he had used his Feral ability to assume control of them. Veyl leapt from her mount, hitting the ground a heartbeat before her father did, and rushed into his arms, knocking him back against the huge kanodrak, who grunted, but stood her ground, displaying an uncommon level of tolerance.

Joyful tears flowed as he hugged her so tightly she could barely breathe, and she loved it. Being smothered in his desperate embrace let her be a child again, if only for a moment, and she clung to him, burying her face in his shoulder.

"Never do that again," he said in a voice choked with emotion.

She sobbed a laugh. "Get abducted?"

"Yes."

"I have no plans to."

He held onto her a moment longer, as if afraid she might disappear. When he eased them apart, she took one of his hands to maintain contact. Niskenya leaned in and nudged Veyl's shoulder with the external bone armor on her head, knocking her a step to the side. It was a powerful show of affection considering the beast had little interest in anyone aside from her father most of the time. He looked her over, a slight furrow forming in his brow that she suspected she knew the cause of. Then he glanced at the rest of the group, his gaze lingering on Jinau a moment longer than the others before settling on Arhk.

"Did they send anyone else back?"

"We should discuss this in a less public setting," Arhk evaded, glancing meaningfully toward the palace.

Her father nodded, releasing Veyl's hand long enough to swing up on Niskenya. Then he removed his foot from the stirrup and reached down to her. Jinau was staring at the kanodrak with the look of a formerly blind man seeing the world for the first time as she swung up on its back behind her father. What was it like for him to encounter this beast, a creature his ancestors had revered, in the flesh for the first time?

Veyl wrapped her arms around her father and leaned against his back. Niskenya carried them through the city, too large and untamed to be comfortable in the enclosed side passage. The kanodrak was more of a partner to her father, with express opinions of her own about how to do things, than a companion like Irith. Speaking of whom…

A flicker of panic rose in Veyl. "Where's Irith?"

Her father had one hand over her arm where it rested around his waist, maintaining the reassuring contact, and he gave it a small squeeze. "He's with Jethan. Niskenya wanted to escape the habitat and I the city, so we went out for a run. Irith's gotten a little old for such energetic adventures. I spotted your group approaching with the sandhawk I was scouting with." His grip on her arm tightened along with his voice when he added, "I could hardly believe what I was seeing."

Fresh tears stung her eyes as she hugged her arms more firmly around him. They had so many urgent matters to discuss, but those could wait a little longer. She simply wanted to appreciate being home.

"*Did* they send anyone else back?" he pressed, his low voice making the question for her alone this time.

Veyl heaved a sigh, but she couldn't be angry with him for denying her the chance to bask in the moment given all that had happened. Her parents had a responsibility to Vanris and its people. "They let me bring the twins and their tehnaaks back with me, but Sarketi ships attacked us off the coast and… They killed Lorek." Her voice cracked.

"Three Sarketi ships," Arhk confirmed, having eased back beside them to listen. "Your daughter effectively disabled them with her Frightener ability. We had a simple task of taking them prisoner from there, but such a public incident could force a confrontation sooner than we would like."

Her father nodded, saying nothing more, though Veyl could feel the fresh tension in his back. That he didn't question the comment about her Frightener ability told her Jaysen must have shared what he knew of it with them. When they reached the palace, Arhk passed their horses to the stable hands, and Niskenya settled in the courtyard, an intimidating sentinel. Inside the entrance, her father beckoned over the first attendant he saw.

"Khemron Kasiel." The woman's eyes widened when they lit upon Veyl before she bowed. "How can I be of assistance?"

"Find Khevarin Velara and Khesran Tavin and send them to the…" He hesitated, looking at Jinau, then at Veyl, or rather at the uniform she wore, as if genuinely considering the implications of it all for the first time. His expression darkened. "Send them to the war room."

"Yes, Khemron." The attendant bowed again before hurrying off.

The moment the woman left, he turned to Jinau, who had been taking in the elegant interior of the palace with its marble floors and polished black stone walls. Lush floral arrangements sat on tables along those walls and in tastefully decorated alcoves, adding splashes of vibrant color. He was too observant not to notice that her father's attention had settled on him, so he faced the khemron, inclining his head in a gesture of respect.

"I am Ahndhomen Charmer Jinau, Khemron."

"Ahndhomen? You're not part of the ahnkreth's fleet, then?"

"He is not." Veyl inserted herself into the conversation. She wasn't ready to confront the zenyal issue with her parents, though with Arhk there, they likely wouldn't avoid it for long. "Ahndhomen Jinau–"

"Veyl!"

She spun. "Uncle Jeth!"

Her father's tehnaak caught her up in his arms and lifted her, spinning her around in a manner entirely inappropriate for greeting a visiting ahninveth and ambassador, but she didn't much care. When he set her down, he drew her into a hug for an instant before releasing her. Irith, her father's aging cliff cat, nudged in and came up on his hind legs, setting his paws on her shoulders. He licked her twice in the face with his abrasive tongue before she giggled and shoved her hands between them to shield herself from the onslaught.

At a fond, but stern, glance from her father, likely accompanied by some mental direction, the cat dropped to the floor and Veyl crouched with him, wrapping her arms around his neck long enough to press her cheek against his fuzzy head.

"I missed you, old beast," she murmured.

As she straightened, she caught a candid look of un-ease that passed between her father and his tehnaak. She also noticed the shadows under her father's eyes and the lines of worry that etched his brow. Guilt twisted in her chest, knowing she brought him the welcome news of her return, drizzled like a sauce over the top of a foul-tasting wagonload of complications.

"Let us continue to the war room," Arhk prompted.

Veyl and her father answered with the same nod.

They were almost to the door when her mother and brother, along with their tehnaaks, Keyla and Ellaris, Jethan's wife and daughter, came around the corner. Veyl rushed to them, losing herself in another series of warm, tearful embraces. Something about that overwhelming load of affection and emotion was exhausting. Not that she would trade it for anything else in the world. Being once again among the people who loved her was more than she had dared to hope for as little as a week ago, but her heart and mind were growing fatigued, and they hadn't even gotten to the difficult parts yet. She yearned to curl up on a couch with her family and cry until her tears were spent, and she could laugh again.

Her mother wouldn't let go of her hand when they turned to enter the war room, keeping hold of it so Veyl had no choice but to accompany her to the head of the table alongside her father, all the while using her free hand to dab at tears that trickled down her cheeks with a handkerchief. Her mother cast a venomous look at Jinau when he took a spot at the oval table to Veyl's right. The Thaelian ahndhomen remained unnervingly calm as they gathered in the oval war room around a large oval table with a massive stoneglass and crystal candelabra of the same size and shape hanging overhead. Wherever Jinau got his composure, she wished he would share some of it. Although not if it came from the same place that made him able to kill without remorse. Arhk possessed a similar bearing. How much darkness did one have to accept in themselves to perfect that?

Just as Arhk opened his mouth to speak, the door flew open and Jaysen rushed in. Where there should have been only happiness at seeing him, there was a troubling mix of joy and uncertainty, the latter a cruel blade twisting in her chest. Extracting her hand from her mother's, she stepped around the table and let him pull her into his arms, returning his embrace and clinging to memories from their childhood for a moment to quell her unease.

"I'm never letting you out of my sight again," he whispered.

Veyl swallowed back more tears. By the Break, she was tired. She let him hold her a second longer, then eased away and gestured to the table as she returned to her mother's side.

"Seh'hali," Jinau murmured.

Veyl drew a deep breath and leapt into the storm before Arhk could do so ahead of her. "There are a great many matters we all need to discuss. Chief among them is the fact that the vessel we arrived on was set upon by Sarketi ships in Vanrian waters. An attack that cost Lorek his life."

Ellaris gasped, and Tavin stepped closer to his teh-naak, though he didn't seem aware that he had done so. Jaysen, who had taken a spot on Tavin's other side, across from Veyl, lowered his gaze, anger in the set of his jaw that matched what she saw in her parents' eyes when she looked at them.

"As much as I wish I could be here with you solely as your daughter and a khesran of Vanris, I'm afraid that is not the case, as I'm sure you suspected from my attire. I have accepted the role of Ahninveth na sek and Ambassador for Thaelis. For reasons I will explain as we move forward, the Thaelian council could not meet your demand to send the rest of the Vanrian abductees home at this time. To help resolve the situation, I volunteered to return to Vanris and negotiate on their behalf, along with Ahndhomen Jin–"

Jaysen slammed a hand down on the table. "Why would you help them?"

Arhk gave him a sharp look, the hint of black at the edges of his eyes warning him to silence.

Veyl met Jaysen's eyes, anger stirring like poison in her blood. "Why didn't you stand up for them? Ahn-kreth Kyril brought you here to warn Vanris about Thrasser's actions at my request. I asked you to work with him. Why didn't you vouch for him and his fleet?"

"They attacked Deepwater! They killed people and tore us away from our lives!" Jaysen's fist hit the table this time. "How could you expect me to offer them my protection?"

Veyl looked at her parents. "You must have interrogated the Thaelians. You know what I'm saying is true."

Her mother's hard gaze offered no support. "Ahnkreth Kyril did claim to have come here at your behest," she admitted, "but the members of his crew that we have had time to question could not corroborate his story. His beast companion provides him with a remarkable level of protection from our Evokers, even with them separated. We could not verify his claim."

"The creature denies all my efforts to take control of it," her father added. "It has the mental fortitude of a kanodrak."

Veyl found a spark of hope in the note of admiration in her father's words, and a fond smile curved her lips. "And you would never harm it."

He met her eyes. "The beast is innocent of its bonded companion's crimes. To be honest, we also haven't had the time we needed to deal with the Thaelian prisoners properly. Between investigating Sarket's activities and handling the increasing unrest up north—"

"What unrest?" Veyl interrupted.

Her parents exchanged a look with Arhk.

"We would like to speak with our daughter alone," her mother said then. "Dhomvalen Arhk, can you see to arranging guards and quarters for our guest?" She gestured to Jinau. "The rest of you may leave. We will summon the council when we are ready to engage in more formal discussions."

Tavin and Ellaris walked out with Jethan and Keyla. Jaysen stared at Veyl, looking like he wanted to argue, but when she avoided his gaze, he allowed Arhk to usher him out.

Jinau turned to Veyl, leaning close and keeping his voice low. "Remember the people you risked your life twice to protect."

She nodded. "I ask you to trust me, Jin. I will do

everything I can for both our countries. Please believe that."

"I am linked to you, Seh'hali, so I know when your heart speaks true. I also recognize that these people have a powerful, and justified, hatred for my country right now."

She realized suddenly what he was really getting at. If they did something to him once they had him away from her, he wanted reassurance that she would still follow through for Thaelis.

"Dhomvalen." She paused until Arhk turned to her, aware of Jaysen stopping in the doorway to listen. "Please ensure Ahndhomen Jinau is treated as a political guest and not a prisoner."

Arhk cast a glance at her parents, waiting for a nod from each of them before responding. "Of course, Ahninveth."

"Thank you." She wasn't sure she liked the way he spoke her new title, but she inclined her head in a gesture of respect, first to Arhk, then to Jinau. "I will seek you out when we finish here, Ahndhomen."

"Ahninveth." Jinau offered her a partial bow and left the room, Arhk accompanying him with his personal guards and a few of the dedicated palace ones following.

The moment the door closed behind them, she turned to her parents. "I am sorry if I've made this more difficult."

Her mother pulled her into a hug, and her father wrapped his arms around them both.

"You are home," she murmured, placing a kiss on Veyl's forehead. "That's what truly matters. We can figure the rest out together."

Veyl drew back from them. "What were you saying about conflict in the north?"

"You know that, before your disappearance, there

was a growing movement demanding that your mother and I step down and let you take the throne. They want a leader who better represents most of the population. Someone who is not a mind-crafter. Although if what Jaysen told us is true..." he trailed off, inviting her confirmation.

"It is. I am a Frightener, which will make me exceptionally unpopular, I'm afraid. But Grandfather has agreed to work with me on controlling it."

He nodded thoughtfully. "As extraordinary as it is to have two mind-crafter children in one family, it also means you are no longer what these people hoped you would be. After your disappearance, they spread rumors that we had conveniently disposed of you so we could make Tavin our heir and keep a mind-crafter on the throne. There were demonstrations that turned violent. We put most of our Evokers and Charmers to work trying to weed out malcontents who were using this as an excuse to promote chaos. We've faced many challenges in your absence."

He shook his head then, his gaze sweeping over her, lingering on the tokens in her hair the longest. "You can't truly mean to argue on behalf of a country that violently attacked two of our towns and took innocent people—took you—captive?"

Her parents looked faintly hopeful, as if they suspected she might have merely said those things because Jinau was watching. How she hated having to be the one to disappoint them, but she couldn't abandon the people of Thaelis any more than she could her own.

"I can. I signed an agreement with the Thaelian council stating as much. The residents of Thaelis have suffered terrible losses. What their leaders ordered done to us was reprehensible. I won't try to deny that, but the populace is not to blame for their actions. I intend to see our people returned to their homes here, but I do not want the citizens of Thaelis hurt in the process. For their sake, I will represent Thaelis as agreed. They need someone whose voice carries weight here to do so."

Her father's expression hardened a fraction. "Veyl, you can't—"

"Save everyone? I know. I also know that back when Arhk told you that, you didn't listen, either."

Her mother arched a brow at him, and he gave a tired chuckle and shook his head at Veyl. "This is a lot to process. I'm still trying to move past the fear that I'll wake up in a minute and find that having you back was all just a dream."

"As am I, my love," her mother said, taking his hand and twining her fingers through his.

Veyl drew a deep breath, hoping they would take her next words as well as they had taken the previous ones. "There's more. I would like Ahnkreth Kyril released to assist with negotiations."

Her mother yanked her hand free, using it to cut the air in a sharp gesture. "Under no circumstances!"

Her father's jaw tightened, a dark, predatory anger rising in his eyes. "Jaysen told us what that man did to you in Deepwater and during the voyage. I will not permit him to be anywhere near you."

"Jaysen? He witnessed very little of what happened on the crossing. They barely allowed us to be around each other during that time. Ahnkreth Kyril brought him here to warn you that Thrasser was up to something after I asked him to. If he hadn't, you still wouldn't know where to find me, and I would certainly not be standing with you now. He risked everything because he realized what they had done to us was wrong and wanted to help me protect my people. All of that aside, as a higher officer of Thaelis, he possesses a knowledge of Thaelian culture that could help expedite the negotiation process, and it would provide Thaelis more representation at the table."

"You have the ahndhomen to assist with that," her father countered.

"Ahndhomen Jinau doesn't have the extensive knowledge of their naval complex that Ahnkreth Kyril does. Thaelis is an island country. That information could be invaluable." Technically, Nalika shared that knowledge, but she was Kyril's subordinate. Besides, her parents didn't know about Nalika yet. She hoped they wouldn't hold the omission against her later.

"Veyl." A ready argument hung in wait behind her mother's tone.

It was easy to want to give in and relent to the comfort and safety of the life she had once known, but the people of Thaelis would suffer if she did so. Kyril and Ceris would suffer. "We've all gone through a lot of unnecessary misery because of what Thaelis's council did here, using Ahnkreth Kyril and his fleet as one of their weapons, but I believe this can have a peaceful resolution. Perhaps one that is even beneficial to both sides. We're dealing with Sarket and internal conflict in Vanris. They are recovering from massive population loss because of illness and the threat of attacks from hostiles in the region. Neither side needs more problems." She ran a hand through her hair, reminding herself not to touch the spiral shell. "Please don't force me to let everyone down without at least giving me a chance to prove that I can make this work for all of us. Please."

Her father let out a heavy breath. "It's moving on toward evening. We can set a time tomorrow afternoon to bring everyone together to look over this agreement and open discussions. Tonight, I would like to put it all aside and have dinner as a family for the first time in far too long."

"That sounds amazing." Veyl smiled, though she still wasn't finished yet. "Before we do that, can I at least check in on the wave dancer?"

Her father narrowed his eyes slightly. "The ahn-kreth's companion beast?"

She nodded.

He looked at her mother, who exhaled softly and said, "I don't see any harm in it, do you?"

"No." He narrowed his eyes at Veyl. "Though that mostly makes me wonder what we're missing."

Before going to see Ceris, her father left them to return Niskenya to the kanodrak canyon. Veyl stayed with her mother, who called upon a few attendants and gave orders to begin preparations for a special dinner. Tonight, they would limit family to Veyl, her grandfather, her parents, her brother, and their associated tehnaaks. Once again, she found herself without a tehnaak, though with Arhk there, she wouldn't be the only one. With that arranged, once her father returned, the three of them went out into the evening city with an accompaniment of four guards. Veyl and her parents were all capable fighters, but recent events inspired greater caution, even within the walls of their own city.

They strolled to the cliff cat habitat, where they had the wave dancer locked in a smaller enclosure used for separating out injured or sick beasts during their recovery. Along the way, Veyl told them what she had learned about the amphibious canines, starting with how tribal Qwilki on Thaelis revered them much as people in Vanris revered the kanodraks. She recounted her experience watching Ceris communicate with the whales and seeing him chase off the beautiful but deadly serpents, though she amended that tale to leave out her own interaction with the creatures at the time. Those stories and the resulting questions kept them occupied along the way to the enclosure, as she had hoped they would. By controlling the conversation, she ensured they didn't have time to inquire about other subjects that might lead to more challenging conversations.

Given that cliff cats were naturally alpine creatures, the canyon habitat they resided in had plenty of overhangs and rock shelters for shade and more water than the tethdrak and kanodrak areas. Since the wave dancer also wasn't a desert animal, they had placed Ceris there to give him more options for escaping the baking sunlight, with a stone pool to provide additional water. But, for all their efforts to make him comfortable, they had still separated him from the ocean and his companion, and it showed.

The wave dancer lay panting in the shade of an outcrop, his glossy black coat and scales dull and dusty. Those bright sea-green eyes, when he raised his head to watch them approach, had lost their brilliant shine.

Veyl walked to the bars and crouched there. "Ceris."

He stood, peering at her, and she thought she felt the faint touch of his presence within her, the way she had when she was zenyal to Kyril, though it shouldn't be possible in the absence of that connection to his companion.

"He hasn't expressed an interest in anyone other than his bonded companion," her father warned.

"You separated them and locked them up. Did you expect him to love you for that?" She held a hand through the bars.

"Veyl." Her mother sounded worried now.

Ceris padded over and stopped before her, his long drooping tail drifting tentatively from side to side, sweeping the sandy ground. Reaching his nose out, he licked her hand, then shifted his weight back and regarded her expectantly.

Veyl stood. "Unlock it."

"I can't control him," her father stated, as though he expected that to be adequate to deter her.

"You mentioned that earlier." Veyl fought back a somber smile. How it must frustrate him, the most powerful Feral in Vanris, to encounter a beast other than a kanodrak that he couldn't influence at will. "He won't hurt anyone. I promise you. Ceris was my one comfort aboard the ship to Dagony. I can't bear to see him locked up like this. Look at him. His coat's dull, his eyes listless. He's miserable."

Her father walked up to the gate, digging a key from a pouch at his belt. "The stupid things I do for love of you," he muttered. When it was unlocked, he stepped back and placed a hand on the hilt of his sword, something he hadn't often worn around the city before her abduction, back when there weren't threats coming at them from so many quarters. "If he attacks, I will not hesitate to cut him down, even as magnificent as he is."

"You won't have to." She placed a hand on the gate, wary of her ability reacting to her nervousness when she opened it and stepped through, but the moment she looked into those sea-green eyes again, she calmed. "Ceris."

Her father followed her in, and she heard him lock the gate behind them.

The tall canine walked up to her and pressed his head against her hand, emitting a melodic, sorrowful whine that reminded her of his interaction with the whales that she had been telling them about. Heart aching, Veyl sank down next to him and wrapped her arms around his shoulders the way she had the night he slipped his head between her shackled arms to comfort her. It was her turn to do the same for him now.

"I'm sorry," she whispered. "This is my fault."

The wave dancer leaned into her embrace, and she closed her eyes. All this suffering, heartache, and loss.

All this separation. And why? Because a few people thought they could take whatever they wanted and not pay a price. She would never be one of those people.

Veyl released him and stood, turning to face her parents. Her father specifically this time, where he waited inside the gate, his hand now drifting away from the sword hilt. Ceris stepped up beside her, and she set a hand on his shoulders.

"You understand the torture you're inflicting on the two of them, keeping them apart like this. Reunite them and let me offer Ahnkreth Kyril a place in the negotiations. When that is done, I can tell you over dinner the many reasons I am willing to represent the people of Thaelis in this process."

"The man has a dangerous bearing, Veyl. There's something about him that's…" he trailed off as though searching for the right word.

Dark and beautiful. She kept that thought to herself. "Confident and somewhat predatory. He moves a little like a wild animal." She smirked and glanced at her mother. "Remind you of someone else, Mother?"

The barest hint of a smile touched her mother's lips when she looked at her husband. "Your words hold truth, darling, but perhaps those similarities lead you to trust where you should not."

"Please. Let me offer him a place in the negotiations. If he accepts, we can keep him under guard just like Ahndhomen Jinau and give him quarters in the palace as we would any foreign dignitary." The resistance in their eyes faded a fraction, so she leaned into the one factor that might nudge them in her favor. The problem of finding time to handle all the issues vying for their attention. "I believe his knowledge could significantly expedite this process."

Her father shook his head again. "Veyl, Jaysen told us how the ahnkreth nearly strangled you to death the night they took you prisoner in Deepwater. We didn't put him to death because we thought he might be useful for bargaining with his people, and I was loath to do that to his companion. Even then, it was sorely tempting."

She bit back her frustration. "But did Jaysen explain to you that I had just broken the mind of one of Ahnkreth Kyril's crew members with an ability I told him I didn't have? Did he tell you that the ahnkreth had lost his tehnaak, his parents, his brother, and the woman he loved in recent years to a sickness that killed nearly half their population in Thaelis? He had legitimate cause to react violently to losing someone else, especially when he had every reason to believe I had just lied to him. I don't forgive him for what he did, but I understand why he did it.

"And," she continued, holding up a hand before either could speak, "when everyone else on board those ships pressed him to kill me because my ability was too dangerous, too unpredictable, he refused to do so. Instead, he tried to help me control it, despite my attempts to kill him. I do not excuse the wrongs he and his people committed through their actions in Deepwater, but I would not have made it to Dagony alive if he had not been willing to fight for me."

Her mother was watching her father now, who was considering Veyl with a stern gaze. "It is hard to be comfortable hearing you defend the man who took you from us while you stand before us dressed like one of them with his beast waiting willingly by your side."

"I know how painful this is for all of us." She walked a few steps closer, Ceris matching each step. "But I am still your daughter, and I love you both so much," her voice cracked, and she swallowed. "I want your guidance, but I also need you to see that I am not the same person I was when we parted ways outside Deepwater. I hope you can both still love me as I am now and recognize that you can trust me."

He walked to her, pausing a step away to look down at the wave dancer. Veyl closed the remaining distance, and he put his arms around her, pulling her close.

"Of course, we love you, but this situation makes everything harder. Knowing how terrified you must have been when those bastards attacked Deepwater, then hearing some of the awful things they did to you from Jaysen. All we could do was wonder what else they might have done in the time since he last saw you. It's a lot to work through."

"It is." She hugged him tighter.

"If you two don't come out of there and let me partake in this, I will never forgive you."

Veyl drew back from him and smiled at her mother. "With pleasure."

He cleared his throat when she headed toward the gate. "You can't take that creature out of here."

Veyl glanced down into the trust-filled, sea-green eyes gazing up at her. "He'll be fine. I imagine he knows this is his chance to see his bonded again. Wave dancers are extremely intelligent beasts."

"He is remarkable, I'll give you that. I never dreamed I would encounter another creature as incredible in its own way, and as headstrong, as Niskenya."

Veyl kept her hand on Ceris's shoulder as they approached the gate, eyeing her father expectantly. The wave dancer sat patiently beside her, his attention riveted on the lock.

Her father walked up next to them, the key in his hand. "I think I preferred you in your younger days, when you let us lead the way more."

Her mother cleared her throat softly. "You may be confusing her with Tavin, love."

One corner of his mouth quirked up. "You may be right."

A jittery energy surged through Veyl. She believed Ceris understood enough to recognize she was trying to help, but what if she was wrong? What if he attacked someone or simply bolted the moment the cage opened?

The wave dancer nudged her hand. His coat didn't feel as sleek and smooth under her fingers now. How much of that was depression because of his separation from Kyril and how much suffering from being subjected to the dry desert region? She hoped it was mostly the former. *That* she could do something about. The latter might not be solvable for some time. Simply convincing her parents to humor her and let both Ceris and the Feral ahnkreth out would be an extraordinary achievement under the circumstances.

Her father swung the gate open and stepped out ahead of them, moving between the beast and her mother. His hand sank to his sword hilt again. Ceris didn't bolt for the exit. Instead, he remained alongside Veyl, matching her steps and placing his trust in her. Whatever compelled him to do so, she was determined now not to let him down.

When she stopped, Ceris sat next to her again, and her father blew out a soft breath before shutting the recovery enclosure.

"Beasts have always been fond of you," her mother commented.

Was that why Kyril fancied her? Veyl smothered a smile and turned toward the exit. "Shall we commit an act of kindness before dinner and reunite him with his bonded?"

Her father glanced at Ceris, then met her eyes. "I'm not convinced this is a good or wise decision, but if your mother is willing to give him a chance, I will as well. You need to understand that we will not allow him a single misstep."

Veyl nodded.

At her mother's suggestion, they went to a moderately sized audience chamber in the palace. It had four black stone thrones on the dais at the front set up to accommodate the current ruling family. They shared some of the aggressive, angular design elements that made the city walls so intimidating. Each throne had a cushioned, deep purple seat and back, and sparing silver accents worked along the arms and sides, representing the colors of Vanris. Down the long walls to the left and right, with guards moving into position between them, were statues of the twelve council members who had overseen the founding of the first Vanrian settlement on Pandrea. Veyl couldn't help wondering if they were the same people who had outlawed the zenyal bond here or who had clashed with the district of Thaelis in their homeland.

On the way to the room, her father had sent four guards to collect Ahnkreth Kyril, and an attendant to summon Arhk and Jethan to join them. Jethan, with her father's cliff cat, and her grandfather arrived together, the dhomvalen's three black-clad guards adding to the abundance of security already in the room. It struck Veyl as excessive, but her father was also a Feral and had accomplished impressive feats in the war with his ability. Some of them were awful, but impressive all the same. Perhaps they weren't wrong about being cautious.

For her part, Veyl feared she might bounce out of her own skin with the mix of uncertainty and excitement at the prospect of seeing Kyril again. She stood at the edge of the dais, too restless to sit. Would it please him to see her? How could it not, given that she was freeing him from his prison? But what if that was the only reason? What if the connection between them in Dagony was nothing more than a naïve young woman's fantasy? He wouldn't have risked everything coming here if that were the case, would he?

"What do you think of Ahndhomen Jinau?" her father asked Arhk.

Ice raced up Veyl's spine. If Arhk told them about the zenyal bond now, it wouldn't put them in the most receptive mood. She glanced over at her grandfather. He caught her look, a faint tightening of his jaw the only indication that he might have understood the pleading in her eyes.

"He is strangely forthright for a Charmer."

"Let's not be insulting." Jethan leaned against the side of her father's throne. "Not all Charmers can be as skilled at deception as my cousin and me," he added with a wink for her mother.

Arhk gave him a vaguely disdainful look, an expression no one had mastered better than he had. "The man is challenging to read, but Veyl appears to trust him, despite… We can talk more about it in the morning." He turned toward the door at the sound of footsteps approaching. "I suppose we shall see how decent a judge of character your daughter is in the coming days."

His callous tone stung and did nothing to soothe her screaming nerves. Next to her, Ceris stood, shifting from one paw to the other now, his fin-like ears perked forward as far as they could go. His long, flowing tail wagged, tentatively at first, then faster. When the door opened and Kyril stepped in ahead of the four guards, the wave dancer bolted across the room like a loosed arrow. The guards put hands on their weapons, but her father signaled to them to hold as Kyril sank to one knee to meet the beast's charge.

Veyl's breath caught. Had the ahnkreth always been this unfairly handsome? Despite what had to have been at least two weeks of imprisonment, he still looked statuesque and fierce. Black hair, with braids and streaks of deep blue worked through it, hung long around his chiseled features. In the strangest of ways, he reminded her of her father's nightstar eagle—confident, dangerous, and aloof—even as he let Ceris lick his face and rub his head against his cheek in a distinctly cat-like manner.

Kyril murmured to the wave dancer in Qwilki, intentionally locking them out of that part of their reunion, something she couldn't entirely blame him for. Then he looked directly at her, his intense silver-blue eyes effortlessly unmooring her from the life she had barely reconnected with. "You have our gratitude, Khesran Veyl."

For the briefest of moments, she couldn't find her voice, but nothing would turn her family against him faster than seeing her blushing and stammering before him like a love-struck girl. "You are welcome, Ahnkreth Kyril."

Her mother stood from her throne, her voice cutting across the room like a blade, cold and sharp. "You should be extremely grateful, Ahnkreth, that the young woman whose life you did so much to destroy can look past your cruel deeds and find something of worth within you."

Kyril stood and walked forward, stopping a few feet from the dais with Ceris pressed against his leg as if the beast feared he would disappear. The Thaelian Feral kept his attention on her mother now. "Khesran Veyl is the one who helped me see the depth of the wrong in my actions, Khevarin. As I told your Evoker, she is the reason I brought Prince Jaysen to Vanris against the orders of my council."

There seemed nothing to be gained from allowing them to engage in verbal sparring for long. The risk that he might say the wrong thing was too great. Veyl took a step back toward her throne, catching their attention with her movement and putting a little more distance between herself and the cause of her racing pulse.

"Ahnkreth Kyril, I return home with a specific task. I have agreed to represent Thaelis in negotiations with Vanris and carry the title of Ahninveth na sek Veyl, Ambassador of Thaelis, for the duration of this assignment." The faintest hint of a smirk touched his lips for a moment, as though he found that amusing, and a flush of anger heated her blood. Or was that longing? She pushed past it. "I would like to offer you a place at the table during those negotiations in an advisory capacity. Will you accept it?"

"They did not send you to Vanris to represent them on your own."

It wasn't quite a question, but she chose to treat it as such, hoping that bringing up Nalika at this moment wouldn't be enough to make her parents reconsider. "Ahnkreth Nalika and Ahndhomen Jinau will also attend these sessions."

She caught a slight pinching of his brows and what she thought might be surprise flashing in his eyes at Jinau's name. If only she knew him well enough to decipher that subtle reaction.

"I doubt Thaelis wants me negotiating on their behalf at this point."

Arhk and her parents were watching her now. Why wouldn't Kyril shut up and accept the offer? She inhaled, trying to hide her growing frustration. He was going to get himself dumped back in a prison cell. "Nowhere in the agreement I signed does it say I cannot fill in the gaps in my knowledge of Thaelis using the resources available to me, of which you are one. It looks to me as though you have no other pressing demands on your time. However, if you would prefer to return to your cell..." She didn't bother finishing the sentence.

There it was again, that faint smirk as he bowed his head to her. "It would be an honor to represent my people and assist you in any way I can, Ahninveth Veyl."

Her father stood now, coming to the edge of the dais with Irith at his side, the beast gazing curiously at the wave dancer, who looked equally intrigued by the slightly shorter, more densely muscled cliff cat. "This represents your one chance to earn your freedom, Ahnkreth. If you make a single mistake, trying you here for crimes against our people will become a non-negotiable term of any agreement we come to with your country."

Kyril's gaze flickered to Veyl, meeting her eyes for an instant. He had done what she asked of him, and now both their countries wanted him dead for it. Had he realized this would be the cost of helping her? The fact that he kept his plans from his crew suggested he had at least considered this outcome. Then why had he done it? Certainly not all for some woman he barely knew. Regardless of his motivation, keeping him alive was going to be no small challenge.

Kyril bowed to her parents. "I thank you for the opportunity to prove myself, Majesties."

Her father answered with a curt nod. "Find him quarters and put him under guard like the other one. We will deal with the rest tomorrow."

"What of his beast?" Arhk asked.

Veyl looked at her father, and he met her eyes, shoulders rising and falling with a deep breath. "He may keep his companion with him. See that their needs are provided for and add a few extra guards."

Kyril's eyes flickered to her once more, and he nodded, recognizing her silent input in her father's decision before he turned to leave with the guards. She watched him walk away, wishing there was some way she could justify going to him, to talk to him, and thank him for what he had done. For what he had sacrificed. One brief exchange to tell him she would find a way out of this for him, though she wasn't sure how yet. But she stayed silent on the dais with her parents, accepting that she had at least gotten him out of the prison cell and reunited with Ceris. One battle at a time.

When the doors shut behind them, her mother arched a brow at her. "Who is Nalika?"

This would be her one opportunity to head off the irritation rising in her parents' regard. "She's a subordinate ahnkreth in his fleet who is traveling with the twins and Iyvalin. She has proven more resistant to the idea of negotiating with Vanris. Having someone with his rank and willingness to cooperate involved should help keep her from obstructing the process."

They didn't look entirely satisfied with the explanation, but neither chose that moment to berate her for her earlier omission.

Her father came to put an arm around her shoulders. "You say you asked Ahnkreth Kyril to come here and warn us about Thrasser?"

Veyl nodded.

"Why did he do it?"

A few potential motivations came to mind that she couldn't share, which didn't leave her with much. "He just admitted to realizing what they did to us was wrong. I don't think he appreciates what the Thaelian council sent them out to do and wants to make amends for it. I suspect there may be more to it, and I hope to figure that out in the coming days. Once I do, I will share that information with you."

Her mother came up on her other side. "Be careful, Veyl. I am not convinced we can trust him."

"Of course, you're not. He kidnapped your daughter. But good people sometimes do bad things while following orders. That doesn't make it all right, but he may try that much harder to make up for those wrongs."

She moved out from under her father's arm and turned to face them. "The agreement we can leave until tomorrow, can't we? I'd like one night to just be your daughter."

"Yes." Her mother's fond smile held an edge of sorrow. "We will settle nothing tonight. We can simply enjoy the opportunity to be together again as a family."

"Thank you. You know what I would really love right now?"

Her mother arched a brow at her. "What?"

"I would love for you to send me to my rooms to clean up for dinner."

Her father chuckled and pulled them both into his arms. Veyl closed her eyes, letting the rest of the world slip away for a moment to lose herself in that loving embrace.

A hot bath was exactly what Veyl needed, though it was hard to relax when she yearned to spend time with her family. Some bruises and scrapes from her encounter with the kel'inuk were still healing. When she had undressed, her attendant, Lanis, panicked and was ready to run to her parents to tell them someone had beaten her, which led to the first recounting of that story for the night. The second came at dinner. She attended in one of the simple dresses with an open skirt and fitted pants beneath that she had acquired a preference for from her mother. Seeing her out of the Thaelian uniform seemed to put her family a little more at ease, though she still wore the shells Kyril and Nagi had gifted her in her hair, setting the third aside to give to Kyril.

She spent most of the alternately tearful and joyous dinner answering questions about everything that took place since the day she and the others arrived in Deepwater. As much as she didn't want to relive many of those experiences, she recognized both the genuine parental concern and the need to understand the opposition that drove their interrogation. Hoping to change their adversarial view of the Thaelians and help them make sense of her desire to protect them, she leaned into tales that might nudge them in that direction.

Besides her daring rescue of Nagi, she told them of the confrontation with the Unclean on the voyage to Thaelis, and what she knew about the Devastation and other torments the Ukhen'kya had inflicted upon the people of Thaelis. As the evening wore on, she reluctantly told them about losing control of her Frightener ability with Gannon in Dagony, and the Sarketi attack on their ship coming home that cost Lorek his life.

To ease the sorrow that hung over them after that, she shared her experiences working in the fish market and helping people around Dagony with Kitria, and all the gifts they had lavished upon her in return. Stories intended to clarify how she came to care for the people there. At some point, she realized her parents now knew she had met with Jaysen in Deepwater, but they didn't call her out for it. Perhaps it struck them as less important now.

By the time they parted ways for the night, Veyl could barely keep her eyes open long enough to appreciate the hugs they gave her. Arhk, her parents, and their tehnaaks retreated to a study to talk. It stung a little to realize that they would be picking apart her every word and action from the evening while she was trying to fall asleep. It made sense, though. Right now, the Thaelians were still the enemy, and she was representing them. Everything she did would be under scrutiny.

Her brother and Ellaris wandered off to their own rooms. Veyl followed familiar hallways back to chambers she hadn't spent a night in for some time to find Jaysen waiting outside.

He opened her door for her. "After you, Khesran Veyl."

The energy in his smile leeched away what little she had remaining. "I'm sorry. I don't think I have anything left in me tonight." She strode partway across the sitting room before turning to face him.

He walked up and placed a hand on her shoulder, his gaze sinking briefly to her lips. He was still the handsome young man who had long been her tehnaak and best friend. The man she had willingly kissed in Deepwater. That spark of romantic curiosity was absent now, smothered by a much more potent flame. An entanglement even less appropriate than her brief intimacy with Jaysen had been. The sorrow caused by that truth only amplified her longing for the Feral ahnkreth's company.

"I hated leaving you in that place," he said, his voice soft and thick with emotion.

He was going to try kissing her. She could see it in his expression and feel it in the forward energy of his stance. Taking a step back, she looked up into his bright blue eyes. "Jaysen, I am truly overjoyed to see you, but I'm thoroughly exhausted. Can we talk tomorrow?"

For an instant, disappointment broke his smile, but he rallied quickly, his gaze warming again as he moved in to brush a lock of hair behind her ear. "We can." He placed a soft kiss on her forehead. "Get some rest."

Veyl took his hand and gave it a gentle squeeze. "Thank you."

It was a long time before she fell asleep after he left. She couldn't entirely blame him for not supporting the Thaelians. They never gave him an opportunity to see the side of their world that she saw. On top of that, knowing Thrasser tried to have him killed, and his people believed him dead, had to weigh heavily upon him. He couldn't simply declare he was alive and return to Sarket without a plan for dealing with the king regent and whoever was working with him. That would be suicidal. However, the longer he hid away in Vanris, the harder he would have to fight to regain the support of his people and the more time Thrasser would have to secure that same support. She needed to figure out how to help him deal with all of that while discouraging the intimacy he appeared to still want.

That was only one of many challenges she had to tackle, but the ones that kept her up the longest as she lay in bed were two terms in the agreement she had signed that the Vanrian council would review the next day. Specifically, the zenyal bond and her commitment to return to Thaelis when negotiations here ended with no clarity regarding what would happen after Kyril's trial, beyond her personal plan to keep his head attached to his body. Neither of those terms was going to sit well with her parents. By the time she finally drifted off, she at least had an idea of how to get ahead of the zenyal problem. That bond, as much as she disliked it, was serving an unexpected purpose.

When morning came, she went to dress and noticed the Thaelian uniform she had hung upon the wardrobe was missing. Wrapping a satiny robe around her, she stepped out into the sitting room to find Lanis arranging a breakfast plate for her from the tray of food that she had brought in. The scene was strikingly ordinary. At once familiar and yet newly made foreign by the part of her that had despaired of ever being in this place again.

Veyl burst into tears.

Lanis ran to her as she sank to the floor sobbing and knelt beside her.

"Oh dear. What can I do?"

Veyl grabbed hold of her, clinging to her as she had so many times in her childhood, the tears coming in a flood. Lanis held her close, murmuring softly as she stroked Veyl's hair. It was absurd to break down over something so mundane, but it was merely the catalyst for the realization that, after everything that had happened, after being torn from her life and thrust into a world of fear and chaos, she was finally home safe again, reunited with the people she loved.

Lanis settled there, prepared to hold her for as long as she needed. "It's all right. You're where you belong now."

Her words, showing she understood why Veyl was crying, made the tears come faster. For several seconds, she could do nothing but hold on and weep in the arms of this woman who had helped raise her, where it felt safe to do so. When the sobs finally subsided, Lanis supported her to her feet and dabbed at her tears with a handkerchief before handing it to her, so she might blow her nose.

"Thank you," Veyl said, her voice altered by her now stuffy nose. "Do you know where my uniform is?"

Lanis took the soiled cloth after Veyl blew her nose one more time, frowning briefly at the two shells in Veyl's hair. "I took it to be cleaned."

"Will it be ready by this afternoon?"

"I'll make certain of it. Have yourself something to eat. I headed your father off on the way here. Told him not to smother you. I can take you to see your parents if you like once you've eaten and freshened up."

Veyl touched her arm. "Please don't tell anyone about…" she trailed off, glancing at the floor where she had been weeping.

Lanis pressed her lips together for a moment, but she nodded. "If that's what you want. Just know I'm here for you."

Veyl smiled. "You always have been."

Once she had eaten a light breakfast, she put on another of the open-skirted dresses, this one a satiny charcoal gray with dark purple embroidery along the bodice, hem, and lower part of the pant legs underneath. Lanis returned and helped arrange a couple of snug braids above Veyl's right ear, which she then attached the two shells onto the ends of. The third shell, she tucked in a pouch tied to the black and silver belt, then grabbed the Thaelian agreement and followed Lanis to her parents.

They were in an elegant sitting area that looked out onto the large, enclosed garden along the western side of the palace. Jethan and his wife Keyla sat across from them, and Irith lay at her father's feet, grooming one paw. All of them stood when she entered, a hint of relief in her parents' eyes, as if they feared she might have vanished again in the night.

"Good morning." She offered a smile she hoped would help put them more at ease.

They returned the greeting, settling back into their seats when she claimed a chair to one side, angling it in such a way that she could face her parents.

"It's uncanny how much older you look," Jethan commented.

She frowned at him. "I'm not sure that's a compliment."

"I believe he means you carry yourself differently, and there is more experience behind your eyes." A hint of sorrow muted her mother's smile as she made the observation.

Choosing not to follow that line of thought, Veyl leaned forward. "I brought the agreement I signed with Thaelis." She held it clasped in her hands, not offering it yet. "Although there is something I'd rather you heard directly from me before you come upon it in this." Assuming Arhk hadn't already told them, but he had always provided her a chance to handle matters with her parents on her own before he would intervene. She suspected he was staying true to form now, given that they hadn't confronted her with it yet. "I am bound to Ahndhomen Jinau through a zenyal bond."

Her mother was instantly on her feet. "I will kill that calloch," she hissed.

Her father stood as well, though with much less

conviction. "Hold on. What's a zenyal bond?"

Veyl didn't give her mother time to answer. "It's a type of unequal bond that allows one party the ability to inflict debilitating mental pain on the other as a means of control. I–"

Fury twisted her father's features. "I'm summoning a Bondmaker."

Veyl rose to intercept him when he took a step. "No. You're not."

They stared at her as if doubting that they had heard her correctly. Keyla and Jethan stayed seated, the latter munching on a fruit tart.

"Please sit." Veyl waited until her parents had done so, then she sank down again herself. "There are two reasons I wish to leave the bond as it is for now. The first is that I agreed to do so by signing my name on these pages. The second is my tehnaak bond with Jaysen. In our brief time in Balarus, that bond reformed, and was severed again by the Thaelian Bondmaker. If the zenyal bond remains in place, the other cannot reform, and I don't want it to. I still see Jaysen as my tehnaak, but I doubt either of us can stand having our pairing broken yet again, as we all know it would have to be."

"Veyl." Her mother's sad look overflowed with sympathy. "I can see why you would not want to suffer such a loss for a fourth time, but to remain bound to this Thaelian…"

"I know you don't understand, but Jinau holds the bond only because his council ordered him to do so. He would never use it unless my ability burst out of control again, which is the main reason for its creation. Honestly, until I'm confident that I can manage it on my own, I'd prefer someone to have that power. I've broken many people with my Frightener ability already, and I don't want to do that to anyone I care about the way I nearly did with Gannon. What I ended up doing to him was awful enough."

"Doesn't this give him power over you that could be used to Thaelis's advantage in negotiations?" Jethan asked.

"It would if I feared the bond or him, but I don't. If that changes, I will be the first to ask for a Bondmaker, I promise you."

"You can safely assume that none of us likes this situation," her father stated.

"I know, and I'm sorry, but this is how I want it to stay for now, to protect people from my ability and prevent the tehnaak bond from reforming with Jaysen. I hope you can respect that." She held out the agreement to her parents. "Here. I imagine you'll want to go over this with the council before we start formal negotiations."

Her mother accepted it and placed it on the table, regarding it with a look of dread.

Jethan leaned forward and took a cup off the tray on the table, setting it before Veyl. He lifted the teapot. "Would you care to sit and enjoy the morning with us?"

Veyl smiled at him, warmed by his not-at-all subtle effort to move the conversation away from problematic topics. "I would love that, Uncle Jeth, and a tart if you're willing to share any."

She stayed for most of an hour, and, though the northern unrest and the brewing troubles with Sarket entered the discussion a few times, they avoided the subject of Thaelis, allowing her a chance to enjoy being with them. The dynamic had changed, however. They didn't treat her like a child in the room, instead engaging her in all aspects of the conversation and soliciting her thoughts on various topics. She appreciated that, though she disliked the price she had paid to get it.

Eventually, her father set a hand on her mother's arm. "We should gather the council. We have a lot to go over before we'll be ready to meet with the group representing Thaelis."

"On that subject, I would like to speak alone with the Thaelian contingent prior to our meeting." Veyl was more than prepared for the immediate arguments rising in her parents' eyes. She had practiced this encounter in her head at least a dozen times. "I am supposed to be an ambassador for Thaelis. How exactly do you see that working if I cannot engage in private counsel with the rest of the group?"

"I don't much care," her father countered.

Veyl shifted her gaze to her mother. "Khevarin Velara, how many of the political negotiations you have been a part of have forbidden one party from holding counsel with their fellow dignitaries?"

Her mother let out a sigh. "The circumstances here are highly unusual, but," she paused, turning to Kasiel, "she is correct."

He clenched his teeth and glanced down at Irith, who looked back up at him, his gaze serene and bright. "All right. You can meet with them in one of the smaller council chambers for now, with an abundance of guards on hand."

"Outside the doors," she countered.

He gave her a scowl of warning. "Veyl."

"The Thaelians need to feel as though our discussions are private, or they won't be open with me. I can call for help if there are problems, but if they wanted to hurt me, do you honestly think they would be foolish enough to do so here, in the middle of our palace? Besides, I am still a khesran of Vanris. If I learn something that is of critical importance to Vanris's safety, I will share it, and I am more apt to discover such things if they feel like they can speak openly."

"Again, my love," her mother said, grimacing as if her own words tasted unpleasant, "she's—"

"Not wrong. I know." He shook his head. "You can have a council room with palace guards outside once the last member of their group arrives, but those guards will be under orders to enter if they hear any noise that could be a sound of distress."

That was the most she could ask for now. "Thank you. Is there anything you would like me to do in the meantime?"

Her mother, very much the khevarin of Vanris in that moment, gave her a stony look. "Since you are representing Thaelis, you cannot sit in on the Vanrian council. Perhaps Jaysen would be up for a game of Feral's Folly."

A hint of a cutting edge in her voice betrayed how much the situation pained her, even though she had argued in favor of Veyl's requests. It stung to have earned her mother's disappointment, but she meant to win her approval by the end of this. Somehow. Not today, though. Not once they read the terms Thaelis wanted. Today was only going to get more difficult.

Suddenly, searching out Jaysen sounded like a fine idea, but not for Feral's Folly. It had been too long since the last time she sparred properly, and right then it would be the perfect activity to help clear her head.

She bowed slightly to her parents and offered a nod to Jethan and Keyla. "I hope the council meeting goes well. If you will excuse me." Without giving them time to say more, she swallowed against the tightness in her throat and left the room to search for Jaysen.

·

"Are you sure you wouldn't prefer to talk about whatever's on your mind?"

Veyl didn't answer. Instead, she shifted into a fighting stance across from Jaysen. She had returned to her rooms to change into more suitable clothing and had almost literally run into him coming to look for her on her way out. Under different circumstances, that might have heightened her frustration, but right then she had wanted to find him, and his seeking her out sped up the process.

Recognizing she didn't intend to answer him, Jaysen tossed his head to flip his dark auburn hair away from his eyes and came at her. She blocked and shifted to the side, lunging in for a quick strike. The aggression in her attack nearly earned her a hit on him, but he leapt back at the last second, his eyes narrowing a fraction.

"Feeling feisty, are we?"

Again, she didn't respond, taking advantage of his pause to go on the offensive and drive him back with a flurry of fast strikes. He retreated to the edge of the ring, his brows creeping up, and adjusted his grip on the practice weapon, taking her more seriously now. Veyl grinned and lunged at him. They exchanged a quick sequence of attacks, their violent dance moving them around the circle. She had trained with the top fighters in Vanris, but he had trained with those same people for several years and with some of the best Sarket could offer since, which had noticeably changed his style. Still, he couldn't fight with both hands as effectively as she could, and that was the edge that earned her the first disarm.

Jaysen picked up his practice blade and faced her again. They both lunged in, and Veyl abruptly pivoted to a parry, knocking his weapon aside and coming in with a quick thrust. He sidestepped the attack, and her sword glanced off the side of his ribs, scraping the training armor. The tip of his blade skimmed the back of her armor when he spun around behind her. Twisting, she ducked to the side to avoid his next swing, switching hands with her weapon to find a better angle, and swept out, catching the crossguard of his sword with her blade and tearing it from his grip.

A few more rounds had similar results, with them both landing glancing strikes, but her ability to fight with either hand gave her the edge needed to slip in a killing blow or disarm.

"Havaad curse you and your changing of hands." Jaysen leaned back against the rail for a moment, panting as he wiped sweat-dampened hair away from his eyes.

Also breathing hard, Veyl walked to the bench where they had left water skins and took a long drink from one. She used a cloth to dab at the moisture on her forehead, giving him a sideways glance when he came up next to her. "I recall you being better than this at predicting my changes."

"In my defense, we haven't sparred in some time, and I had no one with your particular talent to practice against in Sarket." He took a long drink before continuing. "Are you going to talk to me yet? You're clearly close to bursting with frustration about something. Why don't you tell me which of the items on the admittedly long list of options is bothering you most?"

"I..." She stared at the bench where she had dropped the now dampened cloth. Living in Sarket for the last several years had changed him. Not in the best of ways, she feared. That more loving, supportive side was still there, but buried how deep? Did she have any hope of digging it out? She sighed. Undoubtedly not, at least when the subject was Thaelis. "You wouldn't understand."

She started turning away, but he caught her arm, keeping her there. "Then help me understand. I know you're upset about how I handled my arrival here with the Thaelian fleet, but you're too smart not to see why I did what I did. You can't have suffered through the things they put us through and not see why I couldn't stomach helping them. I realize that your experience and mine were different. From what I saw, it looked like you had it worse, but that's not the message I'm getting from you. Maybe if you explained it to me, I could make enough sense of what's going on here to stand beside you the way I want to."

Looking at him now, she saw hurt and cautious hope in his eyes and recalled all the times he had followed along with her insane ideas and defended her when she landed them in trouble as children. "You're right. You have always stood by me in the past. I became used to not having that after you returned to Sarket. The twins and their tehnaaks have long been my friends, but none of them ever understood me as completely as you did. I had to learn to live without someone like that in a place where nearly everyone has a tehnaak to fill that role. It's also hard not to keep my guard up when I know your being here won't last."

"Maybe not. Almost certainly not, but I don't want to see us pushing each other away when we both desperately need that support." He gave her a roguish grin. "Besides, I could just stay dead and remain in Vanris."

She answered with a wry smile. "And allow Thrasser to continue ruling Sarket?"

He blew out a heavy breath, running one hand through his hair, a hint of his distress rising to the surface. "A sound argument against it, I suppose."

"I—"

"Khesran Veyl."

She turned to see an attendant striding across the training grounds toward them. "What is it?"

The man stopped at the edge of the ring and offered a slight bow. "The second party from the coast has arrived. I was told to let you know that Ahnkreth Nalika from Thaelis is being provided with rooms and an opportunity to refresh. The khemron said that the smaller meeting chamber near the war room is available for your use when you are ready."

Finally. Butterflies danced to life in her chest at the thought of seeing Kyril. She would have to find some way to stop that reaction or at least ignore it. What occurred between them in Thaelis could never happen again. "Thank you. Have the Thaelian representatives brought to the meeting chamber in half an hour and arrange for food and drink to be delivered there as well, please."

He bowed again. "Consider it done, Khesran. It is good to have you back," he added before hurrying off.

"You're meeting with them?"

The disdain in Jaysen's voice brought up a crackle of energy in her chest. Veyl closed her eyes and leaned her head back, letting the sun fall full on her face. She imagined the ocean breeze, the salty tang of sea air, the crash of waves. Her ability calmed. She opened her eyes, coming back under the scalding desert sun, and gave him a hard look.

"Maybe you could defer your judgment until after I have the chance to explain to you why I believe this is the right course of action."

Jaysen lowered his gaze. "I apologize. I'll try to keep my personal biases in check until we can speak more. Perhaps after dinner tonight?"

Assuming any of them were still willing to talk to her by the time they finished their first negotiation session. "Thank you for trying. Hopefully, we'll have time to talk later."

Veyl hurried to her rooms in the palace and washed up. She changed into the Thaelian uniform that someone had hung back on her wardrobe, knowing she might not have time to do so between this meeting and the first formal session. Then she hurried to the room a little early. A guard met her there with what turned out to be a copy of the agreement she had signed that the Vanrian council must have produced. It made her stomach flip, wondering what her parents thought of the words on those pages. Did it mean anything that they had kept the original?

The attendants had set out four mugs of Vanrian Black Mead, along with plates and utensils, on a rectangular table that could seat up to eight, with trays holding food and two additional bottles of mead in the center. Veyl set the agreement on a sidebar, then took a long drink from one mug and started pacing.

inau and Nalika arrived within seconds of each other, both escorted by two guards, one of whom pointedly assured Veyl they would be right outside if she needed assistance.

The moment the guards left the room, Nalika turned her icy gaze on Veyl. "How does it feel to be the one with all the power?"

Irritation flared in Veyl, bringing that taste of lightning to her tongue. "Considering this is the first time I've had any since the day we met, I suspect you know the answer to that better than I do."

"Fighting amongst ourselves will gain us nothing," Jinau remarked, taking a seat to the right of the head of the table. After sniffing at the contents of the mug there, he smiled and took a long drink.

"She's not one of us," Nalika snapped.

Before either of them could respond to that, the door opened again, and four guards escorted Kyril and Ceris in. Veyl's core temperature seemed to rise when he stepped through the doorway, making her feel feverish. He had cleaned up and wore simple black pants and an ivory shirt that someone had provided for him. One of his guards approached Veyl as Nalika rushed over to Kyril, grasping his arm in a warrior's greeting, only to be pulled in for a brief embrace.

A sting of envy shot through Veyl.

"Calloch! We were afraid they had killed you." The tension in Nalika's voice hinted at the familial bond he had with his crew.

"Would you like some of us to stay in the room?" the guard asked Veyl.

She watched Jinau stand and step in when Nalika moved back, also taking Kyril's forearm in a warrior's greeting, then pulling the Feral ahnkreth into a rough, one-armed embrace.

"It is good to see you," the Charmer said.

"And you, my friend," Kyril replied.

Of course, they were friends.

Veyl absently placed a hand on Ceris's shoulder when the tall beast walked up beside her. "I'm fine. I'll call if I need anything. Thank you," she said, dismissing the guards.

As the door shut behind them, Jinau returned to his chosen seat. Kyril's gaze moved to Ceris, then to her, and her chest tightened, making it substantially more difficult to draw a breath. When he walked toward her, memories swept in, putting her back in his room, his hands exploring her bare skin. She flushed, and the corner of his mouth quirked up in a knowing smirk. Those silver-blue eyes held her prisoner, keeping her pinned to the spot when he stopped before her, standing closer than appropriate. She yearned to reach for him, but she had to abandon that part of their relationship. They both did. If his people considered him not good enough for her, hers were going to have even stronger opinions about it.

Trying to focus past the longing to step into his arms, she said, "Be aware that my father can—"

"See and hear through the eyes of his beasts," Kyril interrupted. "I know, and I already checked. For now, we have no spies."

"When I heard you had come here, I..." The fear

that she had kept hidden from everyone, even herself, rushed to the fore as she stared into his eyes. The rest of the room disappeared. "Why did you do it?"

He chuckled. "I seem to recall you asking me to."

"I should not have done so. If something had happened to you, I never…" She swallowed hard, grasping for her composure. Distance. Their relationship was purely about politics now. "It would have destroyed Kitria."

His smile said she wasn't fooling him. His gaze shifted to the spiral shell in her hair. "You're still wearing it."

For all her good intentions, when he leaned in, she didn't hesitate, meeting him halfway, the touch of their lips lighting a fire that swept out from her core to her extremities. His hand moved into her hair, and she parted her lips for him, deepening the kiss. All her thoughts of maintaining a proper distance between them burned to ash in a fire she seemed to have less control over than she did her ability.

When they parted, he stayed close, his hand cupping her cheek. "Do you have any idea how glorious it is to be kissed by you here?" he murmured.

"Why is it different here?"

"Because you're in control. You have no reason to fear me, and you need nothing from me, yet you still chose to do so."

She met his intense gaze and said softly, "You may be mistaken about what I need."

Kyril kissed her again, pulling her closer with a gentle pressure on the small of her back.

"Deeps spare us! Do we have to watch this?" There was a thud as Nalika dropped into a chair.

Kyril drew back and smirked at his subordinate ahnkreth, who was now drinking deeply from a mug. "You're free to look away at any time."

Veyl flushed. Here she was, not only kissing him,

but doing it in front of the people she was supposed to be leading in negotiations. Though it didn't ultimately matter who they were, it wasn't proper behavior regardless of who was watching. How could she hope to have a productive conversation with them now?

"Look at it this way, Nali," Jinau said. "We can count on her to put genuine heart into fighting on our behalf, given her clear personal interest."

Nalika took another swallow from the mug. "At least the mead is decent." Her gaze moved from the drink to Veyl, their eyes meeting for a moment in which Veyl realized the woman was offering her an opportunity to change the focus of the conversation.

"It's Vanrian Black Mead, made using evalis fruit." She walked to the edge of the table, gesturing to the tray that held two stoneglass bottles with overlapping wedges of the juicy black fruit arranged neatly around the edge.

Kyril moved the second and third chairs on the right away from the table, then he sat in the first one and claimed a piece of fruit. Ceris sat on the floor next to him in the newly created space, his head rising above the height of the table like a regal addition to their gathering. The wave dancer looked healthier already, his coat showing a little of its former luster now that he was back with his bonded companion.

As Veyl settled in the seat they had left for her at the head, Kyril peeled a chunk of meat off a grilled pheasant and handed it to Ceris. She couldn't hold back a fond smile.

He turned to her then. "I imagine you're hungry after that sparring session with your prince."

"You saw that?"

He nodded. "It turns out my room has a better view than I initially realized. The academy is impressive, but watching you fight was even more so. You do it exceptionally well, Ahninveth."

"Thank you," she said, heat rising in her cheeks again, "but he's still not my prince."

He picked up the open bottle and topped off their mugs. "Eat."

In truth, she was famished, and therefore grateful when Jinau broke the stalemate by piling food on a plate for himself. The rest of them followed suit, focusing for a few minutes on partaking of the generous meal before moving on to less pleasant affairs.

"The academy outside... is it for mind-crafters?" Kyril asked.

Veyl nodded, washing down her last bite with more mead. "We have another one in the city for everyone else, but the one by the palace has instructors for all the different mind-crafting abilities."

Kyril's eyes met Jinau's for a second. "The city is astounding, at least what I have seen of it. If they ever trust us enough, I would love to see more."

"I hope we can reach that point, but before we discuss our strategy for doing so, I need to understand something." She waited until Kyril gave her his full attention. "Why did you come here? I can't believe you're foolish enough to have risked everything for the sake of a pretty girl."

"You are much more than just a pretty girl, Veyl."

Jinau snorted and shook his head at them. "To answer your question, Seh'hali—"

"What?" Kyril interrupted, his piercing gaze cutting into the other man.

The satisfaction in Jinau's expression made Veyl wonder if he had intended to catch Kyril by surprise. "That's right. You missed that part." Jinau's gaze shifted to her. Something in the way he looked at her then, as though she was a cherished treasure, made her uneasy. "The murmurings began amongst the tribal Qwilki after Veyl drove off the Ukhen'kya. A few days later, your sister offered to take her in because an incident with her ability put her in danger of being executed by the council. The two of them started helping people out around Dagony and the surrounding areas, which earned her more attention and respect. When she got dragged into the sea by a kel'inuk after saving Nagi's life, and a wave dancer pulled her back out, there was no longer any doubt. She is Seh'hali ne Kunua."

Veyl expected Kyril to scoff at that. Instead, he answered with a solemn nod and took her hand, placing a kiss on the back of it. "I had my suspicions when Ceris reacted to her like he did."

"Enough superstitious horseshit." Nalika scowled at Kyril. "Why do I get the impression Jinau knows more about why you insisted on bringing that prince here than your own crew?"

Kyril turned his attention to her, keeping hold of Veyl's hand. "Because he does. Don't take it personally, Nali. We couldn't risk too many people knowing in case it ended badly. One can't be too careful when two of the countries they are courting the wrath of have Evokers."

"This isn't about..." Her jaw clenched and she glared at Veyl. "You don't honestly intend to bring your little Vanrian khesran into that?"

Jinau pinned Nalika with his stare for a moment. When she grabbed her mug and took another swallow of mead, he spoke into the tension-filled silence, his attention moving to Veyl.

"You already noticed that the council does not represent the true population of Thaelis. To be considered for a seat on it, you must have pure lineage traceable to the original Vanrian homeland. Before the Devastation, a resistance was gathering, planning to strongly encourage a change in leadership. But then the Unclean brought the sickness. While it ravaged the populace, the council quarantined, along with their most loyal soldiers, on one of the smaller islands, leaving the rest of us to fend for ourselves. The Devastation killed too many members of our movement and left all of Thaelis weakened. We no longer had the numbers to risk provoking a civil war, especially with the Ukhen'kya lurking on our doorstep, so we have been biding our time, trying to rebuild."

Kyril took over from him. "Seeing how Sarket's leaders resented and feared Vanris's might, then hearing you speak of your country, rekindled a faint hope in me. After you and I spoke that afternoon, when you asked me to take your prince—" a glint of amusement lit his eyes when she frowned at him "—back to Vanris to warn your people about Thrasser, I sought Jin out. It was a long shot, and a risky one, but if Prince Jaysen would vouch for us, we might leverage the warning we carried on your behalf and his history with your family to open negotiations with Vanris and seek an alliance to overthrow the Thaelian council that ordered us to attack and take your people."

"Only Jaysen threw you to the tethdraks once you got here." Veyl closed her eyes and extracted her hand to rub at her temples, trying to fight the headache these new revelations inspired. Somehow, she had landed herself in a room full of Thaelian insurgents. As if the entire mess hadn't been complicated enough already.

"Yes, but now that you're here..." Kyril let his unspoken suggestion hang in the air between them.

She opened her eyes and went to pick up her copy of the agreement, tossing it to him. "I wish I had known some of this before I signed that, though it might not have made much difference. I had to accept terms I would have preferred not to in order to convince them to send me here."

Kyril unfolded the pages and started skimming

through them. When he finished, he left it on the table and got up, coming to stand in front of her. He brushed his fingers down her cheek and brought them under her chin, gently urging her to look up at him.

"And did you plan to fulfill every line of that agreement as it's written?" he asked.

"I…" She met his eyes, realizing what he was getting at. "No. I will not see you put to death. I had hoped to convince my parents to protect you, although right now I suspect they would prefer to execute you themselves."

"If we can persuade Vanris to ally with our side in this, those pages are meaningless. The council will cease to exist."

"But what would that mean? What exactly do you want my country to do?"

"We may find the answers in that very agreement. If Vanris sends ships to collect your people, maybe they could aid us in overthrowing the council and help us hunt down and destroy the Ukhen'kya." A fire sparked in his eyes, ignited by deep-seated hatred for the Unclean, who had taken so much from him, and perhaps for the Thaelian council as well.

"What makes you believe we can talk them into such an undertaking when there is unrest in Vanris and King Thrasser is clearly planning something?"

His regard remained confident and composed. "That's where your knowledge of your country comes in. With you helping us, we have a much better chance of winning them over than we would have had otherwise, even if Jaysen had stood up for us."

Before she could respond to that, he leaned down and kissed her, an achingly soft and lingering kiss that made her determined to prove him right. When he drew back, she met his eyes, lifting her chin away from his touch. Digging into the pouch at her belt, she pulled out the opalescent shell and put it in his palm, folding his fingers around it.

"Kitria sent this for you." Reluctantly releasing his hand, she returned to the table and looked from Nalika to Jinau. "If I am to have any hope of winning my parents over, I need to understand exactly what our goal is."

•

Nearly two hours passed before an attendant knocked on the door. The food and mead were long since gone. The man entered at Veyl's invitation and bowed to her, casting an anxious glance at her companions.

"Khesran Veyl, the council is ready for your group to join them."

The rest stood when she did. "Give us five minutes, please."

When the attendant bowed and stepped out, shutting the door behind him, the other three eyed her curiously, and Veyl pinned them with her gaze one at a time.

"As agreed, we will not mention the insurgency today and instead focus on the contents of the Thaelian council's agreement to see how they respond to it. That will provide us with valuable information we might use to our advantage in the next session. It will also give the council here a chance to adjust to the three of you while you help me try to make a positive impression and keep the discussion from turning hostile. Are we all in accord?"

"A positive impression might be a lot to ask for, Seh'hali." A faint, teasing grin curved Jinau's lips. If he was nervous at all, he didn't show it.

She shook her head at him, longing for that level of composure. "There will be at least one Evoker in that room, aside from Nalika. Keep that in mind. We need to stay consistent and united in our thoughts and our words." For Veyl, the risk of her mind wandering to Kyril's kisses was a greater one than any danger of exposing her Thaelian companions' planned rebellion.

"You must be skilled at that type of deception to be an insurgent when your opposition has Evokers," Kyril offered as reassurance.

A consideration that might be worth pointing out to her parents in their dealings with the anti-mind-crafter groups in Vanris. Later though, after they deemed it safe to disclose the truth to them. "I suppose we are nearly ready, then." Veyl glanced toward the door. What if she proved to be the weak link in this chain?

"What else is there? We didn't need five minutes for that," Nalika grumbled. The woman appeared to hide her unease behind her temper.

Veyl turned to the primary reason she had asked for that time. Stepping around the table corner, she looked up into Kyril's eyes. He had made it quite apparent that it was pointless pretending she didn't long to be close to him, at least behind closed doors. The slow smile that eased across his lips sent a shiver through her.

"I'll only have so many chances to be alone with you," she said, moving to kiss him.

This time he wrapped his arms around her, pulling her tight against him. She melted into that embrace, savoring the strength in him that was intimidating, arousing, and reassuring all at once. Sliding her arms around his neck, she opened her mouth to encourage a more intimate engagement, moving one hand into his hair where he had added Kitria's token to a braid. The need pulsing through her threatened to overwhelm her, the demand in his kiss and how tightly he held her telling her he felt it too. How she wished this would all disappear. That they could be together without complications and politics. That could never happen, though. This was certain to end in heartbreak, but she couldn't resist the temptation of him. She was like a wave, destined to crash upon his shore again and again, but never to stay.

When she pulled away, slightly breathless, he brushed his fingers along one cheek. "You can do this, Seh'hali."

"Don't you start calling me that too." She stepped back from him, despite how desperately she wanted to stay close to his warmth. "I've trained for this most of my life. I'm more concerned about the three of you." She managed a grin that projected far greater confidence than she felt. Now if she could only pull that deception off during negotiations. She met his eyes, lingering within reach of him. "I could simply tell my parents the truth."

Kyril met Jinau's eyes and shook his head. "No. Not yet. The fate of our country hangs in the balance. Let us have today to observe the people we would ally ourselves with first. Then we shall see."

Veyl considered arguing, but it was their home they were fighting for now, not hers. She would let them make that call.

They exited the room together, the other three staying a stride behind Veyl as the attendant and guards escorted them to one of the bigger meeting chambers. Her parents allowed Kyril to bring Ceris, something she found surprising until they entered the room and saw six tethdraks positioned around the perimeter. One of the large, hound-like reptiles rested in each corner of the rectangular chamber with two more midway down the longer sides. Irith was also there, to the right of her father's chair, where he sat beside her mother at the head of the table. With the beasts and a selection of Vanris's elite guards present, one wave dancer wasn't much of a threat.

There were two similar meeting rooms in the palace.

This one she had dubbed the Intimidation Chamber as a child. It had black stone columns inset at intervals between panels of stormy gray marble. Dark metal sconces crafted to look like large spearheads were affixed along the walls. The floors were a patterned blend of the same dark marble intermixed with the black stone. Two curved tables of polished deep red wood sat facing each other, creating most of an oval with a separation at either end to allow entry for attendants serving refreshments and to provide a central space where someone could give a speech or stand for questioning. The massive stoneglass candelabra that hung overhead looked like a spike trap waiting to fall upon some unsuspecting victim. A room designed to intimidate. With the tethdraks in attendance, it did so today more than usual.

The attendant announced them when they entered. As they took their seats, Veyl stole a glance at Kyril, noting his intense focus on one of the tethdraks. Her father was also watching him, eyes narrowing.

"Stop it," she hissed under her breath as the Feral ahnkreth sat on her left.

He glanced at her. "I've only ever seen the beasts in our history books. They're larger than I expected them to be."

"Stay out of their heads," she warned in a low voice. "You're not gaining any points with my father."

Kyril looked at her father and inclined his head in a gesture of respect as Jinau settled on Veyl's right. Nalika took a seat on Jinau's other side, leaving the space next to Kyril for Ceris to nudge his way into, the wave dancer bumping aside the chair that sat there. His ears perked up when he peered across at Irith. For his part, the cliff cat shrank back a fraction, appearing far more skeptical of the new beast.

Her parents sat opposite them, facing her as the khemron and khevarin of Vanris, with Jethan alongside her father on the other side of Irith. Arhk was there, along with Kince and Darro. Ahndhomen Adnar, the Feral who had been her father's first commanding officer, had a seat at the table next to his tehnaak, Dhomen Nevias. Adnar's companion tethdrak stretched on the floor behind his chair. Two Evokers, Yserra and Zafyr, part of her father's and Arhk's personal guards respectively, were present as well as two naval officers from Delaphine who had apparently accompanied the group that Nalika had arrived with. Jaysen sat next to Arhk.

They gave introductions first, providing rank and mind-crafting ability where appropriate. Once that was done, her mother drew a deep breath, her expression flat and chilling when she met Veyl's eyes. The ties of family faded before the duties of a ruler. As Khevarin Velara, she touched her fingertips to the agreement laid out on the table in front of her and Khemron Kasiel.

"We see no point in easing into this. It is obvious Thaelis disregarded our initial demand for the return of our citizens. Can you give us any reason not to do as we promised and use Ahnkreth Kyril's navigational charts to travel there and take them back by force? While you are at it, we would like to hear your rationale for why we should not pass judgment on Ahnkreth Kyril and the members of his fleet for the crimes committed against those people?"

Kyril pressed his knee lightly to Veyl's under the table. It wasn't enough to alleviate the anguish of having her parents looking at her as an opponent, and not a very well-thought of one at that, but it helped her find her voice. "Thaelis would prefer to avoid either of those outcomes. Unfortunately…" She hesitated. To have any hope of success, she needed to present herself as one of them, not as someone acting as part of and independent of the two sides. "A recent attack by the Ukhen'kya, also known as the Unclean, if it pleases the council, rendered us unable to spare the ships necessary for transporting so many when one of our fleets was already absent. We returned four of your citizens as a gesture of our willingness to negotiate a solution amidst these challenges."

The khevarin's icy look didn't thaw in the least. If anything, it grew colder. "The Unclean, while their alleged crimes against Thaelis are undeniably appalling, are not Vanris's concern beyond the potential danger they present to the Vanrian citizens still being held hostage in your country. Regarding the people you returned to us, one is now dead because of an attack by Sarket. An incident that might not have occurred had Ahnkreth Kyril not chosen to strike a deal with King Thrasser upon his first visit to Pandrea. You have bound a khesran of Vanris to Ahndhomen Jinau using a zenyal bond that is illegal in our country, and compelled her to not only represent Thaelis, but to return there after completion of negotiations here, per the terms of this agreement." She arched a brow. "Not the grandest of gestures in the end, now, is it?"

How could her mother speak of her as if she weren't the person in question? A khesran of Vanris. Their daughter.

Frustration and hurt flared in Veyl, accompanied by that crackle of lightning in her chest. Arhk smirked. A hint of black moving into his eyes warned her he could sense her reaction. Veyl drew a breath, conjuring up the crashing of ocean waves in her mind to help her calm the storm.

Arhk gave a subtle nod, and the darkness in his eyes retreated.

Veyl looked at her mother, their ruler, keeping one hand clenched beneath the table. "Neither of our countries needs to invite greater conflict at this time. Thaelis faces an ongoing threat of attack from the Unclean. Vanris is dealing with internal strife and the possibility of a confrontation with Sarket. We—"

"Sarket might feel less emboldened," the dark-skinned Delaphinian admiral, Ansen, interrupted, "if Ahnkreth Kyril had not agreed to dispose of the heir to the throne for them, a deed they currently believe he accomplished."

Veyl refused to be discouraged by his interruption. "Considering how quickly he took advantage of the situation, I believe we can confidently assume King Thrasser would have tried something, whether or not the Thaelian fleet had shown up off his shores."

"Can we be confident of anything at this point?" Kince countered. "None of us would have believed our khesran could turn traitor, yet look where we are."

Veyl winced. The sting of such harsh words from one of her father's tehsheyn, a man she had called uncle growing up, was like a blade in her chest.

Kyril stood, his unforgiving gaze cutting into Kince. "I will ask you not to disrespect Ahninveth Veyl. That she could earn the admiration of so many of my people and come to see the good in them enough to want to protect them, despite everything she has been through—"

Jaysen shot to his feet. "Despite everything you put her through!"

Kyril snubbed Jaysen. His gaze shifted to her parents instead. "I will not deny my guilt. What our fleets did to your people was wrong. Although Khesran Veyl lost everything when we took her, she has never stopped fighting for her countryfolk. It was the power of her conviction that convinced me to bring Prince Jaysen here to warn you of Sarket's actions at the risk of being branded a traitor to my people. I can only hope to earn the place she has given me at her side throughout these proceedings. A place I could not be more honored to have." He looked down at her, his gaze filling her with a warmth free of desire this time. "She is many admirable things. A traitor she is not."

When he sat next to her, she noticed the slight tightening in his jaw, the only hint that he had wanted to give Kince a far harsher reprimand.

Veyl looked at her parents. "If I may…"

The khevarin gestured for Jaysen to return to his seat. "Continue, Ahninveth."

She tried to ignore Evoker Zafyr, who leaned over to whisper something in Arhk's ear. Whatever the woman had gotten from their thoughts was already out there. She hoped it was nothing damaging.

"With Delaphine's aid, Vanris can send a fleet to Thaelis along with me and Ahnkreth Kyril's fleet. The Thaelian council has agreed to let all Vanrians who wish to leave do so."

"No," her father said, contributing for the first time. "You will not be returning to Thaelis."

Anger blossomed in her chest, and the smell of lightning filled her nose. "You would hold me prisoner, then?"

The Delaphinian general and a few others shifted in their seats.

Arhk regarded her with increased interest.

"Seh'hali," Jinau murmured.

Veyl wrestled her unruly ability back under control again.

The khemron didn't answer her volatile question. "What assurances do we have that if we allow Ahnkreth Kyril's fleet to return with the ships we send, they will not turn upon us once they have the rest of their force to aid them?"

"Thaelis does not have the might to fight Vanris," Kyril answered. "They would not dare attack, and I, for one, welcome the opportunity to make amends. I will not allow my fleet to act against you."

The khevarin turned her freezing gaze on him. "You will not be returning to Thaelis either. As leader of one of the fleets that attacked our shores, you will stand trial here. Thaelis will also release the commanding ahnkreth of the other fleet into our custody for the same purpose."

Veyl drew a shaky breath. This was going to be a lot more challenging than she had hoped.

Veyl sat a few feet up from the eave on the rooftop above her bedroom windows. It wasn't the easiest and certainly not the safest climb, but she had done it dozens of times growing up. Cool evening air was welcome after hours in the stifling tension of the meeting room. The perch wasn't high enough to have a view of more than the academy, but it wasn't the scenery that brought her up there. It was frustration and the need to escape everyone. In all her years calling it the Intimidation Chamber, she had never imagined she would sit within those walls feeling like an enemy of her own country… her own parents.

They had resolved nothing in the session. Not that she had expected them to on the first day, but, if anything, she felt like the situation had drifted further from any solutions by the time they wrapped than it had been when they started.

When they dispersed, Arhk had drawn her aside to suggest meeting with her in the morning to help her with her ability. By the time she got away from him, the guards had already escorted the three Thaelians back to their rooms. She would get to speak with them in private again before the negotiations resumed the following afternoon, but she desperately wanted to talk to them tonight. The khevarin and khemron—her parents, they were still her parents—forbade her from visiting their personal rooms. It was unfair. Members of the Vanrian council would have any opportunity they desired to consult with one another, but she could only meet with her group with their permission.

As a khesran, she had rights within the palace, assuming her parents hadn't revoked those. Maybe at some point she would try pushing that line. Tonight, it was all too fresh. She would wait, no matter how much she wanted to speak with Kyril and the others.

Veyl moved her hand away from the spiral shell in her hair when Jaysen poked his head over the eave where his bedroom windows were.

"Is there room for two up there?"

"I suppose," she answered halfheartedly as he pulled himself up and came to sit cross-legged beside her.

"Since we were stuck in the meeting room for dinner, I thought you and I might have our chat up here."

"Because you knew where I would be?" She flicked a twig that some passing bird had dropped onto the roof, sending it flying over the side.

He smiled, but the expression faded when she didn't reciprocate. "How are you holding up?"

"A member of my father's tehsheyn, a man I grew up regarding as one of my uncles, called me a traitor earlier. How do you think I'm holding up?" She could still hear Kince's harsh voice, his words cutting through her.

"Then stop this. Let the Thaelians fight for their own country. You've already given them more than they deserve."

She watched a bird circle in the distance, riding the higher wind currents. "You didn't experience the side of Dagony that I did. The people were kind and welcoming to me. They didn't know what their council had done to bring us there, and they were so excited to have us. I enjoyed helping them. I can't let them come to harm because their council members are a bunch of callochs. If I weren't willing to fight for them, my parents wouldn't be giving them any chance at all. Not after what they did to us."

"Ironic, isn't it?" Jaysen chuckled, though there was little actual humor in the sound. "Gannon was asking about you."

She looked at him, daring to allow herself a spark of hope. "Gannon? Really? How is he doing?"

"For once, he didn't have it in him to mock or insult me. I'm guessing that's a bad sign. He has his family and Iyvalin keeping a close eye on him, though."

Veyl nodded, swallowing against the tightening in her throat. She watched the bird arc around and come their way, moonlight glinting off the silver that tipped its wings. "I'm glad. He's going to need all the support they can give him to get past this."

Jaysen followed her gaze, frowning as the nightstar eagle let out a cry. "And that was a brief chat."

She reached over and squeezed his hand. "We'll have our chance. There's just a lot going on right now." Letting go of him, she slid toward the eave above her window.

"Need a hand?"

Veyl smirked at him. "Just worry about getting yourself down in one piece. I imagine you're out of practice."

A grin tugged at his lips as he slid toward his window.

Veyl took hold of the edge and lowered herself down onto the sill, climbing inside to find her father waiting, watching her. She turned her back on him to shut the window and hide the unexpected sting of tears. "What do you want?" she asked, emotion giving her words a sharp edge.

"Today wasn't as fun as you hoped?"

She turned on him, a crackle of energy rising with

her anger. "I never expected it to be fun! All I want is to get our people home without hurting theirs. Why is that wrong?"

Irith growled low in his throat, his ears lying back. It was the first time the cliff cat had ever growled at her with any seriousness. Her father eyed her warily, retreating a step. A loud roar sounded out across the city from the kanodrak habitat, Niskenya reacting to her bonded companion's alarm.

Facing the window again, Veyl gripped the sill and closed her eyes, imagining the sound of the waves crashing on the rocks and Dampener Erkhan's forced darkness surrounding her. She wrestled with the energy that raced through her, flickering out to her fingertips and threatening to reach beyond.

"I'm sorry. Your mother retired early so no one would see her crying. Kince and I nearly came to blows a few minutes ago over his calling you a traitor today. This is difficult for all of us."

She drew a trembling breath, finally wrestling her ability back under control. "Kince was just being Kince." The rawness in her voice undermined her dismissive words.

"He was out of line," her father said, anger in his tone that turned to concern when he spoke again. "I appreciate that Ahnkreth Kyril defended you today, but he risked a great deal for you by coming here. I'd like to understand why. What's in this for him?"

Struggling to keep her tone and expression neutral, she turned to face him. "I told you, he protected me on the voyage to Thaelis and tried to help me with my ability..." she trailed off when he shook his head.

"And I don't need to hear all the other things he's done for you again. I want to know why he did them."

Far too many potential missteps lurked within this conversation. "At first, he defended me because I was everything they were hoping for. A powerful mind-crafter of royal Vanrian lineage. But he's not the awful person you think he is. I believe he genuinely regrets what they did. When the council told him to come back here, he tried to make up for the wrongs they committed by helping me. Look at how devoted that wave dancer is to him. You of all people know a Feral bond that strong requires true empathy."

"You're not a beast, Veyl."

She grinned. "I've been called a little beast by you plenty of times."

He cracked a smile. "And so you can be, but no changing the subject."

She blew out a breath, latching quickly onto a different approach. "He is also like Ahndhomen Jinau, almost more Qwilki than Thaelian. The Qwilki, because of the things I told you about, believe I am special. Seh'hali ne Kunua. Daughter of the Ocean."

"You are special, but I prefer to think of you as my daughter."

She took a few steps closer, and Irith walked up to meet her, rubbing his head into her hand, no longer defensive now that her ability was quiet. "It's comforting to hear you say that after today."

His gaze sank to the cliff cat as she scratched behind the beast's ears, coaxing forth a loud purr. "We can't be gentle with you just because you're our daughter. Not in that room. Right now, our responsibility is to ensure the safety of all Vanris."

She lowered her gaze. "I know, and I would expect no less. I just… I didn't realize how hard this was going to be, but I swear to you that the people here are still my priority."

He nodded. "It pleases me to hear you say as much. Now, back to the subject of our guests. One of them in particular."

Dread coiled in Veyl's gut. She had to get him off the line of questioning he had fixated on, and the only way she could think of doing so was to hint at the truth the others had asked her to hide. If she approached it carefully, she wouldn't be entirely betraying their trust. "Please don't mention this to anyone yet, because I'm uncertain myself, but I've gotten the impression that the three of them may not want to support their leaders. The Thaelian council doesn't represent all the people of Thaelis. They only allow those with pure lineages traceable back to the original Vanrian homeland to sit on the council, but the populace is far more mixed. When I was there, I noticed that the council members appear to have lost touch with the people they lead. I'm trying to earn enough trust to convince the others to speak openly with me about it."

His brow furrowed. "That information could be extremely relevant to these negotiations." Stepping closer, he put his hands on her arms and looked her in the eyes. "You're a smart young woman. I believe you can do this, but you're going to have to tread delicately. If your suspicions are correct, they would be admitting treason."

"Ahnkreth Kyril already faces accusations of treason against his country. The other two don't have that hanging over them. Regardless, I will figure it out." She let him pull her into his arms and rested her head against his shoulder, closing her eyes. "I'm just glad you can still love me when we aren't in that room."

"We love you inside that room too," he whispered, his arms squeezing tighter around her. "More than you could possibly imagine."

●

Veyl had just finished dressing the next morning when

there was a knock on her door. The muscles between her shoulder blades pulled tight, and she briefly considered pretending not to be there. But no attendant had delivered the usual early meal, which meant someone, almost certainly her grandfather, had told them not to. Chances were good it was him outside her door now.

"Come in."

When Arhk walked in, the tightness in her back eased some. Whoever it was she so desperately dreaded seeing, it apparently wasn't him. Was it Jaysen and the difficult conversation they needed to have? Or perhaps her mother after the meeting yesterday?

Arhk looked her over once, taking in the finely made but functional attire she had selected in case an opportunity arose to spar with someone. The amount of nervous energy she had buzzing through her gave the idea significant appeal.

"Good morning. I hoped you might join me for something to eat."

"Because you're worried I'll Frighten someone to death during negotiations later?" The query, meant to be jesting, came out far sharper than she intended, exposing some of her underlying stress.

Arhk nodded, a disconcerting trace of pleasure in his smile. "That possibility had occurred to me. But you are also my granddaughter, and I am glad to have you home, regardless of the complicated nature of your return."

Veyl lowered her gaze. "I'm sorry. I need to work on concealing my emotions better."

"No. Not when we are alone, at least. You should never have to hide yourself from your family."

If he only knew the things she was hiding.

She drew a deep breath and let it out.

One corner of his mouth quirked up. "Except for whatever that was, apparently. You cannot carry all the weight of the world on your shoulders alone."

Veyl grinned. "I find it ironic to hear those words coming from your lips."

His smile held the familiar hint of sorrow he had carried with him her whole life. From talking to others, she got the impression he had carried that weight alone since the day a group from Sarket murdered his wife and kidnapped his son—her father—as a child. Getting his son back twelve years later hadn't erased that pain, though she hoped it had eased it some.

"I am always the exception to my own rules." He gestured toward the door. "Shall we?"

"Lead the way."

He didn't take her to the sitting area of his chambers as she had half expected him to. Their route led them past the hall that split off to the guest quarters. Three of the doors in that first section had guards in front of them, Kyril's with four compared to only two each on the others. Did Ceris find their wariness of him amusing? Those rooms weren't located where she could reach them using the rooftops, not that she should even consider doing so. Besides, her father would be keeping an eye on the palace from inside and out with the aid of his many creatures while the Thaelians were there.

Arhk took her to the same sitting area looking out on the vast enclosed garden that she had visited her parents in the day before. Attendants were finishing setting up a selection of food with hot tea and sweet wine to accompany the meal. Once they left, she settled in a chair facing Arhk, each of them taking a moment to sample a few of the offerings from the table.

Veyl washed a bite down with a sip of wine and asked a question that had nagged her since his intervention on the ship, when she had become trapped by her power. "Typically, mind-crafters can't affect or be affected by someone who shares the same ability. How were you able to use your ability on me to break me free of my own?"

"In ordinary cases, that is true. In that specific situation, your ability had taken control of you, which left you vulnerable to outside influences, even those of a like nature. Normally, you would have been immune to my efforts."

Veyl slathered jam across a piece of bread and took a bite, delighting in the natural sweetness of the berries used to make it. Despite the comfort she got from enjoying familiar meals being prepared for her, she missed the simple pleasure of discovering new dishes. She missed Kitria, under whose patient tutelage she started learning to cook some of those unfamiliar foods for herself.

"Would you care to share the thoughts that bring that wistful smile to your lips?"

For a second, she considered whether he might hold the truth against her, but she had always enjoyed a bond with her grandfather, whom so many people feared—a bond that took on new depth with the awakening of her Frightener ability.

"I was thinking of a woman in Thaelis, a little younger than me. Ahnkreth Kyril's sister Kitria, who welcomed me into her home and was teaching me how to make some of the traditional Qwilki dishes."

Arhk chuckled, biting into a juicy orange wedge.

"What do you find funny about that?"

He swallowed, then a faint, teasing smile curved his lips. "I am merely trying to imagine you cooking for yourself."

"It was fun, and I wasn't half bad at it," she answered with a deliberately dramatic pout.

"You excel at most of the tasks you put your mind to, though I have gotten the impression your Frightener ability is proving more resistant."

She gazed past him into the jungle of foliage beyond

the glass wall, thriving within the carefully managed enclosure. Plants that provided food or medicine, and some simply for decoration, in a vibrant garden that burst with life year-round.

"Have you ever broken someone's mind with your ability?" she asked, finally meeting his eyes.

"Yes. A few times after it first awakened, and on several occasions in the months following the loss of Kasiel and his mother." Though his tone remained almost disinterested, she caught a quick tightening around his eyes and in his jaw before he moved on. "Most abilities have the potential to destroy a mind in that way if they are powerful enough. As a Frightener, I am afraid you will find few who appreciate the strength of your ability."

Veyl nodded, poking at a savory pastry on her plate that had looked far more appetizing a moment ago. "Do you see their fear?"

"I do. You must learn to accept that fear and blend it into a single experience in your mind the way the sounds from an array of different instruments can come together to create a song." As he spoke, he applied jam to a piece of bread, meticulously spreading an even coat to every edge. "Then use your ability to play that song back, if you will, to the people you wish to influence. When your ability—your song—takes hold of them, their minds will transform it into whatever sparks terror in their hearts."

Veyl stared at him. "When you speak of it, you make it sound much more beautiful than it is."

"Because I learned to accept what I am. You must do the same if you wish to control it." He passed the bread to her and picked up another to spread jam on for himself. "Master their fears. Give them a form, an image or sound in your mind that pleases you. One that will help keep you focused and in control."

"Like the ocean breaking upon the shore." She took

a bite of the bread, delicious enough on its own that the jam made it an overindulgence of the most delectable kind.

His brows rose a fraction. "If that pleases you."

They finished the bread in companionable silence. Before they could resume their conversation, the door opened, and her father entered with Irith at his side.

"A pleasant morning to you both."

Arhk stood, so Veyl did the same, though, given the familial bonds between them all, the formality seemed out of place.

"Good morning, Kasiel."

"Father," Veyl added, letting Arhk's greeting serve for her as well. She glanced past him to where three of his personal guards, including his Evoker Yserra and Dampener Minera, stood waiting on the other side of the wide hall. "Are you going somewhere?"

"I'm meeting..." He trailed off, his focus turning inward in the way it did when one of his beasts passed information to him, and Irith glanced back down the hall, his ears swiveling in that direction.

After a second, Veyl heard several sets of footsteps approaching. Then Kyril and Ceris came into view, stopping outside the door in the company of four guards.

Her father faced the other Feral. "I was heading out to visit the habitats, and I thought your wave dancer might enjoy an opportunity to stretch his legs."

Kyril bowed his head respectfully. "Your consideration is appreciated, Khemron Kasiel." His hand came to rest on Ceris's head. Though he never looked directly at her, somehow she could feel his attention on her, like the heat of the summer sun.

"We shall go then." Kasiel glanced back at her. "Why don't you join us, Veyl?"

Panic twisted her gut, and she turned to her grandfather. "I would, but we were having..." she trailed off when Arhk extended a hand toward her father.

"Feel free to accompany them. I have other business I should attend to."

She realized then that she hadn't thrown her father off the scent after all. This was a trap, set up to try figuring out what sort of connection, if any, existed between her and the Thaelian ahnkreth. Kyril's wary look said he saw it too, but there was no reasonable way to escape it now that wouldn't draw more suspicion. She couldn't even use her need to meet with the other Thaelians as an excuse to beg off because her father was taking one of them with him.

Forcing the appearance of composure, she inclined her head. "Thank you, Father. I would enjoy the walk." She accepted the arm he offered her.

They wandered out through the garden, her father's guards and the four accompanying Kyril falling back far enough to offer some privacy for conversation while staying within range to react to threats. Veyl strode along next to Irith on her father's right, while Kyril walked on his other side with the wave dancer between them. Ceris peered over at Irith now and then, ears perked with an eagerness that made her wonder how young the beast was.

"Dhomvalen Arhk was helping with your Frightener ability, I assume?" Her father inquired, breaking the uneasy silence.

"We discussed it a little?"

"The dhomvalen is a Frightener?" Kyril asked.

Her father nodded. "The strongest in Vanris."

Kyril gave Veyl a sideways look. "Even now?"

Her father glanced at her as well, his brow furrowing. "You incapacitated the crews of three Sarketi ships, as I understand it. That's no insignificant feat."

"You should have seen the fleet of Ukhen'kya she drove off." The glimmer of pride in Kyril's tone brought warmth to Veyl's cheeks.

"I should like to hear more about that."

Veyl had told him some of that experience, but Kyril was more than happy to indulge him in a retelling from his perspective without embellishment, while still framing it as an extraordinary accomplishment. To her relief, he emphasized his gratitude for her selfless defense of his people, which might lend a more straightforward legitimacy to his desire to help her.

At the cliff cat enclosure, they let Ceris out into the recovery area to run. He sprinted around the perimeter twice before settling into pace along the barrier between him and the rest of the habitat to observe Irith and a few other big cats. The cats watched Ceris from a distance, curious but wary of the strange amphibious canine.

"You attempted to interact with my tethdraks in the meeting chamber yesterday," her father commented a short time later as they were leaving the habitat.

"Apologies, Khemron, I meant no disrespect." Kyril smoothly deflected the accusation in her father's stern regard. "It was merely curiosity. I have only ever seen them in illustrations in our history books."

Opportunity lit her father's eyes. "Then you've never seen a kanodrak either, I assume."

Veyl caught a trace of almost childlike eagerness in his voice. A boy who had just discovered someone to whom he could show off the toy he took the greatest pride in. Not that Niskenya was a toy, or even his in essence, but the effect was still quite similar, allowing tension between the two Ferals to fade for the moment. If Kyril were Vanrian, she suspected they might easily learn to get along.

"You assume correctly," Kyril answered, a flicker of cautious interest in his eyes. Next to him, Ceris's ears perked up, the animal responding more openly to his companion's emotions.

"Come with me."

Her father led them to the enormous building that overlooked the tethdrak canyon. It took them a few seconds to get Kyril past the life-sized kanodrak statue in the center of the structure. When they reached the open back wall and viewing platform, he stood gazing out at the habitat, lost in awestruck contemplation for several minutes before they led him to the complicated lift mechanism that would carry them to the canyon floor, which created another prolonged distraction. At the bottom, they passed in front of the tethdrak habitat, and a few of the reptilian beasts approached the barrier, watching the wave dancer curiously. Ceris bounded closer, giving off some of the strange calls he had used with the whales. One of the younger tethdraks sprinted back and forth along the bars several times, excited by the new sound.

Ceris bolted back to Kyril, looking immensely pleased with himself. The Feral ahnkreth sank to one knee in the dirt and scratched the beast behind both ears. "Are you trying to make friends again?"

Ceris licked him on the nose, and Veyl smiled, glancing over in time to catch the thoughtful look on her father's face. The sun brought out the lighter shades in his long red hair, pulled back into two braids like the ones she wore. In his case, it exposed one of his ears, which ended in flat scars from being cut short by the people who kidnapped him as a child. Did he remember what it was like to be ripped away from his home? Her mother said he had been almost five when it happened, and the trauma of the event seemed to have erased most of his memories of that time and his life before it. Regardless, she could see how the experience wouldn't endear him to Kyril or his people. Arhk either, who had his son stolen away as she had been, only at a much younger age. They faced an uphill battle with the two men.

Kyril stood, the sunlight drawing out the blue in his black hair. He looked at the canyon habitat, then back at the lift they had ridden down on. "This place is impressive. Thaelis is a much simpler land. I'm afraid our isolation has encouraged a certain level of ignorance about the world beyond our shores."

"No amount of ignorance should lead your people to believe that stealing others from their homes is acceptable," her father remarked, his tone cutting, though Veyl caught a slight softening there of the teaching voice he often used with her when she got into trouble. Something she suspected he had picked up from his tehnaak. Speaking of whom.

"Why isn't Uncle Jethan with you?"

He faced her. "Jethan and your mother are having a conversation with Ahndhomen Jinau."

Charmers for a Charmer, naturally, and a Feral to handle the Thaelian Feral. Maybe he wasn't still suspicious about Kyril's support of her after all. But then, why would he have brought her along if he didn't have an underlying motive?

"Divide and conquer." A smirk curved Kyril's lips, the barest hint of admiration in his tone. "I have to ask, who did you subject to Evoker Nalika's sharp temper?"

"Evoker Zafyr and Dhomvalen Arhk should be able to handle it," her father answered, and Veyl instantly felt sorry for the Thaelian Evoker. "Come, I'm curious to see how your wave dancer responds to the kanodraks."

At the door leading into the tunnel that cut through to the kanodrak canyon, he ordered Kyril's guards to wait, taking only his three elite ones with them. It surprised her he was letting the wave dancer come, but, as a Feral who could control almost any beast, she could see where his curiosity regarding the creature might be too much for him. Perhaps he sought Niskenya's impression of it.

When they stepped out into the canyon on the other side, the kanodrak was at the front of the enclosure, waiting. No matter how many times she saw the beast, Veyl remained in awe of her. Larger than a horse, but built more like a cat, she had long upper canines that dipped below her jaw, a silver-gray scaled hide, and exposed bone armor over part of her head and neck. There was nothing like her, aside from the other kanodraks, one of which lurked several yards away, curious about them, but respectful of the alpha female.

Kyril took a few steps toward the bars and bowed to the beast. Niskenya watched him with her milky white eyes, letting out a low growl at his approach. His gaze turned inward for a second, and he chuckled when she growled louder.

"Quite forceful, isn't she?" he asked, not taking his eyes from the kanodrak.

"Kanodraks choose their companions and let no one in without permission," her father explained, watching the Thaelian Feral intently. Then his gaze lowered to Ceris. "Much like your wave dancer, it turns out."

"Hm, yes." Kyril touched the tall canine's shoulder. "No wave dancer has ever been forced to do anything."

Kasiel nodded, a thoughtful furrow forming in his brow. "This is Niskenya."

"It is a great honor," Kyril said, looking her over with open, almost childlike awe.

Ceris trotted forward, approaching the bars without fear, and made a trilling sound. Niskenya lowered her head, sniffing at him, and answered with what sounded like a purr, only a little higher pitched than anything Veyl had ever heard from her. The wave dancer reared up on his hind feet, placing his front paws on the bars, and pushed his nose between them to lick her head. The kanodrak responded with another high purr, rubbing her face forcefully against the bars.

Her father looked taken aback by the instant bond between the two very different creatures. Kyril, however, didn't appear even a little surprised, his lack of reaction taking Veyl back to the wave dancer's interactions with the whales. She had assumed there was some natural relationship between the two ocean species, but maybe it was more than that.

"I've never seen Niske take to another creature like that." Kasiel stepped closer to the bars, his attention riveted on the two.

"Something in the way wave dancers communicate seems to be like a common tongue for many beasts. Most intelligent creatures react positively to them."

The other kanodrak crept a little closer, also watching Ceris and Niskenya. The wave dancer bounded back and forth along the bars as though inviting the larger beasts to play. Niskenya rose in a half-rear, landing with a grunt and vocalizing again. Ceris's tail wagged enthusiastically.

Her father chuckled. "You are fortunate to have the favor of such a creature."

"It appears we are both fortunate in the bonds we have made," Kyril answered, his gaze flickering briefly to Veyl while her father's attention was on the beasts.

She avoided his eyes and walked up to the bars next to Ceris. Niskenya calmed, her gaze settling on Veyl for an unnervingly long moment. Kyril approached on Ceris's other side, his focus on the kanodrak farther back. The second beast huffed, staring at him and digging his claws into the ground.

"Don't even consider it." A hard edge came into her father's voice.

"You needn't worry." Kyril's grin was disarming and unfortunately handsome. "I've never been on a mount of any kind. I'm not eager to start that education with one of these."

"Wise choice." Her father's laugh, though it still carried tension, gave her a glimmer of hope. Maybe this could come to a peaceful resolution after all.

On the way back, Veyl quietly observed while the two Ferals amiably chatted about the different beasts they had worked with. Kyril seemed most intrigued with her father's ability to see and hear through the creatures he connected to, questioning him about it for at least half the walk. When they reached the guest hall in the palace, the guards escorted Kyril back to his room at her father's bidding, and he continued with Veyl to hers. She didn't need to go there, but she got the sense he wanted to speak to her in private, so she let him determine their destination.

"Well, what did you think?" she asked as they walked through the door into her sitting area.

"I think you were rather attentive to him."

A flush of alarm swept through her. She had been so busy worrying about the impression Kyril would make with his words and actions she hadn't stopped to consider what her own behavior might give away.

"I was merely..." she trailed off before the stern shake of his head.

"Niskenya could see a few threads reaching between the two of you. One similar to the link you have with Ahndhomen Jinau that looked to have been intentionally severed, and another more natural bond that appears to be in the early process of forming. Would you care to explain these to me?"

Veyl turned and walked to the empty pass-through fireplace that warmed the sitting room and bedroom in colder months. How careless could she be? She knew Niskenya had abilities akin to a Bondmaker's, and that her father could see through her eyes, but her excitement for Kyril to meet the kanodrak and for her father to see the Thaelian Feral in a different light made her careless. She hadn't considered exactly how much he might learn from watching them that way. That he had been willing to introduce Kyril to his cherished companion had struck her as a positive development, but in truth, it was just a clever method for extracting information. If she had thought it through, she might have tried harder to come up with a way to avoid going with them, though she doubted he would have allowed it. Now she had to give him at least some portion of the truth.

"After I broke one of his crew members in Deepwater, Ahnkreth Kyril had me made his zenyal to protect his fleet from my ability on the way to Thaelis." Watching her father's expression darken, it occurred to her to wonder why Jaysen hadn't mentioned that detail. They really needed to have that talk, if for no other reason than to find out what he had and hadn't told her parents. "In his defense, I did attack him in a manner that would likely have proven fatal after that. It wasn't an irrational precaution."

"And he deserved to be broken by you," her father growled.

Any progress they had made today disintegrated before her eyes. Veyl absently touched the spiral shell in her hair, and his eyes narrowed.

"What about the other bond I saw developing?"

He would hate the full truth behind that, but she didn't have to tell him everything. "I don't have an answer for you that you're going to want to hear. On the way to Thaelis, he showed me patience and stood by me in moments when most of his people would have written me off for being too dangerous. He defended and protected me. He saved me when…" she cut off abruptly, realizing what she had been about to admit.

"When what?" He took a few steps closer, the dread in his look suggesting a little too much perceptiveness.

"I…" This was one incident she had meant to keep from her parents forever, but she had to give him something, and it was either that or the truth about Kyril. She looked away, straining to breathe past the constriction in her throat. "At my lowest point, when I believed I would never see any of you again, I tried to kill myself. Kyril and Ceris saved me."

"Veyl," his voice cracked, and he rushed to her, pulling her into his arms and holding her as though he feared he might lose her at any moment.

Her head came to rest against his shoulder. There were no tears, at least not for her. Perhaps her eyes had simply run dry. She would never grow tired of knowing how deeply her father loved her, but it hurt to acknowledge how much pain this experience had brought her parents. Still, no matter how much of this was his doing, she couldn't find it in herself to hate Kyril for it. What she felt for him was quite a long way from hate.

They stood there in silence for a time. Then he kissed her head before he spoke again. "How can you feel gratitude toward that man for saving you when he was the reason you were miserable enough to want to end your life?"

She gently extracted herself. "Because I understand now what his people lost, what he lost, that drove them to come looking for us. I also know a little of what they were told about us. Most importantly, I believe he regrets what they did, enough that he risked defying the council's orders to come here and warn you. They grow up being taught to view the other original Vanrians—our people—as enemies. We are the descendants of those who tried to suppress their ancestors through violence. Their council drilled into them that the only way to bring us there without us destroying their way of life was to capture some and ensure the rest never discovered where they took us."

"That's absurd."

She met his eyes, forcing herself to hold the contact. "Is it? Why don't our history books or classes talk about the political strife that drove the people from the province of Thaelis to risk evacuating the homeland on their own? Why did we erase them if we did nothing wrong?"

He broke eye contact. "I don't know. I wasn't around when those choices were made."

She could tell he was thinking about it, considering that there might be more to the mistrust the Thaelians had for Vanris than was immediately obvious. "But doesn't it make you wonder?"

"It does, but we may never have answers to that, and it still doesn't excuse what they did." A sudden discomfort became apparent in the way he looked away and in the slight fall of his shoulders. "I hate to have to ask you this, but my understanding is that they took all of you to reintroduce pure bloodlines and more mind-crafters into their country. Were you forced to be intimate—"

"No!" She hoped he would take the coloring of her cheeks as embarrassment over the subject in general rather than a symptom of the truth she was trying to hide. No one had forced themselves on her, that was true, but she had been intimate with someone. "The Thaelians wanted us to integrate and become part of their society. They truly believed we would do so, given time, and I'm not sure that they were wrong about that."

He arched a brow in question, so she elaborated.

"It is beautiful there, and the people, at least in my experience, were mostly welcoming, generous, and kind, aside from the delusional, self-important councilors." Should she tell him she suspected the council had given some of the Vanrian prisoners to the Ukhen'kya? Without proof, maybe that was something best left unsaid for now, especially considering how tense the situation already was.

"I'm glad some of them treated you well, and they at least didn't sink to that depth of cruelty. I don't think we could negotiate any further with them otherwise. It's hard enough, given the things they did do." His gaze took on a greater intensity, reminding her of his eagle when it was hunting. "Tell me you haven't developed feelings for that man."

How she hated keeping secrets from him, but nothing would make him understand and accept how she felt about Kyril or what she had done with him. Something she would be happy to do again if the opportunity presented itself. She sighed. "I am grateful for some of the things he did for me and what he sacrificed by coming here. That's all."

"That he saved your life in an intensely traumatic moment could explain the fledgling bond, but we should work to prevent any further development of that connection. Are you certain you can maintain an emotional distance between you while continuing to interact for the sake of these negotiations?"

"Father." She gave him a flat look, lying to him with her eyes, her expression, and the set of her shoulders, even her tone, but not with words. She could at least avoid that.

He considered her for a few seconds, still apparently hesitant to take her at her word. Eventually, he nodded. "All right. You may wish to meet with the Thaelian contingent soon. We would like to start at noon today to see if we can make any headway. Our Delaphinian allies are eager to return to their own waters. If you can persuade the Thaelians to disclose to you whether they support their council, that might help guide our path forward."

"I don't suppose you would allow us to meet in a more comfortable space. One of the drawing rooms, perhaps?"

Kasiel's lips quirked up in a smirk. "Are you going to teach them Feral's Folly?"

His touch of humor relaxed the muscles between her shoulder blades that she hadn't even realized were tense. Maybe someday she would be able to have a conversation with her father again without it inducing anxiety. "As apropos as that sounds, I was hoping the casual atmosphere might help encourage the openness we're hoping for."

"I'll have attendants set up food and drink in the south drawing room. Just keep your wits about you while around them, all right? You've got a Charmer and an Evoker in there."

He had a point, although it was the Feral who was addling her wits. "I am aware. If Ahndhomen Jinau were to try something, the zenyal bond would let me know, so there's some benefit there."

His scowl told her how little he thought of that. "Be careful and don't give them more trust than they deserve." With that warning, he gave her a hug and left her to prepare.

Veyl took a few minutes to don her Thaelian uniform. Doing her best to ignore the increasingly frantic flutter in her chest, she struck out for the south drawing room. When she arrived, two attendants were finishing setting up an assortment of fruit, cheese, and teacakes, along with tea and sweet wine. Veyl considered the selection and the people she was meeting with for a moment, then beckoned one attendant over.

"Could we exchange the wine for mead?"

"Yes, Khesran."

As that attendant departed with the wine, she turned to the other. "Please ask Ahnkreth Kyril's guards to escort him here."

The woman bowed her head, but she didn't leave. "Only the Ahnkreth, Khesran?"

"Yes, please. There are a few matters I want to clear up with him before the other two arrive."

"As you wish, Khesran."

The woman left her, and Veyl started pacing behind an elegant ivory and black couch, pausing briefly when the first attendant returned to drop off the mead. She traced her fingers along the carved, black-stained wood edging as she paced, feeling the notch toward one end on each pass. Tavin had dropped an ornamental dagger he wasn't supposed to be playing with on it when their parents walked into the room. He had been about eight at the time. She and Jaysen had been watching him try to show off his skill with the weapon to Ellaris and giggling to themselves. Ultimately, they had also gotten in trouble for not intervening and setting a good example.

At a knock on the door, she took a moment to compose herself, then called for them to enter.

The attendant opened the door. "Ahnkreth Kyril, Khesran."

She forced herself not to watch him as he entered with Ceris at his side, keeping her gaze on the attendant. "Give us ten minutes before you send for the other two, please."

"As you wish." She bowed out and shut the door.

Veyl counted down a few seconds, aware of Kyril watching her curiously from where he now stood near one chair. Then she went and slid the bolt on the door quietly into place before facing him.

He arched a brow in question, though he didn't approach.

Veyl walked closer and met his eyes. "Is it safe?"

His focus turned inward, telling her he understood what she was asking. After a second, he nodded.

Clinging to her resolve, she stated, "There can be no more intimacy between us."

"Because?"

She narrowed her eyes at him. "You know the answer to that. I am a khesran of Vanris. I can't have a casual fling with anyone, let alone a man who has committed crimes against my people. Should I someday be allowed to choose my own match, you would never be an acceptable option. You're not even Vanrian."

"No, I'm not. Nor am I noble, and I have no khesran." He closed the remaining distance, his fingertips caressing her cheek as he brushed a lock of her hair back behind one pointed ear. "You realize that was one of the strongest arguments I had against coming here."

"What was?" Her voice came out as a breathless whisper that lit a spark of hunger in his eyes. She should step back, look away, break the moment somehow, but she didn't.

"Knowing I would lose any chance I might have had of a future with you in it."

He leaned toward her, and she mirrored the movement as if enthralled. Their lips touched, engaging in the very intimacy she had just tried to deny him. His fingers traced a line of fire down the side of her neck, and she shifted closer, molding her body to his, ignoring the voice in her head now mocking her for how utterly she had failed at establishing boundaries between them. But she felt instantly stronger and more alive when his arms moved around her. He was the rocky shore she wanted to break upon. How had it gotten to this point?

She slid her hands into his hair, holding him close,

and deepened the kiss, bombarded by heated memories of that afternoon in Thaelis. After a moment, she drew apart from him, lingering with her lips mere inches from his, their breath mingling.

"No matter what happens, I am yours." She made herself step back. "But we are in Vanris now. Things are different here. What transpired between us in Thaelis… I believed I might never leave there. No longer a khes-ran. Just a woman like any other. If I could not have the life I lost, I hoped I could at least have you."

"And were you ever going to stop trying to find a way back to that life?" He cupped her jaw, running his thumb across his cheek, the warmth of affection in his striking silver-blue eyes.

Veyl pressed into his hand, savoring that contact. "Maybe," she whispered, "for the right reason."

He chuckled. "Lie to yourself if you must, but don't expect me to believe it. You would never have stopped fighting. That doesn't change how I feel about you. If anything, your fierce determination is one of the things I love most about you."

How she wanted to give herself to him again.

Responding to her unspoken longing, he captured her lips in another kiss. An achingly soft and lingering one this time that made her eyes sting with desperate tears. In Thaelis, there might have been a chance, but not here. Never here.

A knock on the door made her startle away from him.

"Khesran Veyl, the others have arrived," the attendant called.

It was faster than she wanted, but there was nothing for it now. "One moment." Meeting Kyril's silver-blue eyes, she did her best to sound stern as she said, "No more."

He brushed his thumb along her lower lip and

winked, his grin making her want to slap him… or kiss him again. She pointed to a chair, waiting until he walked toward it to slide the bolt carefully free and open the door. She let Jinau and Nalika in as Kyril sat and poured mead into their mugs, Ceris settling on the carpet alongside him. The other two Thaelians wore knowing looks as they joined him.

"I understand you all had visitors this morning," Veyl prompted as she sat in a chair opposite Kyril, far enough away to avoid the temptation for contact.

Nalika turned the mug in her hands, a faint smile curving her lips as she inhaled the aroma of the dark liquid. "Your dhomvalen is an intimidating man."

"He's my grandfather, and yes, most people feel that way about him. He was one of Vanris's greatest assets in the war, along with my father."

"Doesn't that consolidate a substantial amount of power into one family?" Kyril asked before taking a drink from his mug.

Veyl opened her mouth to dismiss his words, then paused, considering them for a moment, aware of Jinau and Nalika watching her. "I suppose it does, but my parents make very few weighty decisions without the input of the council, though their position grants them the power to do so. I don't see where it has brought any harm or hardship to the people of Vanris. My father accepted the role of khemron only because it came with the woman he loved." Her gaze shifted to Kyril as she spoke those last words, and he returned her regard without expression, taking another drink of his mead.

Veyl glanced up above the quiet fireplace to her left at a painting of the lake behind the northern capital of Doran. She had visited there with her family dozens of times when she was younger, often with Jaysen, Tavin, and Ellaris. Sometimes the twins and their associated tehnaaks came with them too. Swimming in those waters, enjoying the simplicity of childhood adventures, she never dreamed she would end up in a position like this.

She needed to talk to Jaysen. He had been her confidant throughout much of her youth. The one who stood by her and supported her in the years after she lost her tehnaak. Events in Deepwater before the arrival of the Thaelians had altered their friendship. Now Jaysen desired something more, but he had to recognize that a relationship between them was as impossible as one between her and Kyril. Even if they both wanted it, they could never be together romantically when they were destined to rule their very different countries. What did he hope to gain from continuing to pursue her in that way?

"Seh'hali?"

She looked at Jinau. "Apologies. I got lost in thought. Did you say something?"

Jinau nodded, his regard offering patience and acceptance of her distraction. "I said your mother is a shrewd woman, protective of you and the country she leads. And your father's tehnaak cleverly hides his perceptive and thoughtful nature behind a disarming wit. I, for one, believe we could do much worse than to ally ourselves with these people, if they will consider it."

Veyl nodded, giving Nalika and Kyril expectant looks. "It pleases me to hear you say so, because it's time to leave off playing games if we want to avoid creating a greater division between our two sides. If we do not plan to negotiate based upon the terms I agreed to with the Thaelian council, we should make that clear now. We are wasting time while the threats of the Ukhen'kya and Sarket loom over us."

"There remains a substantial barrier to seeking an alliance with your kingdom," Nalika said. "We do not control our country yet, but even if we somehow convinced Vanris to help us overthrow the council, Thaelis has little to offer a country this powerful."

Veyl drew a deep breath, pushing back discomfort at the idea of betraying the Thaelian council. She owed them nothing. They had destroyed her life without remorse, but she had signed her name on those pages. Would casting that agreement aside cheapen the value of her word? She found it difficult to feel good about the deception required. But, ultimately, it was about making the right choice for the people, and she trusted these three more than she trusted the Thaelian council. "We had best start working on our approach, then. We only have a couple of hours to figure out what we can offer."

●

Much sooner than she was ready for, Veyl stood at the meeting room table facing her parents, her grandfather, Jaysen, and others she had known for most of her life. They all listened to a brief recap of the previous day's discussion before she requested the floor. Her palms were damp and her legs as wobbly as jellyfish, but no one needed to know that. Well, aside from the three Evokers in the room, who were certain to catch some of her anxiety in her surface thoughts.

"The representatives of Thaelis would like to propose a different option to the council, if we may."

"Proceed," Khevarin Velara said, glancing down at the Thaelian agreement on the table before her rather than at Veyl.

Her father, not fully engaged in his role as khemron yet, offered a nod to show his support.

"The Thaelian council ordered Ahnkreth Kyril and Ahnkreth Eavara out with their fleets to find and take some of Vanris's citizens without the knowledge of the general populace of Thaelis. Its members also went into hiding during the Devastation when their guidance was most needed, leaving the people to navigate that disaster on their own. That council has not acted in the interests of the population of Thaelis. No one in this room wishes to stand in support of it."

A ripple of tension moved through the Vanrian representatives, and a few of them shifted back from the table, brows furrowing, jaws tightening. Veyl didn't give them time to consider their reactions.

"We would like to propose that, rather than bending to the demands of the Thaelian council for the sake of getting our people back, we could negotiate an agreement of a different kind. An alliance between Vanris and the Thaelian delegates here, who represent a larger group seeking to unseat the current leadership and replace them with one that is of, and for, the people of Thaelis."

Silence hung over the meeting room for what seemed an eternity until Khemron Kasiel leaned forward, folding his hands on the table. "What would this alliance look like, Ahninveth?"

"We propose that Vanris send ships back with Ahnkreth Kyril's fleet, as detailed out in the agreement. Under the guise of following their terms, we could dock in Dagony and connect with the resistance in Thaelis. Working together, we could overthrow the council and open the way for a new one. We could also eradicate the Ukhen'kya threat. Afterward, any captives who wished to return to Pandrea could do so with the cooperative Vanrian and Delaphinian fleet. Thaelis would offer open trade to Vanris and the aid of its fleets, if necessary, in dealing with Sarket or any other naval threats, easing the burden on Delaphine to always meet that need."

"Please take your seat, Ambassador." Her mother leaned over to whisper something in the khemron's ear as she watched Veyl settle back into her chair. When she spoke, her cool tone made it clear she did so entirely as the khevarin of Vanris. "Considering what the Thaelian side stands to gain, what you offer is uninspiring. It makes no sense for us to assume such risks for a country that can give little in return. Unless…" she paused, eyes narrowing a fraction. "If Thaelis were to become a Vanrian territory, it would then be in our best interest to intervene."

A chilly silence surrounded Veyl. "You want us to give up… everything?"

"All we require is our people back, and we will accomplish that, either by trading the crew members of Ahnkreth Kyril's fleet or by force. You are asking us to help overthrow the current government and assist in neutralizing an outside threat of uncertain strength. If we are to take part in resolving these matters, it makes sense that we should remain involved in the outcome of our investment. You have offered trade and military support. This would not be dramatically different. Your local leadership would be subject to our oversight. Your military would become a part of ours, left in defense of the islands and leveraged only if necessary for the mainland. Some goods you produce would be transported to the mainland, just as those produced here would become available to the Thaelian territory. So long as the new council does not abuse its people, our influence shouldn't significantly change any aspect of life in Thaelis."

"No." Kyril's tone offered no room for argument, and Ceris growled, shifting closer to his bonded.

"The council may have been right about Vanris after all," Nalika muttered.

Feeling the thin thread of calm unraveling around her, Veyl hastily stood again. "We would like an opportunity to speak among ourselves in private to discuss your counterproposal."

The khevarin rose, and the rest of that table stood

with her. "Granted. We will pause negotiations for the time being. You have until tomorrow afternoon to accept our proposal or come up with a compelling alternative."

Nalika started shouting the moment they were back in the drawing room. "If we agree to this, we will forever be under Vanris's heel. They will force their culture upon us, just like the council warned."

Veyl stood near the door, watching Kyril. He ran a hand through his hair, his focus turning inward for several seconds, checking for her father's spies perhaps, then he approached the Evoker. He didn't raise his voice, but there was an intensity and aggression in his forward posture that was more intimidating somehow. Ceris sat a few feet behind him, ears partly back, looking as uncomfortable as Veyl felt.

"Or maybe, if we agree to this, they will set the rest of my fleet free and let us return home. We would be free of the council and have a chance to set up a new one that supports all the people of Thaelis. And we could finally stop living in constant fear of the Ukhen'kya."

His words surprised Veyl. Only minutes ago, he had firmly negated the idea. Why had he changed his mind?

Nalika didn't back down, a fact that raised Veyl's respect for her considering the man she faced. "But the controlling power behind that new council, the Vanrians, still won't represent the populace. Have you seen any non-Vanrians living here? Have you spotted anyone of mixed blood among them who isn't merely an agent from another country? Do you honestly believe they'll support all the people of Thaelis?"

Jinau rested his hand upon the back of the couch, his thumb settling in the notch there. Like Arhk, he only raised his voice as much as necessary, somehow commanding attention without the need for volume. "And what do you think happens if we don't agree, Nali?"

The two looked at him, Kyril gesturing to the other man as if he had proven his point.

Jinau's gaze stayed on Nalika. "Vanris doesn't need anything we have. They only want their people back. Kyril is right. If we refuse this, they will imprison us and use his navigational charts to retrieve their citizens using force. Thaelis will fall and still become theirs, and the fleets involved in the attacks here will face trial for crimes against the Vanrian people. The khevarin made the offer far too quickly for it to have been an idea she just came up with. They intended to propose annexation at some point in these negotiations."

Something twisted in Veyl's chest with the realization that he was right. Her parents and the council had planned for this, and they had told her nothing.

"We should have gone to Sarket with an offer of alliance," Nalika growled. "At least there they would have helped us in exchange for aid in fighting Vanris and let us keep our home."

Kyril shook his head. "Sarket lost to Vanris before when they had two countries allied with them. What makes you believe they'll do any better with us? Our few mind-crafters are nothing compared to what Vanris has."

Veyl walked to the couch and sank down on it with her back to them.

"Were you aware of this, Khesran?" Nalika spat out Veyl's title like it tasted foul.

"No," she answered in a small voice, burying her

face in her hands. Her parents hadn't even hinted at it. In all the time she had been alone with her father, he had kept her in the dark, never even alluding to this outcome. Was this supposed to be some lesson, or had she lost their trust completely?

Kyril sat next to her. "It's what any country would do under the circumstances. I hoped to meet potential allies when I brought Jaysen here, but he painted us, not entirely undeservedly, as the enemy. Once I saw how powerful Vanris is, I knew there wasn't much hope for it." He took her hand in his, trying to comfort her when it was his country being taken over. "You were our one chance at convincing them to listen, Veyl, but we made ourselves a threat, and this is how they will bring that threat under control."

"Kyril speaks with wisdom," Jinau said. "The choice they have given us isn't one, but if we go about it right, if we cooperate, we might maintain enough independence to better our situation in Thaelis."

Yanking her hand away, Veyl snapped to her feet and stormed to the door, throwing it open. She looked around at the startled guards. "Show them back to their rooms."

"Yes, Khesran."

Not giving anyone time to question her, she strode swiftly down the hall, heading for a study her parents often used when they wanted to discuss political matters away from their personal chambers. The two guards standing outside the room were enough to confirm they were within. She stopped abruptly when they dropped their halberds into her path to block her from entering.

"Apologies, Khesran Veyl, but we have orders. Please wait."

Trembling with frustration and anger, she stood her ground as the guard knocked.

An attendant peeked out, his gaze landing instantly

upon her. "One moment." He ducked back inside.

A few seconds later, Kince, Darro, and Arhk walked out. None of them tried to speak to her, and Veyl refused to meet their eyes, afraid she might lose her temper or her nerve. When they had passed, the attendant stepped out and held the door open for her, remaining outside when he shut it after her.

Her parents sat together on a couch, calmly watching her enter.

Veyl strode up to stand behind a chair facing them, the piece of furniture providing a barrier between them. "You were going to do this all along."

Her father took her mother's hand, uniting them against her. Veyl raised her chin, trying to pretend the gesture wasn't a dagger in her heart.

"Yes," the khevarin answered. "They have shown us they will harm our people. We are generously offering to help them remove the council behind the atrocities they committed against us and establish a new one. We are even offering to aid them in dealing with these Unclean, who, judging by what they have allegedly done to the people of Thaelis, pose a threat to anyone who might encounter them. But, given their crimes, Thaelis will need to earn the right at this point to live free and independent again. If not for your return and defense of them, we would likely have made a similar offer directly to the council in Thaelis while holding Ahnkreth Kyril and his fleet here to face our justice."

"What was this morning, then? I thought you were talking with them to determine whether you would consider allying with them. What was that really about?"

"We had already settled on this course." The khemron's placating tone ignored all the opportunities he'd had to share this information with her before now as her father. "This morning was to decide if we would consider making this offer to them in place of the existing council."

"You've given them no choice. Do you know how that must feel?"

Her mother's stately composure crumbled, and she snapped to her feet. "How did you feel about the choice they gave you in Deepwater?"

A shudder swept through Veyl. Suddenly, she was back in the coastal town when that first explosion displaced fear of Jaysen's friends and brought forth a different terror. Vivid memories raced through her mind. The bomb that separated her from Jaysen. Kyril's hand around her throat, pinning her to the wall after she broke Illis. Her freshly reformed tehnaak bond with Jaysen being severed again. Despair upon walking out onto the ship's deck to see her home already so far away. The overwhelming hopelessness that had driven her to jump into the water with the serpents, intending to end everything.

With a crushing sense of failure creeping in, she wiped roughly at the tears that trailed down her cheeks. "I only wanted to avoid doing more harm than has already been done. I didn't know that would make us enemies."

Her voice cracked, and she bolted from the room, slamming into Jaysen in the hall with enough force that they both nearly hit the floor. He caught her by her arms, barely keeping them on their feet.

"Are you all right?" The worry in his regard told her he could see that she wasn't.

"Veyl, wait!" Her mother rushed into the doorway.

Yanking free of Jaysen, Veyl sprinted down the hall, leaving them all behind. She didn't head toward her room. Instead, she struck off in another direction, trying to come up with a place her parents wouldn't think of looking for her. After turning down several halls, she hurried past the drawing room she had spent so much time in as a child, playing Feral's Folly and other games.

Someone caught hold of her arm and pulled her back through the doorway. Twisting, she jerked away, ready to run again, but hesitated instead when she met familiar, haunted blue eyes.

"Gannon."

He guided her away from the door. Ahrin and Iyvalin were there too. Ahrin came and peeked out into the hall, then ducked back in and nodded to Gannon.

"Behind the couch," Gannon whispered, taking her shoulders and turning her toward the suggested article of furniture.

Feeling somewhat foolish, Veyl did as directed, sitting behind the couch with her knees pulled to her chest and her head down. Gannon and Ahrin rejoined Iyvalin at a table and resumed the game of dice they had been playing. A few seconds later, a guard entered the room.

"Have any of you seen Khesran Veyl?" he asked.

"Not today," Iyvalin answered, sounding convincingly disinterested.

"If you do, tell her Khevarin Velara needs to speak with her immediately."

"We will." Ahrin's tone was dismissive, a young man eager to get back to the game.

They waited several seconds after the guard left before Gannon got up and peered into the hall. He waved for Veyl to come out. She stood and walked around the couch, considering the three of them.

"Why did you do that for me?"

"We haven't seen you since we arrived in Etrion," Ahrin said. "Maybe we just hoped for a little time to catch up. You may have questionable new friends and substantial obligations to deal with, but you're still one of us."

Her throat tightened, and she faced Gannon. "Am I?"

He met her eyes, a storm of emotion raging so

fiercely in his that she couldn't hope to make sense of it. "Yes. Would you care to spar?"

"Right now?"

"Right now."

Veyl nodded.

Ahrin got up from the table. "No. That's not a good idea."

Ignoring him, Gannon leaned out the door, then glanced back at Veyl. "It's clear."

"Shit," Ahrin grumbled as Veyl followed his brother from the room.

The four of them made their way along the halls with Gannon in the lead, checking each passage and ducking into alcoves or through doors when necessary to avoid palace guards. Eventually, they reached a side entrance to the palace and slipped out near the training grounds by the mind-crafter academy. Avris was at the sparring rings when they arrived, watching Merrin work with a student. When she noticed the four of them, she perked up, coming around to intercept them.

"Are we sparring?"

"They are." Ahrin gestured to Veyl and Gannon with a resigned wave of his hand.

Avris grinned. "Fantastic. There's extra armor in the building. I'll get your weapons."

Several minutes later, after discarding the outer layers of her Thaelian uniform in favor of the practice armor, Veyl met Gannon in the ring. It would only be a matter of time before someone found her here. Sparring on the academy grounds wasn't exactly a secretive endeavor. But she needed this, and she suspected Gannon, now standing across from her with a disconcertingly blank expression, needed it at least as much. He wasn't one to ask for support, but this might be a way she could help him work through some of the emotional turmoil of losing his tehnaak.

Gannon attacked without warning, his initial strike glancing painfully off her shoulder armor as she tried to leap out of the way. A second fierce attack followed that, and another, both of which she barely evaded. He wasn't holding back. Veyl ducked in under his next swing, using her lesser height to her advantage, and struck him with a powerful blow to the ribs. A satisfying grunt of pain answered her effort, but he didn't back off to regroup as she thought he would.

That expectation left her unprepared for the series of rapid strikes that followed, and somehow she ended up face down in the dirt. She stood, ignoring the shouted admonishments targeted at Gannon from Avris outside the ring. When Veyl touched her stinging lip, the fingers of her leather gauntlet came away stained red with blood. It had happened so fast she wasn't sure if Gannon had struck her in the face or if she had split it when she hit the ground. It didn't matter. She welcomed the clarity the pain brought.

Veyl focused more intently on her opponent. They engaged again, alternately forcing each other on the defensive. Gannon slipped in close, locking with her in a brief grapple, but she shoved him off, following it up with a kick to the chest that sent him sprawling in the dirt. He was up again almost instantly, spitting blood to one side, likely from biting his lip or tongue.

"Are they trying to kill each other?" She heard Avris ask with far more curiosity than concern.

"Maybe." A hint of worry strained Iyvalin's voice.

"Should we stop them?"

"Not yet," Ahrin answered.

Veyl attacked first this time, swapping hands with her sword to try catching him by surprise, but he was ready, dodging the strike and managing a glancing blow to her side. Recovering quickly, she feinted another switch, getting him to change his guard before she struck again with the same hand, catching him in the back as he tried to twist clear. His flat, intense expression broke, the barest hint of a grin curving his lips as he dove in with a series of varied swings.

They exchanged attacks for a while longer, neither securing the advantage, though each gained an increasing collection of bruises. Sweat dampened her clothes under the armor. She became aware of several additions to their audience. Several people, including her parents, now stood at the edge of the ring watching them beat each other into exhaustion. Finally, she pulled off a swift hand switch and knocked Gannon's weapon from his grip. He immediately caught the hilt of her sword, trying to wrest it free. They struggled for a moment, then he twisted his lower body and swiped her legs out from under her. Veyl kept hold of him, hooking one leg behind his knee as she fell, taking him with her.

They hit hard enough that she lay stunned for a second before coming up on her elbows. Gannon was getting to his knees. He sat back on his ankles and shook his head as if to clear it, then he chuckled and held a hand out to her.

"I never want to be your enemy, Khesran."

Veyl cracked a weary smile. "Nor I yours." She accepted his hand.

She wasn't sure if they helped each other stand or if their attempts to do so actually made it more difficult. Once they were upright, both still breathing hard, Gannon put an arm around her shoulders.

"Feel any better?" he asked.

She leaned into him, her body stinging all over from an array of fresh bruises, muscles trembling with exhaustion, but her mind was clearer and her emotions calmer. "Some. You?"

He nodded, brushing sweat-dampened hair away from his face with his other hand. "A little. Sorry about the lip."

She licked her bloodied lip with her tongue and shrugged. "Sorry about the cheek."

He touched a scrape on his cheek and glanced at the trace of blood on the fingertips of his glove, lips curving in a faint smile. "Looks like we're even."

"Veyl."

She glanced at her mother. "I'll be right there."

After changing out of her practice armor and brushing off the dust from the ring, Veyl gathered the rest of her uniform and accepted a cloth Avris gave her to dab at her still bleeding lip. Then she walked out to where her parents waited, turning to the twins and Iyvalin.

"We'll catch up soon."

Iyvalin's delicate brows pinched together in an adorably stern expression. "Promise?"

"Promise."

Her parents fell in on either side of her heading back toward the palace, Irith padding along beside her father. They walked in silence until they were inside the private quarters.

Her father pointed toward her room and met her mother's eyes. "Why don't you help Veyl clean up? I need to take care of a few things."

That was an obvious attempt to encourage them to talk. Veyl nodded, not saying anything, and headed toward her room. Her lip had at least stopped bleeding. Inside, she tossed the rest of the uniform and the bloodied cloth on the bed. She had gotten the pants dirty enough that she wasn't sure she could wear them again today, but since they weren't supposed to meet now until tomorrow afternoon, there would be time to have them cleaned. She could smell the fragrance of hot, scented water wafting out from the bathing room.

Her mother shut the outer door and followed her as far as the open doorway to the bedroom. "When I heard where you had gone, I asked an attendant to have a bath prepared."

"Thank you."

Veyl discarded the last few articles of clothing, pulled out her braids, and climbed into the steaming water. Her mother wandered out into the sitting room to give her privacy. She was still waiting there when Veyl dried off a short time later. As she slipped on a dressing robe, her mother joined her in the bedroom.

"I'm sorry we cut you out, but this situation is challenging for all of us. You seem to have gotten concerningly close to your new Thaelian companions. We feared that they might have manipulated your recollection of events, but your expression when I brought up Deepwater earlier tells me you have extremely vivid and unpleasant memories of that experience."

"I remember every waking moment, Mother, I assure you." Veyl used a towel to start drying her hair.

Walking to the bed, her mother reached out to touch the wave dancer clasp on the Thaelian cloak. "You need to trust your own people, Veyl. This does not have to be an unfortunate outcome for Thaelis. They gain our aid in accomplishing their goals. How involved we are after that depends entirely on them. They'll have our military to call upon if necessary, and our oversight need only become a burden if they make it one."

Veyl eyed her slightly swollen split lip in the mirror. Not the most attractive addition to her appearance, but far from the worst injury she had suffered in the sparring ring. "I'm not certain they see it that way. As I mentioned before, they all grew up learning that our ancestors were their oppressors, which, in this case, it sounds like they may have been. They were told to expect the same from us, and, in their minds, your demands justify those warnings, making it appear that their council may have been right all along."

"What I would like to understand is how the Thaelian council has held power for this long if they are so disliked." Her mother walked around behind her.

Veyl heard her opening the wardrobe. She drew a brush through her hair. "I believe the destabilization caused by the Devastation played a part, but I haven't had the opportunity to learn all of their recent history."

"If we are to get involved, we will require that information. We need your Thaelian companions to tell us everything they can about the council and its supporters, as well as how many will unite against them. Oh, and any knowledge they can give us of these Uk… Unclean."

"Ukhen'kya," Veyl offered.

Her mother came up beside her, carrying one of her split-skirted dresses. It was deep blue with black embroidery along the bodice and the edges of the split that ran down the right side. The pants underneath were the reverse, black with blue embroidery reaching partway up the lower legs. A panel of sheer black material filled in the deep V of the neckline, hinting at modesty or perhaps its opposite.

Veyl's gaze caught upon the blue. "That color matches—"

"The streaks in his hair?" Her mother arched a brow, and Veyl's traitorous cheeks grew warm. "That's what I was afraid of."

"You can't deny that he's attractive. Any woman with a pulse would notice." Veyl turned to the mirror, trying to brush off her mother's concern with a dismissive tone as she began redoing the braids along the side of her head.

Her mother hung the dress on the outside of the wardrobe and took over braiding. "I would be lying if I said he wasn't, but it requires a lot more than good looks to make a good man."

Defensive anger crackled through Veyl. "I understand that, and I know Ahnkreth Kyril far better than any of the people judging him here do." In the reflection, she saw the slight flickering of lightning in her own eyes and the rising of her mother's brows as she finished the first braid along the side of Veyl's head and started the second.

"And how well does he know you?"

Veyl changed tactics, searching for a less risky way to approach defending the Thaelian Feral. "Did Father not do some terrible deeds when fighting for Vanris?"

"He did, though I am not convinced this is the same. Regardless, I hope you are keeping your head about you around him and his companions. You can't afford to let emotions or desires influence this process. Besides, they will be out of your life before long, one way or another."

Veyl tried not to let show the sorrow that comment inspired. "Why the dress?"

Her mother finished the second braid and picked up one of the two shells Veyl had set on the counter. "Who gave you these?"

Veyl took the other shell and worked it onto one braid. "Nagi gave me this along with several other gifts after the incident with the kel'inuk."

"And this one?"

"Ahnkreth Kyril gifted it to me the day we reached Thaelis." She struggled to keep her tone indifferent.

"Why?"

"I don't know for certain, though he expressed a desire to present a united front before the council," Veyl evaded, accepting the shell back and putting it on the other braid. "Why the dress?" she asked again.

"We've arranged an early private supper for you and your Thaelian companions. If the ahnkreth is attracted to you, and I can't imagine why he wouldn't be," she added with a fond smile, "he might prove more receptive to hearing positive arguments for accepting our proposal if he finds the scenery pleasing."

"What?" Veyl abruptly faced her mother. "Didn't you just warn me against him?"

"I'm not telling you to seduce him, Veyl. In fact, I would cut his hands off myself if he dared to touch you. I'm suggesting that you might take advantage of that attraction to put him in a better mood and encourage him to look at this situation in a different light, but only if you feel safe doing so. When Jethan and I spoke with Ahndhomen Jinau, he seemed to hold you in surprisingly high esteem, which may mean he is more open to hearing what you have to say already. Arhk didn't have as much luck with their Evoker, but if you can get the other two to see how this might be a favorable outcome, I imagine she will come around."

"You want me to manipulate them over a pleasant meal?" Veyl asked as her mother helped her into the dress.

"I dislike leveraging his interest in you in this way, but we need to move forward with this quickly so we can turn our attention toward Sarket and our own internal strife before those situations get out of control." She selected some earrings and a necklace to match the dress. "If we cannot come to an agreement on this soon, the alternatives are likely to be worse for them. I encourage you to call upon your knowledge of our history to help them understand we do not wish to dominate them, merely to ensure the effort we put in is not wasted or turned against us in the future. I get the impression the other two will follow the ahnkreth's lead. Making you look nice is merely a way to soften a message he may find hard to accept." She stepped back and looked at Veyl, frowning at her lip. "That's unfortunate, but you put on quite a show acquiring it, one I'm sure our Thaelian

Feral could appreciate."

Realization struck her like one of Gannon's blows. "You put them on that side of the hall on purpose."

"We did. It couldn't hurt to let them see our people training for combat even in times of peace, fragile as it now appears. We didn't expect you to put on so many shows for them yourself, though we probably should have." She smiled fondly again and brought some of Veyl's blood-red hair forward over one shoulder. Hair that matched her own. "Seeing you fight earlier should be enough to discourage any man from trying to take liberties with you, but there will be the usual guards at the door as a precaution."

Her smile faded, and she rested her hands on Veyl's shoulders, the scars on her face giving greater gravity to her somber expression. "I wish none of this had happened, but we are where we are. Please know that your father and I will never be your enemies. We couldn't possibly love you more, and we are proud of how courageous you have been through all of this. No matter what side we are negotiating on, you can come to us as our daughter at any time."

Her mother put her arms around her, and Veyl savored that embrace, hugging her back.

"I love you both too," she whispered. "I'm sorry this has been so hard."

"You have nothing to apologize for. You found a way home to us. That alone is an admirable feat. You have also shown empathy toward the people who harmed you and proven yourself to be a skilled negotiator at such a young age. Your father and I could hardly be more proud of you." Her mother stepped back, brushing at the tears that balanced precariously on her lashes, then took Veyl's hand. "Now, let's escort you to your dinner, shall we?"

They walked together to one of the smaller, more intimate dining rooms in the private quarters of the palace and stopped outside the door. Her mother took her hand and turned Veyl to face her.

"We will all find our way through these challenges. This is not what they wanted, but I am confident you can make it more palatable for them. I am not entirely convinced that they deserve such courtesy, but your father and I believe in you." Her mother unnecessarily straightened Veyl's necklace and smoothed the shoulders of the dress. "If you are confident that allying with them over the Thaelian council is the right course, we will trust you."

Veyl caught one of her hands to stop her fussing. "I'll be fine. What happened in Deepwater came from a place of desperation and misunderstanding. None of them would hurt me now." She wasn't sure that was true in Nalika's case, but there was nothing to be gained from saying as much.

"Even so, remember there will be guards waiting outside if you need them."

"And tiny spies?"

Her mother breathed a soft laugh. "No. Although your father has tried to sneak rodents into your meetings a few times, Ahnkreth Kyril has been remarkably attentive and quick to redirect them. As odd as it may sound, I get the sense Kas rather enjoys the game and is developing a grudging respect for the skill with which the man wields his ability. I asked him to stop trying, however. I want you to see that we trust you."

A grudging respect. That was better than hatred. "Thank you."

She kissed her on the cheek. "Enjoy your dinner. I asked the kitchens to make a few of our finest dishes."

Veyl watched her walk away before entering the room. It was a cozy space, with dark wood furnishings and trim around wall panels painted a deep rust red. An elaborate pattern of wooden tiles ranging from almost black to slightly lighter reds and browns made up the flooring. A large carpet underneath the couch and two chairs near the fireplace carried over the color scheme. The dark dining table had the same pattern as the floor inset in the center and at each corner. Ornate wood panels that made up the high ceiling helped to darken the room and shrink it, working with strategically placed candles and sconces to add intimacy to the setting.

Three attendants were finishing laying out the meal. The rich aroma of spiced meat contrasted by the delicately sweet sauce they had sauteed the vegetables in made her mouth water. Veyl went to where a decanter of dark red wine and two pitchers of Vanrian Black Mead waited. She poured herself a glass of wine, sipping at it as she carried it over by the fire. It wasn't noticeably cold out, but the dancing light of the flames and the soft crackle enhanced the welcoming atmosphere. As the three attendants stepped out, Kyril entered, one of his guards lingering until she dismissed him.

Ceris trotted over, stopping to let her scratch his head before he lay on the carpet, gazing into the fire. Kyril prowled toward her, shamelessly admiring her, pleasure sparking in his eyes. He wore a fine set of black pants and an ivory shirt under a fitted black, thigh-length jacket with subtle silver and blue embroidery on it. It made her wonder that his outfit so finely matched her dress. It had to have been something they found to loan him, given the distinctly Vanrian cut, and it looked enticingly handsome on him. They had grossly overestimated her ability to resist their mutual attraction.

She watched him approach in silence, letting her eyelids fall shut as he neared the fire, so she might imagine, for a moment, that this dinner was solely for the two of them. That their story wasn't destined to end in sorrow. The closeness of his body brought a searing heat, far more intense than that of the fire. His hand settled on her shoulder and slid down her arm over the thin, sheer fabric of the sleeves. She parted her lips in anticipation of his kiss.

But it wasn't her lips he kissed. His fingertips grazed her skin as he brushed her hair back, and his lips touched her neck, eliciting a soft gasp from her.

"I know you said no more," he murmured, "so if I misread your invitation just now…"

"You did not," she whispered, sliding her fingers into his hair. She opened her eyes long enough to meet his, closing them again when he kissed her lips, the sting of the split barely noticeable past the ache in her chest.

Parting her lips, she invited him in, savoring the taste of him and the electrifying fear of being caught like this. Some desperate, reckless side of her wanted everyone to know. She longed to tell them all her heart was hopelessly his, but she couldn't. Not with everything that was at stake. The instant she heard voices outside the door, she parted from him. They stepped back from each other, and she turned her attention to the guard who came in ahead of Jinau. The man held the door open a moment longer, allowing Nalika in as well. Then he looked at Veyl.

"A few of us can stay inside if you like, Khesran Veyl."

"No. We will be fine. Thank you." Could he hear the pounding of her heart?

The guard nodded and backed out, giving each of her companions a warning scowl before he left them.

When the door was closed, Kyril stepped in again and brushed his thumb lightly under the split on her lip. "I hope you didn't spend all of your anger in the sparring ring."

"Why?" She smirked at him. "Did you want some of it?"

He chuckled. "I was hoping your parents received their share, but now that you mention it…"

His mischievous grin made her pulse race, and she stepped back when he came forward, putting a hand on his chest to keep him at a distance. Why did all her better senses have to abandon her the moment he was near? "They did, not that it changed anything."

"What are we doing?" Nalika snapped, gesturing toward the lavish spread on the table.

"Having a pleasant dinner." Kyril walked over and poured himself a glass of wine.

"You're having wine?" Jinau sounded genuinely bemused.

"Mm-hmm." His gaze moved to Veyl. "I got a little taste and decided I might like a glass of my own."

Veyl's cheeks warmed.

Nalika blew out a breath of frustration. "I was referring to their proposed annexation of Thaelis and what this has to do with that."

Kyril pulled out a chair and met Veyl's eyes, gesturing to the seat. When she started walking over, he turned his attention to Nalika. "We're accepting it. That's all we can do, and they have provided us a grand meal to enjoy while our lovely hostess tries to help us feel better about giving up our country." He leaned close to Veyl as she stepped in front of the chair and sank into it. "Isn't that right?"

She couldn't discern from his voice or expression how any of that made him feel, but she wasn't about to lie. Not to him. "Why don't we eat while I tell you more about my country and my family? Afterward, we can discuss any specific terms we want to argue for in the final agreement. We have very little to work with, but my parents aren't unreasonable."

The other three sat, Nalika slumping into the chair and glaring at the food. "Is this our last night as Thaelians, then?"

"We will always be Thaelian," Jinau said, "but remember that many of our ancestors came from Vanris just as theirs did. It is the Qwilki in our blood that separates us. The ocean will remain our home, and our Seh'hali will do her best to see that we are treated fairly by the people who raised her."

Veyl almost corrected him. Her people, not the people who raised her. But maybe this was the right time to let it pass. It was becoming more apparent that Jinau truly looked upon her as someone special, somehow connected to Qwilki beliefs she knew little about. Nalika, judging by her sneer, wasn't at all convinced, but Kyril? What did the thoughtful look he was giving her mean? Did he share the same conviction as Jinau that she was the Daughter of the Ocean? If what Jinau told her was true, the Qwilki had similar views regarding him. Maybe she should learn more about these beliefs and what it meant to be Seh'hali ne Kunua. But right now, she needed to bring them into her world and figure out how to make this situation work for all of them.

As they dined on a selection of the finest Vanrian dishes, from crimson cactus salad to a roasted pheasant with a glaze made from evalis fruit, she told them about her homeland. She started with the story of her father and how a group from the south killed his mother and kidnapped him as a child, raising him in Fallend until his recovery twelve years later. A tale intended to help them see how their abduction of her might have had a more profound impact upon her father and grandfather. Given that history, was it any surprise that they were reluctant to grant the Thaelians their trust?

"It's a wonder Dhomvalen Arhk didn't execute me on sight," Kyril remarked when she finished.

"Thankfully," Veyl commented too quickly, her cheeks coloring at the warm smile he gave her in response.

His expression changed abruptly, his attention turning inward. After a second, he smirked and gestured toward the bottom of a cabinet on one side of the room. "Your father's checking to make sure we aren't mistreating you."

Veyl glanced over and caught sight of a mouse peeking out from under the cabinet, even after her mother's assurance that he wouldn't do so. She hoped he hadn't been there long enough to hear their prior exchange. "Thank you for the vote of confidence, Father. Could you send in more mead?" she added, watching Nalika empty one pitcher into her mug. After the mouse disappeared, she turned to Kyril. "How long was he there?"

"Only a moment. I allowed him a glimpse to appease his worry and burning curiosity."

Jinau chuckled and emptied what remained of the other pitcher into his mug. "I understand your father and his tehsheyn ended the war?"

"They played a significant role, and my father struck the blow that led to Sarket's surrender."

"Sarket seems to be growing weary of their station beneath Vanris." Nalika's expression suggested she sympathized with their plight.

"Vanris could have brought down the southern

kingdoms long before that had we wished to, but it would have been a costly victory. All we wanted was to live peacefully in our own lands. We didn't come here seeking to conquer anyone. It was the southern kingdoms that refused to allow mind-crafters to exist on their doorstep."

Someone knocked on the door. Veyl moved her hand away from where it had somehow ended up next to Kyril's on the table before calling them in. They hadn't been touching, not quite, but still close enough to potentially draw attention. Fortunately, the mouse hadn't been at an angle to see such details.

An attendant entered, carrying a platter with two fresh pitchers of mead on it. "Would you like us to remove some dishes, Khesran?"

She glanced around, receiving nods from the other three, though she caught both Nalika and Jinau snatching last bites as she turned her attention back to the attendant. "Yes, please."

The woman gestured to two more who were waiting outside the door. They hurried in and started collecting dishes while she swapped out the pitchers. "Should we place dessert here or by the fire?"

Her mother was giving them the full treatment, it seemed. "By the fire," Veyl answered, avoiding Kyril's gaze. The seating there consisted of two chairs and a cozy couch. She wouldn't dare suggest sitting with him, but the desire to do so was enough to warm her cheeks. At least she could blame the wine for that.

"It speaks well of Vanris that they didn't leverage their might to crush the opposition at any point during the war and were open to negotiating with Delaphine when they came in search of an alliance, despite all those years of hostility," Kyril remarked, watching the attendants go efficiently about their work.

Nalika narrowed her eyes at him over the rim of her

mug. "How do you know so much?"

"The war and the relationship between the four kingdoms were a few of the topics Jaysen would discuss with me on our voyage here." His gaze shifted to Veyl. "He was very close-lipped about you, Khesran, and any personal details about your family. It's clear he cares for you."

"He is…" She averted her gaze, refusing to let the sudden spark of resentment take hold. How much easier might all this have been if Jaysen had simply trusted her? The attendants finished arranging the dessert and ducked out with their trays as she tamed that flare of dark emotion. "He was my tehnaak. It would surprise me more if he wasn't protective."

Kyril's hand folded over hers, squeezing gently. "I am sorry. There are several things I wish had been different about the way you entered my life, Seh'hali."

His warm hand and the remorse in his tone deflected her frustration far better than her efforts had. She looked at him, into those piercing eyes, and for a heartbeat, it was just the two of them. Sentiments of affection balanced on her lips, begging to be spoken.

"We should discuss what we want to ask for from our new rulers in exchange for our country." Nalika's bitter words fractured the moment.

Veyl looked away and extracted her hand. "Let's move to the fire."

When she stood, they did the same, each of them taking their chosen drink with them, though a decanter of sweet wine waited on a tray there that also held a selection of delicate tarts and tiny cakes. Jinau sat in one side chair and Nalika claimed the other, leaving the couch open.

Veyl hesitated, glancing uneasily at the remaining option.

"Don't worry, Khesran," Nalika said, a crooked

smirk on her lips, "if anyone comes, I'll switch with you. We all know this torrid affair has no future, but as much as I disapprove, I'm willing to help you steal a few moments together for the sake of my ahnkreth."

Veyl hesitated as Kyril sat on the end closer to Jinau. "What if my father sends another spy?"

Kyril gestured to the spot beside him. "No creature will get near this room without my being aware of it."

She should still refuse, and his smirk told her he knew she wasn't going to. Blowing out a breath, she sank down next to him. "You realize their catching us together would be far more disastrous for you than me?"

"They won't." Kyril reached over and brushed the backs of his fingers lightly across her cheek and down her neck, sending a shiver through her.

Veyl glared at him. "You are a horrible man."

Kyril chuckled and collected two tarts from the tray, passing her one of them.

"If we're moving forward with my parents' proposal, we need to figure out what we want to argue for. I also need to understand more of what Vanris will face when they arrive in Thaelis. Who will fight for the council if it comes to open conflict? How many will stand against it? Is there a way Vanris could take over without bloodshed? And of course, anything you can tell me about the Ukhen'kya."

Jinau leaned forward, eyeing the offerings on the table as he spoke. "The council has a loyal elite military force that supports them. Most of them are from pure or nearly pure bloodlines. They have priority access to the best jobs and the nicest housing for their families. When the Devastation came, most of them pulled back into quarantine with the council, hiding from the sickness while the rest of our people suffered. There are some others who may support them, but that group represents the greatest threat. The tribal Qwilki stand with the resistance, though most have never trained as warriors."

Veyl settled back to sip at her second, or was it her third, glass of wine. She let the other three talk about Thaelis as it was now and their hopes for it, as well as the ways the council had let down the people who lived there. A couple of hours later, she was curled against Kyril with his arm resting comfortably around her shoulders, her glass of sweet wine nearly empty again, a blizzard of new information swirling through the fog in her head.

"You look about ready to fall asleep, Seh'hali," Jinau observed, his fatherly tone striking a chord of affection in her.

"Mm-hmm. I'm a little wine-weary, but there's still more we need to work out."

"Sleep on all we have discussed. There is time for us to gather again in the morning." Jinau stood, and Nalika followed his lead.

Veyl lingered a moment longer, reluctant to leave the comfort she had found nestled up against Kyril.

"It would be pleasant to stay here, wouldn't it?" he murmured, his arm tightening around her.

"A girl can dream."

"You're no girl."

"Hush. Don't tell my parents," she whispered.

His deep chuckle sent a flush of desire through her, which struck her as a solid reason to extract herself from her spot there. She got up and bid Jinau and Nalika good night as they left first with their guards.

Kyril stepped toward his waiting escort, then hesitated, turning back to her. "Might I have one more word in private, Khesran?"

A thrill of anticipation swept through her. She met the eyes of the guard holding the door and nodded. "A few minutes, please."

The guard bowed his head and retreated, shutting them inside.

Kyril approached, stopping a few feet back. When Veyl moved to close the remaining distance, he held his hands up to discourage her, his expression unreadable.

"A word, Khesran. Merely a word."

Disappointment twisted in her chest, but she stood her ground. "Yes?"

"I imagine you have realized that your family will not want you returning to Thaelis with us."

An ache spread in her chest. Not only from the idea of being parted from him. She would miss Ceris too, and she yearned to return to the ocean to ride upon its waves, and to walk the beaches of Thaelis and explore the tide pools with the Qwilki women. The sorrow expanded at the thought of not seeing Kitria again, or Mardi and Quillon.

She lowered her gaze, tucking her hair absently behind one pointed ear. "I have."

"There might be a way to convince them otherwise."

She wouldn't let herself hope, not yet, but she wanted to hear him. "You have an idea?"

"Our best opportunity to avoid violence is to let the council believe everything is going as they requested in the agreement, at least long enough to move the required pieces into place."

Veyl nodded, several scenarios now racing through her head. "Yes, and my returning there is an explicit component of that agreement." She gave him a discerning frown, setting a hand on one hip. "You could have saved this for our meeting in the morning."

He stalked to her like a predator closing in on its prey. "I could have," he murmured, sliding one hand along her jaw and back into her hair, "but I wouldn't have had another chance to defile your royal Vanrian beauty with my lowborn caresses."

Pulse racing, she moved into his arms and tilted her head back. "Please do."

He kissed her hard, his hands sliding over the sides of her breasts and sinking down to her waist to pull her closer. The sting from her lip became a mere nuisance before the surge of longing racing through her. Veyl moved her arms over his shoulders, wrapping them around his neck. His mouth tasted of sweet wine, his hips pressed against hers, every muscular inch of him heightening her desire. She couldn't catch her breath, but he was all the air she needed. It took all her willpower to keep from pulling off his clothing, but the underlying fear of discovery held her back, even though the abundance of wine urged her to recklessness.

His lips moved to her neck, and she tilted her head to the side, letting his arms support her as his kisses lit fires in every part of her. She stifled the moan that strained to break free. He paused, drawing back enough that she could face him, his long black hair a curtain shading them from the light of the nearest sconce.

"You're trembling," he whispered.

"I want more of you. I hate that we can only have brief moments like this in secret."

"What would you do if you could have more?"

"I would give you everything," she answered in a breathless whisper.

Mischief glinted in his eyes. "That again?"

Veyl smacked his arm and tried to pull away, but he held her close, his gaze turning molten. One hand slid into the split in her skirt, fingers brushing along the inside of her upper thigh, eliciting a gasp of surprise. "And I would savor every second. I do savor every second I can be near you, even when I can't touch you."

He kissed her again, fingers moving up and gently teasing her, drawing her desire to a single burning point. Then he stopped with a deep sigh, lingering a moment longer as she traced his jaw with her fingertips before backing away. His eyes closed for a second, perhaps searching in the darkness behind them for the self-control that she also struggled for.

"We need to be cautious." The huskiness in his voice betrayed the desire he was trying to rein in. "Your parents have noticed there's an attraction here. If they suspect it has strayed beyond that, the rest of these negotiations will fall apart."

She nodded, trying to ignore the heat that still raced through her, the longing. "I am the one who said this had to stop before, remember?" And after they resolved things between their countries, an ocean would divide them again. There would be no more of these moments, secret or otherwise.

"You lacked conviction." His smile had a solemnity to it that made her wonder if his thoughts had followed the same path as her own.

Ceris, apparently sensing that the evening was truly over, got up from his place by the fire, stretched, and joined Kyril.

"Goodnight, Khesran."

"Goodnight."

She watched him leave in the company of his guards. Breathing a heavy sigh, she refilled her glass with sweet wine. Taking it and one of the few remaining fruit tarts, she wandered out. She had little doubt her parents were aware they had dispersed for the night. Her father might not have checked on them inside the room again, but he would have some tiny creature lurking in the shadows outside. What would he think of Kyril not leaving with the others? At least they hadn't lingered overly long.

She finished the tart by the time her unhurried stroll brought her back to her chambers. In the sitting room, her eyes caught a glint from something on the mantel above her fire. Relenting to its lure, she set her wine on the table and went to pick up the ornate dagger Jaysen had given her when he left Vanris before his fifteenth birthday. They had been so close back then. Nigh inseparable. When they reunited in Deepwater, the distance of those years apart had seemed to melt away. But had they really? He was here in the palace again, sharing this place as they had in their youth, and she had never felt so far from him.

Veyl startled, nearly dropping the knife when the subject of her thoughts stepped through the doorway from her bedroom.

Jaysen's gaze took in the dagger before moving to meet hers. "I was beginning to wonder if you would ever show up."

She set the weapon down, a faint flicker of lightning sweeping through her. Why? He had long been her best friend. What was it that made her so uneasy around him now? "What are you doing in my room?"

"I was out wandering the rooftops when I noticed your window was open and there were still sconces burning." He smiled, though it wasn't quite the amiable smile he usually had with her.

"My parents wouldn't approve of your being in here so late." And unlike Kyril, he had no way of knowing if her father was watching. She glanced around the room, noting the myriad places a rodent could hide. There were the windows too, through which a bird might easily observe them. If only her parents truly trusted her enough to let her be, but the incident in the dining room made it clear they didn't, despite what her mother had said. Then again, maybe that wasn't such a bad thing in this case.

"I needed to see you, Veyl." He came closer, stopping a few feet back from her. "Every time I think we'll finally get to talk, you're whisked away by the unfortunate role you have in these negotiations."

She had only ever been this nervous in his company once, on that night in Deepwater, before they embraced, when she wasn't sure if he was still the young man she had known growing up. Something in his bearing or tone was off. Almost menacing. She drew a deep breath, forcing the appearance of confidence before him. "This role is one I volunteered for. Who else in Vanris would stand up for the Thaelians? Who here would lend them a voice and push my parents and the council to acknowledge their humanity?"

He shook his head, brow furrowing. "How can you even want to after what they did to us?"

"The people of Thaelis are not bad, with a few obvious exceptions. Unfortunately, those exceptions have significant power there. Everyone in Thaelis doesn't deserve to suffer for the actions of their leaders, and if we can help them change that leadership, we can make their lives better while also removing them as a potential threat to Vanris."

"You have a remarkable ability to remain objective considering what they put you through. I hope what you say is true." He took another step closer, his hand rising slightly as if he wanted to reach out to her. "But Kyril and Nalika? They are part of the rot we should be weeding out. How can you bear to stand beside them?"

Her defensive temper flared, and she clamped aggressively down on it, fearful of another incident like what had happened with Gannon. "How many times after your return to Sarket did you commit actions you knew were wrong? Things you felt you had to do to protect yourself from people bent on destroying you because of your time in Vanris? How many people did you hurt?" She pushed ahead when he averted his gaze. "Kyril and Nalika were following orders, doing what they were told was necessary to help their country after it suffered tremendous losses. Once the true cost of their actions sank in, they tried to mitigate some of the damage they had done by bringing you here."

"All right." He placed a hand on her shoulder and met her eyes. "All right. There may be an argument for giving them a second chance. We can all do awful things out of fear and desperation. But they helped Thrasser get me out of the way, and now he has a potentially unbreakable grip on Sarket's throne." He took his hand away, running it through his lengthening hair. "My people believe I'm dead. If Thrasser learns otherwise, he'll stop at nothing to make it true. He could erase me from existence right now, and no one at home would even know to blame him. I doubt they would care if they knew."

Guilt caused an uncomfortable pang in her chest. She pulled him into a hug. "I'm sorry. I've been so wrapped up in trying to solve the situation between Thaelis and Vanris that I lost sight of what all this has done to you and your country, not to mention our relationship with Sarket."

He put his arms around her and held on as if she were the only boat in a sea full of wreckage. "You were everything to me when I lived in Vanris, Veyl, and thoughts of you were all that kept me going most days after I returned to Sarket. I wish we had run away together that night in Deepwater."

"You know I could never have abandoned my family like that," she whispered.

"Yes. I do." He drew back, though he didn't retreat far. One hand came to rest on her shoulder again, closer to her neck this time, its presence there strangely uncomfortable. "Your family is the truest family I've ever had. I couldn't ask you to hurt them." He brought his thumb up, brushing it along her jaw, open affection in his eyes.

His touch only made her yearn for Kyril again. Veyl

turned away and walked to the window, searching the sky for any of the raptors her father used in his scouting.

Jaysen came up behind her. "When Kyril had you pinned against that wall, I feared he was going to kill you. I can't forget that. I will always hate that man for hurting you, and for severing a cherished bond that had only just reformed." He rested his hands on her shoulders, stepping in close enough that she could feel the warmth of his body against her back. "If we aren't honoring the council's agreement, why haven't you had them remove the zenyal bond with Ahndhomen Jinau?"

Her gut clenched. She took one of his hands as she moved out and turned to face him. "You know as well as I do that if our bond reforms, they'll have to sever it again. I don't want either of us to have to go through that. Twice was enough. It can't happen while the zenyal bond is in place."

Adoration softened his gaze and warmed his smile. "You're putting up with that indignity to protect us?"

For the briefest instant, she feared she might have to reject him, but he cupped her cheek with one hand and leaned in to kiss her forehead. Had he also realized they should never have taken their relationship beyond that of spirit siblings?

As he moved away, his gaze drifted to her lips. Then he started leaning in again, and she shied back from him, running into a small table behind her. When she threw her hand out to catch herself, she struck the candleholder there. Pain tore a cry from her when liquid wax spilled across her wrist, burning the skin as it rapidly started hardening there.

Veyl snatched her arm to her chest, startled by the searing pain. Jaysen grabbed the hand and went to work peeling away the drying wax. He barely had time to remove one large portion before the door flew open and her father rushed in with her mother close behind. Their swift arrival making it obvious her father had been spying on them.

"Out of the way," he snapped, and Jaysen immediately obliged, holding up his hands as though declaring surrender. Her father's gaze locked on the wounded arm she held before her, the remaining wax clinging to red, blistering skin on the inside of her wrist.

"I knocked over a candleholder."

The glare he shot at Jaysen told her who he blamed.

"Bring her to the couch," her mother ordered, emerging from the bedroom with the basin, a towel, and a pitcher of water from the bathing room.

Her father took her other hand and guided her to the couch as her mother set the basin on the table and poured water into it.

"Submerge it in this. It will help ease the burning," she advised. "Then we can take a better look at it."

The moment Veyl had sat and done so, her father turned to Jaysen. "I should not have to say this, but our daughter is not for you. I expect you to get that through your head immediately."

Even with the cool water, the pain was searing, but Veyl couldn't leave Jaysen to fend for himself. Not after all the times he had defended her mistakes over the years. "Father, please don't. Nothing happened. Besides, if we wish to cast judgment here, you should also face some for spying on me at dinner and again in my own rooms."

Velara narrowed her eyes at him. "At dinner? Even after our talk?"

Before he could respond, a guard raced in through the doorway, her gaze picking out Veyl. "Khesran, are you all right?"

Her mother's brows pinched. "Are you not supposed to be watching Ahndhomen Jinau?"

"Yes, Khevarin." The guard offered her mother a

deep bow. "The ahndhomen insisted Khesran Veyl was in pain and that one of us should check on her."

"He felt it through the zenyal bond," Veyl murmured, gazing down at the angry blisters rising on her skin beneath the water, bits of wax still clinging in places.

Her mother nodded to the guard. "Please send someone for one of the palace healers and return to your post. Let Ahndhomen Jinau know she is being cared for and that we appreciate his concern for our daughter."

As soon as the guard left, her father turned to Jaysen again. "You are like a son to me, but that does not give you permission to take liberties with Veyl. She is heir to the Vanrian throne, just as you are heir to the Sarketi one. I don't know what freedoms they allowed you in your homeland but, no matter the bonds that have grown from your experiences together, there can never be an intimate relationship between you. Do you understand?"

Jaysen's gaze flickered to her, frustration and a hint of anger in the set of his jaw, but she gave a tiny shake of her head, pleading with her eyes for him not to make matters worse. "Yes, Khemron," he answered.

"Good. You may leave us. Her mother and I have things handled here." Once Jaysen had stalked out, her father came to sit next to her. "How is your wrist?"

"Far more in need of attention than my virtue," she snapped.

"Have the two of you been intimate?" her mother asked.

The question made the burn hurt worse somehow. The water was no longer helping, so she pulled it out, her parents grimacing at the injury. Might a little truth here gain her some leeway in the future? "We kissed once, but it was a long time ago. I don't feel that way about him. I was just... curious, I guess, and perhaps naively thought it wouldn't lead to anything." Now it felt as though her wrist was burning anew. The water had been helping more than she realized. She dunked it back in.

"It never doesn't lead to something." Her father's contemplative gaze lingered on her mother.

"Your father was my first kiss——"

"And we all know you weren't supposed to be kissing him any more than I was supposed to kiss Jaysen. If I recall correctly, you were being considered for a political marriage at the time." She shot a look at her father. "And I know Mother wasn't your first. Nerith has told me a few stories."

"Oh." Nerith stood in the doorway, her cheeks flaring pink, a satchel hanging from one hand.

Her mother smiled a welcome at the healer. "I imagine she has. Come in, Nerith. You are part of the family, and this young woman could use your expertise."

Nerith brushed a few strands of unruly silver hair away from her lavender eyes and came to join them, shooing Kasiel out of the way so she could take his spot next to Veyl. The healer glanced at her submerged injury and winced, then began pulling items out of her satchel.

"I'll have a longer conversation with Jaysen tomorrow," her father said.

"Please don't. We're not children anymore. Let me talk to him."

Her parents shared a look, and he reluctantly nodded. "All right, but be firm. If something like this happens again, there will be repercussions. We didn't hesitate to shelter him from his enemies in Sarket despite the political volatility of the situation because he is like family to us. Taking advantage of that to indulge an apparent infatuation with you is unacceptable."

"I understand that, and so will he."

Nerith laid the towel across her lap and reached for Veyl's arm. "Let's look at this burn, shall we?"

•

Veyl walked past the guards through the open door to the drawing room the next morning to find the three Thaelians already waiting for her. She had slept longer than intended, largely because of the sedative painkiller Nerith had given her to ensure the burn didn't keep her awake through the night.

When she shut the door behind her, Kyril walked over, worry etching lines in his brow. "Are you all right?"

Her gaze flickered briefly to Jinau before she nodded and held her bandaged wrist up between them. "I spilled hot wax on my arm. It's nothing serious."

"How?"

She met Kyril's eyes. "Does it matter?"

"Jin said he felt a moment of panic from you before the pain."

She gave Jinau a searching look. "How much can you feel through the bond?"

"The longer it remains, the stronger it becomes," he answered.

"Not the most helpful response. Why is it I only have a faint sense of you?"

"There is always a moderate amount of sharing both ways, but this bond is intentionally imbalanced, designed to give the holder more control and awareness of their zenyal." His expression was unexpectedly apologetic. "I do not want or deserve to have that power, Seh'hali, but if we wish to misdirect the council upon our return, it might be wise to let it remain for now."

Kyril had obviously been speaking with them already. Veyl pushed aside her discomfort. "Yes. You're undoubtedly right." And there was the complication of her tehnaak bond with Jaysen to consider.

"Why the panic?"

She frowned at Kyril's persistence. "It doesn't concern you." A touch of guilt stung her at his faintly wounded look, but she couldn't involve him in this. The relationship between him and Jaysen was fraught enough. "We should get to work. The afternoon will be upon us all too soon."

She sat at the table, avoiding the inquisitive looks they gave her. None of them joined her. Veyl glanced around at them. Nalika stood with a hand on one hip, giving a slight shake of her head.

"What?"

Kyril held a hand out to her. "Come with me for a moment… please."

She blew out a breath and stood, taking his hand and allowing him to guide her to the far corner of the room amidst some tall bookshelves.

"What is going on?"

"By the Break," she snapped, the heat of anger flashing through her. "It doesn't matter. It isn't like this is a genuine relationship. You don't need to know every detail of my life outside these meetings."

His silent, steady regard worked its way rapidly under her skin.

She blew out another breath. "We have no future together. We both understand that." She couldn't help the yearning in her chest that wanted him to tell her she was wrong, and she despised it.

"Let's worry about the present then. This has something to do with Prince Jaysen, doesn't it?"

His perceptiveness dumped water on the fire of her anger. "Why would you say that?"

He answered with a patient smile. "Because I have eyes. I saw how you two were on the ship heading to Thaelis, and I see how your energy toward him has changed, but his toward you has not, at least not in the same way. Tell me what happened."

"We shared a few poorly considered intimate moments in Deepwater before the…" She caught the tightening of his jaw and rushed ahead. "He visited me in my room last night and tried to kiss me. I knocked over the candleholder when I moved to avoid him. The injury isn't his fault. It was just an accident," she added when his expression darkened. "I opened that door as willingly as he did, but I need to make him understand that isn't what I desire from our relationship. And yet, I don't want to hurt or alienate him. He has fewer genuine allies here than you do, despite all the years he lived within these walls. He will always be Sarketi, and the new friction between our countries isn't helpful."

"Lying to him will only make it worse, as I'm sure you know. The two of you were tehnaak. Tell him you care, but not in that way. Be his tehnaak." He reached out and brushed his fingers across her cheek.

For a second, she almost gave in to the temptation to lean into that caress. Instead, she caught his wrist and moved his hand away. "Even if I wanted that from Jaysen, he would not be an appropriate partner, but neither are you. I can't keep doing this. Sneaking these moments with you when I can never truly be with you. It's too painful. I'm sorry." Her throat tightened, nearly choking off those last two words before she got them out.

"We face a great deal of uncertainty about the futures of our two countries. I find it easier to confront each day knowing that every once in a while, I might have a moment alone with you, but if this is hurting you, maybe it is time to end it. Is that what you want?"

She stared into his silver-blue eyes, a desperate ache spreading through her chest. "No," she whispered. "I want you to be the ocean I drown in."

The words barely passed her lips before he pulled her in and kissed her, a deep, devouring kiss that stole her breath away. No matter what else was going on, no matter how tense their situation, and how overwhelming her responsibilities, the desire to be close to him was ever present. Fighting it made it harder to focus on tasks that required her attention. This, basking in the delicious sensation of being wanted by him and wanting him in return, indulging in their forbidden attraction, was the fire that fueled her.

He drew back and brushed his finger lightly below the split in her lip. "I didn't hurt you, did I?"

"I was too distracted to notice," she whispered.

He chuckled and lightly kissed the injured lip. "We will get through this."

"We won't. Not together."

A reassuring confidence backed up his patient regard. "Will you give me your trust?"

"Am I a fool if I say yes?"

"No. I will not allow this to destroy what we are working for. I promise to protect both you and Thaelis as best I can from this moment forward."

His words had a weight to them that reminded her of the sharing of vows. Her throat tightened as she responded. "Then I give you my trust." She would give him her heart too, if he hadn't already taken it.

He grinned and slid his hands around her waist. "I also promise to lure you into my arms every moment it is safe to do so." He pulled her in for a soft kiss full of tender longing that sent a not- unpleasant shiver through her.

When they parted, she put her arms around him and rested her head against his chest, smiling as he enfolded her in his secure embrace and simply held her for a moment. But the weight of responsibility finally forced them apart, and they rejoined the other two, falling into a long discussion about how they wanted to approach the afternoon conversation with Vanris's leadership.

Though nothing had changed, Veyl was more at ease. Somehow, simply hearing him put into words that he was prioritizing the negotiations and their safety gave her permission to enjoy the time they had and not dwell on the risks or the inevitable separation. They had something to accomplish for all their people, and they would do it together. That confident ease spread to the others, drawing the four of them into a cohesive unit working toward the same ends.

By the time they met with the Vanrian council in the afternoon, they had a list of demands for the proposed annexation of Thaelis as a Vanrian territory. Chief among them was an emphasis on Vanrian oversight as opposed to direct engagement, particularly in the selection of new leadership and the governing of the populace. They insisted that the next council be elected by, and made up of, the people of Thaelis—pure-blooded, mixed, and Qwilki—and that any Vanrian involvement stay at the level of neutral supervision barring matters presenting a clear violation of agreed upon terms or a threat to the mainland.

Ceris sat between Veyl and Kyril this time. A visual separation intended to encourage the perception of distance between them. Somehow, she felt more connected to the Feral ahnkreth with his companion close enough to place a hand on the beast's shoulder or scratch behind his ears, though she had to be careful not to do so at the same time Kyril did. She imagined the wave dancer as a tether binding them.

Confidence infused her. Kyril, Jinau, Ceris, and even Nalika, to a lesser degree, stood united as the Thaelian delegation, with her as their primary voice. Veyl felt motivated and empowered to fight for what they wanted out of this arrangement, and several of those across from her, Arhk chief among them, appeared impressed, if slightly vexed by her composure and persistence.

They discussed conditions all the way through another dinner in the meeting chamber before adjourning. The Vanrian council would take the following day to deliberate and decide how they wanted to respond to the proposed terms. Once they reached an agreement, they could start the deeper information gathering and planning that would precede an actual voyage to Thaelis.

Veyl made a point of not watching the Thaelians as their assigned guards escorted them out, though, after the high from their rapport during the meeting, it felt as if some of her own flesh were being torn away to part from them. One of them in particular. When she started toward a different exit, she immediately spotted Jaysen coming toward her on a course to intercept. He stopped several feet away, his expression darkening when her father reached her first.

In contrast with the prince's sour look, her father wore a pleased smile. "You are welcome to speak with the Thaelians before you retire tonight, if you wish. They must be impressed with how you stood your ground for them today. I know I am. I also want you to make certain you get plenty of rest, though, so keep it brief."

Veyl's heart soared at his praise. "Thank you. Might I meet with them for a few minutes in your reading room?"

"Why there?"

"I told them about Sylaryth and your fight with King Lodmund. I would love to show them his claw, if that's all right."

He chuckled and kissed her on the forehead. "You're welcome to use that room if you wish to glorify the accomplishments of your father and his companions. Just don't stay too long. I've asked Nerith to visit you in your rooms in half an hour to check that burn and redress it. I will send a scout to look in on you if you aren't on time."

"Yes, Father." She kissed him on the cheek and hurried to catch an attendant, asking the woman to have the Thaelians brought to her father's reading room in five minutes. That should give them all a brief opportunity to freshen up.

She glanced around before she headed for her rooms, expecting Jaysen to still be waiting for her, but he had disappeared. After a hasty visit to her chambers, she went to the reading room and found the other three inside, standing by the case that held Sylaryth's claw. For once, Ceris wasn't with them.

Veyl shut the door behind her and walked up next to Kyril, who slid his arm around her, his hand settling warm and welcome at her waist. "I see you found the claw."

"This is the one from your father's first companion?" A hint of reverence tightened Kyril's voice. "The one he used to kill Sarket's king?"

Veyl leaned against him. "Yes. It's why I asked to use this room. I thought you might like to see it."

"Your father is a remarkable man," Jinau stated.

"One surrounded by people who care deeply for him." Nalika's thoughtful tone gave Veyl the impression that she was talking more to herself.

Kyril faced Veyl then. "Speaking of remarkable, you handled yourself extremely well in there today. One might assume you had been disarming foreign dignitaries with your words all your life."

Veyl's cheeks warmed, and she glanced around for a distraction. "Where's Ceris?"

"He's resting in the room. He had an exhausting afternoon."

Something in his regard made her suspect there was more to the statement that he wanted to see if she would figure out on her own. What had Ceris been doing that might have exhausted him? He had merely sat between them.

"The connection?"

He smiled. "Yes. He can create a sort of artificial tehnaak bond using himself as the link between two people, though it requires sustained effort from him. I thought you might appreciate the support if he was open to giving it, which he seemed eager to do. I'm not sure you needed it, though. You truly were incredible in there."

"He speaks true, Seh'hali," Jinau added. "If your efforts today did not convince them, nothing will."

"You did all right," Nalika allowed, walking to a shelf to look over the books there.

Veyl accepted all three comments as high praise. "I want to be sure Thaelis still feels like it's your country when this is over. With better leadership and no Ukhen'kya, ideally."

Kyril's smile warmed her. "We truly appreciate the effort you've put forth on our behalf. If they accept our terms, you should be able to lean on us more for discussions of tactics and what to expect in Thaelis. As long as we remain unified in our approach, I believe we can make this work for both of our countries."

Nalika let out a small, derisive snort, but Veyl was confident the Evoker would stand with them given what she had seen up to now. The other woman didn't like letting Vanris take charge, but she appeared to recognize it was the path forward with the best chance of getting them home alive and with the prospect of achieving a few significant victories for Thaelis.

The ever-present pain in her wrist flared, as if to remind her she had other places to be. "If you are all satisfied with how today went, we can plan to meet tomorrow morning and discuss some options for dealing with the responses we may receive in favor of or against our proposals. But now, I need to meet with the healer."

"I am satisfied." Jinau inclined his head to her.

Nalika merely nodded.

Veyl faced Kyril.

He moved his hand along her jaw, fingertips tracing lines of heat on her skin that sparked warmth throughout her. "I've told you how I feel, but in case there is any doubt..." His lips met hers in a soft, warm kiss that made her want to curl into his arms and stay there until her world settled. When he drew back, there was a flicker of pleasure in his eyes. "Care for your wounds, Seh'hali. We will meet tomorrow."

Veyl watched them leave, barely resisting the urge to reach for Kyril and pull him in for another kiss. When they were gone, she turned to cast a last glance at Sylaryth's claw. Something shifting in the back of the room behind the bookshelves sparked alarm in her that brought to life the storm within.

Who's there?" Veyl tried to sound confident as she attempted to contain the energy crackling up inside her.

Jaysen stepped out from behind the bookcases, watching her warily. Fear, anger, and hurt waged war across his features. "Your former tehnaak," he said through gritted teeth.

"What are you doing in here?"

"I couldn't make sense of your reaction to me last night. As I lay awake, I started wondering if their Evoker and Charmer might be manipulating you. When I heard you ask to meet with them in here, I hurried ahead so I could see for myself. But it turns out that's not what's going on at all, is it?" His eyes narrowed. "It makes so much more sense now."

Panic burst in her chest, and her ability threatened to break free, energy crackling out to her fingertips. "Why don't we sit down and talk about this?"

"I'm not certain I care to." His gaze flickered to the door as if contemplating how fast he might reach it. "I'm glad I didn't kiss you though, knowing who else has been partaking of your lips."

"Please, Jaysen." Her voice shook with the effort of keeping her ability contained. "Give me a chance to explain this."

"Would you break me to keep your secret?" The

hurt came to the fore, his brows pinching together and a hint of moisture rising in his eyes. Years of friendship that had flirted with becoming something more shattered in an instant.

She blinked against the sting of tears. "I would never break you. You mean the world to me. But what happened between us in Deepwater should not have happened. We both know that. You and I can't ever be together. Our responsibilities lie along different paths."

"And you can be with your Thaelian Feral? Explain that to me, because I'm not sure I'm getting it." He held up his hands. "No, don't bother. Even if your excuses made any sense, I would never understand you letting a man touch you who tried to strangle you the first time you met him. I have a feeling your parents won't understand it either."

"No! Please, you can't tell them about this." The crackle of energy was nearly overwhelming now, so much so that it was almost painful. More than just her voice trembled with the effort of holding it back, and her vision blurred with desperate tears.

The door slammed open, and Arhk stormed in, casting a warning look at Jaysen. "What is going on here?"

"It's nothing," Veyl blurted. "I was just upset."

Arhk stepped between them, facing her. "You should probably leave, Prince Jaysen."

"I expect you're right, Dhomvalen," he answered far too readily.

She tried to meet his eyes as he stalked past. "Please, Jaysen. Promise me we can talk about this."

"We'll see." He didn't look at her on his way out the door.

Arhk placed a finger under her chin, drawing her to look at him. Black moved in at the edges of his eyes, and she could feel his ability crash up against hers. Pressure and a sharp taste of fear and darkness that couldn't quite find entry past her storm.

"After your performance in our negotiations today," he began, his smooth voice far too composed for the situation, "I nearly forgot how young you still are. I do not know what happened in here, but I know you can control this."

Veyl wasn't so certain, but she would try, if only to make him proud. If Jaysen reported what he had seen, it might be the last opportunity she had to do so.

She met Arhk's eyes, normally the same pale gray-green as her own. The blackness filling them in, something that struck terror in most people, brought a sense of calm to her. A visual representation of the Frightener connection they now shared. Staring into that darkness, she felt the storm abating. The trembling subsided as the wild energy slowly faded.

As the last crackle of lightning in her chest flickered and died, Arhk smiled. "There. I told you that you could control it." The dark spread further into his eyes, as it often did when he was angry. "Now, tell me what happened with Prince Jaysen."

Serpents of dread coiled in her gut, their writhing making her want to throw up. "We merely had an argument."

"Does this have anything to do with his attempt to kiss you last night?"

Of course, her parents had told him. Veyl drew a deep breath, struggling to hold the newly rising panic at bay. "It was connected, yes."

"If he tried something—"

"No, there are simply a lot of tangled emotions involved, and emotions are," she paused, suppressing the urge to touch the spiral shell in her hair, "messy."

"A significant understatement." The black faded, and the pressure left the room.

"I'm tired."

"Your manner tells me this is more than the typical weariness from a long day."

She lowered her gaze, a deep, despairing hollow spreading through her chest. If Jaysen told her parents what he had seen, it would destroy the progress made in negotiations, at the very least. Kyril would end up behind bars awaiting trial, and she would lose all the ground she had gained with them. It wasn't fair, really. If she were someone else's daughter, her parents might be a little upset, but they would likely move past it without it destroying anyone's life or throwing the fate of another country into chaos. Because she was heir to the throne, the rules were different.

"If you want to talk about it…" He trailed off, leaving the offer open-ended.

She looked into his eyes. "Is there anything I could do that would make you stop loving me?"

Arhk hugged her, a gesture he rarely initiated with anyone else. Not even her father.

"Never." He held her for a moment, then pushed her out with his hands on her shoulders. "You should get some rest. Whatever has upset you may not seem so dire tomorrow."

Veyl doubted it, but she put on a brave face and forced a smile. "You are undoubtedly right. Thank you."

They parted ways, and she hurried to her room. Nerith was waiting in the hall. Veyl kept up light small talk until she finished changing the bandage and left. For a while afterwards, she sat awake, staring at the swallow of painkiller the healer had left her to help her sleep. She could climb around to Jaysen's room. The weather was pleasant enough that his windows would probably be open. Then again, she would be less sure with her injured hand, and maybe it was better to wait and let him cool down, though she didn't see that happening anytime soon.

When she finally swallowed the sedative painkiller and lay down to sleep, she was more than a little surprised that her parents hadn't come knocking yet. How long would Jaysen wait to tell them? Might he give her a chance to talk to him first? Their friendship deserved that much, didn't it?

•

Veyl crawled awake through the heavy fog of the sedative. She lay on her side near the edge of the bed, someone's hand on her arm, shaking her gently. Something cool touched her neck below her jaw. Forcing her weighted eyelids open, she saw Jaysen kneeling next to the bed, holding the ornate dagger he had given her with the sharp edge of the blade resting against her skin. Icy fingers of fear swept through her, warring against the persuasive lull of the sedative. No energy crackled to life within her. The drug was apparently strong enough to suppress her ability.

"Jay—"

He silenced her with a finger over her lips and a shake of his head. "No. I don't want you to speak or move."

Veyl drew a trembling breath and gave him the barest nod, trying to pull together her sluggish thoughts. Under normal circumstances, she could almost certainly fight him and win. They were well-matched in skill, but she had defeated him in practice more often than not. Now, with the sedative weighing down her muscles and muddying her thoughts, she had little chance of achieving the upper hand without getting to know the sharp edge of that dagger a lot more intimately than she wanted to.

"Good girl," he murmured, praising her like a prized hound.

Keeping the dagger against her neck, he ran his hand over her shoulder and down along her side on top of the thin fabric of her nightdress, pushing the covers off as he went, his gaze following the progress. He rested his hand on her hip and drew a deep breath, letting it out in a sigh.

"You and I are going to share some secrets." He looked her in the eyes, then. "Do you have any idea how much I have loved you? You were the only person who never judged me for being Sarketi in all the years I lived here. When I returned to Sarket, where everyone judged me for the time I spent in Vanris, it was memories of you that helped me find the will to get through each day." His jaw tightened. "And every time I fucked a woman I didn't care about to earn the respect of those bastards, I imagined I was making love to you to keep from hating myself so much."

His gaze moved back to his hand, and he brushed his thumb over the curve of her hip. "But you were judging me, weren't you? Tell me, is it his Vanrian blood that makes him acceptable to you? Those pointed ears I always wished for?" His fingers curled into the fabric of her dressing gown and started slowly gathering it up.

This was only a nightmare. It had to be. Some horrible imagining brought by the sedative and the stress of the day. Veyl squeezed her eyes shut. The drug welcomed her into the darkness, offering her the sanctuary of its embrace.

The blade tapped her neck. "We are still talking. It would be exceptionally rude to fall asleep." He ran his fingertips up the side of her now exposed thigh.

She looked at him, pleading with her eyes and her words. "Please don't."

"Shh." The dagger pressed harder, the definition of its edge distinct against her skin. He brought his other hand down, resting his fingers on the inside of her thigh now. A chilling hunger sparked in his eyes. "I wonder what else you've given him."

Veyl was trembling now, a few tears slipping free. Where was the crackle of energy? The power that overwhelmed her when she least wanted it to couldn't seem to break past the fog subduing her when she needed it most.

He brought his hand up then, his fingertips brushing one breast before moving to wipe away the tear sliding over the bridge of her nose. "I won't do that to you. Not like this. I still love you, after all, so here's what we're going to do. You won't mention this little chat to anyone, and I will, for now, not tell anyone what I saw in that room." He brushed her hair back from her face, the cold calculation in his eyes killing any affection that might have come across in the gentle touch. "How I saw Kyril force himself on you, using his Charmer and Evoker to make you believe you wanted it. I wonder how desperately you want to keep that secret."

Panic sent a jolt through the fog, but it still wasn't enough to shake it off. It would be one thing to say she and Kyril had kissed, but to suggest that she had been an unwilling participant, manipulated by them, would get all three of them executed.

He forced her chin up with the edge of the blade and tapped his temple with one finger. "Keep in mind, if you say anything and Evokers get involved, what I saw in that room today is a death sentence for your Feral. Do we understand each other?"

Not to mention the effect the sedative would have, muddling and calling into question any memories they pulled from her mind of this encounter. She swallowed. "Yes."

"Wonderful. Consider what you're doing, Veyl. Remember who your tehnaak is. Remember who embraced you in Deepwater and who hurt you there."

She squeezed her eyes shut when he leaned in and kissed her, his lips warm and unwelcome against hers. Then he pulled her covers back over her and climbed out through the window, taking the dagger with him. She wiped at her lips forcefully enough to make the healing split bleed again. After that, she curled onto her other side, drawing the blankets up to her ear to cover her neck, silent tears falling until the sedative dragged her back under.

•

Early the next morning, Gannon arrived with Iyvalin and Ahrin following protectively along behind him, the two still keeping a close eye on him in the wake of Lorek's death. He invited her to spar, and despite the burn on her wrist and the lingering grogginess from the sedative, Veyl accepted. She had no desire to be alone in her rooms even a minute longer.

Jaysen's nocturnal visit had left her shaken. Between the distracting pain of the bracer over her bandages and her nightmare encounter with her former tehnaak playing back repeatedly in her head, she found herself on the losing side of several rounds before Gannon lowered his sword, his brow furrowing, and approached her.

"You know what, I'm not feeling this today, and I get the distinct impression you aren't either." He put an arm around her shoulders. "How about we have a little something to eat and relax before they drag you off to negotiations again?"

"That sounds nice." She gave him a grateful look as he turned her toward the palace.

He pulled her closer as they walked, lowering his voice so no one else would hear. "If you need to talk, I'll listen."

Guilt tied knots in her gut. She settled her arm

around his waist and leaned into him a little. "I should be the one supporting you right now."

He breathed a humorless laugh. "I could use the distraction of someone else's misery. Besides, given how much of our lives you've put up with me being a horse's ass to you, I feel like I owe you something."

"You haven't—"

"You don't need to lie to me. Losing..." He fell silent, swallowing a few times before he found his voice again. "I've done a lot of looking at myself and the people around me lately. To think I might drive off someone important to me now that I know how easily they could be taken away..."

"I understand."

After a few thoughtful hours spent in the company of old friends, Veyl mustered the courage to call together the Thaelian group. She had them brought to the rather sparsely furnished meeting room where they had met the first time. It had no hidden areas in which someone might conceal themselves. There were plenty of nooks a mouse might spy from, but she didn't fear that as much now. Besides, Kyril would be on alert for such intrusions.

When she joined them, he moved to kiss her, and she evaded him.

His brow furrowed. "Is everything all right?"

"Yes," she lied, avoiding his eyes. "My lip just hurts."

"It does look as if it may have taken another hit sparring." He took her hand and examined the bandages. "It's likely the blisters also broke out there. You should have it cleaned and redressed."

At least he wasn't trying to chastise her for choosing to spar while injured. She appreciated that. What she didn't appreciate was the looming dread that Jaysen could choose to destroy everything at any moment. It made her nauseous in their company. The three

Thaelian's lives hung upon the whim of a man she had thought she knew until last night. It turned out she didn't know him at all. Not anymore.

"It's fine."

He caught Jinau's eye and gestured toward the door with a jerk of his head. The Charmer walked over and leaned out, asking the guards to call for a healer to see to Veyl's burn.

Kyril shifted closer, bringing his lips up next to her ear. "Something's wrong."

"Now isn't the time," she whispered.

He stepped back, those piercing silver-blue eyes searching hers.

Veyl turned away, going to sit at the table with Nalika, who was far less likely to care that something had upset her. "I apologize for calling you together a little late today. We should discuss the responses we may get from the Vanrian council and how we wish to handle them."

Kyril didn't join them right away. He watched Ceris sit beside her and push his nose up under her arm. Veyl's throat seized as she sank her hand into his odd fur, and she feared for a moment that she would break down in front of them. Then, a sense of comfort and confidence moved through her. She drew a careful breath and let it out, regaining control.

Kyril gave a slight nod and sat at the table.

With something else to focus on, the time passed quickly. The twins' mother, Tath, also one of the palace healers, dropped in to tend the burn. The blisters had burst during the sparring session. She chastised Veyl for trying to fight with the injury, warning her it might not heal as well now, and that they would need to watch it for infection.

When it came time to join the Vanrian council, Veyl's gut twisted into a thousand knots, the snakes of dread multiplying more every second. She didn't want to see

Jaysen. The idea of simply being in the same building as him was upsetting enough, even in a structure as vast as the palace. When she stood to leave the small meeting room, the room spun, and she braced herself against the table to catch her balance.

Kyril placed a steadying hand on her arm.

Jinau considered her with a deepening frown. "You look pale, Seh'hali."

She glanced at the ahndhomen, a moment of opportunity flashing through her mind. Perhaps she could beg off as feeling unwell. But no, Jaysen would know why she wasn't there. Would it please him to know how deeply his actions had distressed her? Would he regret it? Or might her avoidance prompt him to act on his threat? It was far too likely that hiding from him would make the situation worse.

"I'll be fine." She had to focus. With three Evokers in the negotiation room, she couldn't afford to let the source of her distress dominate her thoughts. Not that she hadn't been working until now to avoid revealing her relationship with Kyril, but this would add an additional layer of difficulty. Was Jaysen skilled enough at managing his thoughts to hide all of this from them? Would they even bother paying attention to him when they had the Thaelians to monitor?

When they reached the meeting room, Veyl hung back, waiting to enter behind the other three so she might have a moment to try spotting the source of her upset before going in.

"Good afternoon, Khesran."

Jaysen's voice behind her made her breath catch and her stomach clench. For an instant, she feared she might throw up. If she did, perhaps she could at least do so on him the way she had vomited on Kyril's boots on the voyage to Thaelis. She stepped quickly to the side to move away from him, lightning crackling to life in her chest as she noticed that, sometime since his visit last night, he had cut his hair shorter in a Sarketi style.

Across the room, Arhk's attention snapped to her, abandoning whatever conversation he had been having with Dhomen Nevias. He leaned to his left to whisper something to his Evoker, Zafyr, whose gaze moved to Veyl as well.

"Afternoon, Prince Jaysen." Veyl forced the words out, happy that her lunch didn't follow them. She clamped down on her ability and hurried to join the others.

When they were all seated, her mother addressed them. "The council has reached a decision. We agree that most of the terms you presented are reasonable, with a few slight adjustments. We insist on the addition of three Vanrian advisors to the new council in Thaelis whose roles will be to provide guidance primarily on matters that might affect the safety of Vanris and its territories, or that run any risk of encroaching upon the rights and freedoms of the citizens therein. Regarding military presence, we will, as requested, establish only a single military base on the main island. The appointed advisors will be responsible for determining whether there is a need for more over the course of the first year, at the end of which we will reconvene to discuss the matter. They will also assess trade needs and what goods might be worth transporting to or from the mainland in cooperation with the rest of the new Thaelian council. You may take a moment if you wish to speak among yourselves before you respond."

Veyl focused on the words and on the subtle reactions of the three Thaelians. With Ceris once again linking her and Kyril, she got a faint sense of resignation. It was more oversight and involvement than they wanted, but ultimately less than they had expected. She glanced at each of them, keeping her gaze low as she turned to the right to avoid seeing Jaysen. Their subtle nods were enough, though she noted the tightness of Nalika's jaw. Of them all, the Evoker was the least happy about it, but she had dealt with Arhk and Zafyr, two of the most intimidating individuals in the room, on the day their parents arranged for people to talk with them in private. It was no wonder she was less comfortable than the other two.

"While we would prefer less direct involvement, we will accept your proposed changes for the sake of establishing a connection between the people of Vanris and Thaelis that will hopefully benefit all of us." A weight lifted from Veyl's shoulders as she said it. It was done. If only Jaysen hadn't become a greater burden, his threats bearing down on her chest and threatening to suffocate her.

Ceris nudged her hand with his nose. The gesture, meant to bring comfort, mostly sparked an instant of panic as she remembered to push such thoughts into the background. A glance around at the two Evokers on the Vanrian side assured her their focus wasn't on her at that moment. She couldn't look at Nalika without being obvious about it, so she hoped for the best.

Her mother inclined her head slightly, her eyes sweeping across the Thaelian side of the table. "Very well. We will have agreements written up as discussed for your review and signatures in the morning, after which we can begin planning our approach to Thaelis and action against the current Thaelian leadership. This evening, we invite you to join us for a feast to celebrate the closing of these negotiations."

That sounded positive up front, but when they gathered in the larger dining hall, the rest of her father's tehsheyn, as well as the twins and Tavin and Ellaris joined them, and Veyl's usual spot in the corner next to Jaysen awaited her. At the start of the meal, she focused intently on her food, relieved when Jethan asked her questions about Thaelis, giving her an excuse to ignore the source of her discomfort for a while. When Jethan's attention moved elsewhere, she stared into her plate, trying to keep her thoughts on the meal and the coming military action in Thaelis.

"Khemron Kasiel, you and Khevarin Velara must be quite relieved," Jaysen said, drawing her parents' attention.

"How do you mean?" her father asked.

"Now that the Thaelians are technically citizens of Vanris, and we are moving on from negotiations, there is no need for Veyl to continue meeting with them in private." He nodded to the three Thaelians who had been given places on the far side of the table. "We will all be fighting on the same side from now on."

"That is an excellent point," her mother smiled fondly at her. "Now that we are working together, you can assume your proper role as a khesran of Vanris. That should take some of the burden off your shoulders."

Under the table, Jaysen's hand touched her leg.

Veyl tensed, fighting the sudden urge to kick him or throw up. Maybe both. She set down her fork, any appetite she'd had abandoning her, and began folding her napkin.

"Yes, it is a relief that we can move forward," she answered. She stood, an action that unfortunately drew everyone's gaze to her. Forcing a smile, she said, "Excuse me. My wrist is quite painful this evening. I'm going to retire a little early. Please enjoy the rest of your meal."

"I told you it was a poor choice to spar with it like that." Tath's sympathetic smile softened her words.

"It's my fault," Gannon offered in her defense. "I shouldn't have encouraged her. You know she can't resist a bit of friendly competition."

"If you need anything, let us know," her mother

said, fine lines furrowing the subtle ke'hanoath tattoo on her brow.

Her father regarded her thoughtfully, his gaze searching. "And you are more than welcome to rejoin us later if you find yourself feeling up for it."

"Thank you," she answered as graciously as she could, deliberately not looking at Kyril, Jaysen, or any of the Evokers in the room.

Nerith stood, setting her napkin on the table. "I'll come with you. We can change that bandage and add some fresh salve. That might help."

"No," Veyl protested. "You should stay and enjoy the evening."

"I insist."

Resigned, Veyl left the room, relieved to at least get away from Jaysen. She returned to her chambers alone while Nerith went to collect the supplies she needed. It was stuffy inside. She had closed and latched all the windows that morning. Knowing Jaysen would probably stay at dinner for some time, she dared to open one in the sitting room and another in the bedroom, resenting the roiling in her gut that accompanied that process.

When Nerith returned, they sat on the couch together, and the healer began removing the wound dressing.

"You seem unsettled today." She set the soiled bandages aside and gently cleaned the injury. "Is everything all right?"

Veyl stared at her wrist, afraid Nerith would somehow see the truth in her eyes. "I had nightmares last night on the sedative. I think I'll try to manage without it tonight?"

"With the wound this raw, I doubt you'll get any rest. A stronger dose might help you sleep more soundly."

"No!"

Nerith pulled back from the vehemence in her refusal,

and Veyl drew a deep breath, closing her eyes to try finding some calm in the darkness. Where was the ocean in that darkness, the soothing crash of the waves? A hand touched her shoulder, and she startled, eyes snapping open.

Nerith's brow furrowed. "Veyl, are you all right?"

"I'm fine. There's just been so much stress lately. I'm sure I'll sleep better now that the negotiations have wrapped up." She hated making it sound as if she were unequal to the task of managing those political responsibilities, but she could think of nowhere else to lay the blame that wouldn't inspire more questions.

"All right. I'll leave a dose of the sedative here in case you end up needing it."

There was a knock at the door, and Jaysen poked his head in before entering. "Pardon my interruption, but I didn't want our ailing khesran to miss out on dessert." His smile was bright and far too relaxed. The expression of a man who knew he held the winning hand.

"Isn't that sweet?" Nerith said. "Let me finish up here, and I'll leave you to enjoy that in peace."

Jaysen set the covered plate on the table, his smile for Veyl less warm now that Nerith's focus was on her wrist again. "I hope you feel up for joining us later this evening, Veyl. Your father offered to teach Ahnkreth Kyril Feral's Folly after dessert. It should be quite entertaining."

"Perhaps." Veyl barely pushed the word out past the rage, sorrow, and frustration that squeezed her throat. She hissed as if Nerith's ministrations hurt more than they did, giving herself an excuse to focus on that process and beg off an evening that she would have loved to be part of.

When the two left, she pushed the dessert to the far edge of the table. Then she closed and latched the windows before going to sit on her bed with her legs pulled into her chest, trying desperately not to think about anything at all.

For the next several days, they dedicated meetings entirely to extensive discussions about how to approach the return to Thaelis and overthrowing the council with the least amount of bloodshed. Once the agreements were drawn up and signed by all parties, the three Thaelians became citizens of Vanris. They had their own voices in the conversation now, ones with far more detailed information to offer than anything Veyl could provide. She didn't know the workings of their country like they did. Still, given her role up to that point, and the time she had spent in Thaelis as an outsider, she remained part of the discussions.

Her parents and the Vanrian council, after the first full day of investigating options with the Thaelians, agreed that the best approach would be to arrive in Thaelis under the pretense of going along with the original agreement Veyl had signed. No matter how much they disliked the idea, for it to be convincing, it required her to return to Thaelis with the fleets. She was Thaelis's ambassador and had committed to seeing this through until they tried and sentenced Kyril in Thaelis. If she didn't arrive with them, the councilors would immediately be suspicious.

Now that the Thaelians were Vanrian citizens, the rest of Kyril's crew currently imprisoned in Etrion was to be given a chance to prove themselves. A process that required finding a place to put them all. One of the city's barracks, along with adjacent military housing, was cleared out to make temporary homes for them. The area was put under heavy watch, given the circumstances, and they had orders to stay within the designated boundaries, but they were at least freed from their cells. Considering the importance of ensuring nothing went wrong with that process, Nalika, Jinau, and Kyril moved out of the palace and joined their crewmates to help ease their transition.

With the three Thaelians no longer in residence, Veyl felt more alone in her own home than she ever had. She did her best to avoid Jaysen without being too obvious about it, spending a part of each evening working on her ability with Arhk and going out every morning to spar with Gannon, Ahrin, and Iyvalin. Merrin and Avris were often there training students, and were happy to offer them additional feedback and instruction when they had the time to do so. Despite her abuse of it, her burned wrist slowly healed.

Veyl missed knowing Kyril was watching when she sparred with her companions. Even more, she missed meeting with him and the others, and not only for the moments of intimacy it had allowed them. For a brief time while the negotiations were going on, she had been one of them. Now that they no longer needed her to be their voice, she felt distanced, not only from them, but from the Vanrian side as well, because of the secrets she had been keeping and the fact that Jaysen sat among them.

Internal strife in Vanris had quieted since word spread of her return, though they were making a concerted effort to keep the fact that she was a Frightener from becoming common knowledge for now. With the situation a little calmer to the north, her parents summoned more military and mind-crafter support to gradually bolster forces along the southern border in case Sarket made a move before the mission to Thaelis returned. More aid from Delaphine was also called upon, primarily of the naval variety, to help protect Vanris's western coast.

Veyl kept her windows latched at night, no matter how warm it got, and her door bolted. The first few mornings the attendants came to deliver food and had to knock, they looked puzzled, but word of the new behavior apparently didn't move beyond them, because no one asked about it. It distressed Veyl, however. This was her home, and Jaysen had stolen away her sense of safety within those walls.

Five days after the Thaelians moved out of the palace, Kasiel took Tavin and Kyril to the tethdrak enclosure, relenting to an apparently irresistible desire to see if Kyril could work with the reptilian beasts. Veyl spent most of the morning sparring with the twins and Iyvalin to take her mind off where she would rather be. Later, she attended a few hours of discussion dedicated to logistical planning around the gathering and moving of supplies and soldiers for the voyage to Thaelis. Jinau and Kyril were there. Meyla, Kyril's second in his fleet, had claimed Nalika's place at the table now that she was no longer imprisoned. Jaysen was there as well, taking advantage of the moderately less formal setting to wander over next to Veyl, his nearness making it nearly impossible for her to focus on what was being said.

For a time, he just hovered close to her, then he leaned in and whispered, "If you're lonely without your Feral, I could fill that void."

Veyl tried to pretend she hadn't heard him, but a wave of nausea rolled through her, and she shuddered with the force of it. His faint smirk made it apparent he noticed.

Something snapped in Veyl. She was tired of being

uncomfortable in her own home, but she couldn't create a scene. They had been inseparable companions once. Maybe if she talked to him, she could make him remember that and end this torment. She would get him to see reason. Somehow.

When the session ended, she forced herself yet again not to watch Kyril leave. Every meeting was a punishing process of trying not to look at him in any way that might betray her affection or raise Jaysen's ire. Today, Jaysen rushed out and Veyl hurried after him, pursuing at a distance as he strode back toward the private quarters. He turned down a hall ahead of her. When she reached the corner, she saw him enter her father's reading room.

Nerves lighting up, she followed, stepping through the door to find him nowhere in sight.

"Jaysen?"

Silence met her unfortunately tremulous query. She walked through the room, peering into the shadowed areas amongst the bookshelves. Her nerves on fire now, she hesitantly made her way to the back, peeking around the tall bookcases for him.

"I see you finally rediscovered your courage?" Jaysen stepped out behind her from wherever he had been hiding.

Veyl barely managed not to jump. She spun to face him, her back now to the rear wall, with him between her and the door. "I wanted to talk." Again, her voice trembled, and she hated herself for it.

He took a step forward, already closer than she was comfortable with. When he spoke, his soft, sensual tone sent an unpleasant chill through her. "Do you know how different my life might have been if your parents hadn't insisted on my being a ward here for seven years when Sarket surrendered? But I didn't resent them for that, because I wouldn't have gotten to spend that time with you otherwise. I would have given up my throne in a heartbeat for the chance to stay with you, but you would never do the same. Your family is everything to you. Or they used to be, before he showed up." He moved forward another step, now only a few inches from her, and reached up to brush the backs of his fingers across her cheek. "That's why I'm certain now that they have messed with your mind, Veyl. What else could cause you to lie like this to the family you hold so dear?"

The contact and his nearness took her back to that night in her bedroom, his dagger at her throat, the sedative making her slow and vulnerable, him touching her as if he had every right to do so. She pressed against the wall, her breath coming quicker now, lightning crackling through her without the drug to suppress it this time. She pushed back on it, afraid of drawing Arhk to them again.

Jaysen looked into her eyes, a hint of curiosity in the tilting of his head. "Ah, I see the mind-crafter emerging now. Do you intend to break me, Khesran Veyl? You don't even realize that you broke me some time ago, do you?" He brushed her hair back over her ear, leaning in close enough that she could feel his breath on her lips. "Should I tell your parents what they've done to you? Maybe it's not too late for them to fix this."

"Please don't." The tightness in her throat made it a struggle to force the words out. The same words she had spoken that night. She could fight her way free of him this time, but if he told her parents this story he had made up to rationalize what he had seen, they would launch a full investigation. Once their Evokers pulled the kiss Jaysen had seen from his mind, they would dig harder to find the truth. A truth both Nalika and Jinau were aware of. Would they go so far as to eliminate Ceris to interrogate Kyril? Regardless, no amount of fighting would save Kyril and the others if that relationship came to light. All she could do was try not to give him a reason to expose it. "They haven't altered my mind."

"I think they have." It scared her that he sounded as if he truly believed it now. He leaned back a fraction, his gaze moving down below her lips to her neck as his hand came to rest lightly around her throat in what felt like a casual threat. "All I had without you was my country, but your new lover took even that from me."

"Jaysen," she said, finding her voice, "you and I were always there for each other. You're my tehnaak. Why are you doing this?"

His brows crept up. "Tehnaak? I seem to recall him taking that too." He leaned in, bringing his mouth close to her ear this time, and whispered, "I'm doing this because you were the last dream I had left."

The inner storm abandoned her, leaving a despairing emptiness in its place. Veyl couldn't move when he brought his lips to hers in a soft kiss, his hand still on her throat. A cold sweat broke out over her forehead and the back of her neck, her stomach roiling in protest. Then he turned and walked away, leaving her trembling against the wall in the back of the room.

What if he was right? Would she know if Jinau and Nalika had manipulated her? The Evoker could have extracted her memories of such. But no, her attraction to Kyril, unlikely as it was at the time, had started on the voyage to Thaelis, long before she met Jinau. Nalika hadn't been around for that either, not on the same ship. Not that she remembered.

Veyl wiped her lips and hurried back to her own rooms. It was stuffy there. She cast a bitter glance at the closed windows before grabbing a hooded cloak from her wardrobe and sneaking out of the palace through a side entrance. The light garment was a common soldier's cloak, meant to protect from the sun and blend with the colors of the desert rather than provide warmth. She tossed it around her shoulders, pulling the hood forward enough to at least cover her distinctive hair, and struck out across the city.

It didn't take long to reach the area the Thaelians were staying in. The tricky part was figuring out how to sneak past the guards. This wasn't a visit she wanted to make widely known. Pulling her hood farther forward, Veyl lingered at the corner of a building and watched the two city guards standing at the entrance. They looked bored, meaning they had plenty of time on their hands to question anyone seeking to pass, of whom there were none yet that she had seen. They forbade the Thaelians from roaming outside their area, and didn't allow the city's residents to venture into the Thaelian area unless they were in the company of certain approved individuals, such as her parents or other council members. Technically, that meant she could enter. She just didn't want anyone knowing she had.

An odd but familiar sensation tugged at her moments before Jinau strolled into view. He looked directly at her hiding spot as he walked up to the two guards and engaged them in conversation off to one side of the street. After a few seconds, the Charmer waved her discreetly in with a hand by his leg. Veyl strode quickly and purposefully alongside the buildings opposite them, trusting him to keep them from noting her passage. Then she ducked around the next corner and waited. Jinau joined her a couple of minutes later.

"Thank you, Jin." She didn't meet his eyes for fear he would see her shame in them. Although given the zenyal bond, he could undoubtedly sense that something had upset her.

He gave her a scrutinizing look, then nodded. "Follow me."

Veyl went with him around to a house near the barracks.

He sent her inside and left her there to wait.

The house was cozy and relatively simple in both furnishings and layout. If anyone had been using it before the Thaelians, they had removed all items that might have given the space personality. It was around the same size as Kyril's home near the port in Dagony, though it lacked the brighter ocean-inspired color scheme and decor that was so popular in that city.

She walked to the center of the main room and stood there, recalling her encounter with Jaysen. Her fingertips touched her throat where his hand had rested, the memory of his quiet threat somehow more potent than that of Kyril's powerful grip pinning her to the wall in Deepwater.

When the door opened, she turned to see Kyril enter alone, his self-assurance and vigor barreling over her turmoil as he strode to her. He took her arms and looked into her eyes, the pinching of his brows making it clear he could see her distress.

"What happened? Are you all right?"

Despite all that had happened, just being close to him still felt like coming home. The concern that tightened his voice brought the sting of tears to her eyes, but she couldn't find the words to tell him the truth. Instead, she stepped closer, sliding her hand around to the back of his neck, and pulled him into a kiss. The earnest passion with which he responded, bringing her in tight against him as he accepted the invitation of her parted lips, lit a fire in her. A fire she craved that could help burn away the demoralizing fear and heartbreak caused by Jaysen's actions.

Her hands gathered the fabric of his shirt, and she broke the kiss only long enough to lift it off. Kyril unclasped her cloak and let it fall to the floor along with his shirt. He reclaimed her mouth as if it were a meal he was starving for and guided her back toward the bedroom. His lips erasing all memory of Jaysen's. When he undressed her and eased her down on the bed, his caresses did the same for every place Jaysen had touched her and more.

•

Later, Veyl lay curled against him, basking in the false security his strength offered in this place. It wouldn't be enough to save him if someone caught them like this. Still, she wanted to imagine for a moment that they could protect each other from the world outside those walls.

"Now, will you tell me what's been eating away at you?"

Veyl closed her eyes and pulled herself more tightly against him.

"Veyl, you're worrying me."

She startled at a sound from the next room, and Kyril chuckled. "That's just Ceris or Jin. We share this house. I must have truly enthralled you if you didn't realize he was back."

"Why would I…" It clicked abruptly into place. The zenyal bond. "Oh, by the Break, please tell me he couldn't feel how much I was appreciating your… talents?"

"He probably could, to a certain degree, given how long the bond's been active between you."

It was easy for him to be nonchalant about it, but her cheeks blazed hot at the notion. She tucked her face against his chest. "No. How will I ever look him in the eyes after this?"

Kyril chuckled again, and he rolled on his side, forcing her to shift back from him. He tried to meet her eyes. "What has you so troubled?"

Veyl avoided his gaze. "Can we just enjoy being together for a little while longer?"

"Do you think your body is all I want from you?"

A flash of anger moved through her. "It's all you can have, isn't it? You're not even supposed to have that."

"I see I've woken the storm." He brushed her hair back with gentle fingers, his touch welcome where Jaysen's had not been. "The water in Le'equo Cove is the same color as your eyes, minus the lightning, of course. I would love to take you there someday."

The affection in his smile calmed the crackling energy in her.

"There. Exactly that color." His expression turned thoughtful. "Now, you've had your way with me. Will you tell me what happened since the last time we were alone that has you in such turmoil?"

She drew a shaky breath and made herself meet his eyes. "Jaysen saw us together in my father's reading room the day I showed you the claw."

Kyril stilled, the implications racing behind his eyes. "Deeps take me," he snarled. "I should never have risked it without Ceris there. I can tell if there are creatures around, but I have been relying on him to warn me about other people. Has your prince told anyone?"

"Don't call him that," she snapped. She ignored the querying rise of his brows and shook her head, unable to bring herself to tell him what Jaysen had done. "Not so far, but he's convincing himself that the three of you meddled with my mind to make this happen. If I persuade him otherwise, he'll see it as my betrayal and could expose us out of spite. If I don't, he may decide it's his duty to help me by telling my family, and the results will be the same."

He sat up on the edge of the bed and turned to face her. "That's a serious problem, but there's still more to this. Even at your lowest point, when you were ready to die, you burned with fierce determination. Something has undermined that."

How could he see so much?

Veyl sat up as well, resisting the urge to pull the sheet up with her. It wasn't as if he hadn't seen and touched all of her. "I'm just worried." She chewed at her lower lip, and he arched a brow.

"There was more to your coming here than just wanting to see me, and more to our coupling than just desire. Did he hurt or threaten you, Seh'hali?"

The caring in his voice wasn't enough to hide the tightening of his jaw and slight pinching around his eyes that warned of an immense fury waiting to be unleashed upon anyone who tried to harm her. Lashing out at Jaysen would assure his death as certainly as daring to be intimate with her. She couldn't involve him in this any more than he already was. Somehow, she had to handle Jaysen on her own.

He schooled his expression to patience when she didn't answer. "I realize our situation is difficult, but I will help you in any way I can. I won't try to force you to talk about it right now. Just know that when you are ready to, I will be here."

Veyl moved closer and leaned in to kiss him, a shiver of pleasure racing through her in response to his hand sliding around her waist. "Thank you," she whispered.

He stole another kiss, his body making obvious the effect the contact was having on him. "What I wouldn't give to keep you here."

She smiled, sliding her arms over his shoulders. "What I wouldn't give to be so kept."

For a while longer, she let herself become lost again in touching him and being touched by him. Before things got too heated, he eased away from her, his breath coming a little faster when he pressed his forehead to hers, his muscles tense with the effort of restraint.

"Although I greatly appreciate your chosen method of avoidance, I know you aren't supposed to be here.

We should sneak you back out before someone comes looking."

Veyl closed her eyes, drawing a shaky breath and steeling herself for the prospect of returning to the palace where she might encounter Jaysen.

Kyril became ominously still, the soft growl in his voice making her eyes snap open. "If he touches you again, I will kill him."

"You will do nothing," she countered. "I'm not losing you, and I won't allow this to all fall apart. There's too much at stake."

His eyes flashed, the Feral predator in him rising to the surface. Ceris's fierce growl came from outside the door. "Then he has touched you."

She closed her eyes and drew a deep breath, realizing she had fallen right into that trap. The desperate need to keep him safe helped her force a show of confidence when she opened her eyes again. "He hasn't done anything that terrible," she lied, "and you will do nothing in return. If you get involved, there will be an execution before the mission to Thaelis, and I won't have that. Let me handle this. Please."

He drew a deep breath, some of the alarming wildness in his bearing calming, and slid a hand into her hair. "You shouldn't have to deal with this alone."

"There's no way around that right now, but if I know you're safe, it will be easier for me to face him." She hoped he couldn't see the dread building within her. Coming here had only ever been a brief escape, yet there remained the irrational hope that a way out would present itself if she could just be with him.

He frowned, but even he couldn't deny that their situation left them very few options. "All right. It's in your hands for now."

After they cleaned up and dressed, Kyril and Jinau worked together to help sneak her back out of the

Thaelian area. It was nearing evening, and she had been away too long already. She hoped that those most likely to seek her out would assume she had visited the training grounds and not go looking. Two blocks from the entrance to the temporary Thaelian quarters, she spotted two palace guards heading her way and ducked into the shadows of a building, checking the hood of her cloak. What would she do if they stopped her?

"Veyl!" a low voice called from the alley behind her.

She turned, spotting Gannon in the shadows, and hurried to join him. Iyvalin and Ahrin were there as well.

"What are you doing here?"

"Looking for you," Iyvalin whispered.

"Quiet," Gannon hissed, waving them down the alley.

They made their way several blocks into the city to The Blade's Rest. It wasn't as nice a tavern as The Twisted Vine, her father's preferred haunt, but it was closer and busy enough that they could disappear into the crowd and claim a table in the back corner.

Once they sat and a round of mead was on the way, Gannon shook his head at her. He spoke in a low voice. "I'm not sure if you're brave or stupid, but either way, you almost got caught. You need to be careful if you don't want your precious Feral meeting the pointy end of a sword."

"My precious…" She gave him a long look, then turned to Ahrin and Iyvalin, who both nodded.

"We were pretty sure something was going on between you two that day in Thaelis, when you showed up outside the house with him after disappearing for several hours," Ahrin explained.

Gannon stared at the mugs the serving boy set on the table, sliding one over in front of her before taking another for himself. "I shouldn't have gotten upset with you like I did that day."

Veyl tentatively touched his arm. "That doesn't excuse what I did to you."

He shrugged off her words. "I guess I felt rather worthless knowing you would choose someone like him, despite what he had done to us, before you would consider me. Upon looking back on how I've treated you over the years, I realized it wasn't all that surprising after all."

Veyl didn't know how to respond to that. Losing Lorek apparently had him doing a great deal of self-reflection. They needed to be wary of him judging himself too harshly, whether he deserved it or not. It wasn't uncommon for someone to try ending their own life after losing their tehnaak. "How did you know to come looking for me?"

"We were walking over by the academy when we heard some palace guards asking if anyone had seen you," Iyvalin answered. "We put our heads together and guessed that you must have gone to visit him. If you had, we figured you might need a little help."

Ahrin nodded. "Not that we had the slightest idea how we were going to talk our way past the guards into the Thaelian area to look for you. Lucky for us, you were leaving already."

"We'd have figured it out," Gannon muttered.

"Speaking of guards." Iyvalin took hold of her mug, subtly gesturing toward the door with one finger as she picked it up to take a drink.

Veyl heaved a sigh and took several swallows of mead. "That didn't last long."

"You've been with us all afternoon," Gannon stated. "We were visiting at Iyvy's house until a half-hour ago. No one is at home there to say otherwise."

The other two nodded when she looked at them, supporting the story.

A fond smile curved her lips. "Thank you all. I don't

deserve you."

After a moment of searching through the patrons, the guards spotted them and walked over, bowing slightly. "Khesran Veyl, the khevarin and khemron have requested your presence."

"I'm coming." She appreciated that they went to wait for her by the door, giving her a moment to say goodbye to the others. "Maybe you three could stop by the palace for some Feral's Folly this evening?"

"We'd love to," Ahrin answered for them.

Veyl leaned close to Iyvalin, dropping her voice to a whisper. "Any chance you could pick up a precautionary elixir from the healer's building on your way?"

"A precautionary…" Her eyes widened, pale cheeks turning a soft pink. "Oh! Yes, I can do that for you."

Veyl gave her hand a squeeze. "Thank you." She got up and followed the guards from the tavern, feeling a little less alone. More people knew of her secret relationship with Kyril now, but at least they appeared willing to stand beside her regardless of how they might feel about him.

Veyl's parents were looking for her, but not for any reason that would justify the near panic she had arrived in, fearing Jaysen might have told them something. They wanted her to join them for a family dinner with only the four of them before the journey to Thaelis took her away again. They were remaining in Etrion because of the looming threat from Sarket and sending Arhk to oversee the mission to Thaelis, with several trusted senior officers serving under him.

"Arhk can also help you with your ability more during the voyage," her mother said. "He will make certain you are out of harm's way once Ahndhomen Jinau and the others have everything in place to move against the council as well. You must do exactly as he says. He—"

"Yes. I know." Veyl blew out a heavy breath. "You've told me five times this evening already."

Her father squeezed her arm. "And we lost you once already. That's one time too many. The only way we can stomach the idea of letting you leave again is by knowing that your grandfather will be there to look out for you."

"He'll be your commanding officer as well," Tavin added. "Something to keep in mind in case you're tempted to ignore what your family tells you to do as usual."

Veyl grabbed a roll and threw it at him. "I'll miss you too, you little calloch."

Tavin ducked to the side, grinning.

"No throwing food at the table."

Veyl arched a brow at her mother. "So, if we step away from the table..." she trailed off, reaching for another roll.

Her mother shook her head. "Go ahead, if you wish to spend the last few nights before you depart helping to wash dishes in the kitchen." She cast a warning glance at Tavin, who was grabbing for a roasted beet with a wicked grin. "That applies to both of you."

Her father chuckled. "Here I was thinking you two were growing up too fast. Apparently, I had nothing to worry about."

Veyl gave him a tremulous smile. "I'll always be your little girl, Father."

He reached over to give her hand a gentle squeeze. "Always."

Her mother gazed down at her plate, tears glistening in her eyes. "You'll have some friends with you." She drew a shaky breath and looked at Veyl. "The twins somehow talked their parents into letting them accompany you. They worked their magic on Iyvalin's family as well. I suspect Darro and Tath are hoping the mission will give Gannon less time to dwell on losing Lorek."

That the three wanted to come was a surprise, a much more pleasant one than the one her father dropped next.

"And Jaysen will be there too, maintaining a proper distance."

Her stomach squeezed into a tiny ball, threatening to push out all the food she had just eaten. "Why?" She had to work hard to keep from sounding as distraught as she was. "With everything that's going on in Sarket, isn't it wiser for him to remain here?"

Her father shook his head, the certainty in the

gesture banishing her hope for an escape. "We helped him send off a messenger to someone he trusts in Sarket. The response came a few days ago. He says they told him Thrasser is unquestionably up to something, but since the Thaelians didn't return as agreed upon, and they heard rumors that we have Thaelian ships in our custody, he appears to be reassessing his plans. The contact will try to learn more but encouraged Jaysen to continue being dead for another few months, at least. Jaysen suggested joining the mission to eliminate the risk of his being seen by the wrong people here. We were skeptical too at first, but Arhk supported the idea. He promised to keep him out of any fighting that breaks out in Thaelis, and it will be a comfort to have one more person there committed to seeing you safe."

She barely caught herself before scoffing at that. At least Arhk knew there had been friction between them and was unlikely to permit them to be alone together. The decision was made. There was no point in belaboring it. "You've taken Ahnkreth Kyril out with the tethdraks a few times. Can he control them?"

He opened his mouth to answer, but her mother spoke first.

"You haven't asked him yourself?" She casually cut a slice of roast on her plate.

"When would I have done so?" Veyl countered, just as casually taking a bite of beet.

"When no one could find you earlier, we wondered if you might have gone to visit the Thaelians." She gave Veyl a hard look, her sharp gaze searching for something.

Veyl stared back into those bright silver eyes. Had her mother ever used her Charmer ability on her? She wanted to believe she hadn't, but how hard would it be to resist using such an advantage now and then on two unruly children? Or at least that one admittedly headstrong daughter? "I was with the twins and Iyvalin. We haven't had many opportunities to spend time together lately."

Her father cleared his throat, breaking their standoff. "To answer your question, he controlled them extremely well after only a brief time around them. He's a gifted Feral, though his wave dancer didn't appear to like him working with them."

Veyl smiled to herself, imagining Ceris watching his bonded companion connect with other beasts and squirming with jealousy.

"You're fond of him," her mother said, her tone making it not quite a question.

A spark of anxiety flashed through Veyl, but she held onto her soft smile. "Ceris is a remarkable creature. He can be unexpectedly sweet."

"Not who I..." her mother trailed off when her father took her hand.

They didn't speak of Kyril or Jaysen again that evening, focusing the rest of the time on enjoying the opportunity to be together. It was too late to meet with the twins and Iyvalin when she finally parted ways with them, not that she minded. A chance to be with her family was something to be cherished. She understood that now more than she ever had before.

When she entered her rooms later, the pleasant meal turned to ice in her stomach. Jaysen sat waiting on the couch near the fireplace. A carafe of wine rested on the table between two fine glass goblets in front of a colorful arrangement of flowers from the palace gardens.

She drew a breath, steeling herself to order him out. But thoughts of the man whose arms she had spent a few blissful hours of the afternoon in and what could happen to him if Jaysen exposed them to her parents stayed her.

"It's late, Jaysen." She succeeded at sounding more

weary than afraid. Not an insignificant accomplishment under the circumstances.

"I ask only a few minutes of your time. Come, sit with me."

She glanced out into the hall, momentarily humoring thoughts of running, then slowly closed the door. Jaysen filled the goblets with sweet wine as she joined him on the couch, keeping enough distance from him to be proper without making it obvious how much she wished to avoid even the most incidental contact.

Jaysen shifted closer, handing her a goblet. "I owe you an apology."

Veyl nearly spit out the drink she was taking. It was all she could do to hold back the furious tirade that wanted to burst forth, but she covered her mouth as she coughed and turned away, hoping he would assume she had merely swallowed wrong.

"Are you all right?" Jaysen reached for her arm.

She couldn't stop herself from flinching at his touch, but the reaction was subtle enough he didn't appear to notice. Was it possible he genuinely didn't realize how much she despised him for what he had done?

"Please," she choked out. Lacking other options, she took another drink of the wine, coughed lightly a few more times, and gestured for him to continue. "You were saying?"

"Yes. I've felt adrift and alone since I returned to Etrion. Hopeless, faced with Thrasser's betrayal and the loss of my country. I was certain that if I could just get you back here, it would no longer seem so insurmountable. But then..." He trailed off, taking a swallow of his wine before continuing. "When you arrived, you were entirely caught up in the role you had assumed and in assisting the very people who had helped Thrasser dispose of me. Not that he wouldn't have tried something else eventually," he added. "Seeing that man kiss you though… I'm afraid that was more than I could handle. I was so blinded by jealousy and anger that I failed the one person who has always mattered most to me."

Hope sparked in her chest. Perhaps the awful events since their reunion in Deepwater, piled on top of the constant struggle he had faced in Sarket since returning there, simply pushed him over the edge. Not that it would excuse his behavior, but maybe she could still get her beloved friend back after all. Although earning her trust back after the offenses he had committed against her would take a very long time. The scars he had left on her heart and mind would heal slowly.

He took her free hand, and she resisted the urge to pull it away. "Veyl, let me help you. Even if you don't see it, it's clear to me that these people have manipulated you. We can request an audience with your parents now and take care of this. They must face punishment for what they've done."

Now she did pull her hand away and stood, moving over beside the fireplace. Her gaze caught on the ornate dagger sitting on the mantel. Had he brought it back as part of his apology? Could he honestly believe she still wanted it now? There had to be a way she could discourage him from acting on this without provoking him again.

"Hear me out, please." She downed the rest of her wine and set the goblet on the mantel before facing him. "What if we let the mission proceed as planned? I believe that the annexation of Thaelis and elimination of the Ukhen'kya would be positive developments for Vanris and Sarket. It removes a threat and gives us another naval force we can call upon to help fight Thrasser if it comes to that. And there may be useful goods we could export from the islands. Bringing these accusations to light now could set us back significantly in this process and further delay our handling of the situation in Sarket."

Jaysen got up and came to join her. "You make reasonable arguments. An excellent diplomat, as you've proven in recent negotiations, but we can't allow them to get away with what they've done to you. To me. To everyone they abducted or killed that night."

Veyl clung to her outward calm. She had to be convincing. "They have committed awful crimes, but we must move forward. Kyril, Nalika, and Jinau can provide critical connections to the resistance in Thaelis to help us bring down the council quickly. We need to look at what is best for our countries now."

His jaw tightened, and he shook his head. "But what about what they're still doing to you?"

"I..." She couldn't see a way out of this. Either they were manipulating her, or they weren't. Whichever way she went with it, there were pitfalls along the path. "I don't believe they're influencing me."

Jaysen's regard turned cold. "You wanted him to kiss you?"

They were balancing on a knife's edge again. She could see that in his eyes. The wrong words would push him over, back to that dark place that had driven him to torment her. Perhaps the Jaysen she had known and loved, her tehnaak, truly was broken. She didn't want to believe that, but the situation called for caution.

She swallowed against the twisting pain in her chest. "Of course not. I meant now. I haven't been around them in private since they signed the annexation agreement. If they were manipulating me, they can't be anymore. The zenyal bond doesn't work that way, and the Charmer and Evoker abilities require direct interaction."

His expression softened, and he placed a hand against her cheek. "That may be true, but they violated you. Do you honestly want them to get away with that?"

It took considerable resolve not to pull back from

his touch. "I would like to move forward and not linger on the past." Was there a chance he would realize she was referring to what happened between them as well? Did she dare tell him she didn't want their relationship to be more than friendship? She wasn't entirely sure she still wanted that if this was who he had become. "Please, Jaysen."

"I would do anything for you. If this is how you truly want to handle it, then this is how we shall proceed."

He started leaning in, his gaze sinking to her lips, and her gut clenched. A knock on the door gave her the excuse she needed to move away. Avoiding his eyes, she hurried to answer it, relieved to find Iyvalin standing there.

"Veyl, I got the..." she took a step into the room, halting when she saw Jaysen. Her gaze took in the wine and the flowers, and her brows pinched. "Is this a bad time?"

"No, Iyvy. I asked you to come by this evening." Veyl stepped back to encourage her entry. Though it wasn't precisely the truth, she trusted her friend would play along.

Iyvalin walked in and nodded politely to Jaysen. "It's a pleasure to see you well, Prince Jaysen."

He answered with a tight smile and headed for the door, touching Veyl's wrist as he passed next to her, and leaning in close enough that his breath was warm against her cheek. "We'll talk more soon," he whispered.

The moment the door shut behind him, Iyvalin gave her a searching look. "That was strangely uncomfortable."

Veyl glanced around the room. After being reprimanded by her mother for spying on her, and with the cessation of her private meetings with the Thaelians, her father had scaled back his attempts to check in on her. It still made her nervous, knowing he could easily do so.

Although if he were spying on her now, he would have come bursting in before this.

"Interactions between us have been tense since he saw me kissing Kyril."

Iyvalin's mouth dropped open for a second. "He didn't?"

"He did." Veyl wiped her damp palms on her pants. "You brought the elixir?"

She pulled a small flask out of the pouch on her belt. "I got a little extra, just in case."

Veyl took the flask, surprised at how full it was. She arched a brow at her friend. "I'm not sleeping with the army."

Iyvalin grinned. "No, but while I may have some misgivings about him as a person, your Feral ahnkreth seems like he would be a rather, um, passionate partner."

Veyl's cheeks blazed. "Iyvy!"

Iyvalin laughed, but the humor rapidly faded. She gestured toward the table with her chin. "Want to talk about this situation with Jaysen?"

Veyl nodded, surprised by the sense of excitement that swept through her at the prospect of having someone to confide in. After taking a sip from the flask, she tucked it away in a corner of her wardrobe. Then she wiped the rims of the two goblets and refilled them, giving one to Iyvalin. They sat at the table and talked well into the night, finishing the carafe of wine. She told her friend the secrets she had been hiding from everyone else. All about her relationship with Kyril, and disturbing things Jaysen had done since he caught them together.

"Doesn't he realize what your parents would do to him if they found out about all of this?" They had moved to the bedroom a short time ago, and Iyvalin sat facing her cross-legged on the bed.

Veyl leaned back against the headboard. "I don't

know. Maybe he's convinced himself his behavior is justified somehow, or simply not that bad. The one thing I'm sure he knows is that, after the crimes they already committed against our people, Kyril and his companions don't stand a chance if my intimacy with him comes to light."

"And is it worth it to you to protect them?"

Veyl gave her a hard look.

She held up her hands in a gesture of surrender. "I was just making sure."

Iyvalin was quiet for a moment, staring out a window Veyl had dared to leave open to let in the cooler night air since she had company. Finally, she looked at Veyl, her brow lined with delicate furrows. "You and Jaysen were always so close growing up, but he seemed different in Balarus. Do you think just being back in Sarket could have changed him that much?"

Veyl thought back on the political visit there before the ill-fated visit to Deepwater. The conversation she'd overheard with him and his friends. The convincing distance he'd maintained between them. Even that night in Deepwater, some things about their interaction had concerned her, though she had attempted to ignore them then. Not the least of which being his admission that he had willingly used women to gain the approval of his peers. "I think his mother's death and the treatment he received when he got back to Sarket may have twisted him."

"But none of that excuses his tormenting you this way."

Veyl met her friend's eyes. Would she ever have the words to express how grateful she was to have someone to talk to about all of this? To no longer have to deal with it all alone. "No. It doesn't."

Iyvalin gave her a gentle smile. "Want me to stay here tonight?"

Veyl nodded, and Iyvalin moved over beside her and took her hand. They fell asleep a little while later, hands still clasped, the weight that had rested on Veyl's shoulders now divided between the two of them. While she felt some guilt over putting that burden on her friend, she also felt better prepared to face those challenges now that she didn't have to do so entirely alone.

•

The force heading to the coast under Arhk's command did so over the course of a few days in separate, smaller units. They added a little time to the journey by sticking close to Vareyl's Warning, the black crag formation north of Etrion that stretched across the country from east to west. Traveling near the southern border would raise the risk of their groups being spotted by Sarketi patrols. They had increased the number of Vanrian patrols in the days prior to the first departure to flush out any Sarketi scouts that might have ventured into the area for just that reason.

The group Veyl rode with included Kyril and Jinau, along with about a third of the Thaelians who served under Kyril. They split the rest into two additional groups heading out before and after, putting Nalika as representative for the Thaelians in one and Meyla, Kyril's second, in the other. It made sense to keep Veyl and Jinau together because of the zenyal bond between them and the working relationship required by her role as Thaelis's ambassador. How she had the good fortune to travel with Kyril as well, she wasn't certain, but she chose not to question her grandfather's decision under the circumstances. To her immense relief, Arhk assigned Jaysen to the group heading out after them. He put Ahrin and Iyvalin in that one as well, making the odd decision to keep Gannon with her rather than with his brother.

Kyril, like many of his countryfolk, had never ridden a horse before. They had transported him and the other Thaelians in wagons as prisoners on their way to Etrion. Being a Feral, he had an advantage over his fellow Thaelians in that he could control the animal with his mind. Still, Veyl found his struggles to get comfortable in the saddle amusing.

A half-day out of the city, now too far away for her father to keep watch over her with his ability, and with Jaysen nowhere in sight, Veyl could relax when she approached Kyril and Jinau. For the moment, Arhk had his attention focused forward, not that she cared. Being out of the city and ocean-bound emboldened her.

"You should relax into his movement. Stop resisting it," she said, easing her mount up on the other side of Ceris.

Kyril arched a brow at her. "Relax? You've clearly never been in the mind of a horse, so I will tell you that this poor beast is perpetually on the edge of panic."

"You are asking him to travel in the company of a wave dancer. Horses are prey animals. Ceris," she paused, sweeping an analytical gaze over Kyril a little more boldly than she ought, "and you are anything but."

The cloth they all wore to filter dust churned up by the hooves of the horses hid his mouth, but she could see the grin in his eyes. On his far side, Jinau chuckled.

"What do you find so amusing, Jin?" Kyril inquired, the offense in his voice belied by an undertone of amusement.

The Charmer inclined his head to Veyl. "I enjoy watching the young Frightener telling a Feral ahnkreth how to work with a beast."

"Horses are smarter than most people give them credit for," Gannon said, riding up on Veyl's other side. "As long as you keep in mind that they are prey animals, their behavior isn't all that hard to understand. I've known more than one horse in my time with quite a clever sense of humor, too."

Kyril inclined his head to Gannon. "You show surprising empathy for these animals. My initial impression of you may have been wrong."

Gannon's return regard was severe. "I certainly hope my first impression of you was wrong, Ahnkreth."

Kyril gave a slight nod. "Fair enough."

The Dhomvalen wishes to speak with you.

In response to the voice in her head, Veyl glanced toward the front of their group to where Arhk's speaker was now looking meaningfully back at her.

She considered Kyril and then Gannon, a little more concerned about the latter. "I'm being summoned to the front. Please don't bite one another while I'm away."

"I won't, but I can't promise for Ceris." Kyril's teasing earned him a roll of her eyes.

Gannon nodded more solemnly. "I can be civil when I need to."

Veyl gave him a long look. "Is that so?"

He shrugged. "I've never needed to."

She could see a faint glimmer of humor in his eyes. That was encouraging. "This could be the moment." She hoped he could see the smile in her eyes before she urged her horse faster to catch up with the dhomvalen's group.

Arhk glanced over at her when she trotted up beside him. "You might wish to be a little less playful with your Thaelian friends. There are many among your own people who may find your comfortable interactions with them unsettling." Before she could defend her behavior, he changed the subject. "I would like you to practice with your Frightener ability. I want you to touch on everyone in our company. Only use enough of your power to get their fears to begin feeding into you."

A chill of apprehension moved through her, and her horse tossed its head, reflecting her changed mood. "Wouldn't that be an invasion of their privacy?"

"Not if you do it correctly. I do not want you looking at their fears. You need to practice converting them to something you can dictate and control. The ocean waves, if that is the form you still wish to give them. I expect your touch to be subtle enough that no one notices."

"What about my horse?"

"What about it?"

She set a hand on the animal's neck. "What if he spooks or tries to wander off when my focus is elsewhere?"

"I expect you to learn to control your ability well enough to fight with your blades while using it, but I will humor you for the moment." He glanced over his shoulder. Riding at the front, he didn't have his face covered, so she could see the hint of a smirk curving his lips. "Perhaps we can make this lesson serve more than one student. Our Thaelian Feral is new to working with horses." He turned to his speaker. "Tell Ahnkreth Kyril I would like him to keep the khesran's horse calm while she is practicing with her ability. I expect he will endeavor to do his best."

Veyl glanced back, surprised to see that Kyril had moved Ceris to his other side, and he and Gannon were deep in conversation. The Thaelian Feral's attention snapped to them. His gaze shifted from her to Arhk, and he nodded. Veyl's mount relaxed under her, his head dropping a little lower, his strides becoming uniform and steady.

"Now," Arhk said, "start practicing."

Veyl evened out her breathing and, trusting Kyril to keep her mount in line, closed her eyes to create a semblance of the darkness Dampener Erkhan had put her in when he worked with her on the cliffs in Dagony. In her mind, she could hear the waves crashing on the rocks below, feel the mist in the breeze, smell and taste the hint of salt and sea in the air. All so vivid, it almost became a distraction by itself. The deep rumble of the rolling water met up against the crackle of lightning flickering to life in her chest.

She resisted the urge to retreat from that sensation, forcing herself to reach out around her, cautiously letting her ability touch everyone in their party. When she encountered Kyril and Gannon, recognizing the feel of their fear from previous experiences, she drew back from them, unwilling to risk hurting either of them. Gradually, she began seeing flashes of images, thoughts, and dark emotions. For a few heartbeats, she successfully fed them into the ocean in her mind, letting the rolling waves consume those varied fears. Then they started slipping out of her grasp, and she was falling from a cliff, choking on blood as a sword thrust through her chest, standing shamed before her peers—dozens of nightmares played out in her head.

The storm strengthened, myriad threads of contact spinning out of her control.

A hand came to rest on her arm.

"Veyl."

The storm fractured upon the sound of Kyril's voice. She opened her eyes to find him riding alongside her now. Warmth swept through her when their eyes met until the unease in his expression drew forth realization and panic. She looked at Arhk, still riding on the other side of her, his discerning gaze considering them both. Kyril would not have intervened unless Arhk told him to, which meant her grandfather at least suspected a greater depth to their relationship. Had he deliberately entrapped them? What was Kyril supposed to do when the dhomvalen of his new sovereign country ordered him to call her back from the edge?

Arhk's guarded expression told her nothing before he faced forward. "When I tell you to reach out to everyone in our company, I expect you to do so. That means not excluding your favored companions. Now, try again."

CHAPTER FOURTEEN

For the next few days of the journey, Arhk put her to work, making her practice several times a day. He wasn't at all hesitant about also assigning Kyril the task of controlling more and more of their horses at a time. The Feral ahn-kreth professed to some experience influencing creatures in small groups, primarily dolphins and whales, but he had never, by his own admission, worked with as many at one time as Arhk was pushing him to. He appeared to enjoy the challenge. It made her wonder if the dhomvalen was cultivating Kyril for some specific purpose. He treated the Thaelians like soldiers in his army, which they technically were now, but recognizing that this wasn't the outcome they had hoped for, the development left her feeling slightly uncomfortable on their behalf.

Seeing the ocean again filled her with an unexpected sense of freedom and belonging, though the change in Kyril and his crew upon reaching it left her in awe. They came to life like plants given water for the first time in far too long, a vital energy bursting through them. They laughed and joked, and the somber mood that hung over most of them, which she had not expected to see change until they reached their homeland, melted away. But then, these people spent so much time at sea, maybe the ocean was their true home.

It irrefutably was Ceris's home. The wave dancer sprinted ahead of them at the first hint of salt in the air, vanishing out of sight. When they made it to the beach, they found him lying in the surf with a ridiculous grin splitting his long muzzle, panting so hard from his exertions Veyl feared his sides might burst. Kyril had dismounted and ran with him some more until the two of them were both too exhausted to do much more than sit and stare at the waves. Veyl yearned to join them on that sandy expanse as some of his crew had, but she didn't dare. Instead, she accompanied Arhk to watch and learn from him as he gathered information about their resources to ensure they were being prepared to his satisfaction.

The rest of the following day, Arhk spent dividing up who would be on what ship, so they could depart the morning after the last company arrived. He accomplished the task with input from Kyril, the Delaphinian admiral, and some of the Vanrian officers who would accompany them. The Thaelian crews he divided up, moving some of them onto Delaphinian and Vanrian ships and filling in the ranks on their ships with Vanrian and Delaphinian soldiers. A precaution to ensure the Thaelians didn't forget their new loyalties as citizens of Vanris once they were at sea. Kyril looked unhappy with the arrangement, but if he argued against any specific reassignments, he always offered someone else who could swap ships in that person's place, showing respect for Arhk's authority and reasoning.

To Veyl's surprise and pleasure, Arhk assigned her to the Delaphinian flagship with him while putting Jaysen, who hadn't yet arrived and therefore couldn't object, on a separate ship. It made her wonder what he might have deduced from the night he intervened between her and Jaysen in her father's reading room. Though Arhk was more open with her than with anyone else in their family, even she had little insight into what went on in her grandfather's head.

"Why did you want to bring Jaysen with us?" Veyl asked, standing alongside him outside one of several two-story buildings that made up the officers' quarters within the base.

Arhk was watching Kyril, Jinau, and Nalika, who were a few blocks away, heading in their direction. With his attention on them, she took advantage of the opportunity to observe Kyril as well, appreciating how he moved with an almost predatory confidence and air of danger.

"We do not have to worry about someone learning the crown prince is in Vanris if he is not in Vanris."

"That makes sense, but is it the only reason?" She quickly faced him when he glanced over at her, struggling not to squirm before his discerning gaze.

"I suspect you have had more opportunity than most to see that Jaysen's time in Sarket changed him, and I am not convinced it was for the better. I prefer to have him where I can keep watch over him."

That comment produced a barrage of new questions she wanted to ask, but Arhk looked away again, turning his attention back to the approaching Thaelians. How much did he suspect? How much did he know? She couldn't believe he would have brought Jaysen if he had deeper insight into what had happened between them in the last few weeks. Unless his goal was to take control of that situation as well.

She turned her attention back to the three walking in their direction. "Is there a reason you were having Ahnkreth Kyril practice with the horses so much?"

One eyebrow curved up in a slight arch. "What harm is there in further developing his skills, now that he is a Vanrian soldier?"

She had the feeling again that he wasn't telling her

everything, but she didn't get the impression he intended to elaborate. Was it a coincidence that he had focused his training efforts on the two of them, keeping them both busy along the journey here?

Kyril slowed his pace, turning to say something to Nalika a few strides behind him. At that moment, an object flashed past him, and red blossomed at her throat, spraying from the back and front as the projectile plunged through her neck. Cries of surprise rang out from the people near them. Nalika choked up blood as she fell, the bright red vivid and shocking against her lighter skin. Jinau stepped in to catch her as Kyril spun, scanning for the source of the attack. Ceris focused on something and exploded into a run.

Feeling strangely disconnected from the moment, Veyl followed the beast's direction and spotted a man near a building across the street. He was grabbing and aiming a second preloaded crossbow. If Kyril hadn't turned toward Nalika when he did, the first bolt would have hit him.

A charge of lightning burst through her and out. "Veyl!"

It was too late to heed Arhk's shout. The full force of her ability struck the man. For a heartbeat, his terror fed back into her, then empty silence filled that space. His arm fell limp, and the crossbow dropped from his hand, hitting the street and discharging amidst more cries of alarm. A few people near Kyril and Jinau moved in to help. They were on a military base, so a substantial number of weapons were in hand now, and soldiers were scanning the area, trying to determine if there might be more than one threat. Sudden pressure swept out from Arhk, the street around them growing dark, as if a cloud had passed overhead. How odd that they could see and feel the illusions each other's abilities created yet could not weaponize each other's fear.

"Everyone is to stand down," he commanded, the black spreading across his eyes giving a well-earned aura of danger to his presence. He singled out two soldiers with his gaze and pointed to the man who had fired the crossbow, who now stood staring at nothing. "Guide that man to Dhomen Aitan. I will join you momentarily."

"Yes, Dhomvalen." They hurried to follow his orders.

Arhk turned his cutting gaze on her. "Go with them."

Veyl wanted to run to Kyril and Jinau, who were easing Nalika's lifeless body to the ground, but Arhk's eyes darkened more when she hesitated, so she ducked her head and followed the two soldiers.

The man who had shot the crossbow—a Vanrian with deep shadows under his light hazel eyes—didn't react to anyone around him. He continued to stare at nothing, fine lines of red trickling from his eyes, ears, and nose. Her ability had broken him as thoroughly as it broke Illis and the Sarketi sailors that attacked them upon their return to Vanris, as well as more than a few of the Unclean, though she couldn't bring herself to feel as bad about them. She followed the soldiers in silence on their way to take the man to Dhomen Aitan's office in the building she and Arhk had just come out of.

The structures here were of stone and clay because of the scarcity of timber in the region, and more cramped inside than most of the homes and other buildings she frequented in Etrion. Built early in the war with the southern kingdoms with a focus on fast construction and economy of purpose rather than comfort, the quarters here were simple and stark.

They waited a few minutes before being admitted into Aitan's office, and Arhk came in on their heels with Kyril behind him. The latter had spatters of red on one side of his face and across part of his jacket. Nalika's blood. A member of his crew. His family. He looked straight ahead, his eyes flickering only briefly to the broken man who had killed Nalika before settling on the dhomen behind his desk.

Focused on Kyril, Veyl barely heard Arhk's words as he explained the incident to Aitan.

Aitan considered the broken man for a moment, then looked at one of his soldiers. "Isn't this man one of the refugees who escaped the attack on Deepwater? His wife and their tehnaaks were taken captive, as I recall."

The soldier shifted his feet, averting his eyes. "Yes, Dhomen."

"I also seem to recall ordering that all survivors from the town be moved off base grounds before the groups from Etrion arrived with Thaelians in their ranks to avoid possible confrontations. Am I remembering that correctly?"

The man nodded, his shoulders tightening. "Yes, Dhomen."

It almost surprised Veyl when Aitan's hair didn't catch fire from the fury burning in his eyes. Somehow, he maintained an even, if terse, tone when he turned his attention to Arhk. "Is there no way to reverse this damage?" He gestured to the broken man.

"I am afraid not."

Aitan shook his head and rapped his knuckles on the wooden desktop hard enough that Veyl cringed. "We should delay your departure and investigate—"

"No. There is nothing to investigate. This was an attempt at revenge in which the assailant is, unfortunately, not able to stand for questioning." Arhk's harsh gaze fell upon Veyl, the message clear. If she hadn't broken the man, they would have no trouble confirming that. Instead, they would make that assumption because he was unwilling to hold back their mission. "Send a report to Etrion. This man is to be dispatched as humanely as possible. He will not survive long in this condition." He turned to Kyril. "We can have Ahnkreth Nalika's body prepared for travel if you wish to take her home."

Kyril dipped his head in a nod. His voice was low and tight when he spoke. "Thank you. We will return her to the waters near Thaelis."

The heartache in his words tugged at Veyl. She moved one foot to take a step toward him, pulling it back when Arhk softly cleared his throat.

"We depart as planned. You may see to your people, Ahnkreth," Arhk said.

Kyril bowed his head. He didn't look at her before turning to leave.

Guilt and shame burned hot in her cheeks, and she lowered her gaze, unable to face any of them.

"I would like a moment with Khesran Veyl."

She could feel Arhk's judging gaze on her as the others, even Dhomen Aitan, whose office it was, walked out, guiding the broken man with them. Arhk turned to her, and she forced herself to look at him, knowing he would respect nothing less.

"Is there a reason you chose to condemn that man rather than merely incapacitating him with your ability?"

"I didn't mean to, I—"

"Your power was too much for you," he interrupted. "Would you like to be the one to explain this to his wife and their tehnaaks when we bring them back from Thaelis?"

Tears stung her eyes. "If you feel that's how it should be handled, I will—"

"I do not," he snapped. "I am inclined to advise your parents to make your brother the official heir. Running a country is far too demanding for someone who cannot control an ability as volatile and deadly as yours."

His words threatened to crush her. Not that she had a burning desire to be khevarin of Vanris, but it was an assumption, an expectation she had grown up with. To be denied that because he deemed her too unreliable and dangerous, after she had indeed proven herself to be so, was a devastating prospect.

When she spoke, she struggled to raise her voice, hating how small she felt. How small she sounded. "But you're a Frightener, like me. Can't you help me fix this?"

Arhk shook his head. "You bear the burden of an uncommonly powerful ability. I can guide you. I can tell you what worked for me, but I cannot fix it for you. You will have to figure that out for yourself. If you cannot, it is my responsibility to protect the people of Vanris from you."

Veyl blinked back tears. "I understand."

"For now, return to your room here and remain there until I say otherwise. I expect you to spend every minute you are not asleep reaching out to as many people as you can within the base with your ability. Not one of them had better report being aware of your actions or suffer any ill-effects from it."

"What about…" she trailed off when his eyebrows lifted a fraction.

"Kyril and Jinau do not need you to help them mourn their companion. You have your own problems to solve, Khesran."

Veyl nodded and left him, hurrying to her room in the officer's quarters. Once she was there, she worked through combat forms as best she could in the limited space, trying to burn off the overwhelming distress that threatened her control. The last thing she needed now was another incident. Finally, she settled on the bed and stared at the door. In a way, it was insulting to be sent to her room like this, but she had never felt more deserving of being locked away. She had killed a man or at least sentenced him to death. It didn't matter if she struck the final blow. His blood was on her hands. And it was one of her own people this time. Even her grandfather, a man who struck fear in people everywhere, thought she might be too dangerous.

What would her parents do if she couldn't figure out how to control this ability? Would they make Tavin the heir as Arhk had suggested and hide her away where she couldn't hurt anyone? Maybe Kyril's crew had been right. She was too great a threat to let live. If only her ability had never awakened. Even remembering how distraught she was after her Trial, when she believed she wasn't a mind-crafter, she preferred that feeling of inadequacy to this. What she wouldn't give to not be a mind-crafter now.

A sharp rap on the door made her jump. "I recall ordering you to practice," Arhk called.

Veyl glared at the door and drew on the crackling energy that rose instantly to her need. She reached out to him first, touching his mind and feeling the immediate rejection of his ability blocking hers out.

"That is more like it. Keep at it." His footsteps moved off down the hall.

With nothing else except her misery to occupy her time, Veyl lay back on the bed and focused her full attention on reaching out through the base. She advanced slowly, imagining the ability like the strands of a spider's web, touching one mind and stretching out to the next and the next, connecting them all, but not allowing their fear to feed into her yet. It wasn't until the threads of power wavered at the limits of her reach that she gradually opened herself to them, funneling the responding rush of fear into the ocean she conjured in her mind, and letting the waves churn it into a rumble of white noise.

Her head started throbbing, a headache rising in response to the limits she had stretched herself to. Clenching her teeth, she pushed farther. She had earned this pain. She deserved the residual sense of sorrow and loss that came tied to many of those fears. Tears slid into her hair, soaking into the pillow.

A light knock on the door startled her, breaking the tenuous connection. All the fear she had gathered seemed to settle in her chest, deepening her sense of sorrow and hopelessness.

She sat up on the bed, wiping at her eyes. "Who is it?"

"Ahndhomen Jinau, Seh'hali. May I enter?"

"Jin?" Veyl hurried to the door and opened it, stepping aside to let him in. "What are you doing here?"

He waited until she shut the door and turned to face him, the gentle regard out of place on his rugged features. "I can feel your sorrow, Seh'hali. I asked the dhomvalen to allow me to speak with you."

She walked to a worn side table, fingertips coming to rest on the hilt of her sword she had set there. Such an elegant, uncomplicated weapon. "I'm surprised he agreed."

"You should not torture yourself. You saved Ahnkreth Kyril's life. His crew and I are grateful for what you did today, even if the outcome was not ideal."

She spun to face him. "Not ideal? Nalika is dead, and I killed that man."

His solemn, patient regard didn't change. "Both of these things are true."

"And Kyril, how does he feel about all of this?" Her chest tightened, remembering how he had avoided looking at her earlier.

"That is more complicated. He takes responsibility, as the head of his fleet, for the events in Deepwater, and he is not proud of what happened there. He followed orders that he now wishes he had not, but he cannot undo the past. That man lost the people dear to him, and Kyril accepts that he earned his hatred, but Nalika paying the price for it weighs heavily on him."

That man had lost his loved ones because of Kyril. Now, because of her, those loved ones, if they were still alive in Thaelis, had now lost him. "I wish I could go to him."

"He knows that, Seh'hali."

"I doubt just knowing that brings much comfort." A sudden metallic taste spread across her tongue, and she met his eyes. "Have you ever used your Charmer ability on me?"

Jinau shook his head, holding her gaze. "I told you I would not on the voyage here. Besides, I prefer not to use it. I have applied it in ways that do not sit well with me in my efforts to become a trusted asset to the council. It is because of this that I have as much insight as I do regarding who we can and cannot rely on in Thaelis, but that knowledge came at a high price."

Veyl gazed into those amber eyes for a long moment. She reached out, letting her ability touch his mind. His eyes narrowed a fraction, but he did nothing to stop her. Carefully directing what she found into that ocean in her mind, she avoided looking at what it was he feared and instead let herself feel the remorse and self-loathing that came attached to it. That was enough.

She drew her ability back. "We all have regrets, it seems. Thank you... for letting me in. I am sorry about Nalika. Could you give Kyril my sympathies and my..." She caught herself before saying the word that rested on her lips.

"I will do so. He sent me with his love as well." Jinau took a step toward the door.

She drew a shaky inhale. Did Kyril love her?

"Be patient, Seh'hali. The ocean is mighty. It will help you find your way."

"Thank you," she murmured, watching him walk out.

The ocean? If only she could have faith in the

connection to the ocean that he and so many others believed she had.

She breathed a bitter laugh.

Or maybe they were right, and the power and unpredictability of the vast ocean were part of the problem.

They set sail at night. Veyl stood at the bow and watched the ocean ahead of them. Dread coiled in her gut at the thought of leaving her family again, especially given that she was bringing her problems, specifically Jaysen and her uncontrolled Frightener ability, with her. Though perhaps it was better that her parents didn't have to deal with those things, given all the other problems they had to sort out. Despite those challenges, a sense of exhilaration moved through her at being on the water again. The ocean held a promise of freedom, adventure, and danger that invigorated her. She tried to focus on that feeling and let the dread slip away.

"You don't look back?" Gannon asked, stepping up to the railing beside her.

Veyl kept her gaze on the dark waters ahead. "I will look to Vanris when that is the direction I am traveling. We have a long way to go before then." She glanced over at him. "I don't see you looking back, either."

"That's because I am here to support you. I've failed too many people in my life. I won't do so this time."

"Gannon, what happened to Lorek—"

"Please don't. Lorek was the best part of me. We all know that. I didn't realize how much I could feel his presence until it was gone. Maybe I couldn't have done anything about how he died, but I could have been a far better tehnaak to him while he was alive."

The edge of anger in his voice hinted at a self-loathing she didn't dare challenge. Not yet. Maybe when Lorek's loss was less of an open wound. She said nothing. Instead, she reached over and put her hand on top of his on the railing.

•

Waking on the ship the next morning was disconcerting. A brief panic jolted through her as memories of Deepwater and the first days after those events that changed her life raced in. Not images, so much as remembered fear and hopelessness. She lay on the overly firm bed for a few minutes, eyes closed, moving her focus beyond those traumatic moments to that afternoon in Dagony, when she had gone with Kyril to his house and shared herself with him. The way he had explored her, awakening sensations she never imagined could be so intense… so satisfying.

A sharp knock on the door of the cramped cabin startled her from her reverie.

"Practice," Arhk called, his footfalls continuing past.

"Calloch," Veyl muttered, blowing out a breath. Practice could wait a bit.

She let her racing heart calm before she got up, cleaned off at the basin, and hastily dressed for the day. The Delaphinian flagship was larger than the Thaelian one, with several small private rooms in the area near the captain's cabin. As khesran, she ranked high enough to have one. She hurried out of it now and went in search of Arhk.

On her way up to the rear deck, where he stood talking to the Delaphinian admiral, she spotted Gannon and beckoned him to join her with a wave. Jinau was also on the main deck, leaning on the starboard railing, his amber eyes following them as they continued up together. She led Gannon to the port side rail to wait for Arhk and the admiral to finish their conversation. Arhk glanced their way, giving a slight nod to let them know he was aware of them.

Veyl faced out toward the water, letting the cool, misty air wash over her and closing her eyes to feel the rocking of the waves.

"Morning, Khesran," someone called out.

She opened her eyes to see one of the Thaelian ships coming up beside them with Rel, the man who had tried to warn her away from Kyril on her first voyage to Thaelis, standing near the rail. The Thaelian ships were slightly faster and more maneuverable than the Delaphinian ones, particularly the monstrosity she was on.

Breathing a soft, somewhat weary laugh, she nodded to him. "Morning, Rel," she called back.

"Doin' any deck hopping today? We could use a new ahnkreth over here."

A woman on the Thaelian crew walking by at that moment smacked him soundly in the back of the head. "Have some respect, you disloyal bastard, and get to work."

Rel winced from the blow, but he grinned at Veyl before moving away from the side of the ship.

Her gut tightened with a twinge of sorrow and guilt. The man was on Nalika's ship. She scanned the deck, spotting mostly Thaelians with a few Delaphinians among the crew, but couldn't tell who among them was acting as ahnkreth now.

"You do not know how to run a ship," Arhk remarked, walking up beside her.

Odds were that she knew more about it than he did, after everything she had learned from Kyril's crew on the previous crossings, but she refrained from pointing that out. Facing him, she offered a subdued smile. "Good morning, Dhomvalen."

He looked her over once, his gaze flickering briefly to Gannon, who stood silently at her side. "Is there a reason you are not practicing with your ability?"

"Because it won't work." She held up a hand to stall the argument rising in his narrowing eyes. "I'm not breaking people when I'm calm and focused. It's only when I'm angry or afraid that it spins out of control."

He arched a brow. "I assume from your tone that you have an alternate suggestion."

Veyl breathed deep, drawing confidence from the crisp ocean air. "I do. When I was in Thaelis… Bear with me," she said when he scowled. "For a time, I went to the cliffs every evening, and a Dampener by the name of Erkhan would sit with me. He would take away my sight and have me recount upsetting experiences or provoke me with tales of their attacks on our towns while I tried to manage my ability. He had Ahndhomen Jinau there to stop me if I started losing control. Honestly, I hated it, but I think it may be necessary to put myself through similar sessions, unpleasant as they were, if I want to avoid breaking more people, which I most certainly do. If we could arrange for me to work with Jinau and one of our Dampeners, maybe I could figure out how to keep this under control."

His gaze flickered to Gannon again. "And his role in this?"

Veyl looked at the young man beside her. "I hate to ask it of you, but I had hoped you would help. You know me well enough that I'm certain you could come up with a few memories I would find upsetting or think of other ways to provoke volatile reactions."

A faintly bitter smirk curved Gannon's lips. "You're saying the skill I can bring to this is my endearing ability to antagonize people."

Veyl offered him an apologetic smile. "Not just that. You've been around me all my life. If anyone here knows what might get under my skin, it's you."

"I didn't join this mission to hurt you."

Arhk was watching them, fresh curiosity in his gaze. "She may be right. If you could stomach it, this might be the safest way to avoid more drastic measures. My primary objection is that you and my Dampener would be at risk if something went wrong. We would have to rely upon Ahndhomen Jinau to react fast enough to protect you both."

"What about Ceris? He shielded Ahnkreth Kyril from me."

Arhk's expression wavered somewhere between his usual sternness and a hint of amused appreciation. "Exactly how many times did you try to kill him?"

"I…" A smirk from Gannon brought warmth to her cheeks, and she tried hard not to picture Kyril in her head as he had been when she last tussled with him. "More than once."

Arhk turned away, though not before she caught his faint smile. "Do you think the beast could protect someone other than his bonded companion?"

"It's possible. The wave dancers have unusual abilities, much like kanodraks. It might be worth asking." And not because she yearned to see Kyril. At least not exclusively because of that.

"Let us speak to Ahnkreth Kyril, then."

Veyl and Gannon accompanied him to where he had one of the crew signal the Thaelian flagship, which was following orders to stay near the Delaphinian one. Kyril approached the front as it moved closer, his long black hair weighted down in places by shells and bones affixed to the braids, the wind picking at some of the black and blue strands that hung free. The intensity of his regard and the confidence in his bearing made him look dangerous and, well, feral.

When they were within range, he jumped across with Ceris. Veyl, her pulse quickening, resisted the urge to move closer to him. The wave dancer, not one to be bothered by the formalities of human society, padded over and sat beside her. Somehow, simply resting her hand on his shoulder helped calm her.

Kyril kept his eyes on Arhk, inclining his head a fraction. "Dhomvalen."

Arhk answered with a slight nod, his gaze jumping to her. "If you please, Khesran, explain to Ahnkreth Kyril what it is you wish of him."

Veyl sank her fingers into Ceris's odd fur when those silver-blue eyes settled on her. Why did it feel as if they had somehow become strangers again? She drew a deep breath. "I would like to work on controlling the reaction of my ability to my emotions—"

He interrupted her with a soft, derisive snort.

For a heartbeat, she couldn't find the words to continue. Then Ceris shifted a little closer, a movement so small she might have missed it if her hand hadn't been on him. She raised her chin a fraction, determined not to let Kyril's frosty reception deter her. "Gannon and Arhk's Dampener will be helping. With Ahndhomen Jinau's assistance, they will have some protection, but I had wondered if Ceris, given his unique abilities, could offer an extra measure of safety."

"He might, but he stays on my ship. You can use my cabin." His attention moved to Arhk. "Is there anything else, Dhomvalen?"

"No." Arhk stepped back and gestured toward the Thaelian flagship with one hand, beckoning Jinau and his Dampener over with the other. "You have two hours, Khesran, before I expect you back on this ship."

Kyril jumped back across, Ceris leaping after him. He stopped and waited, offering her a hand, the coolness in his regard unsettling. Veyl nodded to Arhk, drew a breath, and jumped, ignoring Kyril's hand as she landed, silently thanking the mild waves for the fact that she didn't end up on her rear on the deck or worse. Jinau, Gannon, and the Dampener, Rysek, followed.

When they were across, Kyril turned to her. "You know where my cabin is, Khesran." He made a vague gesture in that direction, then, after placing a hand briefly on Ceris's head, he spun and walked toward the stern.

A few minutes later, Veyl sat cross-legged on the floor of the cabin across from Rysek. Being in that space again brought back a surge of disconcerting memories she struggled to push aside. Gannon watched her intently as he sank down on her right and Ceris sat on her left, his webbed front paws neatly placed before him as if he took his duty there seriously. Jinau sat in a chair at Kyril's table, glancing at them periodically as he whittled away at a chunk of driftwood with an oddly shaped knife that looked better suited to violence.

After Veyl explained the process to Gannon and Rysek, the Dampener eased her into darkness, isolating her visually from the world around her, so she might be more deeply immersed in imagery and emotions. When that was done, she took a moment to focus part of her attention on the underlying sound of the waves breaking before the bow. Then she drew upon her ability, letting a little of that crackling energy move through her, and nodded.

"I'm ready."

"Let me take you back to Thaelis, then," Gannon began. He proceeded to paint with words his experience of the incident in which she had attacked him with her ability. A memory that Iyvalin or Ahrin must have shared with him, since an Evoker had removed his recollection of it to repair the scarring Veyl's attack left on his mind. Despite that, she could hear the hurt in his voice and an underlying guilt that shouldn't be his.

In the darkness, she could see him once again, cowering there, his fear turned against him by her failure to control her ability. She felt the storm inside rising with the sorrow and shame that soared within her, gaining strength and sparking out to her extremities, threatening to reach beyond. She struggled against it, her breath coming faster as she tried to pull the power back, letting the ocean around her and within her draw it down into the depths. Another presence lurked in her mind. Not the expected zenyal bond to Jinau, but a peaceful one that immersed her more thoroughly in the mighty expanse of water surrounding them.

Ceris.

Was he doing that on purpose, or was the beast's connection to the ocean simply that strong? Regardless, she appreciated his influence and would eagerly accept it if it helped her move closer to controlling this on her own.

Veyl focused on Gannon's voice, his words making her relive that painful moment, sending tears streaming down her cheeks. Allowing those memories to move through her, heightening the storm within, she embraced the opposing calm of the ocean, encouraging it to wash over her and soothe the ferocity of her ability. Growing more confident, she took hold of that power, daring to try touching the minds of those in the room. A slight increase in tension came from Ceris, but neither the wave dancer nor Jinau tried to stop her.

Gannon ceased speaking, leaving only the sounds of the ocean in the darkness. She had the unnerving sense that someone crouched behind her, confirmed when their breath warmed her ear.

"Tell me," Kyril whispered, "what was it like to return from Thaelis and see your prince again?"

Veyl's grip on the present fractured. In an instant, she was once more lying in her bed in the dark, the sedative weighing her down and Jaysen's dagger at her throat. His voice whispered in her ear as he drew up her sleeping gown, his fingers moving to touch the inside of her thigh, an unspoken threat hanging between them.

Veyl's ability lashed out, only to be cast instantly back at her. She screamed when a lance of pain flashed through her head and the darkness vanished, leaving white-hot agony in its wake. It dissipated rapidly. When she regained awareness, she was on her hands and knees, trying hard not to be sick. A cold sweat broke out on the back of her neck, her body trembling. Someone's arm moved around her shoulders.

"Break-blasted calloch!" Gannon shouted. "What did you say to her?"

Veyl sank back on her heels with Gannon's hands moving to her arms, supporting her. She swallowed against the bile rising in her throat, trying to reach a place where she could speak. Kyril stood back a few feet now, watching them, his cool-eyed gaze providing no explanation for his actions.

She glared at him. "All of you, please leave us."

Jinau and Rysek headed for the door, but Gannon hesitated.

"Are you sure about this, Veyl?"

She nodded. "Thank you for your concern, but I need to speak with Ahnkreth Kyril alone for a moment."

Gannon moved one hand away, then the other, his reluctance palpable, but he finally stood and left them.

"Bastard," Veyl muttered after the door shut, ignoring the hand Kyril offered as she rose unsteadily to her feet. "Why would you do that to me?"

His brows pinched. "I couldn't stop thinking about how desperate you were to return to your family when you were in Thaelis, and yet, you were so relieved to put

Etrion behind you again when we left on this mission. I could only come up with a few reasons you might be that eager to get away from there, and it got me wondering just how profoundly Jaysen had traumatized you. Now I have my answer."

"This was your best idea for how to figure that out," she shouted. Glancing at the door, she lowered her voice. "You couldn't have just asked?"

"And what would you have told me?"

Nothing. Or at least as little as she could get away with. Veyl turned from him, desperately searching for the composure he had taken from her.

"I am sorry, Seh'hali. After what happened at the base, I had to know if your being around him in Thaelis could jeopardize our task. I didn't expect… It seems I vastly underestimated how deeply he wounded you."

The genuine apology might have made her feel better about it if not for the realization that, like most everyone else, he feared her ability now. Not out of concern for himself, but for the people he cared for. Had he finally given up on her? On their first crossing, he had been willing to defend her against anyone who challenged her right to live. Would he still do so now?

She turned away, trying to breathe past the panic and heartache that constricted her throat and the bands of iron squeezing around her ribs.

"Veyl."

He set a hand on her shoulder, and she twisted away, backing up as she turned to face him. When he followed her, reaching out again, she retreated a few more steps, bumping into a wardrobe along one wall.

He took a step closer, putting his hands against the wardrobe to either side of her, an attempt to discourage her from moving away again, and pinned her with his gaze. "I just lost another person who was extremely dear to me. I can't put more people I love at risk."

Kitria.

She could see his sister's name resting unspoken behind his eyes. The person he loved the most. The one he would do anything for, and she couldn't be angry with him for that. She could only long to be someone he cherished that much.

"What do you expect me to do? I can't ask them to change course and take me home to Vanris now."

He leaned closer, his eyes drawing her in. "This is not me turning my back on you. You were doing well today. I could feel that much through Ceris, but the wound Jaysen left in you is considerable. Maybe if you help me understand its nature better, I can try to help you heal it. It's one piece of a larger problem, but I think we proved just now that it's a dangerously volatile one."

He reached toward her face, and she caught his wrist, searching his eyes. Keeping things from him only made this harder, but she wasn't ready yet to tell him everything. Moving his hand down, she pressed it over her heart. "Jaysen wounded me here. He is... Was my tehnaak. There was no one I thought I could trust as completely. I loved him as my tehnaak and my friend, and he betrayed that because he wanted something more." A few tears spilled down her cheeks, the heartache breaking free despite her efforts to hold it in.

Kyril drew her into his arms and held her. "I'm sorry. You deserve so much better."

Veyl gave herself a few seconds to linger in the comfort of his embrace before she pulled away and wiped brusquely at her damp cheeks. "A Vanrian rebel group killed Jaysen's mother when he was returning there. I think that, along with being separated from me, his tehnaak, nearly broke him. The people in Sarket—his peers and the leaders there—made his life miserable because of the years he spent in Vanris. Rather than reject me, I think he turned me into a repository for everything positive, his reason for not giving up despite how unhappy he was there. He made me his sanctuary, his one link to sanity amidst their cruelty. Seeing you and me together shattered that fantasy, and now he is holding the threat of exposing our relationship over my head."

"None of that is your fault." Kyril scowled. "What is it he demands in exchange for keeping this secret? There must be a price."

She swallowed. Admitting how significantly Jaysen had violated the bond they shared made it feel as if it had always been worthless and she merely too much of a fool to see it. "My silence, my tolerance of a dagger at my neck, and a few inappropriate touches or kisses thus far, but I fear where it could progress to from there." Kyril's expression hardened, a dangerous threat rising in his eyes, so she rushed ahead, though she didn't want to understate Jaysen's actions. They didn't have time now to delve into greater detail. "He may be truly starting to believe that you had Nalika and Jinau manipulating me. I convinced him not to risk the mission by making the accusation, since you no longer had access to me. Now that we are in a position to be around one another again, I'm not confident I can keep him from breaking his silence."

"Or what he may demand next in exchange for holding it," he growled, Ceris echoing him with an intimidating vocalization of his own. "I will not let him get away with this."

She shook her head, denying her own apprehension. "Once again, you will do nothing. We have a little time. I won't have to deal with him until we reach Thaelis. Arhk doesn't seem to trust him anymore or want him around me."

"The dhomvalen and I agree on that, at least. Veyl, I can't sit idly by and let him hurt you."

"Unfortunately, I think he feels the same now that he's made you my tormentor in his mind, as ironic as that is."

Kyril's jaw tightened with frustration, anger creating a storm within his silver-blue eyes.

She forced her fears aside, searching for and finding a ready distraction in how close he stood, his body inches away, that innate Feral vigor sparking longing in her. Her pulse quickened, a flash of warmth spreading through her. "Perhaps you should not be idle," she murmured, her gaze sinking to his lips.

"You won't distract me from this that easily," he said, though a hint of a lustful growl crept into his voice.

"Won't I?" She met his eyes and took his hand, moving it to her breast.

The action had the intended effect. Desire surged up, threatening to force out the rage in his eyes, and he leaned in to claim her mouth in a kiss full of pent-up frustration and unbridled longing. Veyl didn't try reining in her need of him. She slid her hands under the jacket he wore, feeling the definition of his muscles beneath his shirt. He pressed against her, both of them eager to forget where they were and who waited outside.

A knock on the door brought an abrupt end to their intimacy.

"One moment," Kyril called before touching his forehead to hers, and taking a second to catch his breath. "At least they knocked."

Veyl exhaled a laugh and pressed a light kiss to his lips. "Neither Jinau nor Gannon would let anyone come barging in here."

"Gannon knows?"

"Not everything, but enough."

Kyril stepped back and reached out to straighten her shirt for her, his hands wandering a little as he did so. "I will follow your lead on this for now, but Jaysen needs to be dealt with. Jinau and Gannon may be able to help as well."

She pressed her lips together, glancing past him at the door. Reluctantly, she moved away from him, not wanting to push their luck further than they already had. "I'm not sure about Gannon. He and Jaysen have a tempestuous history. Losing Lorek seems to have calmed him—nearly broken him, really—but I don't know if this new, more reflective state will last. He might seize too willingly upon any excuse to return to despising Jaysen."

"You need someone you can confide in and turn to, who you can openly spend time with, and Arhk put Ahrin and Iyvalin on another ship. If Gannon is aware of us, and is choosing to keep it secret, perhaps it's worth considering, but you know him better than I do."

Veyl nodded. "I'll ponder it. I should leave."

"One last thing." He stepped closer, brushing an unruly strand of her hair into place with gentle fingers. "I don't think the Dampener is helpful. You won't have that controlled environment under normal circumstances. This may be more effective without him."

"And not having him here will make it easier to sneak in moments like this," she ventured, arching a brow at him.

Kyril grinned. "A convenient side effect." He slid his hands around her waist and pulled her in for one last kiss before letting her go. "If it would help, I can join your session tomorrow, more thoughtfully than I did with my poorly considered efforts today."

"I should hope so."

She placed a hand on his arm, reluctant to give up contact with him. Drawing a breath, she made herself walk away, her fingers sliding off his sleeve. Once outside, Jinau, Rysek, and Gannon accompanied her back to the other flagship. When they were close to Thaelis, she would transfer to Kyril's ship for appearance's sake, but Arhk wanted her where he could watch over her for now. As a result, moments with the Feral ahnkreth would be rare, though perhaps not as much so as she had assumed going into this.

That evening, Arhk questioned her and Gannon about her session over a casual dinner, though she didn't doubt that he had gotten a full accounting from Rysek earlier. She lied when he asked what Kyril had whispered to her, saying he had brought up a moment from her capture in Deepwater. Before they parted ways, she broached the idea of removing his Dampener from the sessions. A proposal he agreed to only after she framed it as too much of a deviation from real-world situations, where she wouldn't have that isolating darkness to improve her focus. It was Gannon who unexpectedly suggested that Kyril joining them might aid the process, given the multitude of upsetting experiences she had gone through with the ahnkreth that remained fresh in her memory. After some deliberation, her grandfather consented to that proposal as well, though she wasn't sure he would have had she been the one to bring it up.

When Arhk dismissed them, she headed straight for her room. Gannon caught up with her at her door, holding a stoneglass bottle and two mugs. "Crack a stone with me?"

The simple offer of friendship in his open smile deflected the rejection that almost slipped between her lips. She smiled back. "That sounds lovely."

A while later, Gannon sat reclined against the headboard of the bed next to her and stared at the door of the cabin, his brow lined with deep furrows. "So, you and Kyril... How did that happen?"

Veyl peered into her nearly empty mug and leaned forward somewhat unsteadily to look at the stoneglass bottle on the side table. "Is there any left?"

Gannon reached over, picked it up, shook it, then squinted into it as if closer scrutiny might garner different results. He set it down and gave her a crooked grin. "No, and I seem to recall you asking me that about ten minutes ago with the same answer." He raised his mug to his lips.

"Oh my," she giggled and settled back beside him. "I didn't think there was enough mead in that bottle to make the room rock like this."

Gannon spat out the drink he had just taken, spraying most of his last swallow over his legs. "We're..." He bent forward, laughing too hard to finish the sentence.

"What?" A reason he might have found her comment so funny danced at the edge of her thoughts, but she couldn't quite take hold of it.

"Of course, the room's rocking. We're on a ship," he blurted, breaking out into more uncontrollable laughter.

"Oh, by the Break." She covered her face with one

hand, heat rising in her cheeks. Her embarrassment faltered before the bombardment of his mirth, and giddiness bubbled up, escaping in a fit of laughter that intensified until she was struggling to breathe.

When they brought themselves under control again, Gannon smiled at her, an expression warmed by affection. "I have a feeling your current state of imbalance has plenty to do with how many glasses of wine you nervously emptied over dinner with your grandfather before we started drinking this." He held out a hand as she finished the last of her mead, putting the mug on the table after she passed it to him. "Which begs the question, why risk so much for this man you'll probably never see again once we accomplish the mission?"

Given who she was speaking with, Veyl deemed it best not to get into detail about her physical attraction to Kyril, which was considerable, or the inexplicable connection that existed between them from the start. "I don't know. At first, I couldn't have despised him more, but when he started working with me to control my ability, I felt his sorrow and saw in his fear how much he had lost. He also defended me against his crew when they wished to be rid of me, and saved me when I..." She hadn't told her friends about her attempt to kill herself, so she pivoted abruptly. "It became harder to hate him. As I came to understand him more and saw how much he regretted following the council's orders, that floundering hatred transformed into something else."

Gannon was silent for a moment. Then he turned to face her, sitting cross-legged on the bed. "Saved you when you what?"

The drunken giddiness faded. "That day on the ship, after they took you away, I guess I gave up. I had lost everything. We all had, but it seemed clear to me at that moment that they didn't mean to give anything back, not even my friends."

His expression was enough to tell her the humor had left him, too. "You tried to end it?"

She nodded.

Gannon shifted closer and slid his arm around her shoulders. "I would rather see you in the arms of someone like Kyril any day than live in a world without you in it. You are one of the few reasons I have to keep going now that Lorek's gone."

She tensed. "Do you mean that? Even after what I did to you in Thaelis?"

"I do. I realize now that your ability had more control over you than you did of it. Now maybe I can help you change that."

Veyl relaxed, leaning against his shoulder. "Thank you." She closed her eyes, the influence of the alcohol exaggerating the motion of the waves. "Lorek would be happy to see us supporting each other," she murmured after a bit, drifting on the edge of sleep. "I think he would be proud of you."

"Maybe," Gannon whispered.

A light knock on the door prompted her to force her eyes open. "Yes?" she called.

Before Gannon could move away from her, Jinau leaned in. "You are growing weary, Khesran. Perhaps I should see your drinking companion to his room."

Gannon hesitated halfway off the bed. "How did—"

"The zenyal bond," Veyl said, sliding down and resting her head on the pillow.

"That's unnerving," he muttered. "Goodnight, Veyl."

The door clicked shut a moment later, and weariness tugged at her. After a few minutes, she half-woke to Jinau spreading a blanket over her.

"Sleep well, Seh'hali."

•

The next several days raced past. For the first part of each morning, Veyl and Gannon stayed busy volunteering their services to help around the ship, taking advantage of the opportunity to learn more about what it took to run a vessel of such size. A pastime Arhk appeared to find amusing, though he insisted on her using some of her time before the sessions on Kyril's ship to practice on her own with her ability.

In the afternoons, she went to the Thaelian flagship with Jinau and Gannon to continue testing her control under stress. Kyril had an unfortunate knack for finding ways to upset her with his words. While it was helping her make progress managing the volatile storm within, she worried she would despise him for it by the time they reached Thaelis. Although if their brief, stolen moments alone were any indication, that wasn't apt to happen. She tried to keep open expressions of their intimacy to a minimum. Gannon might tolerate that her affections were for Kyril, but forcing him to watch that on display seemed like unnecessary torment. The last thing they needed was to push him to the point that he might reconsider exposing their secret to Arhk and others. And yet, with the recent changes in him, she didn't believe he would.

The reality of what they were planning and all the ways it could go wrong crept in when Veyl officially moved to Kyril's ship the night before they were to arrive in Thaelis. They deemed it wise to have her there, with him locked in the brig, in case they encountered other ships along the last stretch. She needed to arrive in Dagony acting as the Thaelian ambassador and ahn-inveth the council expected her to be, bringing Kyril back to face justice for his actions. Technically, given his status as an accused traitor, his Thaelian fleet was under her command now, though they had tasked Jinau with making certain she followed through as required. If only the councilors knew how little loyalty the Charmer ahndhomen felt toward them.

It was unlikely that the council would allow more than a token representation from the Vanrian fleet to enter the city. Most would have to remain aboard their ships. They would maintain the ruse of cooperation for as long as it took for Jinau and some of Kyril's crew to reach out to fellow insurgents within the city and secure enough support to hopefully intimidate the council into surrender or, failing that, remove them by force. That meant Veyl needed to appear to uphold her part of the agreement until they were ready to make their move. A nerve-wracking prospect, given that she suspected at least one councilor might be an Evoker.

The one upside of all this was that Veyl had a valid reason to take over Kyril's quarters on the Thaelian ship. After the evening meal, Jinau conveniently invited Gannon to join him for drinks and a game of dice below deck. The two left them, Gannon more reluctantly, waiting until she nodded to follow the other man out. She couldn't blame him for the warning glower he cast at Kyril before closing the door. Only Iyvalin knew exactly how much of herself she had already shared with her Feral ahnkreth.

"Gannon is protective of you," Kyril commented after the door clicked shut, a hint of approval in his tone. He set his drink down and stood, his faintly predatory regard causing a quickening of her pulse.

Veyl got up and walked around the table to him, bringing her fingers up to run them down one of the shell-adorned braids in his hair. "He is."

Kyril gave her a long, searching look, his hands coming to rest at her waist. "Have you told him about your conflict with Jaysen?"

She shook her head, her worries losing some of their

power as she sank into those silver-blue eyes. "He's always disliked Jaysen. I fear he might try something if he knew what had occurred between us. We can't afford an incident in the middle of our efforts to overthrow the council."

He took a step closer, his voice dropping to a whisper, and slid his hands around to the middle of her back. "As soon as the council has been dealt with, then."

Veyl nodded. His next words became lost in the background as she focused on the movement of his lips and leaned in to kiss them. He didn't seem to mind the interruption, allowing her to lead him in abandoning all pretense of an interest in conversation.

A while later, pleasantly spent and nestled against his naked body, she smiled to herself. "I enjoy being with you here on your ship, in your bed."

Kyril chuckled. "Depending on who you ask, it's your ship right now."

"Hmm. Does that mean I can tell you what to do?"

He turned and came up on his elbow, grinning as he moved his hand down the front of her body, his gentle touch awakening fresh longing. A challenge sparked in his eyes. "Maybe, if you can get your orders out."

She opened her mouth to speak, her intentions becoming lost in a gasp as his wandering fingers found the core of her desire. Then he moved his body over hers and demonstrated how difficult he could make it for her to focus on words again.

She was more than willing to let him win that challenge.

•

"Seh'hali."

His whisper and the caress of his fingers on Veyl's cheek woke her. She lay with her back pressed against his chest, the warmth and comfort of him bringing a sleepy smile to her lips. Without opening her eyes, she wriggled in closer.

Kyril breathed a laugh. "While I agree with the sentiment, if we stay here much longer, they'll find us in a most compromising position. Particularly if you keep pressing yourself against me like that."

The hint of playful threat in his tone made her giggle as she moved away, rolling over to look at him. "Why does being with you make me want to break all the rules, regardless of the consequences?"

He slid his hand into her hair and leaned in to give her a light kiss. "Because we belong together," he said, his breath warm on her lips until he shifted back to consider her. "Unfortunately, it's almost dawn. We need to prepare before the dhomvalen drops in to make sure everything is in order. I believe he expected me to spend the night in a cell in case we ran across any Thaelian ships, not in my cabin making love to his granddaughter."

Reluctance to leave him and unease with the coming encounters tightened her chest. "What if I lose con—"

He placed a finger on her lips, complete confidence in his roguish smile. "You've been showing significant improvement in our sessions. You are strong." He leaned in again, punctuating that compliment and each following one with more kisses. "You are clever. You are brave. And you carry my love with you."

She caught his shoulder, not letting him move away. "Do I?"

He smirked, the intensity of his regard making her his prisoner. "Is there any reason I would lie about that?"

She arched a brow. "Because you hope to lure me into your bed again."

"Every chance I get." He captured her lips in a deep,

consuming kiss that left them both breathless.

Veyl put a hand on his chest, digging within herself for the willpower to push him back. "Up. We need to leave this bed before we do get ourselves into trouble."

He rolled away and stood, holding a hand down to help her up.

Wishing she had more time for him, and for some actual rest, she reluctantly accepted the offer. "Did you get enough sleep?"

He grinned. "As much as you did."

His answer brought a flush of warmth to her cheeks.

"I'd worry more about yourself, Seh'hali. I can sleep on the cot in my cozy cell. You must help manage the rest of the voyage, though Meyla has promised to take care of most of it."

Her smile vanished, and she took his hand. "I don't want to lock you down there."

He pulled her into his embrace, the abrupt action giving her only the briefest glimpse at the troubled look that furrowed his brow. "It will be fine. As soon as the council is unseated, I'll be free. Until then, you have Jin and Gannon, not to mention the rest of your people and mine who will stand with you. This is only a blink in our stories."

By the time they were dressed, Jinau had arrived to take Kyril below. Gannon also came, putting his back to them when she gave her Feral ahnkreth a last kiss before he left the cabin.

They encountered the first local ships near noon. The vessels, Eavara's fleet and another that sailed out of one of the other island ports, formed an escort to guide them into Dagony. Eavara boarded Kyril's flagship with several members of her crew and took him and Ceris into custody, moving them to her flagship. Veyl hated letting her do so, but she couldn't protest the development without drawing suspicion. Kyril's fleet had orders to dock when they reached the port, while the Delaphinian ships received the message that they were to anchor outside the port. They would permit the Delaphinian command vessel to dock, but only after Kyril's crew had come ashore.

Veyl, Jinau, and Kyril's fleet officers, with a man Veyl hadn't officially met standing in for Nalika, disembarked first. She had barely set foot on the docks before one of the Qwilki merchants called out a greeting to her. Quillon and Mardi were among the guards that met them.

"You will accompany us to the Great Hall," Mardi stated.

Veyl dredged up a smile for the merchant, then turned to Mardi. "I would prefer to wait until the Vanrian delegation can join us."

"I am afraid our orders from the council are for you to come before them immediately without the Vanrians." The faintest hint of apology scrunched the bridge of her nose, but the stern set of her jaw made it clear they wouldn't be discussing it further.

Veyl nodded. "Lead the way."

Jinau and Quillon fell into step on either side of her as Mardi led the small procession of ahnkreths and Veyl toward the Great Hall.

"I'm sorry you had to return here," Quillon offered in a low voice, "but it is nice to see you."

An unexpected wave of fondness struck Veyl. Not just for Mardi and Quillon, but for this place and its people, encouraged in part by the greetings and smiles she received from several market vendors and Qwilki they passed along the way. "I feel the same on both counts."

She caught his nod out of the corner of her eye. Knowing he, and possibly Mardi as well, supported her, helped her hold on to her courage, though she wasn't certain if either would go so far as to defy their leadership if they had to choose. Then again, she had no way of knowing who here might be part of the resistance. There was always a chance they were. What would Jinau do if the council pressed him? She hated to consider it, dreading the genuine possibility that he might risk his life for his Seh'hali.

The Great Hall had its doors shut when they arrived, the council once again not allowing the public to be a part of the proceedings. They had more guards along the walls than she had ever seen there at one time. Veyl followed Mardi inside with the rest of Kyril's officers behind her and Jinau at her side. Once they stopped before the council table, the guards moved off to the sides, and Veyl bowed along with the fleet ahnkreths.

"Ahninveth na sek Veyl," Councilor Darith greeted. His gaze lingered briefly on the man who had taken Nalika's position, but he seemed little more than passingly interested in the change. "We are pleased to see you returning to us with Ahnkreth Kyril's fleet, as promised." The doors at the back of the hall opened, and he fell silent, waiting as Eavara and some of her crew escorted Kyril to the front.

Veyl didn't allow herself to watch him walk up. She winced when Eavara and the soldier on his other side put their hands on his shoulders and each rammed a knee into the back of one of his, forcing him to kneel. The crack of his knees hitting the stone floor made her wince, but he tossed his hair back and raised his chin in defiance, as if he hadn't felt it.

By the Break, he was magnificent, and not just physically.

She stared ahead, burying any thoughts that could cause them trouble. Was one of them an Evoker? If so, unless they had an uncommonly powerful ability, they would have to make eye contact to pull much out of her head, so she carefully avoided looking directly at any of them.

Darith came around the table and approached their prisoner, a bitter edge to his smile. "And Ahnkreth Kyril himself. I look forward to presiding over your sentencing, Ahnkreth."

Kyril said nothing.

Veyl's gut twisted. How soon would they pass judgment on him? The plan relied upon having a day or two for Jinau and the others to reach out to allies and assess potential resistance in case the councilors didn't cave to intimidation. In all likelihood, Vanris's force could win a confrontation given the number and power of the mind-crafters they brought with them, but the idea was to avoid violence if possible. They weren't out to cripple Thaelis or risk substantial losses among their own people. What if Kyril didn't have that much time? Could she convince Arhk to risk more bloodshed for one man if it came to that?

"We have much to discuss with our Feral ahnkreth, but that can wait until after we have dealt with our guests."

The way Darith spat out the word guests as though it tasted foul made it hard for Veyl to maintain her neutral expression. Again, she didn't let herself watch as they hauled Kyril to his feet and escorted him through a door at the back of the room. She longed to call out to him, his name resting unspoken on her lips. This would not end in his death. She wouldn't allow it.

The head councilor turned to her. "You brought the Vanrians to collect their people, as expected. We would like a full account of the agreements you came to with them before we allow their representatives to join us."

The Vanrians. He explicitly had not referred to them as her people. "Of course, Councilor," she said. She couldn't quite avoid his eyes with him this close, so she kept her thoughts on a leash and hoped he wasn't an Evoker.

Fortunately, they had worked out a script for her to follow regarding the agreement she reached with Vanris. She passed along their displeasure over the terms allowing Vanrians to stay, should they choose to, and shared a desire for reparations for harm inflicted on the people taken and for lives lost and damage done to the two towns that were attacked. Vanris demanded assurances that if they agreed not to return here, Thaelis would also agree never to visit Pandrea again. Just those few topics should prompt negotiations that would use up the needed time. If things progressed too quickly, Arhk also intended to show interest in local goods based on his brief walk through the port market on the way here and propose the possibility of trade as an alternative to avoiding all future contact. On the unlikely chance that all of that didn't keep the council occupied long enough, he would suggest the installation of a Vanrian military base to stir them up.

Veyl recounted the fabricated outcome of their negotiations that she had rehearsed several times on the voyage over. The points Vanris supposedly agreed to were selected to keep the council from becoming too upset while still setting up enough disagreement to make it appear genuine and promote ongoing discussions. Considering the situation, she had, in terms of the agreement, convinced Vanris to agree to a great deal, but several members of the council still looked mildly disgusted with her by the time she was done.

Darith regarded Jinau, who stood passively beside her. "This is all accurate?"

Jinau nodded. "Ahninveth na sek Veyl handled negotiations admirably, Councilor."

An underlying note of satisfaction in the reaction of the councilors to that brief exchange made Veyl's skin crawl, as if they were trying to groom her for something. They had never discussed her return to Vanris once she met the terms of the agreement, only that of her people. Did they somehow believe they could keep her here?

The councilor inclined his head before turning to her again. "Given your youth and limited guidance, I would say you have done reasonably well. Better than many here expected. I am certain we can resolve the rest now that the Vanrians have arrived." He glanced toward the entrance and called, "Bring them in."

Guards pulled open the main doors enough to allow the representatives from Vanris entrance. Arhk strode in ahead of the guards escorting a group that included other Vanrian and Delaphinian officers and, to her great disappointment, Jaysen, but it was the dhomvalen who captured everyone's attention.

For the first time, she saw her grandfather as the powerful and terrifying man people told her he was. The man soldiers in the southern kingdoms had given names like the Bane, the Waking Nightmare, and Beast of the Break during the war. Though that had been before she was born, the passing of years treated him well, and he entered with confidence, advancing swiftly up the center of the room with powerful, bold strides that forced those following him to stretch to keep up. His long white-blond hair and the full-length black jacket he wore, adorned with dark metal accents evocative of armor, flowed out behind him. A hint of pressure and the slightest dimming of the light in the room added to his aura of intimidation. Subtle manipulations that she had a greater awareness of now because she shared his Frightener nature.

The unpleasant emotions brought by Jaysen's presence vanished before a sparkle of delight at how hastily Darith retreated behind the table when Arhk approached. Maybe threatening them into giving up their seats wouldn't be that difficult after all.

After brief introductions, the council and representatives retired to a large meeting room behind the long table. They spent what remained of the day in tense discussion, each side trying to nudge the other to an agreement. The group from Vanris left most of the talking to Arhk, and he embraced his role. He played the council easily, his skills as a negotiator apparently as sharp as ever, while the Thaelians, given their isolation, had little reason to be practiced at it on this level. The dhomvalen laced his statements with carefully chosen words hinting at cooperation, allowing them to settle into the idea that Vanris might go along with them on one point or another. Then he would strike them with a soft-spoken, compelling argument against the matter in question, sending them scrambling to figure out where the discussion had gone wrong.

Veyl knew her grandfather well enough to see in his eyes and the faint curve of his lips now and then that he enjoyed the game, especially since Vanris had no intention of giving this council anything in the end. All they were doing now was stalling.

"If any of your people wish to stay in Thaelis, there is no reason they should not be given the opportunity to do so," Shyall commented for perhaps the fifth time in the last hour. She had quickly learned not to refer to the abducted Vanrians as newcomers with Arhk.

They had been going around on this one subject for almost two hours, and Veyl could see Arhk's answer in his eyes before he spoke. "None of our people will stay here." His flat tone said, not for the first time, that it was no longer up for negotiation.

Veyl had spoken little throughout the evening, only commenting when she could offer something that would allow her to dance the line between them and not show a strong loyalty to either side. She saw a potential stalling opportunity here, however. One that might move them past it for now, while providing a more substantial delay going forward.

"Respectfully, I disagree with your approach on this, Dhomvalen." Arhk arched a brow at her, and a flicker of pressure swept through the room, letting her know she had displeased him. It was hard not to smile at the way the councilors shifted back in their chairs, as if trying to put more distance between themselves and the powerful Frightener. "These people were taken from their homes against their will once. While it may be extremely difficult to imagine them wanting to stay under the circumstances, would it not be wrong to deny them their right to choose their own fates a second time?"

"Ahninveth Veyl speaks with wisdom beyond her years." Darith's pleased smile made it clear he believed her words supported their side.

Arhk eyed her shrewdly. "How would you handle this, then, Khesran Veyl?"

"Ahninveth," another councilor corrected him.

Arhk didn't acknowledge them with so much as a glance.

"My position among us is unique. I am of Vanris, brought here against my will with the others and trusted by them, but I also represent Thaelis and know some of its people and qualities. With a proper escort, I could go around tomorrow and speak with the Vanrians here personally to discover whether there are any who would genuinely prefer to remain on the islands."

A sneer curved Arhk's lips, though she wondered how much of that was for show, given their actual goal. Did he recognize that her proposal could provide Jinau and the others more time to complete their tasks?

Darith glanced around at his fellow councilors, receiving several nods, some less enthusiastic than others. "We would allow this, so long as Ahndhomen Jinau and guards appointed by the council accompany you to ensure no attempts at persuasion."

"If you wish to waste time," Arhk said with a heavy edge of disdain. "I will appoint a representative from our side to accompany her as well. Given that we will clearly not be resolving this tonight, I suggest adjourning for now. My fleet is weary from travel and in need of sustenance."

Darith nodded, jumping on the opportunity to escape the negotiations a bit too eagerly. "Yes. Of course. We will arrange for Ahninveth Veyl to begin visiting the Vanrians here in the morning. For the time being, we ask that you and your people remain confined to your ships. We can have food and drink sent out if you are in need."

Arhk shook his head and stood, the others following his lead. "No, thank you. We can feed our own." The expression of mistrust behind his refusal was a slight to their hosts, who had already insulted them by not offering lodgings within the city, though Veyl wasn't sure the councilors had an adequate understanding of political negotiations to recognize either as such. His gaze settled on her. "Khesran, if you will join us."

"You are welcome to stay ashore, Ahninveth Veyl," Shyall offered. "Quarters are available."

Veyl bowed her head politely. "Thank you, Councilor.

I wish to speak with the Vanrian representatives before I settle in. It might be easier if I stayed on the ship tonight. I would be happy to consider your kind offer tomorrow."

Several of the councilors' expressions tightened with displeasure, but Shyall glanced briefly at Arhk, then nodded to Veyl. "As you please. The space will remain open for you."

That Arhk alone had set the Thaelians on edge was clear. It was strange to see her beloved grandfather through their eyes, a powerful mind-crafter whose menacing presence had them all desperate to escape the room. Adding the threat of more kingdoms allied against them, with Delaphine representatives and Sarket's rightful heir represented alongside him, they might well have enough already to frighten the councilors off their seats of power if they went about it correctly.

Thaelian soldiers escorted them back to the port. Along the way, Jaysen took advantage of the opportunity to fall into step beside her. Even though Gannon and Jinau weren't privy to most of the details of what had happened between them, she sensed a faint rise in tension from both men as they moved a little closer, as if they instinctively sensed a threat.

"Jaysen, how was your voyage across?" Veyl asked, hoping to keep their interaction friendly and give herself some control of the conversation.

"Uneventful." He glanced at Arhk, walking a few feet ahead of them, eyes narrowing. "Rather lonely and boring, to be honest."

"Weren't Ahrin and Iyvalin on your ship?"

Jaysen shook his head, the pinching of his brows suggesting surprise. His resentful gaze flickered to Gannon. "I assumed all three of them were with you."

"No. Only Gannon." Veyl couldn't stop herself from glancing at Arhk's back. Why had he split them up that way? Gannon parted from his twin and Iyvalin when he most needed their support. Jaysen separated from all of them. He must have had reasons.

Some of the aggression in Jaysen's posture faded, as if he had suspected her of playing a part in his isolation and was now willing to shift the blame entirely to Arhk. As the dhomvalen had been the one to decide who would be on what ship, she couldn't bring herself to argue, especially since it deflected Jaysen's temper away from her.

His expression softened a little when he spoke again. "I hope these negotiations resolve quickly. I doubt we'll have much opportunity to talk until they do, unless I might be allowed to join you in speaking to the Vanrians tomorrow."

"No." Arhk glanced over one shoulder, his soft yet powerful voice cutting across the space between them. "Veyl is the one working for the Thaelian council. There is no reason to complicate the situation now."

"As you say, Dhomvalen." Jaysen inclined his head in a gesture of respect, though she was in a position to notice how his shoulders tightened and his hands flexed with barely restrained anger.

Had his few years back in Sarket twisted him so thoroughly? Enough that he would react with such aggression to her and a man who had helped mentor him for much of his childhood. This couldn't all be because of Kyril, could it?

Veyl touched his arm. "We'll talk soon," she said in a gentle tone she hoped would deflect his temper.

Jaysen looked at her, affection rising in his bright blue eyes in the light of a street lantern at the port entrance. "Yes, we will." Something in his tone gave a little too much confidence to his words. He caught her hand as she drew it away. "I know we will." He gave it a squeeze and released it, turning his attention to the far end of the docks. "I should find my tender."

"Accompany the prince," Arhk said, signaling two of the Vanrians guards.

Jaysen waved them off, gesturing to two Thaelian guards that were already splitting off to go with him. "It's not that long of a walk. I'm sure these two know their way around well enough to get me there." He glanced at her once more, then turned and strode off into the darkness with the Thaelians falling into step alongside him. He engaged one in conversation, and the man pointed toward the heart of the city, leaving her to wonder what they were discussing.

Gannon leaned close to her, speaking in a low voice. "Is it just me, or was there something disturbing about that whole encounter?"

A shiver moved through Veyl, and she hugged her arms around herself. "There was," she murmured.

When they reached the Delaphinian flagship, Arhk requested that she join him in his quarters, a development Veyl appreciated. She had questions for him she meant to get answers to, and she jumped in with the first the moment the door to the main cabin closed behind them.

"Why did you separate the twins, Iyvy, Jaysen, and me the way you did?"

Arhk poured two small glasses of something that smelled stronger than his usual fare and handed her one. "I appreciate the strategic sense you showed today. At every opportunity, you encouraged them to believe you were, at worst, a neutral party and, at best, agreeing with their side. The questioning of our people may have been the perfect maneuver to stall them for as long as we need to. A brilliant tactical maneuver." He took a sip of the drink. "Now, what was it you were asking?"

She refused to let his praise distract her, though it brought a pleased flush to her cheeks. "About the ship arrangements," she prompted again, and took a sip of the drink he had given her. It burned like fire all the way down, striking off a fit of violent coughing. "By the Break, what is this?" she choked out when she could finally talk again.

Arhk chuckled. "It is an acquired taste. Is there something else you need?"

Veyl swallowed her irritation along with another, more cautious sip, then tried a different topic. "How do you manage your ability so precisely? You always know just the right amount of darkness and pressure you need to influence your subjects."

"First, you must remember it is as much an illusion as the lightning you draw forth. I do not truly increase the darkness or pressure around my victims. I merely make them perceive that I have done so."

Veyl lowered her gaze, uncomfortable with his choice of words.

"The people you use your ability on are victims, Veyl. We are Frighteners. There is no benevolent application of that power. You need to accept that." He took another sip of his drink. "Your grandmother, Ellaris, used to encourage me to practice on her. I learned to refine my control very quickly. I would never have forgiven myself if I had hurt her." He swallowed hard and glanced away, his hand tightening slightly on the glass, and it struck Veyl how deeply he must have loved her to still feel her death so acutely. After a second, he drew a breath and went on. "With her feedback, I became quite adept at subtlety. It would please me to assist you in such a way once we resolve matters here."

"Thank you. That would mean a lot to me." Veyl inclined her head in a gesture of gratitude and respect before pressing him again. "Regarding my first question…" she trailed off, hoping he would accept that she didn't intend to let it go.

This time he took a longer drink of the burning alcohol before answering her. "I told you I brought Jaysen here to keep an eye on him. I also felt it could not hurt to illustrate to the council that they risk making enemies of multiple kingdoms on Pandrea, not just Vanris." He gave her a long, discerning look. "However, I am aware Jaysen has taken a more-than-friendly interest in you, and I have, as you may recall, witnessed firsthand the rise of conflict between you because of that. If I assigned Iyvalin and the twins to the flagship with you, while separating him out, he might have suspected you were involved in the arrangement. By dividing you as I did and placing Gannon, who would not normally be your first choice, with you, I discouraged him from coming to that conclusion and possibly adding it to the list of wrongs he thinks you and your parents have done him by rejecting his advances."

Veyl stared at him. Her grandfather was a shrewd man. Listening to him now, confirming some of her suspicions from earlier, she could hardly believe he hadn't yet caught on to her relationship with Kyril. But if he had, he would never have allowed her the various opportunities she'd had to spend time around him on their voyage here. Would he?

Absentmindedly, she took a swig of her drink, hating how he smirked when she broke into another coughing fit.

He held out a hand. "I should not encourage you to develop a taste for that." When she didn't relinquish the glass, his shoulders lifted in a slight shrug, and he lowered his hand. "Tomorrow, when you speak to our people, you will have Ahndhomen Jinau with you. I will send Gannon and two other guards along as well. After today, I am confident that you can manage the process without raising the ire or suspicion of our gracious hosts." The slight sneer in the word gracious told her how unimpressed he was with the council.

Veyl caught herself straightening before his praise. "I appreciate your faith in me."

He walked over to place a hand on her shoulder and looked her in the eyes. "I trust in you, Veyl. I have not misplaced that trust, have I?"

The searching look he gave her turned the alcohol into a snake twisting in her stomach. How she wished she could be honest with him. "No, grandfather… I mean, Dhomvalen," she corrected when he arched one eyebrow.

A faint smile curved his lips. "Alone, you may call me whatever you wish." When he reached for the still half-full glass this time, she let him take it. "Get some rest. You have a long day ahead of you."

Veyl wished him goodnight and retreated, taking her secrets with her.

•

Mardi, Quillon, and two more guards met her group, made up of Gannon, Jinau, and a pair of Vanrian guards appointed by Arhk, at the docks early the next morning. They wasted no time escorting her to the first house, where four Vanrian abductees were living. The two tehnaak pairings greeted her with enthusiasm, eager to hear news of Vanris and their likely return home. She attacked her task with sincerity despite the planned coup, taking them one at a time into a separate room to discuss the matter of their futures. If there were any who wavered about leaving Thaelis, they might be more inclined to stay once it became an official territory of Vanris. For now, she couldn't reveal that to them, but it could be beneficial to have some Vanrian residents remain on the island to aid with the coming transitions. More so if they stayed by choice.

The day swept past, all the conversations eventually blending into one another. There were over a hundred abductees to meet with, so many that it would take a few days to speak to them all, but she worked her way through enough to bring a representative sample to the negotiation table later. The majority had expressed an enthusiastic interest in returning home, though several admitted to finding the island beautiful and most of its people welcoming. Of those, an even smaller number acknowledged that they might not be as eager to leave if Vanris and Thaelis were on friendly terms.

The council insisted on the Vanrian company staying aboard their ships for most of the day. Arhk negotiated a visit to the port market with a modest group to replenish provisions they were running low on. The outing also gave him an opportunity to investigate what unique resources the island might have to offer. Before departing that morning, Veyl mentioned the substance they used to aid their mind-crafter Trials as something that could be of interest, encouraging him to ask the tribal Qwilki about it.

Everyone was present that evening for her report on the results of the day's meetings. Not surprisingly, the paltry number of people in her selection who would consider staying displeased the council. Particularly when she mentioned offering the caveat of a changed relationship with Vanris, but they maintained hope for better in the second batch, encouraging her to try harder, as if her results were because of a lack of sufficient effort on her part. At the end, as they adjourned with plans to meet again once she finished her rounds the next day, Darith called her aside.

Her nerves sparked to life as she approached him, aware of Arhk watching her intently. "Yes, Councilor?"

"Ahninveth, if you would consider making use of the lodgings we have provided here, you could get an earlier start tomorrow. You might feel less rushed."

Again, the implication sat behind his words that the lack of interest in staying on Thaelis was a fault in the process and not a direct result of the fact that they had abducted her people. She kept her tone carefully neutral despite her irritation. "I appreciate that, but my belongings are on the Delaphinian flagship now. I can make certain we are on shore first thing in the morning."

He inclined his head, his gaze flickering to Arhk near the doorway. "If that is what you prefer."

As he spoke, another councilor approached. She held a bottle of wine out to him. "Excuse my interruption, but I believe this is what you requested."

Darith accepted the wine. "It is. Thank you."

The woman lingered a moment, her gaze following the bottle as he tucked it in the crook of his arm. "I was fond of her mother. It is a shame the girl must lose her brother too, after all she has gone through."

Her words set off alarms in Veyl. There was no mistaking who they were talking about. Had they already decided Kyril's fate?

Darith drew a deep breath, his expression solemn. "I am afraid there is no way around it, Jiyan. The ahnkreth made his choice and cannot go unpunished. Perhaps we can arrange a companion to stay with her for a time. Ideally someone close to her age who has also lost their tehnaak."

"I will send out an inquiry tomorrow to start that process. A pleasant evening to you both." Jiyan gave each of them a nod before walking away.

Veyl eyed the bottle, a twisting of guilt in her gut. "That's for Kitria? Do you still intend to give her brother a full trial?"

His lips pressed in a tight line as he nodded. "Yes, on both counts, but the outcome is easy to predict, given his actions. His sister sent a message to the council this morning to plead for her brother's life. With everything she has lost, it will be difficult for her to recover from this. I thought I might take time this evening to have a drink with her and let her speak her mind, even if it will not change what is to come."

Veyl felt her dislike of him fading a fraction. "It's considerate of you to try easing the loss." She yearned to add her voice to the pleas for his life, but knowing they still meant to give him a trial meant there was time to save him through other methods. "I will bid you…" Her focus moved to the bottle when he shifted his hold on it, and she remembered her promise to Kitria that she would get Kyril back. How shattered she must be, believing they would put her brother to death for his crimes?

"Is something wrong, Ahninveth?" Darith prompted.

"Maybe I could take it to her. I lived with her for a time before I left here."

He shook his head. "This requires delicate handling. You, while we have appreciated your efforts, are not Thaelian. You did not suffer through the Devastation as we did."

She wanted to spit in his face for that. He probably assumed no one had told her how they deserted their people and went into hiding during that time. Keeping her tone earnest, she said, "You know she'll find it harder to open up to you as one of her leaders. Please. Let me do this for her."

"Perhaps… You are more of an age with her, and your time together may make her more receptive to your support." Darith considered her for a long moment, then he offered her the bottle. "Very well. Take it. It is one of the finest vintages from our stores. Not one I would normally choose to give away, but this is an unusual circumstance. I hope you both enjoy it. If you wish to stay ashore tonight after you meet with her, something I would encourage given your duties on the morrow, you are welcome to use Ahnkreth Kyril's former quarters near the port. Or you may stay with Kitria, should she offer."

Veyl tucked the bottle under her arm as he had done, worms of guilt still squirming in her gut. Would Kitria even speak to her? The tenuous peace they parted on depended upon her bringing Kyril back, but it seemed safe to assume delivering him to his execution wasn't what the other woman had in mind. If she could at least hint at the truth, that might ease her sorrow and smooth things over between them. Or perhaps Kitria already knew and was merely playing her expected role in this. There was only one way to find out.

"Thank you, Councilor Darith. I appreciate your trusting me in this."

"Do not let it be a mistake," he answered, a little more curtly this time, eyeing the bottle with what appeared to be a hint of distress before turning away. "Good evening to you, Ahninveth."

As soon as Darith was gone, Veyl turned to find Arhk coming up behind her.

"What was that about?"

"I'm going to visit Kitria, Kyril's sister," she added when he arched a brow in question. "I may be there late, so I'll plan to stay ashore tonight." She braced herself, coming up with counters to the arguments he might raise against the idea.

"Be careful," he warned in a low voice. "Don't expose our plan and don't let down your guard. We need only make it until tomorrow night." Speaking at a more normal volume, he said, "I assume Jinau will follow you, but take Gannon along as well, and I will leave you two of our soldiers to act as guards."

Were they that close to moving against the council already? Once again, his trust in her left her surprised and humbled. Part of her suspected that was deliberate, rightly predicting that it would make her more determined not to disappoint him, but it remained effective regardless. "Thank you, Dhomvalen."

She gathered Gannon, Jinau, and the appointed guards, two Vanrian and two Thaelian, and struck out for Kitria's home through the darkening streets. A light breeze carried the scent of the ocean, bringing with it memories of her time there before, not all of them unpleasant. Some of them, in fact, rather positive. She touched the two shells in her hair, a twinge in her heart for Kyril, locked up beneath the Great Hall where she had spent time herself at one point. Was he in the same miserable little cell they had placed her in?

When they arrived at the lovely house near the ocean, one of the Thaelian guards cut her off and went to knock. Veyl wanted to be annoyed with him, but since she dreaded the welcome she might receive, maybe it was better if a guard took the lead up front.

Kitria yanked open the door. Her dark hair was unkempt. Her silver eyes, bloodshot and rimmed in red, went straight to Veyl. She slammed it shut again.

"Kit." Veyl darted forward and pushed it open before the other woman could try to bolt it. "Please, I just want to talk."

Kitria stepped back from the door, leaving room for her to enter, and turned away, walking brusquely into the main room.

The Thaelian guard moved to follow Veyl inside, and she cast a glare at him. "No. Only Gannon and Ahndhomen Jinau."

The man looked like he might ignore her until Jinau placed a hand on his shoulder and pulled him back. The Charmer met her eyes. "You and Gannon go inside. I will wait out here with the guards."

She hesitated, oddly reluctant to be parted from

him, but perhaps it was better not to overwhelm Kitria. Veyl nodded and walked farther in, leaving Gannon to follow.

When he had entered and closed the door behind him, she held up the bottle of wine, meeting the eyes of the woman now standing across the room near the statue of the wave dancer. "Councilor Darith sent this. Can we talk? Please."

Kitria gestured to the couch. As they moved to sit, she snatched the bottle from Veyl and walked into the kitchen. When she returned a moment later, she had a platter holding three mugs made from the shells of large crustaceans called ket'ta, a plate of small pastries, and a different bottle of wine. She placed it on the table before dropping into a chair closer to Gannon.

Now that Veyl thought about it, perhaps it was wise not to drink wine provided by the council. She popped the cork on the new bottle and poured some for each of them, struggling to come up with something to say. Kitria's anger suggested she didn't know about their actual plans yet, which left it on Veyl's shoulders to decide if she could risk telling her and, if so, how much to say. When she finished pouring, they each claimed a mug.

Kitria smirked and raised hers. "To traitors and liars."

"Kit." Veyl watched the other woman slam back the wine and reluctantly took a drink from her own. It had a hint of bitterness to start, but the smooth aftertaste made up for it. She downed another swallow, yearning for the false comfort it would bring in sufficient quantity.

Gannon, sitting unnaturally stiff alongside her, finished his almost as quickly as Kitria had. Then he grabbed a tart and popped it in his mouth, perhaps hoping to avoid having to say anything.

A tense, awkward silence stretched between them all. Though it wasn't the way wine was supposed to be enjoyed, Veyl shrugged and drank the rest of hers. She refilled all three, hoping to appreciate the second pouring at a more leisurely pace, while Gannon and Kitria each took a tart, probably more for an excuse to avoid speaking than out of want for one. Veyl claimed a tart as well, chewing on the surprisingly savory treat as she considered her words. When she washed the last bite down with a swallow of wine, Kyril's image came to the front of her mind. If he learned how distraught his sister was, it would crush him.

"Your brother won't be executed," she said in a low voice, wary of the Thaelians among the guards out front.

Kitria's eyes narrowed, her trust apparently no longer extended to Veyl. "How do you intend to prevent that?" She took another swallow of the wine, the new intensity in her forward posture hinting that she might still have hope.

Gannon touched Veyl's arm, giving a slight shake of his head when she looked at him. She drew a breath, then took a sip of her drink, hoping the liquid would help her find her courage, though it seemed unlikely to do much for her wisdom. Part of her wanted to heed Gannon's caution, but Kitria wouldn't betray them, not with her brother's life at risk.

She slid to the edge of her seat, leaning forward, and whispered, "We have a plan in motion to force the council to step down."

Gannon grimaced, shaking his head, and bit into another tart.

Kitria's eyes widened a fraction, her gaze jumping to the front door as if the guards outside might still hear. "How?" She took a tart and fumbled, dropping it back on the tray, then scowled at her hand as if it had betrayed her.

"I can't… say too much…" Veyl trailed off, blinking a few times. Her vision was blurring, her tongue and lips feeling thick and strange, protesting the formation of more words. She shook her head to clear it, the movement unbalancing her enough that she slid back on the couch a bit more for better stability.

"Veyl." Gannon spoke her name as if doing so required the same effort as climbing a steep mountain, each sound a strain.

"Where did you get this… wine?" Veyl asked, struggling to articulate the words. Or could it have been the pastries?

"The wine and tarts…" A hint of panic rose in Kitria's eyes as her mug dropped from her other hand, spilling red on the carpet. "The messenger… said…" She shook her head, seeming unable to focus on Veyl. "He said …"

A flush of terror swept through Veyl, and she clumsily shoved the tray off the table, nearly falling as she did so. Her ability flickered, weak and uninspiring, like a storm fading in the distance. She sagged against the back of the couch as it became too hard to hold herself upright.

Thuds and a few grunts from outside made her throat constrict. She felt a cutting sensation in her chest. The front door opened, but she could no longer control her muscles well enough to turn and see who had entered. The two Thaelian guards, along with four others, hauled her two Vanrian guards, bloodied and unmoving, into the room. Then they dragged a third person in, dropping him beside the first two.

Jinau. Tears sprang to Veyl's eyes, a raw stinging in her throat. No. Please no.

The words wouldn't pass her lips. Someone shoved their arms up under hers with no apparent concern for her comfort and lifted her.

One man glanced at the mess of pastries and wine on the floor and smirked. "Didn't waste any time, did they?"

Had this all been a setup? Jiyan arriving with the wine exactly when she had. Darith expressing remorse for Kitria's plight. But they hadn't opened that wine. She wanted to ask again where the other bottle and pastries had come from, but she couldn't speak, and she doubted Kitria was in any state to answer.

"Get her to the boat," a male voice behind her ordered. "Hurry. We need to be on our way before the Unclean attack."

The Unclean!

Terror spiked for herself and for her people, but she could do nothing. Whatever drug they had given her left her as helpless as an infant. A sedative of some kind, given how groggy she felt, with apparent paralytic qualities. She was entirely at their mercy. That they were moving her somewhere suggested they at least didn't expect it to kill her, as little comfort as that was.

"What about the other two?" a female guard asked.

"Bring them." This voice she recognized extremely well after listening to it so many evenings in forced darkness. Dampener Erkhan. "We can dump them overboard later if they don't prove useful."

When they allowed her feet to touch the ground outside, Veyl found she still had a small amount of muscle control. Enough for what equated to a drunken stumble if someone else held her upright. Since she had no desire to go wherever they were taking her, she didn't even give them that. Instead, she dug her heels in to make it harder until one of the larger men simply picked her up and carried her to where two boats waited on the beach with more Thaelian soldiers, cursing under his breath the whole way.

He dropped her into one boat when they got there, bruising her hip on the edge of a bench, and climbed in along with Erkhan and two others. The rest tossed Gannon and Kitria even less gently into the second boat, and the two groups wasted no time heading out from shore and north along the cliffs where the Dampener had worked with Veyl on controlling her ability.

Barely able to move and still unable to make her voice obey her, Veyl stared up at the towering rock wall, tears welling in her eyes. Was Jinau dead? The cutting sensation she felt in her chest before they dragged him into the house suggested he was. Who had sent the other wine and the pastries? Were the councilors behind this? They almost had to be, given that she appeared to be their target and she probably wouldn't have gone to visit Kitria this night if they hadn't brought her up. Had someone warned them about the intended coup, or were they merely putting into action a hidden plot of their own? And how were the Ukhen'kya involved?

This time, the motion of the waves was unwelcome. The small boats followed the line of the cliffs, then turned out to where a fleet of six ships waited in the nighttime waters with no lanterns lit upon the decks to draw attention to their presence. The group Veyl was with climbed aboard first, the crew using ropes to help one of the larger men bring her up.

Eavara approached them, her stony gaze offering no insight. Her expression held neither guilt nor gloating. "How much time do we have?"

Erkhan stepped past Veyl and the man holding her upright. "The Ukhen'kya were heading toward the port side to attack the Vanrian fleet when we left. We need to depart now."

At that moment, an explosion rang out from the direction of the port, a gout of flame rising into the night, lighting up the horizon. Panic raced through Veyl, giving her a burst of strength she used to pull free of the man supporting her. Faint lightning crackled as her ability struggled to rise. The man she had jerked away from struck her across the face with enough force to send her sprawling on the hard wood of the deck. Before she could get her bearings, he fell to his knees next to her, holding his stomach and throwing up.

"If you or anyone else dares to hit her again, I will run you through," Jaysen shouted. "Do you under-stand?"

Jaysen?

Her stomach twisted into knots when she looked up at him, his dark auburn hair in disarray from the stiff breeze, wild rage flashing in his eyes. The throbbing in her jaw wasn't nearly enough to distract from the visceral terror that raced through her at the prospect of being his prisoner. Somehow, that frightened her more than the idea of being taken by the Thaelian council. Perhaps because, for all that they were manipulative and selfish, at least they appeared sane. She wasn't sure of that with him anymore.

"She was drawing on her ability even with the drug," Eavara snapped, coming to the man's defense.

"Where's the Havaad-cursed Bondmaker and that Feral? Find them now and move her to a room!"

"What about these two?" Eavara asked.

Veyl tried to turn and see where Gannon and Kitria were, but the effort proved too much. Instead, she rested her throbbing cheek against the cool wood of the deck, closing her eyes and reaching deep within to search for the flicker of power that once again eluded her.

"Take them below and lock them up. They may yet prove useful."

She opened her eyes as Erkhan lifted her with more consideration this time.

Jaysen was staring at her, his jaw set. After a second, he scowled and turned to Eavara. "Shouldn't you be sailing us out of here, Ahnkreth?"

"As per your orders, Majesty." Eavara gave a stiff bow and stalked away, shouting commands to the crew.

Jaysen also walked off as rain started falling, fat raindrops pattering noisily on the wood deck. At least she knew now who had betrayed them to the council. Warm tears slipped down her cheeks to mix with the rain. Her tehnaak, her best friend and confidant as a child, was truly gone, twisted into this. She could only hope Arhk survived the night so that, someday, they could kill the stranger Jaysen had become together.

•

"Veyl."

She crawled awake from a nightmare in which Jaysen had betrayed them, her thoughts thick and sluggish, only to open her eyes and find that it was real. He sat on the edge of the bed in a cramped secondary officer's cabin, the rocking of the ship on the water confirming her fate. A strange Thaelian woman, her dark brunette hair braided back into a long tail, stood near the door, a wave dancer next to her with eyes the color of sea foam. Its head cocked inquisitively to one side when Veyl looked at it.

"Good morning," Jaysen said, his flat expression giving no life to the greeting.

Veyl struggled upright, her muscles still heavy from the aftereffects of whatever they had drugged her with. It was worth the strenuous effort to move a little away from him and lean against the wall.

"Jaysen," she breathed, nausea rising along with her words, "what have you done?"

"I told the council what Vanris was planning and offered them an alternative." He presented the information casually, as though discussing a change in the weather and not an act of vilest treachery.

"What alternative?"

A smile curved his lips, though the expression didn't reach his eyes. "The council, along with many of the mind-crafters and soldiers who support them, and you, are going to help me take back my throne from Thrasser. In return, Sarket will ensure that Thaelis remains theirs."

She swallowed, trying hard not to be sick. "This is madness."

"Is it? Thrasser has already established a cooperative stance with the Thaelians, so arriving in their company should provide me the opportunity to reach Sarket's shores and start spreading word of Thrasser's treason before he even knows I'm alive. With the promise of backing from Vanris, reinforced by our pending marriage, I will soon have my throne."

"There is no pending marriage." She put a hand to her stomach, his words worsening her nausea. "My family will never stand behind this, especially if you mean to subvert their efforts in dealing with Thaelis."

He chuckled. "I expect they'll be more upset by our subversion of their plans for you. By the time news reaches them about what happened last night, it will be too late. Besides, if we allow this to escalate into fighting, the presence of mind-crafters on both sides, along with Sarket's alchemical weapons, will lead to substantial loss of life. You and I can prevent that. This isn't as upsetting as it may seem right now. You," he paused, taking her hand, "will soon remember that you love me. Once we reach land, you will send word to your family stating that you wish to renounce the throne and marry me. As wedding gifts, you will request that they withdraw from Thaelis and elevate Sarket as a Vanrian ally." He gave her hand a painful squeeze then. "And if the damage Kyril and his people inflicted on your memories doesn't fade enough for you to realize that you want this too, there are Evokers and Charmers in this fleet who can fix that."

Veyl jerked her hand away, his words stealing the air from her lungs. A careless Evoker, given free rein to alter her memories, could do enormous damage. Her ability responded, albeit reluctantly, to her rising panic, slowly crackling to life in her chest.

The wave dancer stood with a whine, and the Feral by the door set a hand on the beast's head, giving Veyl a frosty look. "Don't even think about it, Khesran."

"Pardon my manners. I forgot to introduce you." Jaysen gestured to the woman by the door. "This is Feral Ahninveth Heshara. She now holds a zenyal bond over you. Although I hate to continue that practice, with your ability as unpredictable as it is and with the mess they clearly made of your mind, I'm afraid we can't risk letting you be without one yet. And as an extra precaution…" He picked up a mug from the small bedside table and swirled the contents. "For now, I must ask you to drink this. It is a lighter dose than what you received last night."

She eyed the mug warily. "No."

"Veyl." He adopted the tone of a parent about to lose their patience.

"I will not drink that. You cannot keep me drugged forever."

"Not forever. Just for now. If you refuse, I'll have to call in a Charmer. And you might wish to keep in mind that the experience Gannon and Kitria have on this journey depends entirely on how cooperative you are."

Veyl leaned over the side of the bed and threw up.

Jaysen watched impassively, offering her the mug again when she straightened.

"Am I to understand that the Ukhen'kya attacked our fleet?" she asked, wiping her mouth with the back of one trembling hand.

Jaysen pulled a kerchief out of his vest and offered it to her. When she had cleaned herself and passed it back, he silently held the mug out to her once more.

Recognizing it for the transaction it was, her obedience in exchange for the answers she wanted, Veyl accepted it and swallowed the contents, her hands trembling with suppressed rage.

"Good girl." Jaysen took the mug back and returned it to the bedstand. "Yes. They were to cripple the Delaphinian ships and provide a distraction in the port to keep eyes off the other side of the island so we could make our escape. I'm hoping they also thinned the Vanrian ranks in the conflict."

Hatred soared in her, bitter and nauseating. "But how?"

"That's the best part." He stood and walked toward the door. "It turns out that the Thaelian councilors have been in communication with the Ukhen'kya for years. The Unclean attacks have helped them to thin out insurgents over time and keep control of the populace. They had them waiting nearby in case fighting broke out when the Vanrians arrived."

Veyl clenched her hands in the bedcovers, fighting the urge to throw up again. "The explosions?"

"The warehouse where they stored the firebombs Kyril's fleet brought back from Sarket. I arranged that. There was a certain poetry to my destroying the merchandise Thrasser used to try buying my death. It also made for a dramatic distraction, and I didn't want the Thaelians figuring out how to make their own."

"My people were on those ships, Jaysen. My grandfather. My friends." Her voice cracked. "How could you? How could you do to me what they did to us?"

"I do have them to thank for the idea and its execution. This is for the best, Veyl. You will recognize that in time." He opened the door and stopped in the doorway, not looking at her. "I'll send someone to clean up the mess and have food brought in to help settle your stomach. Get some rest."

Veyl pulled her knees to her chest, trying to keep the pressure of her sorrow from bursting free. She had to think. Somehow, she had to stop this. But it was done. She had no way of knowing what losses the Ukhen'kya had inflicted upon the allied fleet. Was Arhk alive? If so, did he have enough ships in working order to give chase? Or was she on her own? For now, she had to assume no help was coming.

Her gaze shifted to the wave dancer. "What's his name?"

"Her name is none of your business."

Veyl lowered her gaze. Already, the drug was making her drowsy and unfocused again. How long did Jaysen intend to keep her this way? Perhaps he planned to have someone hold her upright at their wedding.

She let out a bitter laugh and leaned her head back against the wall, brushing away an errant tear.

•

The next several days passed in a hazy blur. Any attempt to resist further doses of the drug they countered with threats of a Charmer's intervention or harm done to Gannon and Kitria. Veyl remained locked in the room with the Feral. She desperately wanted out, but with the sedative, she was too uncoordinated and weak to force the issue. The constant low-grade nausea left her with little appetite, which compounded her weakness. But what she hated most about the drug was how it destroyed her ability to focus. A side effect that seemed to grow worse with each consecutive dose. She would try to think about or do something, and her mind would slip away to some other place. Several minutes later, she would remember that she had been trying to puzzle out this problem or complete that task and need to start over, only to go through the same process when her mind inevitably drifted again. Her waking hours were exercises in frustration that often left her curled on the bed in tears.

Jaysen didn't return. Nor did anyone she recognized over the course of those days. If she remembered correctly how many times they had given her the drug, they were about five days into the journey when Councilor Shyall came to visit one morning.

Veyl retreated to the farthest corner of the bed and glared at the woman as she entered.

"Khesran Veyl. I understand you are upset about all of this, but I can assure you it is not what the council wanted, either. Your people really left us no choice. We had truly hoped you would come to see the good of Thaelis and agree to stay as a member of the council. With your bloodline and ability, you would have been greatly respected by our people. Now you shall be wasted in wedlock to a foreigner."

"We left you no choice? Look at what you did to us. If you hadn't..." she trailed off, struggling to recapture the point she had been about to make. Her gaze drifted to the beast alongside Heshara by the door. The wave dancer was lighter in build than Ceris. She did look more feminine, really, with a more slender snout and fine ears that had a delicate taper to them. She was a magnificent creature.

"Khesran?"

Veyl startled, genuinely surprised to find Shyall there watching her. "This drug... Does it..." The words drifted away from her.

"Build up with use?" Shyall offered, continuing when Veyl nodded. "It does, though it will wear off in time once they stop giving it to you. It's made from a substance found in a scent pouch under the shell of the female ket'ta. The Ukhen'kya use it to keep their sacrifices subdued during harvest ceremonies."

Veyl latched onto that subject. "Why would you work with them?"

Shyall's brow furrowed. "Because we were their prey. They hunted us for their harvest and took those they caught home to be butchered and eaten. Every year following their first appearance, we struggled to protect our people from them. When we fought back, they punished us with the Devastation. We no longer had enough soldiers left to protect everyone after that. If we had a greater number of mind-crafters than we do, we might have found another way."

Her gaze turning inward, Shyall stared at nothing as she continued. "And that wasn't our only problem. There were whispers of rebellion on the wind, so we reached out to the Ukhen'kya and made a bargain with them. From then on, we had our spies locate subversives and tell the Unclean where to attack to target those elements. A few times, we have taken people we knew were part of that developing uprising from their homes, claiming they exhibited signs of Devastation sickness and had to be quarantined. We gave them to the Unclean as well. It has served to eliminate those who would undermine our leadership and keep the Ukhen'kya from attacking the rest… most of the time."

Veyl struggled to follow everything she was saying, but the message was clear enough. "You feed your own people to them to maintain power?"

Shyall shrugged again, avoiding her gaze. "Never innocents."

"As determined by you," Veyl spat.

The councilor drew a deep breath. "I did not come here to defend our actions to you. The council needs to know if you love that man."

Veyl's brows pinched. "That man?"

"Prince… King Jaysen." The edge of disdain in her voice suggested a powerful dislike for the man they had allied themselves with.

Unease prickled up Veyl's spine. The answer to that question had significance that she wasn't sure she possessed the clarity of mind to fully understand in her drugged state. Her conversation with Jaysen from several days ago felt like a fever dream now. Though some parts of it were upsetting enough to have stuck with her like slivers under her fingernails. Jaysen planned to marry her, and he expected that to be the path through which he both secured Vanris's support and got her people out of Thaelis. That last point was important here. That was why it mattered to this woman.

But she loved Kyril. At least now, with the council out of Thaelis, he would no longer be facing execution. Arhk would have destroyed the Ukhen'kya and set Kyril free. She had to believe that.

"He says you do."

Veyl startled, realizing she had once again lost track of the councilor's presence in the room. "Do what?"

Shyall's lips pressed into a flat, irritated line. "Do you love him?"

Of course, she loved Kyril, not that it mattered now. "I do."

"Then perhaps this will work after all."

The door opened, and Jaysen entered, pausing when he saw Shyall there. He retreated a few steps and held it open, giving the councilor a stern look.

"Yes, Majesty, I was just leaving." Shyall nodded to Veyl and walked out around him.

He stood there a second longer, turning his gaze on the Feral. "If you could give us a moment alone."

"Majesty." Heshara offered a slight bow before leaving with the wave dancer.

When he entered, Veyl saw the mug in his hand. "No. Please, Jaysen." Tears sprang into her eyes. "No more." She despised him for his pitying look as he placed the mug on the table and sat on the bed next to her.

"You must know I hate doing this to you." He cupped her jaw with one hand. "I'm just not confident I can trust you yet. It's obvious to me now that they made an awful mess of your memories."

"I know." Swallowing back the rush of bile that came up with the lie, she closed her eyes and pressed into his hand, trying to imagine it was Kyril's. When she opened her eyes, he was gazing at her with unsettling adoration. She clung fiercely to the memories she could hold on to. A single mistake would ruin everything. "But I… I remember how afraid I was in Balarus that we had lost our wonderful connection. Then I saw you in Deepwater and…" And what? What had happened then? She took a chance on a disjointed flash of memory and blurted, "You pulled me into your arms—"

Suddenly, his lips pressed to hers, and she had to focus hard not to be sick, clinging to Kyril in her mind, grasping at foggy memories of a last blissful night together on his ship. Even with that to bolster her, she couldn't keep the kiss going for long.

Jason's eyes narrowed when she pulled away.

"I'm sorry." She put a hand on her stomach. "The drug… it makes me nauseous."

"Yes. I imagine so." He didn't look entirely convinced when he leaned back, as if he expected his kiss should have transcended mere physical discomfort. "The winds have been in our favor. We'll reach Sarket soon. Perhaps we can start weaning you off. How about half this time?"

Tears spilled down her cheeks in earnest. She could do nothing to stop them. Facing another day, another hour even, feeling sick, weak, and lost in a mental fog was more than she could bear. Jaysen moved over her onto the bed and bundled her into his arms, holding her as she wept from the torment he had inflicted on her. She didn't have it in her to pull away. Maybe for the moment that was just as well. He kissed her head, and she cried harder.

"I have some wonderful news," he said, his tone lifting with a note of encouragement. "One of the Evokers thinks that, because your ability awoke so recently, there's a chance he could reverse your awakening. Not yet, of course. I need you to help me deal with Thrasser first, but after that, we could return to how life was before."

How many times had she wished to be rid of her

Frightener ability? Now, with him dangling that possibility in front of her, she felt only a greater sense of horror. To have him threaten to take it away when it might be the one thing that could save her.

Veyl indulged her heartache, letting her breakdown be her excuse for not responding to that revelation. She cried herself to sleep that way. When she woke later, Jaysen was gone, and a moist black nose was in her face, those bright, sea-foam eyes staring into hers. The wave dancer's body shifted with the tentative wagging of her tail. After a glance around found the Feral dozing in a chair by the door, Veyl reached out to the beast. When the wagging grew more enthusiastic, she gently scratched behind one of those membranous ears, and the wave dancer pressed into her hand.

"Seyn!"

The shout made Veyl jump, and the wave dancer flinched, her ears dropping back for an instant. Since the woman could have called the beast with her mind, it was clear she intended to startle Veyl, who didn't hide her glare now. The wave dancer, Seyn, turned to go to her companion, her long tail sweeping the mug Jaysen had left for Veyl off the table. The beast glanced back at the liquid that spilled across the wood floor and huffed once, looking oddly pleased with herself, before returning to her companion's side.

Heshara heaved a sigh. "I'll have them send more."

"It's not urgent," Veyl said, sitting up too abruptly. A wave of nausea hit her, but a few hours of sleep without more of the drug had given her head a chance to clear a little. Still a long way from normal, but at least moderately functional. She didn't want to lose that. "I won't be able to use my ability to help Jaysen if they don't allow it to wear off."

"That's not my call," Heshara countered, giving Seyn a chastising look.

"There's Qwilki in your lineage, isn't there?" It wasn't really a question. Veyl could tell by the color of her hair, her darker skin tone, and the roundness of her features that Heshara's family tree was probably fifty percent Vanrian at most. Somewhere in that percentage, some persistent mind-crafter blood had gotten through.

"I'm not here to chat with you, Khesran. You are nothing to me but a means to remove your people from Thaelis."

"Funny how eager your councilors were to bring my people to Thaelis back when we had no say in the matter."

Heshara scowled and got up, going to lean out the door. "Tell King Jaysen his little pet dumped her drink and will need more," she said to someone outside.

Veyl surged to her feet. "I did no such…" The room spun around her, and she staggered, catching hold of the side table as she fell, landing hard on her knees.

Seyn stepped toward her, ears and tail drooping. Then she stopped and glanced at Heshara, who had closed the door again and stood staring smugly down at Veyl. The wave dancer shrank back to her companion's side. "Feel free to blame Seyn. Your dear king is suspicious enough that he will doubt your words, even if he says otherwise, and he will wonder if he should let the Evoker fix your memories more to his liking after all."

Knees stinging from the impact, Veyl glared up at her, etching the woman's face in her mind and adding her to a list that included Jaysen, the Thaelian council, Eavara, and Erkhan. The people she would put an end to when she finally turned the tables.

Jaysen brought more of the drug himself. It took him long enough to get around to it that Veyl, with her clarity somewhat improved, had time to come up with an idea. Though his scowl when Heshara told him she had deliberately dumped the last batch made Veyl's stomach twist into knots. Did she still know him well enough to turn this around? She had to. For Gannon and Kitria as much as herself.

He handed the new mug to Heshara and focused on Veyl. "Is this true?"

She could deny it and blame the wave dancer, which would be the truth, or call it an accident, but she could also do better. Embracing the misery of the last several days made it easy to summon a few tears.

She nodded. "It is."

His jaw tightened. "What did I tell you about co-operating?"

"I know, it's just..." She didn't have to fake the tremble in her voice. So much rested on her ability to turn this to her favor. Her next words raced out in a frantic jumble. "I woke up, and you were gone, and my thoughts have been so confused. I didn't know if you had ever been here at all, or if I had imagined the whole thing. Then I started wondering if I had seen you the night they took me or if that too was some drug-induced hallucination. I couldn't bear the thought of not knowing anymore. Jaysen, I'm so, so sorry. I was just afraid and alone without you."

Those last two words were the most important, and they had the desired effect. His expression softened. He came forward to pull her into his arms. "I'm the one who should be sorry," he murmured. "I am here, Veyl. From now on, I will always be here for you." He spoke the words as though he believed she would find them reassuring and kissed her head.

She rested her cheek against his chest and met Heshara's eyes, allowing herself the slightest of smiles in response to the woman's glare.

Jaysen insisted she drink some of the drug that day, but he cut it back enough that she could at least keep track of what was happening around her. It gave her the opportunity she needed to gather her wits and come up with a short-term plan to avoid having her mind destroyed by Thaelian Evokers. Her ability became more responsive too, though she was careful not to draw upon it. Until they were on land, any attempt to escape or to free Gannon and Kitria served no purpose. Once they reached the shore, she couldn't try to run alone. Jaysen would take his fury out on the others if she did. That complicated the situation.

By the time they approached the coastal city of Taro in Sarket, a little farther south than she had hoped they would make landfall, she had convinced him to let her stop taking the drug, despite Heshara's insistence that they couldn't trust her. In a contest of influence, no matter what conflicts had occurred between them in recent months, Veyl still had years of friendship and her former tehnaak bond with Jaysen to draw upon. Not to mention the ability to leverage the fact that he believed he loved her, even if he showed it in the most appalling ways.

Veyl stood on the rear deck of the ship beside him now, appreciating the brisk coastal breeze that cleared her mind and carried with it a spark of hope. "Jaysen."

He didn't respond, glancing instead toward the Sarketi ship to their right, one of several escorting the six Thaelian vessels to the docks. The admiral in charge of the Sarketi fleet had been astonished to find the supposedly deceased crown prince alive and well on the deck of the Thaelian flagship. Even more so upon hearing, with the councilors supporting his claim, that Thrasser had made a deal with the Thaelians, sacrificing the combined community of Deepwater in order to eliminate him. The man, expressing admiration for Jaysen's determination and his resourcefulness in making allies of the people sent to kill him, swore the forces under his command to the service of Sarket's rightful heir.

Though it made her skin crawl to do so, she slid her hand into Jaysen's, finally capturing his attention. "I wanted to ask you for something."

His hand closed around hers, and the tightness in his jaw relaxed a fraction. "What is it, my love?"

She swallowed. He had been right about one thing. If this escalated to war between their countries, a great many lives would be lost. None of her ideas for escape would allow her to prevent that, and still save Kitria and Gannon. The unfortunate reality she faced was that she could only accomplish those goals if she took her own freedom out of the equation. "I was thinking, since we've sorted matters out between us, maybe I could write that letter to my parents when we get to shore."

A smile curved his lips. Lips that had touched hers far too many times in the last few days. "I would appreciate your doing so, but that wasn't a question."

"No." She would have to endure much more than his kisses if she followed through with this. She drew a bracing breath of cool, salty air. "I had hoped you would consider sending Gannon and Kitria to Vanris with the messenger, as a show of goodwill. There's no need to keep them here now." She gave his hand a gentle squeeze, doing her best to feign affection.

His slight scowl and shrewd gaze sent a chill through her. "I'll tell you what. We'll be in Taro for a few weeks at least, possibly much longer depending on how quickly I can gather support. Write the letter. If I'm satisfied with it, I will consider sending Gannon back to Vanris with the messenger."

If he was satisfied? The condition sent a chill through her. What would happen if he wasn't? "What about Kitria?"

"It would make no sense to send her to Vanris. She is Thaelian, after all. I thought you might like to keep her as a lady's maid, but if you have no use for her, I'll let the council decide what to do with her."

Veyl pivoted abruptly. She couldn't trust the council any more than she could him. If he assigned Kitria to her as a maid, at least then she might have a chance of protecting her until she found another way to send her home to her brother. "No. In fact, that's a lovely idea. I think she would make an excellent attendant."

"Lady's maid, darling. You'll be living in Sarket now. You need to learn to use our terminology."

Veyl wrestled down the urge to spit in his face and forced a smile. "You're right, of course. I just need more practice." She turned to watch their approach, struggling to ignore the churning in her stomach when he extracted his hand and slid it around her waist.

Taro was a large city set south of where the Kilden Mountains curved out toward the ocean, northwest of Andaro, Sarket's capital. The range loomed up just north of them now, sweeping around the backside of Taro to continue south farther inland. Clouds hid the highest mountaintops from view—the shape of their snow-capped peaks left to the imagination. Evergreen forests covered most of the steep slopes, bathing the horizon in a dark blue-green. The landscape was breathtaking, and as unlike Vanris as Thaelis was, though in an entirely different way. A view she would have loved getting to see under much better circumstances.

The city itself, stretching toward the hillsides beyond the oceanfront, was attractive as well. Streets lined with buildings built of light-colored stone and wind-worn wood. Rooftops on the houses and businesses came to sharp peaks, and at least three tall bell towers marked churches of Havaad. Hundreds of round-eared Sarketi people went about their daily lives, unaware of how significantly the arriving ships could alter their futures.

As they finished mooring the flagship to the dock and prepared to unload, she glanced at Jaysen. "Do you think Kitria could begin working for me here? I expect she would be amenable to the arrangement if it earned her some measure of freedom, and it would be nice to have the company of another woman." She added the last with a sharp look at Heshara standing a few feet away.

The Feral narrowed her eyes in return.

Jaysen didn't look at her. "We shall see."

Veyl followed his distracted gaze to the deck, where a group of six Thaelian soldiers were bringing someone up from below. Her chest constricted, breath catching in her throat, when she recognized the figure stumbling along with two Thaelian soldiers supporting him.

Tangled and matted with blood, Kyril's long hair obscured much of his face until he glanced their way, revealing so much bruising and swelling he was almost unrecognizable. She clung to her resolve to stop herself from pulling away from Jaysen. When they turned Kyril toward the gangplank, she sucked in a sharp breath at the sight of raw, bloody stripes over his exposed back, where someone had whipped him. Ice moved through her veins. Without considering what she was doing, she reached up to touch the place in her hair where the spiral shell had hung. Given everything else, the missing shells had been low on her list of priorities.

Unfortunately, Jaysen was looking at her now. "Ah. Yes. I threw those trinkets overboard. You are free of them. I had the councilors bring the former ahnkreth along as a wedding gift. I figured that, once your memory cleared, you would be delighted to see the man who attacked Deepwater and upended our lives so horribly put to death. His execution will also serve as a gesture to acknowledge my alliance with the Thaelian council."

It took all her willpower to hold back a sob. Gannon and Kitria she might have a chance of getting out of this, but Kyril too? Jaysen would never agree to let him live. And even if she could break him free, whether they had drugged him or simply beaten him that badly, he appeared barely able to walk.

Seyn let out a soft whine, and Veyl glanced over at the wave dancer, noting how her gaze followed Kyril's stumbling progress on the gangplank. The beast shifted from one front paw to the other, falling still when Heshara glowered down at her. Was the animal reacting because he was a Feral, like her companion, or was there something deeper to her distress?

Veyl swallowed against a painful constriction in her throat, fighting to keep her voice steady and her ability silent. "Did you bring his wave dancer?"

"No. The council deliberately locked the beast in a cell next to him, so they could leave it there. It would have only gotten in the way."

To be separated from his bonded companion like this was one more form of torture, but at least they left Ceris alive. This changed everything, though, adding significant complications to this situation that she had been unaware of until that moment. The weight of despair that fell over her made the simple act of standing upright feel like an overwhelming feat.

Mind racing, she turned to Jaysen, doing her best to pretend a lack of interest in the group now descending to the dock. "Why did we come here?"

"I need to meet with Wavelord Kronach and secure his support. He holds substantial sway over the coastal communities in Sarket. I'm hoping he will grant me use of his messengers to spread word of my return and Thrasser's betrayal."

"Wavelord? He's Eydarith?"

"Yes." His weary tone and the roll of his eyes told her how he felt about that.

"But there are several churches of Havaad in the city. I thought the Eydarith considered Havaad worship to be blasphemy."

"Kronach is the second wavelord of Taro. His predecessor took the city in an honor duel thirty-three years ago from the lord it had been granted to by my father, King Roald Lodmund," he added emphasis to the man's title and name, as if he felt a need to remind her, or perhaps himself, that he was the former king's son. "My father agreed not to challenge the rule of the wavelords here so long as they adhered to certain conditions, one being that Havaad worshipers be allowed to continue practicing their religion unhampered within the city."

"That strikes me as unusually tolerant, given what I know of your father." She looked out over the city toward the tall castle at its heart, also stealing a glance at Kyril's group where they had stopped by the end of the wooden dock. His guards had forced him to his knees, the hang of his head hiding his face within the fall of his long, tangled hair. An ache throbbed through her chest at the sight of him.

"It's said the only thing in Sarket more savage than a werdyn cat is an Eydarith wavelord," Jaysen remarked. "I'm going to guess that my father didn't want to risk an honor duel for the city."

That was saying something, since his late father had a reputation as a fearsome fighter. Although her father had defeated the king in battle. Her father had also controlled werdyn cats with his Feral ability. Maybe those encounters were proof of who was the better man.

Holding back a bitter sneer that threatened to sneak out, she gestured with her chin to a large group of warriors heading toward the docks from the city side. "It looks like Wavelord Kronach has arranged a welcome party for you."

"For us," he corrected. "You will be my queen soon." He offered her his arm. "Come, let us meet our host."

Forcing a smile, she settled her hand on his arm and let him lead her toward the stairs. He stopped them at the top step when another group of Thaelian soldiers escorted Gannon and Kitria up on deck. The two looked tired and unkempt, their hair and clothes a mess. At least they appeared uninjured. They were nearing the gangplank when the inevitable occurred, and Kitria spotted her brother below. She froze in place, the widening of her eyes and the horror on her face making it apparent that she hadn't been aware of his presence before now any more than Veyl had.

"Kyril!"

Kitria broke from the group, managing a couple of steps before a guard swept her legs out from under her with the haft of his polearm. She hit the deck with a solid smack, the sound sending a cringe through Veyl. Gannon, his bound hands suggesting that he had been less cooperative, hurried to her side to try helping her up.

On the dock, Kyril snapped to life at his sister's cry. He surged to his feet, slamming into one guard hard enough that the woman flew off the side into the water.

"Kit!" he shouted. "Don't you hurt her!"

The butt of an axe haft to his gut doubled him over, and the other guards piled on, beating him with fists and blunt weapons until he fell back to his knees.

On the deck, Kitria stumbled to her feet with Gannon's help and tried to run to her brother again. A guard caught her shoulder and spun her, punching her in the face hard enough that she hit the deck a second time. Two others held Gannon back this time.

"Kit!" Veyl released Jaysen's arm and started down the steps, her ability crackling to life like a wild storm.

A bright flash of excruciating pain burst through her skull, and she missed a step, tumbling the rest of the way down. She lay there dazed, ears ringing as the agony in her head faded, and other pains rose to the surface. Struggling to sit up on one hip, she stared at her hands for a moment, at the bloody scrapes on the heels of both palms.

"Veyl, are you all right?" Jaysen crouched beside her, taking hold of her arms, genuine worry drawing the color from his face.

"Veyl?"

She looked up at the sound of Gannon's voice and gave a tiny shake of her head. He stayed where he was amidst the guards, two of whom had Kitria up again and were binding her hands now. A reddish lump was swelling over her cheekbone, and her lower lip bled from a fresh split, one forearm scraped and bloody from her violent collisions with the deck of the ship. She glared at Veyl as if all these wrongs were her doing.

Veyl averted her gaze. Somehow, it felt as if she deserved the blame, and it wasn't a pleasant feeling. "Help me up," she said, her voice flat and cold to match the empty hollow spreading within her.

When she was on her feet, Jaysen brushed some of her hair away from the corner of her mouth, his fingers shaking, possibly from anger given the look of pure loathing he cast at Heshara.

Veyl frowned at her hands. "Your handkerchief, please." When he gave it to her, she pressed it to the bleeding scrapes on her palms, alternating between them.

"Are you all right?" Jaysen asked again.

"I'll survive." She met his eyes for a second, making a point of not looking at anyone else, especially Kitria and Kyril, who had come out of the chaos in worse shape than she had. "I'm certain they'll have someplace I can clean up in the castle."

Jaysen gestured to the group with Gannon and Kitria. "Take them down, but keep them away from the ahnkreth." Once they were moving, his gaze shifted to Heshara. "You and I will discuss this later."

The Feral swallowed hard, a flicker of dread undermining the defiant set of her jaw. Her hand settled on Seyn's head. "Yes, Majesty."

When Veyl took a step, pain flared in one knee, and she stumbled. Jaysen caught her elbow, but she waved him away. "It's fine. Just bruised. I can walk it off."

He let go, but proceeded at a slow pace, his hand out, ready to help if she needed it. "Why did you draw upon your ability?"

She didn't bother looking at him. "I couldn't bear to watch them hurting Kitria when all she wanted was to help her brother." It wouldn't benefit her to admit that she couldn't stand seeing them hurt Kyril, either. "I apologize for acting rashly."

"She's going to have to accept that her brother is beyond her help. He's a traitor and an abuser. He will die a well-deserved death."

It was all she could do to hold back a derisive snort. Abuser indeed. Too bad he couldn't see the irony of his calling someone else that. If anyone there had earned their death, it wasn't Kyril.

"If you feel this will be an issue with her," he continued, "we can find you a different—"

"It won't."

The Thaelian councilors and more guards disembarked with them. They met up with the formation of warriors waiting at the edge of the docks, a hard-looking bunch who reminded her more of mercenaries in their chain and leather armor. Though the leather portions were all stained dark blue-gray, giving them a semblance of uniformity. None of them spoke. The tall, dark-haired man who appeared to be their leader gestured toward the castle with a jerk of his head, then started walking that way, apparently expecting them to follow. The others fell in around them. Kyril's Thaelian guards took him ahead of them where Veyl couldn't avoid seeing his wounded back or noting how much assistance he required to walk, though he occasionally attempted to do without. Gannon and Kitria's escorts kept them at the rear of the column. The rest of the fleet would wait on the ships for now.

All the buildings lining the city streets looked solid and well-constructed, but they still suffered from the fierce winds and storms that often hit that coast. The closer they stood to the docks, the more weather-worn and in need of repair the exteriors were. It reminded her of Vanris in a way, a city embracing its existence and making life work in an environment that could be as harsh as the desert at times, though more plentiful in several ways.

A wave of homesickness struck her, piling on top of the overwhelming sense that she could do nothing to fix this mess. She stumbled a step, her gut tightening with the struggle to fight back a sob. Not now. This was not the place or time to break down.

Jaysen's hand touched her arm, and she had to force herself not to pull away from him. The rest of the walk to the castle stretched on for what felt like an eternity as she waged a war to hold in her emotions. They passed through the inner gates, the narrow passage squeezing them down to no more than five abreast. Her knee and palms throbbed, that pain overshadowed by the rawness of her throat and cramping of her stomach from the effort of holding sorrow at bay.

The Eydarith warrior led them inside to a long, stark stone audience hall, its soaring ceiling and walls decorated with weapons and tapestries bearing depictions of ocean creatures intermixed with occasional scenes of battle. The guards standing on either side wore the same chain and stained-leather armor as their escort, along with helms shaped to evoke what she suspected was some species of ocean beast with boar-like tusks.

A simple stone throne at the back had the skull of a massive sea predator suspended above it. The tall man seated there had long dark hair that showed hints of gray, the top portion pulled into a tail. One half of his face was a twist of thick scars, as if something had attempted to rip the flesh away. The eye on that side was an eerie, dead off-white. The other eye, dark mahogany in color, watched them with keen interest as they filed into the room amidst his guards. He wore rugged leather and chain armor like his warriors and a long, fur-lined cloak, his bare forearms knotted with heavy muscle.

"I don't get the impression anyone has ever allowed that man anything," Veyl said under her breath.

Jaysen's jaw tightened.

The guards stopped them and sank to one knee. The Thaelians with Kyril moved him to one side of her and Jaysen and pushed him down to his knees before kneeling themselves. His head hung, blood dripping onto the stone floor from somewhere behind the veil of his hair.

Jaysen placed a hand on her elbow, keeping her beside him as he stepped forward. "Wavelord Kronach," he greeted in Pandrean Common, sinking to one knee.

Jaysen's position here was precarious. As king, he wouldn't kneel to this man, but he apparently retained enough of his sanity to recognize that he currently held no crown. This man could choose to support him, or he could destroy him to gain favor with Thrasser. Unfortunately for her, neither outcome promised to be beneficial.

Veyl started kneeling beside him, hesitating when Kronach leapt to his feet, the energy and body control behind the movement showing a hint of grace and agility that came as something of a surprise from someone with such dense musculature.

"Not you." His voice held a powerful command that stilled her. Jaysen tensed as the wavelord strode up and looked her over, gesturing to her leg. "You would kneel upon an injury to show your deference, Vanrian?"

Veyl glanced down, noting the bloody tear in the knee of her pants. She raised her chin. "It is your house into which I seek entry, Wavelord."

"And who are you?" He asked, stepping in too close, his gaze lingering on her distinctive hair.

"She—"

He cut Jaysen off with a sharp gesture. "I am asking her."

"Khesran Veyl of Vanris," she answered.

Kronach barked a laugh. "A Vanrian princess kneeling in my hall." He moved closer still, staring into her eyes with his solitary dark one, then he inhaled deeply, as if he smelled something of interest on her. "A wave-touched Vanrian, no less. I never thought I would see the day." She was aware of Kyril's head coming up as he looked toward them in her periphery. Kronach glanced over at him, eyes narrowing a fraction, then he looked at her again. "You may press your wounded knee to my stone, Princess."

Veyl clenched her teeth and sank down onto the tender injury.

Kronach returned to his throne and sat, his gaze settling on Jaysen. "I know you, Undead Prince. Tell me, why do you bring these people here to bleed on my floors?"

Veyl sank, trembling, onto a corner of the bed in one of the rooms the wavelord had provided them. A Thaelian healer had come by to clean her wounds and give her a dress to change into. When that was done, the woman took the damaged clothing and left. Heshara stayed outside with two Thaelian guards, allowing her some privacy. The room had no windows, and she could find no evidence of an entrance to hidden servants' passages that many of the southern kingdoms built into their castles. It was a common feature in Delaphinian castles and palaces that Sarket incorporated less frequently in their construction. All she could do was sit in her comfortable cell and wait to find out what would happen next.

It could be worse. Somewhere, in an undoubtedly drafty cell, Kyril suffered with his many injuries. Reminding herself of that didn't make her situation seem any less awful. If anything, it made it worse.

She couldn't let him die.

The door opened without warning, and her weary heart leapt into her throat, continuing to pound frantically there when Jaysen entered. Two guards followed him in, with Kitria between them. They took her to a chair next to the fireplace and sat her down. She froze there, looking like a wild animal anticipating an attack.

Jaysen gestured curtly toward the door. "Leave us."

The two guards did as ordered, and Veyl stood, stepping away from the bed when Jaysen approached. He slid a hand along her jaw and into her hair as if he had every right to touch her as he pleased. For the moment, she didn't dare dispute the notion.

"If the girl causes you any trouble, there are guards right outside who can drag her to a cell like her brother." He moved closer, his eyes drifting to her lips, and her stomach clenched. "Heshara is in the next room as well."

Veyl shifted slightly back from him. "Is Kronach going to grant you his messengers?"

Jaysen had met in private with the wavelord after their initial encounter in the audience hall. It had irked her almost as much as it appeared to annoy the Thaelian councilors to be excluded from that discussion. Since the Thaelians didn't share a language with the people of Taro, she had offered to translate, assuming he would want to include his new allies in the conversation. He had declined and sent her with the councilors and an escort of Eydarith guards to be shown to quarters within the castle.

Jaysen slid a hand around her waist, seeming to have forgotten Kitria's presence. Or perhaps he just didn't consider her worth noticing. "He is. Everything is proceeding as I had hoped." He leaned in and kissed her, his hand tightening in her hair, holding her there as his tongue sought entrance.

Squeezing her eyes shut, she gave him what he wanted, and he pulled her against him, the taste of something much stronger than mead on his lips striking a note of fear in her. Was he drunk? Would this be the moment he insisted upon more than just a kiss? The hardness of him pressing against her stoked that fear even higher. Could she bear to do what he might ask of her? Could she let him have her body for the sake of possibly saving the people she cared about? The prospect made her stomach turn and her skin crawl.

He released her after several seconds, breathing hard now, a wild, possessive light burning in his eyes. "Not yet," he murmured, placing a finger over her lips as if she had asked him for something. He stepped back and dug into an inside pocket of his jacket, pulling out a rolled parchment, a quill, and a small ink bottle that he set on the vanity. "For your letter." He came forward to steal another brief kiss. "Goodnight, my queen."

It didn't seem to matter to him that she said nothing in return. He hurried out the door with a lightness in his step. The moment it closed, Veyl sank to the floor alongside the bed and the dam broke, setting free a flood of tears. Tears of frustration, of anger she couldn't act on, and of fear for the people she cared about. And some for herself, too. She pulled her legs in and wrapped her arms over her head, weeping uncontrollably until a hand touched her arm and she jerked away.

Kitria crouched next to her, holding up a rough-made goblet full of pale amber liquid. "Here. I thought you might want something to wash away the taste of him."

Veyl accepted it, swishing some of the sweet wine around her mouth as if it could cleanse him away before swallowing. Then she downed the rest of it and handed the goblet back. "Thank you."

Kitria sat on the floor next to her. "I was ready to keep hating you, but after watching that, I can't muster up much more than pity."

Veyl pulled her knees closer to her chest, ignoring the mild twinge in the one she had hurt.

"Do you have a plan?" Kitria asked.

"I was working on one to save you and Gannon, and prevent a war, but that was before I found out they had Kyril."

Kitria nodded. "Sounds like we need a new plan."

•

They brought a cot in for Kitria to sleep on, but after spending most of the night sitting on the bed talking quietly, they fell asleep there together. Waking up to her company was more uplifting than Veyl would have expected. To know she was no longer facing this alone. That she had someone there aware of the secrets she was keeping, someone who would be her ally in trying to save the people that mattered to her, was what she needed to face this.

For the next two days, Jaysen kept them confined to the room while he dealt with the logistics of settling himself and his Thaelian allies in Taro, starting negotiations with Kronach, and preparing to reach out to those he believed he could sway to his cause. It left them with little to do but talk, heal their injuries, and wonder what had become of Kyril and Gannon. On the third morning, Eavara informed them that they now had permission to move about within the castle grounds in the company of their guards. They took turns cleaning up in the bathing room and dressed in clothing provided by their hosts. The outfit they had left Veyl was an interesting garment with a fitted bodice featuring a V-neck and waist. The long skirt was made of varied strips of fabric in shades of blue and light tan, reminiscent of waves crashing upon the shore. A delicately carved shell broach decorated the bottom of the V neckline.

Kitria helped her work some braids into the side of her hair. The token shells were gone, denying her those symbolic connections to Kyril and Nagi, but she could still choose to represent where she was from in some aspect of her appearance.

When they stepped out of the room, the two guards and Heshara were waiting outside. The wave dancer wagged her tail, then stilled, glancing up at her bonded Feral, ears drooping slightly. Veyl walked past them with Kitria at her side. They followed as expected. She turned down a wide hall, drawn by the bright natural light spilling in from an intersection farther along it. With no knowledge of the place and no one to guide her, she simply hoped to learn something useful about her current prison.

At the intersection, they turned into a broader hall lit by large windows along one side and lined on the other with an eclectic collection of arms and armor. Four of the wavelord's warriors loitered in that hall in the company of Kronach himself, the latter leaning against the stone between two windows. Veyl stopped when he gave her a wolfish grin and pushed away from the wall, prowling over to her.

"Wavelord." She bowed her head, keeping her tone casual despite the dancing of her nerves. "I expected you would be busy with Prince Jaysen."

He waved a dismissive hand. "I sent one of my officers to fill his morning with touring my barracks and meeting my messengers."

Rather than stop at a respectful distance, he walked up to her as close as he had come in the audience hall. Her guards and Heshara started advancing as if they intended to intervene, and his warriors moved into their path, hands sinking to the pair of curved swords they each carried. Kronach ignored them all. Stopping within a few inches of her, he leaned in and inhaled deeply, letting out a satisfied sigh before taking a half-step back. Veyl fought the urge to move away from him, suspecting he would only enjoy knowing how much he unsettled her.

"This is not a chance encounter, then?" she ventured.

"Come with me, Princess." He turned and started walking.

Veyl fell into step beside him, weighing the value of correcting his choice of titles when he already knew better and deciding against it.

His warriors closed in behind them, keeping themselves between the two of them and the rest of her group. They formed a barrier and waited, allowing Veyl and Kronach to get far enough ahead that she was essentially alone with the wavelord before following. Her gaze picked out the weapons he wore in case she needed to try relieving him of one. A pair of curved blades like the ones his warriors carried hung at his waist, along with a dagger with a bone handle.

Kronach was considering her with his shrewd, one-eyed gaze when she finished her quick inventory. "You are trained to fight?"

"Yes. I'm Vanrian. I started combat training as soon as I was old enough to hold a blade."

"I expected as much." His tone suggested approval. "Vanris does not suffer its women to be weak. Do you truly wish to be the queen of a weak man?"

A chill raced through her. Was it possible Jaysen knew he was here after all, and had, in fact, sent him to entrap her? "That man would be your king."

"Sarket's king, Princess."

She offered him the same shrewd scrutiny he had given her. "The Eydarith are people of Sarket, are they not?"

"We are Eydarith. Our ancestors were cast upon the shores of this land hundreds of years ago by a great wave for offending the Tempest. One day, when he is satisfied that we have earned our place back at his side, it will rise again and reclaim us." He shrugged, as if that odd glimpse into his religion explained everything. Perhaps to him, it did. "You should be with a man whose strength is equal to your own. One who deserves your gift."

A man like Kyril?

She pondered the wavelord for a moment. None of the Thaelians spoke Pandrean Common or Sarketi, a reality that left her even more on her own, for better or worse. Walking with him was akin to spending time with a tethdrak with no Feral around to control it. The feeling that, at any moment, she might find his blade in her flesh made it difficult to pretend comfort in his presence. She considered asking what gift he spoke of, but dreaded it could be a reference to parts of herself she had already given Kyril, parts that this man had no business concerning himself with.

"Is there something you wish to say to me, Wavelord?"

"I do not believe you desire this symbolic crown the undead prince wants to place upon your head. You arrived here with no shackles on your wrists, but I sense you are bound all the same."

Veyl stopped. Farther down the hall behind them, his warriors halted as well, keeping her guards and Kitria away. Kronach turned to her, and her gaze caught upon the scars covering one side of his face.

His eyes narrowed. "Do my scars bother you?"

Despite his stern gaze, she didn't get the feeling it would upset him if she said yes. It would be a lie, though. Too many of the people she grew up around had facial scars from the war, her own parents among them. "No. Scars are merely part of the story of who we are."

He cocked his head slightly to one side. "Do you have scars in your tale, Princess?"

A flicker of irritation flashed through her. "Khesran," she corrected sharply, losing patience with his use of the southern title.

Kronach grinned. "Do you, Khesran?"

He had been trying to get under her skin, and she let him. She sighed softly. "I do."

"Show me." A hint of challenge sparked in his eyes.

For the first time in her life, she was grateful for the folly that led her to the academy rooftop that day so many years ago. It had left her with a scar that required no removal of clothing to display. She held up her hand, showing her palm where the long white scar from the tethdrak statue was still clearly visible across it. The scrapes from her fall on the ship were bright and angry on the heel of her palm.

Kronach stepped up alongside her, close enough that their arms touched, and cradled her hand in his. As he ran his thumb slowly along the scar, she had the unnerving sense that there was something erotic in that caress for him.

Seyn trotted up on her other side and growled. Veyl absently placed her free hand on the wave dancer's head, taking comfort from her presence. A reluctant sense of gratitude toward Heshara left her unsettled, and although the intervention was welcome, she worried he might take offense at the beast's arrival.

Kronach released her hand and crouched down, bringing himself to eye level with Seyn. "We are all three creatures of the ocean, are we not?"

Seyn whined softly, her ears flicking back and forth as if his attention made her uneasy too.

He nodded as though they had come to an agreement and stood, gesturing down the hall. With some misgivings, Veyl resumed walking with him.

"I have other scars I could show you." Kronach's tone told her that was an offer she would be wise to ignore.

"It pleases me not to expand upon that aspect of our relationship."

He chuckled, the curve of an amused smile tugging

at his scars.

Veyl followed as he turned through a doorway heading out into a small courtyard that was open to the gray sky. Rows of stone benches covered half the area, leading up to an altar at one end before a statue with canvas draped over it. Untended planters around the perimeter held the long-dead remains of decorative plants, and dirt and debris upon the benches suggested an extended lack of use. They might allow Havaad worship within the town, but it appeared they drew the line at the castle grounds.

"What did you mean yesterday when you said I was wave-touched?"

Ignoring the question, he opened a wooden door on the other side of the courtyard and stood aside to let her enter ahead of him. Nerves on fire, she stepped through the doorway into a dimly lit entry, turning to watch as he followed her inside. His warriors formed a blockade before the door as he started shutting it. Veyl met Heshara's eyes, catching the woman's look of alarm as Seyn bolted through the opening. Then the others were gone, blocked out beyond that heavy door. Did they dare challenge his warriors when their futures hung upon his goodwill?

Kronach glanced down at the wave dancer as she stopped at Veyl's side again and nodded. "That's better."

"What are you doing?"

"Do not look so alarmed, Khesran. As you mentioned, you are wave-touched. I will not allow the undead prince to harm you within the walls of my city." He came forward as he spoke until he was inches from her, once again disregarding propriety and personal comfort. She could feel the warmth of his body in the chill of the poorly lit building. "I cannot offer the same if you choose to leave here with him."

Seyn growled.

Veyl stood her ground, bolstered by the wave dancer. "And who will protect me from you?"

"The Tempest defends his own, if they deserve it."

"I do not believe in your Tempest."

He caught her jaw, his strong fingers pressing into her skin. Her heart pounded with fear, her ability crackling to life. Desperately, she wrestled it back. What would Heshara do if she felt that power rising when he had them separated in this way? Would she still use the zenyal bond to subdue her, putting her entirely at the wavelord's mercy? Did Jaysen know he had delivered her into a viper's den?

"Your beliefs do not matter. You are His." He leaned up alongside her, his lips brushing her ear when he whispered, "I can feel the storm in you." He moved back in front of her, close enough that his lips nearly touched hers when he spoke. "I can smell it every time you exhale."

"Get your hands off her."

Veyl's breath caught at the sound of that voice, and she jerked away from Kronach. With her eyes adjusting to the poor lighting, she could see now that they were in a dusty corridor lined with cells. All of them were empty except for the second on the right, where Kyril stood leaning against the bars, as if they were all that kept him upright. About halfway down, two of Kronach's warriors waited at silent attention, barely visible in the shadowy interior.

Her first inclination was to run to Kyril, but she held herself still, glancing warily at the wavelord. What game was he playing?

"That one is also wave-touched. Tell me, what is the connection between you?"

She looked at Kyril, recalling the moment he said they belonged together as they lay naked in his bed. "Our paths crossed by chance in Deepwater," she answered cautiously.

Interest lit his dark eye, and he walked toward Kyril. "You are the one Thrasser recruited to dispose of the undead prince for him?"

Kyril looked at her in question.

Realizing the problem, she repeated Kronach's words in Vanrian.

Kyril said nothing, his wary gaze returning to the wavelord.

Kronach glanced back at her. "You were this man's victim as well, yet you do not despise him as the prince does."

Veyl fell back upon the safety of silence as Kyril had. If only she had the slightest clue where the wavelord was going with all of this. Why had he brought her here?

Seyn moved a few steps closer to the cell, her ears perked and head cocked to one side as she considered Kyril.

Kronach smiled at the wave dancer, the gentleness of the expression out of place on his scarred, brutal countenance. After a second, he turned his hard gaze on Kyril again, pointing at Seyn. "You are a Feral. This beast should be yours."

"She is the companion of another," Kyril said, guessing his meaning well enough from his body language. He sounded exhausted. The beating they had given him at the docks had worsened the swelling and bruising on his face and split the skin in a few places, though it looked as though someone had at least cleaned the injuries.

Kronach glanced expectantly at Veyl, who translated Kyril's words into Pandrean Common for him.

"The woman outside? She is not wave-touched."

"Wave-touched or not, Ahninveth Heshara and Seyn are bonded," Veyl said, feeling a twinge of guilt at leaving Kyril out of the conversation.

Staring at Kyril, Kronach gestured to Seyn again. "Take the beast from her. Now."

Kyril shook his head, looking confused.

"He wants you to take her from Heshara," Veyl explained, unease prickling up her spine.

Jaysen hadn't looked pleased the previous day when Kronach insisted on his warriors taking charge of Kyril. They had escorted him out of the audience hall and apparently deposited him here in this block of cells that didn't appear to see much use, judging by the accumulation of dust and cobwebs. Did Jaysen and his allies know where Kronach had put him? If not, there could be an opportunity in that, though she wasn't sure how to make use of the knowledge yet. If Kyril tried to take control of Seyn for the wavelord's amusement, however, Heshara would find out he was in here and any opportunity would be lost.

"Don't do it." She said in Vanrian, glaring defiance at Kronach when he turned his attention to her again. His predatory grin as he strode back to her sent a flush of panic through her, but she stood her ground, continuing to suppress her ability with grim resolve.

"You told him not to, didn't you? You care what happens to this man." He grinned as though he had solved a particularly complicated puzzle. "Two wave-touched outsiders in my hall at the same time. I knew there must be a connection between you." He moved in uncomfortably close again, as if the concept of respectful distance entirely eluded him. "I wonder what you will do now that you have seen where I am keeping him? How much would you give to prevent the others from finding out?" He brought one hand up, tracing his fingertips along the line of her jaw. "What have you to offer but your flesh?"

The unwelcome touch took her back to her bed the night Jaysen betrayed their friendship. Something snapped in Veyl, and she grabbed one of his swords with her right hand. His reflexes were frighteningly fast. He had his dagger out in the same heartbeat and rammed the hilt into her wrist hard enough to knock the weapon from her grasp. But that had merely been a distraction. With her left hand, she drew his other sword and thrust up toward his chest below the sternum. What she didn't expect was for him to grab the blade with his bare hand and yank it away from her. Casting it aside, he slammed her back into the wall, setting his bone-handled dagger to her throat.

"Veyl!" Kyril grabbed the bars, helpless to intervene.

"Do nothing," she demanded, afraid he would try taking Seyn to help her. Her heart raced, and her wrist throbbed from the wavelord's strike.

"There you are." Kronach's broad smile told her he was enjoying this game too much for her taste. "Those were training swords," he said with a chuckle. "If you were truly wave-touched, I knew you would only put up with so much. I am not such a fool that I would risk provoking you with a sharpened blade in your reach."

The edge of the blade against her neck was sharp enough she could tell the dagger wasn't a training weapon despite his statement, even if the others had been, but he had been right to assume she would go for the swords. Seyn was growling, and she could hear shouting outside, though the heavy door and stone walls muffled it too much for her to make out any words. Seyn's distress would have been enough to let Heshara know something was wrong.

"Get away from her."

Kyril's demand held little weight from behind the bars unless he used the wave dancer to try enforcing it, but so far he heeded her warning not to.

She stared into Kronach's good eye. "What are you after?"

The wavelord backed away and sheathed the dagger. She stepped out from the wall, watching him pick up the two swords that she could now see had blunted edges. That didn't lessen her desire to grab one and club him over the head with it. He sheathed the two weapons and spun to face her, the sudden ferocity in his bearing enough that she pressed back against the wall again, her breath catching in her throat.

"The Tempest placed you in my halls for a reason," he growled. "Look at where you are compared to where you should be and decide what you will do about the fact that the two are not the same." He turned and stalked toward the door.

She stared after him for a moment, processing his words. He had shown her where Kyril was. He believed they were both touched by his god and was encouraging her to correct her situation. Might he be willing to help them? "Wait!"

Kronach turned and shook his head. "Do not mistake me for an ally, Khesran. I am merely the Tempest's messenger. I will not allow the prince to harm you here, but place yourself at my mercy, and you will find I have none." He slipped out the door, leaving her behind in the dim corridor of cells.

She could hear more raised voices outside now. Her guards wouldn't like him emerging without her, and she didn't want to risk anyone else coming in. She had to hurry.

Racing over to the cell, she grabbed Kyril's hand through the bars. His startled reaction confused her, but there wasn't time to question it. She winced at the visible marks from the abuse he had suffered. Perhaps she had caused him pain. "I will get you out of here."

For a moment, he stared at the hand holding his, as if he couldn't figure out what it was, then he looked up and shook his head. "No, you won't. I'm not in any condition to run. I'll only slow you down. Take my sister and flee this place."

The weakness in his grip supported his words, but Veyl refused to give up that easily. "I'm not leaving you in Jaysen's hands. If you can't escape, I won't either. I'll send Kitria and Gannon without me."

"Don't be a fool. What he will do to you is worse than the death that awaits me."

Veyl met his eyes. The voices outside were growing louder, the argument becoming more heated. Seyn raced to the door, snarling in distress.

"I need to go, but I will be back." She yearned to kiss him, but with his injuries and Kronach's warriors watching, it would be a poor choice. Turning from him, she hurried toward the door, feeling as though some piece of her was being left behind.

"You haven't got a key," Kyril said, barely loud enough for her to hear and despise the truth of his words.

CHAPTER TWENTY ONE

Veyl ducked out through the door and yanked it shut behind her to avoid anyone seeing what, or who, was within, though the stark contrast in lighting would undoubtedly be enough to prevent that. Heshara had her sword out and was bleeding from one corner of her mouth as if someone had struck her. Seyn bolted over beside her companion, taking up a defensive posture and baring her teeth. The other two Thaelian guards had their weapons out as well, though they looked reluctant to engage the wavelord and his four warriors. Unarmed as she was, Kitria had the sense to stay behind them.

When Veyl emerged, Kronach straightened, lowering his swords. He still carried the training weapons, though she wasn't sure if the others had noticed that yet, and she had a feeling he could do plenty of damage with them, even lacking a sharpened edge.

The wavelord gestured to her with one blade. "There, your princess is unharmed."

Veyl scowled at him for switching back to the southern title, his faint answering smirk telling her it pleased him to annoy her again. She faced the Thaelian Feral, speaking in Vanrian now. "I'm all right. He was merely showing off his power."

Heshara turned her anger on Veyl, the less threatening target. "You will not leave our sight again outside your private chambers." Perhaps to emphasize the point, a spear of pain pierced through Veyl's skull, knocking her to her knees.

The wave dancer snarled. It almost seemed as if the beast directed her anger at her bonded companion, though Veyl couldn't focus well enough past that flare of agony to be certain. Then Heshara hit the ground in front of her, and the pain stopped. Fresh tension charged the air as Kitria hurried to Veyl's side to help her up.

Kronach stood over the Thaelian Feral, the end of his blunted blade hovering inches from her nose. "Whatever that was, if you do it again within my halls, you will die for it. There is no place for your mind-crafting here. As I understand it, your people need the undead prince to get your land back, and he requires my support to help him secure Sarket before he can do that. Do not make yourself the reason he fails."

He looked pointedly at Veyl, and she translated his words for Heshara exactly as he had spoken them. When she finished, she offered him a nod to let him know as much.

Without waiting for a response, he returned to his warriors and traded sword belts with one of them. "Show the princess the rest of the castle grounds," he told them before stalking away.

She watched him leave, not as comforted as she wanted to be by the fact that he appeared to mean what he said about protecting her here.

Kitria leaned close and whispered, "Are you truly all right?"

Veyl rubbed the tender place on her wrist where he had struck her with his dagger and quietly answered, "We'll talk about it later."

Though a significant amount of tension remained among the Thaelians, the Eydarith warriors, who appeared to share their warlord's confidence, provided her group with a thorough tour of the castle and grounds. Veyl paid keen attention to everything they showed her, watching carefully for any promising escape routes. The closer to Kyril's location, the better. She asked about the areas they visited at every opportunity, making her questions frequent enough that no one was likely to wonder when she inquired about where a certain hall led or what was behind any one door.

When the Eydarith warriors showed them back to her room a few hours later, her mind raced with possibilities, all of which presented challenges, the most obvious of those being the obstacle of freeing Kyril from his cell. Heshara watched them enter the bedchamber without saying a word, though the look of loathing she gave Veyl when she shut the door behind them sent a chill through her. The moment they were alone, Veyl filled Kitria in on what had happened when the wavelord isolated her from them and who else had been there.

While they discussed ideas for escaping Taro, she worked on the missive to send to her family. It said what Jaysen wanted it to, declaring that she was with him by choice and desired a marriage that would unify their countries. She made a point of professing her love for him, because it would please him to see it written and hopefully blind him to the subtle clues she wove throughout to expose the lie of it to her parents, assuming it ever reached them. In it, she also included an earnestly phrased request for an alliance with Sarket and the release of Thaelis back to the council's control. How he could believe Vanris would ally with him after what he had done in Thaelis she couldn't imagine, but maybe he had a plan for trying to manipulate that narrative. She was hesitant to ask and risk pointing out a flaw in his plan that might anger him.

She had barely finished it when the door flew open and Jaysen stormed in. He slammed it behind him, his features flushed when he turned on her.

"Did Kronach lock you in a room alone with him?" he demanded.

Veyl stood, a metallic taste spreading over her tongue. "He did, but—"

He got in her face, his voice rising to a shout. "Did he touch you?"

She forced a placating smile, all too aware of how thin an edge he balanced on. "The wavelord was merely testing to see what he could get away with, but he didn't try anything. Not that I would have let him had he done so."

"I will kill him."

She caught his arm when he turned toward the door. He spun back, raising a hand as if to strike her, but in his moment of hesitation she stepped closer, placing a palm against his cheek and meeting his eyes. "You won't." She made her voice gentle, but firm. "He can help you reclaim your throne. Use him now. Punish him later when you have the power if you feel it is necessary, but do not let his games stand in the way of your goal."

His shoulders heaved with his fast, angry breaths, but he held her gaze. When she brushed her thumb over his cheek, the tension eased and his shoulders sank a fraction. "I don't want him near you again."

Veyl nodded, keeping her voice soft and placating. "We'll be more cautious from now on." She gestured to the desk. "Here, I wrote the missive you asked for."

Jaysen stepped past her and picked it up, reading over it. Though she yearned to move away from him, in his explosive state she feared the action might raise his ire again, so she stood her ground, staying close enough to watch his pinched brows relax and a faint, victorious smile curve his lips as his gaze moved over her words.

After a moment, he set the missive down and turned, taking her in his arms and kissing her greedily. Her stomach twisted, and she suppressed her hatred and the threatening tears as she forced herself to kiss him in return. One of his hands slid to the small of her back, pulling her closer. With the other, he brushed her hair out of his way. Releasing her mouth, he trailed kisses down her neck in an alarming display of passion. His hand slid up her side to cup her breast over the dress, and it took all of her will to keep from pulling away or tensing in his arms.

She couldn't bear to let him do this, but how was she supposed to justify stopping him and still maintain her ruse?

He released her abruptly and drew back, breathing hard for a different reason now. "My apologies." He adjusted the front of his pants as his gaze raked over her, never reaching her eyes. "I don't want our first time together to be in that man's castle."

"I understand," she answered, making it the breathless whisper he would expect to hear. Silently, she thanked Kronach. It seemed the wavelord was protecting her in ways neither of them could have possibly anticipated.

He picked up the missive again. "This is perfection. As you requested, I will send Gannon with Kronach's messenger to Vanris this afternoon."

Touching his shoulder, her pulse racing with trepidation, she asked, "Since I won't be returning to Vanris, might I speak to Gannon before he leaves? I'd like to give him a personal message for his brother and Iyvalin. Nothing substantial enough to need writing out, just a few words to carry back to honor our friendships."

He reached out and cupped her cheek, the sympathy in his gaze making her hate him more. "You realize they may not have survived the Unclean attack, and, even if they did, there's a fair chance they won't be in Vanris when he arrives there."

She supposed he wouldn't like it if she bit his hand, but imagining doing so helped her keep her expression from souring. "Yes, but if they did survive, they may return—"

"Fine," he snapped. "I'd rather watch Gannon choke on his own blood for how he treated me when I lived with you, but because you asked and…" he paused, his tone softening again as he stroked her cheek with his thumb, "and because you are remembering your love for me, I will allow him to be your messenger. You may speak with him briefly before he departs, but you will keep this in mind next time you want to ask me for favors. I can't give in to all your impulses."

How desperately she wanted to hurt him. "Thank you," she choked the words out past the bitter taste of resentment on her tongue.

"We'll see him off together later. For now, I need to meet with the council and our most offensive host."

He wouldn't let her meet with Gannon alone, then. Not that she had expected him to, but it was still disappointing. "Remember, get what you want from the wavelord now. You can punish him for his behavior later."

He smiled and leaned in to kiss her one more time. "You will be a marvelous queen," he said before walking out.

Veyl put a hand to her stomach, trying not to be sick.

Kitria came over with a goblet of more sweet wine that someone had delivered while they were gone. "You look like you could use this."

Veyl took it and used some to rinse her mouth before downing the rest in one swallow. "If I have to kiss him many more times, I may throw myself from the highest tower."

"If I have to continue watching you do so, I may join you. I'm afraid he's going to push for more one of these days, regardless of how he claims to feel about taking you in Kronach's castle. We need to get you out of here."

Her stomach clenched at the thought. "I know."

"You could bite his tongue off."

Veyl snorted a laugh. "That's disgusting."

"True, but it would serve him right."

A servant came to add wood to the fireplace in the sparsely furnished sitting area and delivered a light meal. After eating, they turned their attention back to discussing options for escape and how they could free Kyril from his cell. One of the two warriors Veyl had seen in that corridor might have the key. But they had no way of knowing that for certain, so they tried to plan for the possibility of the key being somewhere beyond their reach. If they bolted in the middle of the night, most people would be asleep, which meant any overflow from the use of her ability would present itself merely as nightmares.

The first significant challenge was how to escape the bedroom. Two Thaelian soldiers were outside the door at all hours, and they had no windows to try climbing through. Veyl could neutralize the guards with an excessive application of her ability, its absurd strength offering a rare advantage in this situation, but that would also alert Heshara, who was staying in the next room. She and Kitria were both combat trained, so they might defeat the guards outside without utilizing her Frightener ability, but the risk of making a racket that someone could overhear increased with that approach.

"What about luring Heshara in here with a light use of your ability?" Kitria suggested. "After what happened in the courtyard, she might be more circumspect about defaulting to the zenyal bond as her first response."

Veyl ran a finger around the rim of the goblet she had been drinking from. "That could work, but it still requires gambling on a lot of uncertainties. What if she doesn't react as expected or if a guard cries out before we can silence them? What if we can't find the key? We only get one chance at this. I shudder to think what Jaysen will do if we were to try and fail."

"You should shudder," Kitria said, a visible shiver moving through her. "He would simply kill me, along with my brother. Not that I have any desire to die, but I expect he would be a lot more creative with your punishment, since he needs you alive."

Veyl set down the goblet, her stomach turning. A knock on the door made her jump. Heshara opened it without waiting for a response.

"We're to escort you to the courtyard to see off your messenger." Her tone was flat, her hard gaze making it clear she still held Veyl at fault for Kronach's actions.

They both stood and followed her from the room. The current two guards fell in behind them, and Heshara took up position on Veyl's left, with Seyn between them.

Part of the building Kronach was keeping Kyril in was visible from the courtyard they walked to. That corridor of cells connected to the wall that enclosed the castle grounds, making that gate their best choice for an escape attempt. In that respect, she was grateful for the opportunity to revisit the space, even if it required being around Jaysen.

Three horses waited with two of Kronach's people and Gannon. She suspected they were sending an extra warrior along with the messenger in case Gannon caused any problems. Given how confident the Eydarith were in their skills, the addition was most likely Jaysen's idea. It was unfortunate, but Gannon would have to make his own decisions on how to deal with that.

Jaysen was there with a few of his Thaelian soldiers. He smiled and held a hand out to her when she entered the courtyard. Forcing a smile in return, she walked up and accepted his hand, allowing him to draw her close to him. He placed a light kiss on her lips, then drew back and gave Gannon a smug smile, making it clear he had done so to provoke him. Judging by the tension in Gannon's bearing and the way his face flushed, he had succeeded. Jaysen passed her the missive.

"Here, my love, I will let you do the honors of sending this on its journey."

It was so hard to keep that smile on her face as she took the letter and turned to meet Gannon's accusatory glower. She walked up to him, coming a step closer than necessary, and held the missive up.

"Please see that this ends up in my parents' hands."

He snatched it from her and nodded, saying nothing as he tucked it into a satchel they had provided him with.

Veyl's nerves danced. "Also," she said, stopping him when he started turning toward the horses, "could you tell Ahrin and Iyvalin that I miss and love them, but that I am well?"

His gaze flickered to Jaysen and back. "If I see them."

"And be careful." She stepped in, wrapping her arms around him in a friendly hug, and leaned close enough to whisper in his ear. "Kitria and I will try to escape tomorrow night."

She felt the slightest tensing in him, then he hugged her briefly back.

"Take care of yourself," he said as they parted, holding to his gruff tone, though she could see the burning desire to say more in his eyes now.

Before he could do anything that might rouse suspicion, she turned away and walked back to Jaysen, letting him slide a hand around her waist and pull her close. Gannon mounted the horse they provided for him, not looking at her as the Eydarith messenger and accompanying warrior swung up on their mounts. She watched the three trot out of the courtyard, wishing she could have said more. If their escape attempt was unsuccessful, she might never see him again.

That evening, Kronach invited them all to a formal dinner to recognize his alliance with Sarket's rightful king. An event which, in his halls, turned out to be what she would consider a casual affair with much drinking, boisterous telling of tales, and laughter. The Eydarith women looked as fierce as the men, and their voices appeared to be granted as much weight, an unusual sight within Sarket's borders. The people of the Eydarith—children of the Tempest—were less like other natives in their country than her academic studies led her to believe, though Sarket's leadership had long downplayed their presence in the kingdom. A deliberate effort, perhaps, to keep outsiders from learning how separate from the rest of Sarketi culture they actually were, and how strong. They didn't seem overly concerned by the outsiders in their midst, and an open acceptance of and respect for one another supported their authentic, fearless demeanor.

Throughout the evening, whenever Jaysen wasn't looking in Kronach's direction, the wavelord watched Veyl, a challenge in his gaze that left her shifting in her seat. To the rest of his people, she could have been invisible. For her part, she tried to avoid meeting Kronach's eyes and said little, speaking solely when Jaysen asked her to translate something for the Thaelians. Otherwise, she sipped at her drink and smiled at Jaysen when his attention turned her way. Under the table, her left hand ended up in Kitria's much of the time. She wasn't sure which of them initiated that contact, but it offered them both comfort in a place where they had little outside of each other.

When Veyl begged off late into the evening to get some rest, Jaysen rose as if intending to join her. He stumbled, his balance sacrificed to too much drink, and grinned at her with a hunger that chilled her. One hand clumsily cupped her cheek, the gesture lacking any trace of gentleness.

"I'll walk you…to your room," he said with a distinct slur to his speech.

"Tell us about Thrasser, King Jaysen." Though Kronach also slurred his speech, the sharpness in his one-eyed gaze suggested he wasn't anywhere near as inebriated as he sounded. "He seems an impotent man to me. How do you plan to be rid of him?"

"Ha! An appropriate choice of words!" Jaysen turned to him, dropping back into his chair and raising his mug.

As he began enthusiastically recounting some tale to illustrate Thrasser's incompetence, Veyl ducked silently from the hall with Kitria. Heshara and two guards followed them. Back in the room, she sank into a chair, resenting the tremble of fear in her hands.

Kitria scooted another chair closer and placed a hand on her arm. "Do you think he might seek you out later tonight?"

Veyl nodded, swallowing against the bile that rushed up in her throat at the prospect. "I don't know if I can let him…"

"I suspect Kronach will try to keep him until he's too drunk to follow through." The slight faltering of Kitria's smirk didn't inspire confidence. "You know, I doubted the Qwilki when they started calling you Seh'hali, but I can't help wondering if there's something to it now. The wavelord clearly believes there is a connection to their ocean god in you. Whatever it is, it's working in our favor right now."

Veyl barely heard her words. She shuddered, remembering Jaysen's hand on her breast, his lips against her neck. Every time he kissed her, she despised it more.

How much longer could it go on before her willpower faltered at the wrong moment?

Kitria squeezed her hand. "Let's get some sleep. Tomorrow, we'll finalize our plans and leave this nightmare behind."

Veyl merely nodded.

•

Sometime late in the night, Veyl opened her eyes to Jaysen standing over her, licking his lips like a man ready to dine. He threw off the covers and drew up the skirt of her sleeping gown, exposing her. Clumsy fingers crept slowly up her inner thigh, his lips parting slightly when he stopped mere inches from the top. Something in his slow, cruel smile sparked a terror that paralyzed her. She couldn't move or speak. She could barely breathe as he stripped off his clothes and climbed onto the bed over her, using his legs to force hers apart. Tears trickled from her eyes, running down into her hair, screams of protest locked in her mind. When he pressed himself against her, fingers drunkenly fumbling to help him find his target, lightning sparked to life in her chest.

Veyl startled awake from the nightmare to a violent flare of pain in her skull that disrupted her power and left her writhing in agony. Heshara settled on the edge of the bed, staring down at her in the dim, flickering light of the one candle they had left burning.

"Drawing upon your ability in your sleep now? I wonder what dreams you were having."

"Let her go, Ahninveth." Kitria demanded, sitting up next to her on the opposite side of the bed. "She obviously wasn't trying to hurt anyone."

"That makes it worse, don't you agree?" Heshara's

expression didn't change, but the pain increased. "Tell me, little khesran, did you find it amusing to have that bastard attack and threaten me earlier?"

Veyl's skull felt like it was breaking apart. She squeezed her head, tears streaming from her eyes as she curled in on herself, her ability unable to save her from this assault. "Stop," she whimpered.

Seyn came to the edge of the bed and took her companion's hand gently in her mouth with a low whine. Heshara jerked it away, smacking the wave dancer across the muzzle.

"It's not so humorous now, is it?" she snapped.

The pain soared to greater heights, and Veyl could no longer do so much as draw a breath. The room blurred.

"You've made your point. You're going to do permanent damage if you don't stop." Kitria started around the foot of the bed as if considering physical intervention.

Heshara ignored her, continuing the torture for what felt like an eternity, though it had certainly been mere seconds. "Remember this, Khesran." The assault stopped when she stood and headed toward the door.

Veyl was shaking uncontrollably, her cheeks damp with tears.

Halfway to the door, Seyn stopped and met Veyl's eyes. The wave dancer sank to her belly and pressed her head to the floor between her forelegs, closing her eyes and pinning back her ears as though bracing for something.

"I will remember," Veyl murmured.

The storm within her burst to life, striking out at Heshara, violent and pure. The wave dancer made no effort to intervene and protect her Feral companion. Heshara stopped in her tracks. The door flew open, and the guards rushed in, drawing their swords. Veyl lashed out at them as well, watching as their alarm disappeared, their features going slack. The weapons fell to the floor. Blood trickled from their ears and noses, and from their eyes like strange tears.

Veyl stared at the three Thaelians, the crackle of her ability fading away. There hadn't even been enough time for her to get caught up in their fears.

"We leave tonight then." Kitria hurried to the door and peeked out. She ducked back in and took one guard, guiding the catatonic man toward the hall.

"Wait." Veyl got unsteadily to her feet and rushed over, using one loose sleeve to wipe the blood from the guard's face. When she was done, Kitria sheathed the man's weapon and took him back to his place outside the door while Veyl cleaned off the face of the second one.

Seyn stood beside Heshara now, nosing her hand and whining softly.

While Kitria guided the second guard out, Veyl crouched before the amphibious canine. "I am sorry. I can't imagine what that cost you, but I thank you for not stopping me."

The wave dancer's head and tail hung, her ears drooping. She whined softly, the sound replete with sorrow. Guilt twisted in Veyl's chest. For a bonded beast to betray their own companion was unheard of. What must it have cost the poor creature to hold back at that moment and allow Heshara to be broken?

"Come with us," Veyl whispered.

"We have to leave now." Kitria shut the door and started changing into the pants and shirt she had been wearing when they arrived.

Veyl followed her example, pulling off the bloodied sleeping gown and hurrying into the dress she had worn during the day. It wasn't ideal for an escape, but the strips of fabric that made up the skirt allowed for greater freedom of movement than most dresses, and it was long enough to obscure the tall boots she pulled on. If they were lucky, anyone who saw them from a distance would see the Eydarith attire and not pay them any attention. Someone closer would hopefully not make the immediate connection that this was an escape attempt, at least not before they could neutralize the threat.

They weren't ready for this, not really, but what choice did they have now? No one else had come running yet, which meant anyone within range of the overflow from her ability was asleep. They may have experienced a dark turn in their dreams, but that shouldn't be enough to wake them. Still, the moment someone wandered by and noticed something was wrong with her two guards, the game was up. She wasn't sure whether they had patrols checking these halls at night or not. That was one of several details they had intended to investigate during the day. Now they would have to take their chances.

Before they left the room, she knelt in front of the wave dancer again. "I don't know that I deserve the sacrifice you have given me, but if you join us, I will do everything I can to make it up to you."

"Veyl," Kitria urged.

She stood and joined the other woman by the door.

Kitria cracked it and peered out into the dimly lit hall beyond. After a moment, she pulled it the rest of the way open. Veyl grabbed the sleeping dress and handed it to her.

"Take their daggers and wrap them in this. We might need weapons at some point."

Kitria nodded, and they made fast work of tucking the weapons out of sight in the bundle. Their swords would have been preferable, but harder to hide, and any-one glancing this way at a distance might notice the guards were unarmed and come to investigate.

Veyl looked back one last time, meeting the wave dancer's eyes. When they snuck off down the hall, Seyn came with them.

CHAPTER TWENTY TWO

It was a short walk to where they were keeping Kyril, but every step was fraught with tension. Twice they had to hide, once in an alcove and again in a sitting room, when they heard someone coming. Seyn hid with them, her careful, alert manner making it clear she understood the need for caution. Both times, the patrols were Kronach's Eydarith warriors. One of them glanced in their direction as he passed, and Veyl would have sworn he looked right at them, but he didn't slow or give any indication he had noticed anything amiss.

In the small courtyard, Veyl paused outside the door leading to the prison corridor. Kyril would undoubtedly still have guards. The question was how they would respond. Would they attack, or might they sound an alarm? Kitria claimed to be competent in a fight, and Veyl had little choice but to believe her. Something about the Eydarith made her reluctant to face them in combat, but if they wanted to free Kyril, she didn't see how they were going to avoid it. In the end, she would rather take her chances fighting them than risk one of them slipping away and alerting the rest of the castle. But that assumed there would still be only two of them.

She met Kitria's eyes. The young woman nodded, and Veyl's chest tightened. Kyril would never forgive her if she led his sister to her death while he looked on.

Although he might be able to help now if Seyn would consent to working with him.

She eased the door open enough to slip inside. With it dark outside, her eyes didn't need to adjust. Kyril lay on the hard cot in his cell. Two of Kronach's warriors stood in the hall just past it. Neither moved, though they were looking directly at her when she advanced to make room for Kitria and Seyn.

"Give those to me," she whispered, reaching back.

"Both of them?"

"Yes."

Kitria unwrapped the daggers. Neither guard moved until Veyl reached for the weapons, then they both placed their hands on the hilts of their swords in nearly perfect unison. Veyl stopped short of taking them. Slowly, she brought her hands back to her sides, and the warriors did the same, letting their arms relax. Kronach claimed that she and Kyril were wave-touched, favored by the Eydarith god. Exactly how much protection did that afford them here?

"Put them away," she said, advancing again.

"Veyl?"

The edge of worry in Kitria's tone plucked at her nerves, but she continued forward, gesturing to the occupied cell without taking her eyes off the two warriors. "Wake your brother."

At the sound of their soft voices, Kyril shifted and sat up. He stumbled to the front of his cell when he saw them. Kitria hurried to him while Veyl advanced down the center, watching the Eydarith. In her periphery, she saw Kitria grab her brother's hands through the bars.

"Kit, you shouldn't be here. Neither of you should."

"I'm not losing you too," she hissed back.

Veyl was a few feet from the two warriors now. Not far beyond them was a side alcove. She could see two rows of rusty keys hanging on equally rusty hooks on the far wall. More evidence that this area saw little use.

She stopped, searching their eyes. "Will you let me pass?"

The two stared ahead, expressions unchanging, bodies unmoving.

Swallowing, she continued forward, Seyn at her side. The warriors stood still as statues, saying and doing nothing as she passed between them and hurried to the wall of keys. There appeared to be the same number of keys as there were cells. Assuming some rationale to their arrangement, she guessed they lined up to match the cells, but did the top row represent the left or the right, and which end of the corridor corresponded with which end of the rows? After a moment, she grabbed the four keys in the positions that would align to his cell for each possibility.

When she moved between the guards again, it was impossible not to dread the agony of a blade in her back, but it never came. Racing to Kyril's cell, she pushed the first key into the lock, casting it aside when it wouldn't turn.

"Seh'hali."

Veyl glanced up into those silver-blue eyes within the mass of bruises and cuts. Her chest tightened, and tears threatened. She focused on the lock through the blurring of her vision, trying the next key and tossing it aside when it failed to work.

"I'll slow you down."

"Shut up," Kitria snapped at him. "Hurry, Veyl."

Veyl tried the third key, gasping with relief when it turned, and the door clicked open. She stepped back, casting a glance at the two Eydarith as Kitria rushed in, sliding a shoulder under her brother's arm to help him. When they were free of the cell, Veyl did the same on his other side. She longed to kiss him and hold him, but reunions would have to wait. They were far from free yet.

Kyril was limping and unsteady on his feet. She could feel him struggling to carry most of his own weight. They helped him along, passing between the two guards who made no move to interfere.

"Why don't they stop us?" Kyril asked, his voice strained, likely with pain from unseen injuries.

"Later," she managed.

The walk to the door that would take them into the wall surrounding the keep was agonizingly slow. They were near the courtyard she had sent Gannon off from. During part of their tour of the grounds, they had walked along the outer battlement atop the wall and spotted a stable alongside a tavern outside that they both marked as an option if they needed to steal horses. Given Kyril's condition, it was safe to assume they did.

When they reached the door, she glanced down at Seyn. The wave dancer stepped up to it, going still as her ears perked forward. After a second, she looked up at Veyl, giving a slight wag of her tail. Hoping that meant what she thought it did, Veyl left Kyril and eased the door open a crack to peek through. The passage within the outer wall was empty and cold. Flickering light from a torch affixed near the far left corner barely reached them. The one near the end on the right, where the hallway stopped at the gate, provided more illumination to navigate by.

They entered and turned toward the courtyard and the gatehouse. There would be an exit there. Most likely a guarded one.

"Do you want the daggers?" Kitria whispered.

Veyl glanced over at them where they were now tucked awkwardly in the other woman's belt. "Yes."

They stopped, and Kitria passed her the weapons, which she shoved into the belt of her dress. It wasn't ideal, but it would have to do. She didn't intend to touch them unless the guards attacked at this point. It might be foolish to believe Kronach's people would let them simply walk out, but starting a fight if it wasn't necessary and risking injury or death struck her as equally foolish given what had, or rather, hadn't happened in the prison corridor.

Kyril stood silent through their exchange, the furrows in his brow suggesting his focus was on staying upright. As they slipped into position to move again, the sound of footsteps behind them set off a surge of panic, bringing her ability crackling to life. Veyl twisted under Kyril's arm to look the other way. An Eydarith warrior stopped at the corner and stared at them for a few tense heartbeats, then he turned and headed back the way he had come, his strides measured and unhurried.

With her stomach in knots, she met Kitria's gaze in front of Kyril, and they both resumed moving. Before they made it to the corner, she could hear voices. She extracted herself and crept forward to peek around.

Two women and a man, all wearing the armor of Kronach's warriors, were in the main room of the gatehouse. One woman stood near a window looking out. The other two sat at a table, their chairs facing the one at the window. To Veyl's surprise, the language they spoke wasn't familiar, though it made use of some Sarketi words and one or two she caught in Pandrean Common. It sounded like a blend of the two languages with something else mixed in. Eydarith was, based upon her studies, a less prevalent Sarketi religion, overshadowed by Havaad worship, but what she had seen so far in Taro suggested they were their own well-established culture. Under different circumstances, she would have loved to dig into it more.

Drawing a shaky breath, Veyl stepped out from the corner. The woman by the window glanced at her companions, her gaze flickering briefly up to Veyl. Her conversational tone didn't change, though it was impossible to tell if she said anything about their newly arrived company. Neither of the other two turned to look. It was as if they were pretending not to see her. Out of curiosity, Veyl placed a hand on one dagger. The woman's gaze shifted to her, eyes narrowing a fraction. When she moved her hand away, the warrior gave her attention back to the conversation.

On the far side of the gatehouse was a door leading out of the castle grounds. It would put them in a position to sneak to the stable alongside the tavern. It felt absurd to even humor the idea that Kronach's warriors might allow the three of them to walk past and leave, and yet none had attempted to stop them so far. The most they had done up to now was discourage her from drawing a weapon.

Nerves on fire, she returned to the other two.

"We're walking out. Let me have that side." She shooed Kitria over to Kyril's left. If the Eydarith did attack, she needed to be in position to react quickly. "There's a door in the far wall. If they try to stop us, I want the two of you to get out of here."

"No." Kyril gave her a hard look. "We're not leaving you."

She scowled at him. "Kit?"

Kitria positioned herself under his left arm and nodded to Veyl. "I'll make sure of it."

Veyl moved into place on his right, and they entered the gatehouse. The warriors continued their conversation without the slightest pause or glance in their direction, as if three escapees walking slowly past was a daily occurrence, so they continued ahead, Kitria reaching out to unbolt the door and push it open. The disconcerting behavior of the guards left Veyl feeling like she didn't exist, or perhaps she was dreaming, and this was all part of the nightmare that began with Jaysen standing over her bed. What if she had never woken up?

The steps leading out the front of the gatehouse required their full attention, so Veyl didn't bother shutting the door behind them. They were halfway down when one warrior closed it. This wasn't the primary entrance into the castle grounds, which meant the road was narrower and not as well-lit as the other might have been. Still, wary of being spotted, they hurried into the deeper shadows and approached the stable from behind. If they were to have any hope of sneaking out of the city before someone who cared noticed their absence, they needed to move faster. That meant acquiring at least one mount for Kyril, if not more.

When they slipped quietly in through the back entrance, Veyl spotted a horse tied in an open stall near the front, saddled and ready to go. A common practice when someone didn't plan to stay long. The animal was big and solidly built.

Veyl tapped Kitria's arm. "Can you ride?"

"I've ridden kednu two or three times."

The large deer Jinau had mentioned on their way to Etrion from the coast. The thought of him caused an ache in her chest. "That'll have to be sufficient."

Moving fast, they helped Kyril up onto the animal's back. Kitria climbed awkwardly up to sit in front of him. Given their height difference, she couldn't sit behind him and still see where they were going, so they had to trust that Kyril could hold on to her.

Veyl put a hand on Kyril's arm. "Can you get Seyn to scout ahead?"

His focus turned inward. The wave dancer's ears perked up, and she whined softly, but after a moment, Kyril nodded. "She'll work with me."

"Good. You two get moving. I'll grab another horse and catch up."

"Veyl." His strained voice held the tone of an argument.

She avoided his gaze. "Kit?"

Kitria nodded. "We'll see you in a few minutes."

Veyl walked with them to the back entrance and peered out to check for danger before sending them off. She watched the gelding head up the backstreet with Seyn in the lead, then ducked back inside to find a mount for herself. Bareback she could do, but she wasn't confident she could direct an unfamiliar animal without a proper bridle, so she slipped into the tack room and grabbed the first two she saw.

A noise near the front of the building caught her attention as she was stepping back out. When she turned to see what it was, she heard the soft, familiar sound of a crossbow releasing behind her. She twisted, dropping the bridles. Pain flared as the bolt skimmed across her cheekbone, lightly nicking her ear on the way past. Her ability crackled to life, and she hastily suppressed it, afraid of drawing more unwanted attention, but not before it crashed up against a mind she couldn't touch. Another Frightener.

The person with the crossbow ducked out of sight in an open stall to reload. The other, the Frightener, was coming at Veyl from the front, a Thaelian man with hair as black as Kyril's, only shorter. But the Thaelians didn't have any Frighteners, unless the council had lied about that too.

Drawing the daggers from her belt as warm blood ran down her cheek from a line of pain, Veyl charged the man. He drew a sword and dagger, also fighting two-handed. Her usual ambidextrous advantage might not be as useful here.

Desperation fueled her speed. She blocked the sword with one dagger, striking out with the other. He twisted, barely avoiding her blade, and made a quick attack of his own. The sting of a shallow cut along her forearm reminded her that, unlike him, she wore no armor. Shuffling behind her warned her that the one with the crossbow had stepped back out. With the speed and intensity of her opponent, she couldn't focus enough to try addressing the ranged threat with her ability. Instead, she twisted clear of a strike and maneuvered around the Frightener, putting him between her and the crossbow.

A slash hit his chest armor, leaving a deep gash in the leather, but lacking the power to cut through. He was too fast and skilled with both hands for most of her usual tricks to work. They were relatively evenly matched, but his sword and superior height gave him greater reach, and his armor allowed him to take risks she couldn't.

The sword made contact, drawing a searing line of agony across her ribs below one breast. Veyl darted to the side, struggling to catch her breath past the pain. She moved in front of a post and launched herself back into it, bringing both legs up to kick him in the chest when he charged. The added leverage of the post against her back gave her the power to send him reeling. She leapt forward and came in with another kick, knocking him flat on his back. When he tried to roll away, she lunged on him, dropping one dagger and driving the other into his side with all her weight on both hands. She yanked it out, letting the blood flow, and stabbed him again in the neck.

Panic flared, and her ability crackled to life again as she jumped to her feet and spun to face the one with the crossbow. The abrupt movement brought searing pain where the sword had cut in, and she staggered, sinking to her knees on the dirt floor. Directly in her line of sight, the crossbow hit the ground, and the Thaelian woman who had been wielding it fell on top of it, her head still attached by a narrow strip of flesh.

Panting, each breath bringing more pain, Veyl pressed a hand over the bleeding wound below her breast, watching Kronach shake the blood from his blade. Four of his warriors followed him up the aisle, three stopping behind him when he sank to one knee in front of her, closer than necessary, as usual. One continued past them.

"I considered allowing her to shoot you for being careless enough to let them spot you when you were so close to freedom, but you fought well." He took hold of her wrist in an iron grip, pressing on the shallow cut on her arm, and pulled her hand away from the wound over her ribs. With no apparent concern for the pain he caused, he tugged at the blood-soaked hole in the fabric to look at the cut beneath. "You have earned yourself some admirable wounds this night. I'm tempted to keep you here so I might watch them heal." Leaning in, he whispered in her ear. "I could tell the undead prince you escaped and hide you away, just for my pleasure."

"Except you won't." Her voice trembled with pain and fear, but she was not helpless here. Not with Heshara and the other Frightener dead. "Because I will unleash my storm upon your entire castle, and your Tempest will watch you fall before that fury."

He drew back to look her in the eyes, still close enough that she could feel the warmth of his breath on her lips. "There you are," he murmured, echoing his words from their prior confrontation.

For a moment, she feared he would kiss her, and, for all that she didn't want him to, she also had no desire to break him and his men. He had let her leave and saved her life, but it was all a game to him, wasn't it? "Let me go."

He inhaled deeply, exhaling again with a satisfied sigh. "You could still place yourself at my mercy."

"You have none." She wavered slightly, then took hold of the hilt of one of his swords and drew it out. "I'm taking this."

Kronach chuckled. "Smart woman." The wavelord stood, pulling her none too gently to her feet with him. Then he took the sword away from her and cut two strips of fabric from her skirt. These he folded and pressed over the wound. "Hold this."

When she did so, he cut another strip and handed the weapon back to her, apparently not at all concerned that she might turn it against him. He used the material to wrap around her ribs and tie the bandage firmly in place, his rough manner causing more pain than seemed necessary. After he finished, he reached up, and she sucked in a sharp breath when he brushed his calloused thumb over the cut on her cheekbone.

"Hurts, doesn't it?"

Veyl glared at him. "Of course it does."

"War is painful, Khesran, and you have declared war against the man who would be Sarket's king."

Did he truly expect to get away with this? "Have you not done the same by letting me leave?"

"The undead prince arrived in my halls with you on his arm as his chosen queen, not as his prisoner. Before dinner, he confronted me in anger and demanded that my men and I treat you as Sarket's queen. He said that we were not to touch you, speak to you, nor even dare to look upon you. Perhaps he will learn to be more cautious with his commands in the future."

"But you still mean to help him?"

Kronach held her gaze as he nodded. "I do not like him, but he is the rightful heir. Thrasser tried to have someone else dispose of him. That is not Sarket's way. If he wishes to keep the throne for himself and maintain the support of the people now that word is being spread of his cowardice, he will have to face the undead prince the proper way."

She was trembling, though she wasn't cold. Pain clouded her mind. Blood had painted a trail partway down her skirt. Fresh warmth trickled from the place his thumb had rubbed her cheek. It was time to leave if she was going to have any hope of reaching the others. "Do you think Jaysen can win?"

"If he relies upon the skills he learned in your country, he has a chance." Kronach backed away from her.

One of his warriors tossed a full pack at her. Veyl caught it, gasping with the burst of pain as the movement pulled the gash over her ribs. Another led a saddled horse out of a stall and handed her the reins.

"Find your companions while you still have the strength." Kronach grinned, an odd glimmer of pleasure lighting his one good eye. He undid his belt with the second sword still sheathed in it and tossed it on the ground between them. "Tempest guide you." With that, he and his warriors departed through a side door.

Veyl attached the swords and pack behind the saddle, every movement bringing more pain. Then she led the animal out the rear door and struggled up onto its back, the warmth of fresh blood soaking into the rough bandage against her side by the time she situated herself. A drizzle had begun to fall, and thunder grumbled in the distance. The walls of the castle overshadowed the stable. She wasn't free yet.

Tears of frustration stung her eyes as she turned the animal the way Kitria and Kyril had gone. Her intent had been to follow right behind them, so Seyn might help lead them all out of the city. She had a vague sense of the direction she should head, though it would have been easier if the night had provided her with enough light by which to see the distant mountains, but the weather saw fit to deny her that.

Trusting to limited memories of their arrival and instinct, she set off, the horse's movement shifting the cut over her ribs, keeping the pain fresh. The trembling grew worse with the addition of the chill from rain slowly soaking into her hair and clothes. That too increased the agony of the deep wound, though the less severe ones on her cheek and arm were growing numb with cold.

She made it a few blocks before the drizzle turned into a full downpour. It became harder to see more than a few buildings ahead in the gloomy rain. Thunder rumbled directly overhead now, a flash of lightning bringing a bright glare to the night that made everything darker in the aftermath. The horse spooked, and she had to wrestle him back into line, tears spilling hot down her cheeks amidst a surge of hopelessness and more pain.

Desperate, she offered a silent plea to the ocean that raged not far away. Perhaps, if there was any truth to what Kronach and the Qwilki believed, she would find guidance in that.

She continued for a few more blocks before stopping the horse. Everything looked the same in the rain. She wasn't sure which direction she needed to go now or even which one she had been traveling in.

A pair of bright eyes appeared at the next corner, practically glowing in the darkness. For an instant, fear sparked in Veyl, until Seyn trotted out. The wave dancer approached the horse, and the animal tensed, then they sniffed noses and it relaxed again. She looked up at Veyl, taking the reins between her teeth and gently tugging on them. Veyl let them fall, turning her energy to staying in the saddle as the beast led her mount out of the city.

CHAPTER TWENTY THREE

Veyl was shivering so violently she could barely keep herself upright on the horse's back, lost in a haze of pain and cold, when a familiar voice called her name. Seyn and her mount both stopped, and a figure rushed out of the darkness to her side.

"We feared something might have happened. I was heading out to search for you."

"G-G-Gannon?" The chattering of her teeth gave a stutter to his name.

"Let's get you inside."

He grabbed the reins Seyn had dropped and led the horse into the dubious shelter of a half-collapsed barn. It was darker in there than it was out in the stormy night, except within a small circle of light from a candle set on one post. Once out of the rain, she moved to dismount, half falling from the stirrup when the effort shifted the bandage over the wound. Gannon caught her, one hand landing precisely upon the injury, wrenching a cry from her.

"Are you hurt?" As soon as she had her balance, he turned her into the light, his gaze falling first upon the cut on her cheek. "Shit. What happened?"

She pulled back from him, escaping the agonizing touch of his hand on the lower wound, and leaned against the horse, grateful the animal was calm enough to stand for it. Gannon grabbed the candle and brought it closer, his attention moving to the blood that had soaked down her skirt.

"By the Break, Veyl, you need help."

The door opened, and Kitria stuck her head out. "You made it!" As she hurried to them, her eyes widened. "You've got blood all over you. I hope that's not yours." She reached for Veyl's arm. "Let's take you inside and see how bad this is."

"The p-pack on the h-h-horse…" She wanted to say more, but it was too much work for the moment. Shivering and pain were sapping what little energy she had.

Gannon moved around to Veyl's other side. "I'll help her. Secure and feed the animal and grab the pack."

Inside, he sat her in a creaky chair that had seen better days and draped a dry blanket over her shoulders. Everything in the cramped room was thick with dust. In places, she could see grass and weeds growing up through the floorboards. Two of the four chairs around an old rotting table were too broken to use. He brought a couple more candles over to provide additional light.

"That's the worst one?" He pointed to the cut below her breast.

She nodded. "Kyril?"

"He's sleeping in the next room," Kitria offered, walking in with the pack and sword belt. "We thought he ought to get as much rest as possible while we were waiting for you, since we can't risk staying here long." After setting the pack on the table, she held up the belt with the two swords in it. "I'm a little confused by this."

Veyl spoke slowly to keep from stuttering. Just being out of the rain helped, as did the blanket, but only so much with her dress and hair soaked through. "I was attacked after you left the stable. Someone with a crossbow and a Thaelian Frightener who had apparently followed us."

"There are no Thaelian Frighteners," Kyril said, now leaning in the doorway leading to the next room.

Seeing him alive and free made the pain a little less overwhelming. She had accomplished what she had set out to do. Gannon, Kitria, and Kyril were away from Jaysen. That was what mattered. There would be repercussions for everything that occurred this night that could lead to war. Although Jaysen's actions probably would have ended them up there, regardless. Now he had to face Thrasser with two fewer Frighteners in his arsenal and without the promise of Vanris's allegiance that he had hoped to force by marrying her.

She sucked in a sharp breath when Gannon began removing the wrap. Kitria was digging through the pack, pulling out a shirt, jacket, and pants, all in the colors of Kronach's warriors. On top of the clothes, she set a dagger, flint and steel for lighting a fire, a few basic supplies for tending injuries, and various food items. A second shirt, clearly cut and sized for a man, Kitria offered to Kyril.

He made his way unsteadily to the table and took it from her. "Who is your benefactor?"

"First—Ah!" she cried out when the fabric Gannon was peeling away stuck to part of the wound.

"Shit. Sorry." He moved the soaked cloth, trying to catch the blood that ran fresh from the gash with it.

Veyl closed her eyes to ease the sudden spinning of the room. When it calmed, she looked at Kitria. "There most definitely was a Thaelian Frightener. The council may have been keeping more secrets than you realized." She shuddered, the pain making her nauseous now.

"And all this stuff?" Kitria gestured to the pack and weapons. "Where did this come from?"

She closed her eyes again, fighting another dizzy spell. "Kronach. He and some of his warriors also followed us."

Someone moved up beside her, and she opened her eyes, glancing up at Kyril where he stood with his jaw clenched, pulling the shirt on over dark bruises and whip lacerations that were beginning to heal. When that was done, he leaned on the table next to her, careful to stay out of Gannon's light, and took her hand, a concerning hint of hesitation in the contact. One eye had swollen nearly shut after the beating on the docks, and the inflammation and bruising over the rest of his face made her stomach tighten with a pang of sympathy.

Gannon pulled the dagger from his belt and widened the slice in her dress to take a better look at the wound, then glanced over his shoulder at the items on the table. "That won't be adequate for this. You need stitches, Veyl."

"It has to be enough." She rested her head against Kyril's arm, trying not to read anything into the way he tensed when she did so, as if it made him uncomfortable. "We can't stay here, and we can't head back to town. The moment Jaysen discovers I've escaped, he will start hunting for us. For me."

"I wish I could argue differently, but you're right." Gannon stood. "We need to at least get you out of that dress. It's soaked, and we can't bandage this as well as we need to with it in the way."

Veyl breathed a pained laugh. "I see you finally discovered a way to get me out of my clothes."

"Trust me when I tell you, this is not what I had in mind," Gannon answered with a wry smile. He caught her hand when she moved to get up. "Wait. Let's clean and wrap the one on your arm first, then Kitria can help you change in the other room. Hold this."

He placed a dry, folded cloth against the gash in her ribs. Veyl pressed a hand over it, wincing. None of her prior injuries had ever hurt quite like this one did.

Gannon chuckled. "Other hand. I need that one."

Extracting her hand from Kyril's, she held the cloth in place as Gannon worked. It took him a few minutes to clean and wrap the smaller cut on her arm. Afterward, Kitria led her to the next room to strip off the soaked dress. Veyl kept pressure on the bleeding wound while the other woman helped her into the pants from the pack. They were a decent fit, if a couple of inches long and slightly loose at the waist, which was preferable to being too tight under the circumstances. They put the shirt on too, Kitria gathering the fabric to one side and tying a knot in it to preserve some modesty for her while keeping it above the gash.

When they came out, Kyril was sitting in one chair. He got up, his grimace and deliberate movements speaking to the pain of his injuries. Veyl sank into the seat and let Gannon take the folded cloth away. He looked at the wound and shook his head.

"This really needs to be stitched. It's never going to stay closed with all the moving we need to do."

"We haven't got a choice," Veyl said through clenched teeth, Kitria echoing the sentiment.

Kyril watched in silence, making his way around the old table to offer her his hand again. Veyl took it, fully aware of how much this was going to hurt, regardless of what Gannon did with the wound.

"We can't stay here long," Veyl continued. "I don't know if Kronach will choose to help or hinder Jaysen's search once he realizes we're missing, but we shouldn't stake our lives upon his benevolence. Wrap it the best you can."

Gannon muttered under his breath about Vanrian healers and proper care as he grabbed some bandaging material, folded it, and handed it to her. "Press that to your cheek. It's still bleeding a little."

She did as he directed with her free hand as Kitria prepared a bandage for the larger cut. "I seem to recall sending you off with a message for my parents. How did you end up here?"

Gannon began cleaning around the wound, drawing a few soft cries from her. She squeezed Kyril's hand. Considering how much injury he had sustained, it seemed cruel to add the crushing of his fingers to the list, but she couldn't help it.

Gannon answered her as he worked, giving her something to try focusing on other than the pain. "There's not a lot to tell. Kronach's men escorted me away from the castle grounds like a prisoner under guard. Once we were clear of the town proper, they started conversing in a language I'd never heard before and trotted past me. When I stopped my horse to see what they would do, they kept going as if I didn't exist. They left me behind with a mount and the supplies in my saddlebags, so I found this place and settled in to keep watch over the road, since this is the only logical route for someone wanting to head north. Everything else is too rugged unless you cut down and around to Andaro, which would make no sense at all, considering that's the direction Jaysen will want to go soon. I should have missed these two coming through, since I wasn't expecting you until tomorrow night, but the storm woke me. I went out to make certain the barn wasn't falling in on my horse, and I saw them and the wave dancer coming up off the road in search of shelter where they could wait for you. All of which tells me we need to get out of this place soon. It's much too obvious."

He fell silent, focusing his attention on figuring out a way to keep the wound from splitting open. Because the cut was nearly horizontal below her breast, it made holding it closed without stitches especially challenging. Veyl squeezed her eyes shut, clenching her teeth until the seemingly endless, agonizing process ended. Gannon turned to cleaning the wound on her cheek, the discomfort negligible by comparison.

"Are these all from a sword?" he asked as he worked.

Kyril moved closer, inviting her to lean more of her weight against him while he braced himself using the back of the chair.

Veyl didn't open her eyes when she answered Gannon. "That one was from a crossbow bolt."

"By the Break, Veyl, you're lucky to be alive." His voice became a little more distant, as if he had leaned back. "That's the best we can do for now. Why don't you two rest a little before we move on." Veyl opened her eyes, and he looked away, busying himself with picking up the rest of the bandage materials. "The bed in there should be able to hold both of you if you don't mind settling in close. I'll make sure the horses are ready to go."

Kitria placed a hand on Veyl's arm. "I can help you."

"Come, Seh'hali," Kyril murmured, a depth of unexplained sorrow adding weight to his words.

Seyn followed them into the next room, and Kitria left them there, shutting the crooked door as best she could behind her. After Kyril laid down, he held his arm out, offering her a place at his side.

She shook her head. "I saw the bruises on your ribs. I don't want to hurt you."

"You'll be more comfortable on your side with something to brace yourself against. It's the closest we're going to get to elevating that wound."

It bothered her that his reasoning had nothing to do with wanting her near after what they had both suffered through. But perhaps he was simply too fatigued from pain and worry. She didn't have the energy to argue, particularly when she knew he was right. As carefully as she could, she lowered herself down alongside him, trying not to hurt either of them. The occasional groan or intake of breath from each of them proved she was only marginally successful. They had thrown Gannon's bedroll on the bed, but it didn't make the hard surface much more comfortable. She couldn't imagine it felt pleasant against Kyril's wounded back, but, given the bruising and lash wounds over much of his upper body, there were no good options for him.

Once Veyl had nestled there with her head on his shoulder, trying not to let her weight press against his ribs, Seyn stretched out on the floor by the bed with a soft whine.

"What happened to Heshara?"

"I broke her." Veyl's voice cracked as she said it. She couldn't be proud of the lives she had taken, regardless of what those people had done.

"The wave dancer didn't protect her?"

"No. Heshara was torturing me with the zenyal bond. I don't think Seyn approved."

He was quiet for a few seconds, during which Veyl silently ached for him to put his arm around her, though he might be refraining to avoid putting pressure on her injuries, or his own. "Heshara found Seyn as an injured pup and nursed her back to health. That's how they bonded, but she changed during the Devastation, growing bitter and cold. At times, I wondered if Seyn might choose to break the bond. I guess it was fortunate that she waited to do so until now. I'm not sure this escape would have gone as well as it did without her." Kyril looked down at Veyl as a few tears slipped from her eyes. "Don't mourn Heshara or any of the others you had to harm tonight. They chose their fate."

"I'm not sure we would have escaped at all if Seyn hadn't made the choice she did, but I was going to try." She wiped carefully at the tears. "Jaysen said they left Ceris behind."

Another long silence stretched between them, and he breathed a shallow sigh. "They did. I'm glad they didn't hurt him, but…"

"It must be awful to be separated from him. I'm sorry." She carefully placed her hand over his heart, hoping its weight wouldn't cause him pain. Why did it feel as if an ocean lay between them?

After a few minutes of heavy silence, he placed a hand over hers. "There's something you should know."

"What?" she whispered, dread tightening an icy fist around her heart. Not the most pleasant sensation with the wound near there.

"Jaysen had Evoker Halin, one of the council members, try to take you from me the way he believes I had Nalika take him from you. Every day on the ship, he came down with Halin and sat just out of my reach where they had me chained up. He would talk about you the whole time, often while someone else beat me like a hated dog. I tried not to think of you, but between the pain, the drug they force-fed me, and listening to him tell lies about you, I failed too many times."

She could barely breathe past the sorrow and anger cinching in around her ribs now. Fear constricted her throat, preventing her from asking him how much they had taken. Did she honestly want to know?

He continued after a long pause. "I have no way of telling how much damage they did. I don't believe Halin is exceptionally skilled, or maybe he just wasn't that invested, knowing they meant to execute me in the end. All I am certain of is that there are things missing, gaps that make no sense, and the memories I still have of you, of us, are… fragmented and… confusing."

Veyl yearned to say something supportive. She could hear in his voice that he held himself at least partially accountable for not being able to protect those memories. She wanted to reassure him and tell him it didn't matter because what they had together would overcome this, but she was tired and in so much pain. Not only physical pain now. Squeezing her eyes shut did nothing to stop the stream of tears.

His arm slid carefully around her, holding her tentatively. Was that caution merely for her injuries, or could it be because he no longer remembered how powerful their connection had been?

Despite pain and sorrow, she eventually succumbed to exhaustion. Much too soon, she woke to Kyril giving her shoulder a gentle squeeze.

"Veyl, it's time. We need to leave."

Forcing her eyes open, she looked around, trying to orient herself. She felt groggy and weak, with a hollow in her chest as dark and deep as the night that crept in through cracks in the walls of the broken-down building. Unable to meet his eyes, she let Kitria and Gannon help her up, the two taking care to avoid putting strain on the cut. She made her way into the next room with Seyn as they assisted Kyril up behind her.

A few minutes later, Gannon walked up beside her, placing a hand on her arm. "You should ride with Kitria. We only have three horses, and you two are the lightest."

Unable to escape the numbness that had fallen over her emotions, she gestured toward Kyril. "Is he capable of riding alone?"

"I'll manage. I can use my Feral ability to control my mount."

In the partially collapsed barn, the three horses waited, saddled and ready to depart. They had stolen two of the animals. Another reason to get farther from town before the weather calmed too much and morning chased away the night. Gannon secured the bedroll behind his saddle. With the help of a rickety stool, they got Veyl onto the horse with Kitria without causing too much pain. Once the animal started moving out into the ongoing drizzle, that changed. Every step was agony. She sucked in a breath, clenching her teeth as her hold on Kitria tightened, and the other woman stopped the horse.

Gannon, aware of their position in his periphery, turned his mount to face them. "What's wrong?"

Kitria was shaking her head. "I don't know if she can do this."

Gannon moved his mount over alongside them. "We have to leave. If we remain here, they will find us."

"Maybe…" Veyl could see Jaysen in her mind, the gloating in his eyes every time she let him kiss her. The minute Heshara was dead, she should have hunted for him in those halls, should have broken him and everyone helping him. They might have killed her, but it would have been worth it.

"Veyl."

To see Jaysen's bright blue eyes staring at nothing, blood running from them. The last tears he would ever cry. Eyes she had gazed into throughout her childhood with trust and love… Her best friend. Her tehnaak. Did she have it in her to break someone who was already so irreparably damaged?

"Seh'hali."

The edge of alarm in Kyril's voice snapped her back. The two men had moved their mounts up on either side of them, both staring at her. Kitria was breathing faster, with fear, not exertion. Power crackled through Veyl, her ability sending its own lightning flashing out into the night. She caught her breath and pushed back against it, stamping it down.

Meeting Gannon's eyes, she said, "You should leave me here. This wound is going to split open again." And if she let Jaysen's soldiers take her back without the zenyal bond to control her, she could kill him. She could make him pay.

"Horse shit. We're not leaving anyone here. Let's

move." Gannon turned his mount and urged it forward.

Kyril lingered a moment beside them. "I'll keep the horses calm and see if Seyn will scout for us. We're getting out of this place. All of us."

Between the soaking rain and constant motion, it didn't take long for the bandage over Veyl's ribs to become damp and warm with something other than water. The pressure of the wrap kept it from getting too far out of control, even though it made it a little hard to breathe. Gannon made an informed decision to risk traveling on the road for as long as they could, knowing it would provide a smoother ride for her. A few hours out, as dawn's light was adding a glow to the gray sky, the pounding of many hooves came up the road behind them.

Seyn led them into the trees on the mountainside, the wave dancer guiding them toward a spot within a dense stand where they might go unnoticed in the low light. Moving over the rougher terrain led to more substantial shifting. Veyl felt the edges of the wound pull apart and sucked a breath between clenched teeth to hold back a cry and avoid alarming the others. Right now, their attention needed to be on the approaching danger.

When they were in the trees, Gannon and Kyril dismounted, the latter with a grunt of pain, and guided the animals close together. If someone spotted them, they would have a better chance of fighting than running with one of their horses carrying two riders. Veyl drew on her ability, wanting to be ready for that eventuality. She was in no condition for physical combat, so she would have to fall back on her mind-crafting. Only now, the crackle of that power was faint, like a distant storm drifting away, her pain, weakness, and exhaustion impeding her ability to call upon it.

Fortunately, the approaching riders didn't slow, all of them leaning low over their mounts at a hard gallop as they swept past. The group consisted of seven Sarketi soldiers, none of whom wore the colors of Wavelord Kronach's warriors. These were not Eydarith men, though they were coming from Taro. Thrasser had plenty of his own soldiers stationed in that city to ensure the wavelord wasn't persecuting Havaad worshipers or overstepping his bounds. It made sense that Jaysen would turn to them now, since Kronach's people had allowed her and the others to slip out under their noses. More literally than he probably realized.

They waited in the trees for a short time after the pounding of hooves faded down the road, listening for any more riders approaching from the south.

"They're not wasting time." Gannon stared in the direction they had ridden, his brow furrowing deeply before he turned to look at Veyl. "How fast do they think you can travel in your condition?"

Veyl leaned against Kitria and closed her eyes, focusing hard to keep from exposing the extent of her agony in her voice. "They expect us to have gone farther. Kronach won't have told them I'm injured. That would require admitting that he had been there in the stable and allowed me to leave. Besides, while he does seem to find all this entertaining, I get the sense that he truly believes I am favored by the Tempest. He doesn't want Jaysen to have me."

"That's something we can all agree on." The distance in Kyril's voice made Veyl's chest ache, though the sensation had a lot of other pain to compete with for her attention.

"The downside of all this is that they are ahead of us now. We don't know how far they intend to go, where they might stop, or when they'll turn back. We need to stay off the road and away from settlements, but..." Gannon trailed off.

He didn't need to finish. She could tell the two men were looking at her even before she opened her eyes. More specifically, their focus had gone to the growing spot of red on her shirt where blood was soaking through the bandages beneath.

"We need to stay off the road," she echoed. "We haven't got enough fit fighters to confront them directly, and we can't outrun them. What other choice do we have?"

"You are a Frightener," Kitria offered. "An extremely powerful one, from what I understand."

Veyl blinked against the sting of frustrated tears. "I'm having trouble drawing on it in this state." She hung her head, the weight of disappointment heavy on her shoulders. If only she could gain adequate control of it at any point other than when she was in good health and calm, maybe she wouldn't feel like such a failure.

"That power helped you save my life and Kitria's." Kyril's voice was firm, pushing back against her self-loathing. "In your condition, most people would find it difficult to draw on their ability." He urged his mount closer. "Can you make it a little longer?"

His words took Veyl back to the days when her father let her accompany him on scouting trips as a child. Any time she complained of growing weary, he would give her a fond smile and ask if she could handle going for just a little longer, regardless of whether "a little longer" meant twenty minutes more or half a day. Somehow, she suspected this would be exactly like that, so she replied as she always had back then when she wanted to prove to her father that she was tough enough to join him on patrol.

"I'll outlast you." Her voice held a level of conviction that surprised even her, but words were often easier than deeds.

The unreadable stare Kyril gave her set her adrift in his silver-blue eyes. How desperately she wanted to know what thoughts wandered through his mind at that moment. But she didn't have the energy to pursue it, and she wasn't sure she would have dared to with Gannon and Kitria watching anyhow. When he looked away, she was left with only pain and the depressing reality of what he had told her in the night. How much had the Evoker taken from him? Enough to destroy everything they had? Maybe it didn't matter. Her chances of surviving this were looking bleaker with every passing hour.

Gannon started them moving again. From that point forward, Veyl sank into a haze of misery. The battle against pain and, as the day wore on, weakness and cold, required all her focus. Though she began the ride behind Kitria, by the end, she was in front of Gannon on the same horse, his arms around her all that kept her from falling off. She didn't recall them switching out or any rests they may have taken along the way to eat and drink. She only remembered that she had eaten and drunk a few times because someone made her do so by holding food or a water skin to her lips.

It was late afternoon when they stopped in a sheltered area to set up camp. Gannon and Kitria cleaned and covered her injuries as best they could before doing the same for Kyril. Exhausted, Veyl lay down on a bedroll to rest, and Seyn stretched out along her back, supporting her. She lost track of Gannon, but she could hear Kyril and Kitria talking in low voices, then Kitria crying.

When she woke sometime after dark, it was to the

sound of an unfamiliar female voice speaking in a low form of Pandrean Common.

"Yeh said it were a horse that were injured. I told yeh, I only do animals. I don't have the trainin' to work on people. I won't tell nobody I saw yeh, but ye'll have ta find someone else."

"She won't make it like this." Gannon's voice had an earnest edge of pleading to it. "Please, just look."

"I knew I shoulda ignored it when yeh beckoned me over." The woman huffed, and footsteps approached. "Standin' at the edge of the trees with yer hood up. More the fool am I."

"Seh'hali," Kyril murmured, stopping Veyl from trying to sit up with a hand on her shoulder. "This woman's going to look at your wound."

Seyn had disappeared, though Veyl could still feel the wave dancer close by. Although that made no sense. Perhaps she was becoming delirious.

The woman, her face lined with hardship more than age, set a lantern down next to Veyl and looked her over. Her gaze lingered on Veyl's pointed ears and blood-red hair for almost as long as it did the cut on her cheek. Then she glanced down at her side as Kitria knelt next to her and pulled the shirt up. Veyl reached out, uncertain whether she simply got lucky and found Kyril's hand or he caught on that fast and took hold of hers. Either way, his firm grip provided comfort and gave her something to squeeze as they peeled away the bandages.

"Sure. That's a bad 'un."

"And? Can you help?" Gannon pressed.

"This girl should be seein' a physician." The woman frowned at Veyl's side. "But yeh can't do that, can yeh? Yer the ones those soldiers are lookin' for." She shook her head and sighed as if all the troubles of the world had landed on her shoulders. "The light's shit, but I've worked in worse. Bring my packs over." She looked Veyl in the eyes. "I got somethin' that'll numb it a bit, sweet-heart, but it's still gonna hurt. I can't help that."

Veyl nodded. "Thank you," she whispered.

The woman snorted. "We'll see if yeh feel that way when I'm done."

Veyl made it most of the way through the cleaning of the wound before she begged Gannon and Kyril to hold her still, because she couldn't do it on her own any-more. The pain that followed as the woman stitched it was an unending scream in Veyl's mind. Tears streamed from her eyes, and she was distantly aware of Kyril and Gannon, both offering alternating words of encourage-ment and apology as they held her in place. An endless period of suffering later, she lay sweaty and exhausted, without the energy to even open her eyes as the woman finished covering the wound.

"Tha's probably my best work yet." She sounded pleased with what she had accomplished. "Keep it clean and covered. Put this salve on it once a day. It ain't as good as what yeh've got up north, but it's the best we got."

"Thank you. Come, we'll finish up and let her rest."

Gannon's voice moved away, and Veyl let herself drift. The intense pain in her side calmed as whatever salve the woman had put on it took effect. Enough so, sheer exhaustion had the power to drag her down into a fitful slumber.

"Seh'hali."

Her eyelids felt weighted down, but she forced them open. "A few minutes."

"We can't assume she won't tell anyone we're here," Kyril said gently.

"But she helped us."

"For coin. And she stands to make a tidy sum more if she turns us in."

"Shit," she muttered, letting him carefully help her

to her feet. "Where did we find the coin to pay her?"

"I don't know." Kyril guided her to the bigger horse. "I'm going to assume it was another gift from the wavelord, but given the lengths I believe Gannon would go to for you, I chose not to ask."

They had moved the animal up next to a rise in the ground to make it easier for Veyl to mount. Kyril steadied her on one side with Kitria ready to assist from the other. Even with that, the pull on the fresh stitches was agony, but at least they held. To her surprise, Kyril climbed up behind her this time. He wrapped an arm low around her waist, keeping clear of the injury, and pulled her close.

"Lean on me. I don't need my hands to guide him, so I can use them to keep you upright."

"You're injured as well." It bothered her how much effort just speaking required.

"My wounds are not as deep, and Kronach had a physician tend what they could after his men took me from the Thaelian guards." His voice tightened with anger on the last two words.

She couldn't imagine what it must have felt like to be treated thus by his own people. Then again, given that she was in her current condition because of Jaysen, perhaps it didn't require that much imagination after all.

Seyn paced up alongside them and looked up at Veyl with those bright sea-foam eyes. Then she trotted ahead, going to the front to find them a route through the woods with her superior night vision.

"But the bruises over your ribs—"

"Quiet."

The horses started moving. Veyl did as Kyril had suggested and leaned back against him, feeling him tense when she did so. The reaction brought with it a pang of sorrow.

"What do you remember?"

He was silent long enough that she wondered if she had only imagined speaking aloud, then he asked, "Of us?"

"Yes."

"You shouldn't worry about it right now."

"Indulge me."

Every muscle in his body that she could feel tightened even more. "I remember Deepwater and most of the journey to Thaelis, as well as the awful things I put you through along the way. I recall in unfortunate detail the feel of my hand around your throat when I had you pinned to the wall after you broke Illis. I dragged you away from your life and the people you loved, making you miserable enough that you tried to kill yourself. Those memories are powerful."

"Kyril—"

"Quiet." Without the energy to argue, she closed her eyes, focusing on the vibration of his voice against her back when he spoke again, sorrow forming a vast hollow in her chest. "There are fragmented memories that suggest moments of connection in Thaelis and in Vanris and working together to find a solution for protecting your people and mine. I have occasional flashes in my mind of holding you, and touching you, of being kissed and touched by you, but they feel like fever dreams. The kind that slip away soon after you awaken. Fantasies. They make no sense in the context of what I do remember, and I have trouble believing them. I don't see how you could do anything but despise me."

"I did despise you in the beginning," she murmured, struggling to keep her voice steady as the horse's movement on the uneven terrain caused pulling and pain.

"And you still should."

She tried to think of a way to ease his mind as she drifted somewhere between the beckoning sleep of weakness and pure exhaustion and the nightmare of losing him. "I love you."

He said nothing.

•

Veyl didn't recall stopping and dismounting. Nor did she recall the others setting up camp in the shelter of an overhang or lying down on the single bedroll they had among them to sleep. When she woke, she was warmer than she would have expected. She lay on her side with Seyn stretched in front of her, one arm resting on the wave dancer, and someone against her back. Somehow, just from the feel of his chest, she knew it was Kyril. Her arm and shoulder under her were numb from the hard ground, but she didn't want to move. Not yet. And not only because of the pain that effort promised to cause. They had apparently decided that she required warmth, and after her, he, with his injuries, was next most in need of a slightly softer, warmer spot to sleep. For a moment, with him pressed against her, she could pretend he was there because he wished to be closer to her and believed that she wanted him there.

She let her eyes fall shut again.

"Unfortunately, I can't let you do that."

She opened her eyes to look at Gannon, who now crouched in front of her on the other side of Seyn. Veyl held out a hand. After a moment's hesitation, he took it, and she squeezed gently… weakly.

"Thank you for finding that woman."

He shrugged. "Are you feeling better?"

"Not a lot," she answered honestly, "but I don't feel worse, and I think that's where I was heading."

Kyril stirred, placing a hand on her shoulder to support her as he sat up, taking away the warmth of his body.

"We'll do everything we can to avoid hurting you

anymore, but we're still not safe." Gannon released her hand and moved back to let Seyn get up.

The wave dancer turned and licked Veyl full in the face before trotting out of their way.

Gannon chuckled. "Under different circumstances, I'd say that was gross, but I suspect you may have the cleanest face of all of us now." His gaze shifted to Kyril. "Help me?"

The two of them worked together to help Veyl sit up without straining her side, then Kitria held out a wooden bowl toward her and Kyril as if uncertain who to offer it to. Kyril nudged it toward Veyl.

"You first."

Kitria's smile was apologetic. "We need to share the same bowl. Gannon and I already ate. It's not much. A few bites of thin stew. I caught one of those little fuzzy hopping critters..." She looked at Gannon.

"A rabbit," he offered.

"That's right."

"You don't have rabbits on Thaelis?" Veyl glanced at Kyril, but his focus had turned to carefully stretching the stiffness out of his muscles. Her gaze moved to Kitria.

"No. Never heard of them before this. They're kind of cute with those absurd ears." She held her hands upright against her head and wiggled them as if to illustrate for Veyl. "I almost felt guilty for killing it."

Sitting up had caused enough pain to curb Veyl's appetite, but she made herself eat as much as she could stand to before passing it to Kitria to refill for her brother. She watched Gannon and Kitria clean up the camp and prepare the horses. It took only a few minutes. They had tried to stay ready for a hasty departure. When they stole a moment to sit as Kyril finished eating, Veyl pondered the two Thaelians.

"Did you have any idea the council was working

with the Ukhen'kya?"

Kyril stalled mid-bite.

Kitria shook her head. "That's absurd."

They really didn't know? Of course they didn't. Why would Jaysen or the councilors have told them anything? She was the one Jaysen wanted. Gannon and Kitria were mere victims of circumstance, used to manipulate her, and Kyril, an act of revenge and a token to acknowledge his agreement with the Thaelian leadership.

"Councilor Shyall said they had been using the Unclean to eliminate subversives within Thaelis. The night they took us, they sent them to attack Vanris's fleet to keep their attention off what was happening on the other side of the island."

Kitria paled, looking like she might be sick. "The explosion? I thought that was the council's doing."

Kyril only nodded. "I'm surprised she admitted it to you. Jinau suspected there was something of the sort going on. There were several instances where people they asked him to investigate conveniently fell victim to Ukhen'kya attacks." He used a little water to rinse the bowl he had emptied and held it out to Kitria.

"You knew about this?" Kitria snatched the bowl from him. "How could you keep this a secret?"

He gave her a hard look. "They were taking out subversives, Kit. The more you knew, the more likely you were to disappear some night. I couldn't risk losing you."

"I think Jinau's dead." Though Veyl spoke softly, she had Kyril's immediate attention.

Kitria lowered her gaze.

Gannon nodded. "Right before they took us, they dragged him into the house. There was a lot of blood. I couldn't tell if he was breathing."

Kyril turned south and strode a short distance in that direction, his hands balling into fists. Veyl reached out to Gannon, and he helped her to her feet. With shaky, tentative steps, she walked over beside Kyril, also peering to the south.

"I feel the same." She murmured, her words meant for his ears alone.

He glanced down at her. "You want to go back and make him pay?"

"I want to make them all pay."

Kyril nodded. His hand shifted closer, as if he considered taking hers.

Seyn came bolting out of the trees. She gave a high whine and lunged in Veyl's direction, then leapt away toward the horses, her ears back and tail low.

Kyril turned abruptly. "We need to go. There are several hounds coming through the trees, and I suspect they aren't alone. I can divert them, but we shouldn't take chances."

"Agreed. Can you continue supporting Veyl on the horse?" Gannon asked him.

Kyril nodded.

Minutes later, they were fleeing again, Kyril using his ability to guide their mount, so he might help her balance in the saddle and minimize the stress on the newly stitched wound. If only he realized how often she had yearned to have his arms around her in the light of day. Their circumstances made a mockery of that desire.

CHAPTER TWENTY FIVE

They followed Seyn for the rest of that day. The wave dancer was their first warning whenever danger approached, and she frequently bolted ahead to scout the path and ensure they didn't end up in terrain the horses couldn't navigate without too much difficulty. That night, the wave dancer hunted with Gannon and Kitria. They ate in relative silence, all of them too exhausted to have much to say. Seyn slept with Veyl again. Kyril also lay on the bedroll next to her as he had the night before. He seemed to feel stronger, though she caught the occasional grimace or wince when he moved suggesting that his injuries still caused him pain.

The next day found them traveling the coastal woodlands between Balarus and Deepwater. Veyl had studied the map of this area before she came here with her parents for the negotiations with Thrasser what felt like an eternity ago. She knew where Sarket's watchtowers were. Unfortunately, the woods gave way to grassy dunes along the coast, heading into the Crimson Break and barren desert a little farther inland. The terrain wouldn't offer much cover once they left the shelter of the trees.

When they checked it that morning, the cut over her ribs was turning a hot, angry red. None of them bothered to point out that it wasn't a positive development. They didn't need to. If they could make it across the Break to one of the Vanrian watchtowers, a healer with the proper knowledge and access to Vanris's medicines could tend the injury. They had little weaponry. Just the two swords she had gotten from Kronach and a dagger his men had given Gannon. They would face odds heavily stacked against them if they got into a confrontation now.

"We haven't got much choice." Gannon stood alongside his mount, staring out through the trees at the nearest watchtower northeast of them. Another towering structure stuck up from the landscape farther out to the northwest. "If we follow the road, we'll have to deal with border guards. We all know they won't let us pass. If we cross elsewhere, any watchtower guard who spots us is going to suspect we avoided the roads for a reason and come to investigate. We can assume the men Jaysen sent from Taro brought them orders to watch for and apprehend us."

"We could wait until evening. It's only a few hours away now," Kitria suggested.

"That's probably our best choice. We have Seyn. She can guide us around hazards in the dark." Kyril adjusted his arm where it rested low around Veyl's waist, avoiding the wound as best he could. Their mount shifted one leg, even that tiny motion bringing her more pain. "Veyl and Kitria can ride together on this gelding for the crossing. They're light, and he's strong enough that he should be able to keep up a decent speed if we need to run."

"It's likely they'll still spot us, but our odds might be marginally better in the dark." Gannon glanced over his shoulder at Kyril and nodded. "We should find a spot to rest and eat before we try it."

Some measure of respect showed in Gannon's regard when he looked at Kyril now. Would that grudging appreciation remain once they were in Vanris again? He got along with Kitria well enough, but then, she hadn't taken him hostage and dragged him off to a strange land. A traumatizing experience by itself and one that had ultimately led to him losing his tehnaak, a fact Veyl didn't intend to remind him of. Although none of that mattered if they never made it home. Perhaps it was best to focus on the challenges directly in front of them.

Kyril glanced down at Seyn, who stood beside their horse, as she often did when they weren't moving. "Can you find us a secure place to rest?"

The wave dancer looked at Veyl, who nodded in support of the request. For whatever reason, the beast always checked in with her now. It was both disconcerting and flattering.

With Seyn's guidance, they settled in a modest clearing amidst a dense patch of trees. Kitria and Gannon slipped off for a quick hunt to see if they could find something more filling to eat, leaving Veyl and Kyril in the camp. After touching her black nose to the back of Veyl's hand, Seyn also trotted off into the trees.

"She's bonded to you," Kyril remarked.

Veyl looked for a stump or log where she could sit without having to do so on the ground where her injury would make getting up again more difficult. Besides the pain, a general malaise had come over her, likely connected to the infection developing in the wound.

"I'm not a Feral."

He shifted a broken section of a fallen tree, moving it onto a flatter spot to serve as a seat. "Wave dancers aren't like most other beasts. They can create a bond with anyone, though they typically choose to do so with Ferals when they do so at all."

"Then why me?"

He gave her a long look that said he thought she was being deliberately obtuse. "Seh'hali."

Frustration flared, bringing a feverish warmth to her

face. "I am not the Daughter of the Ocean or wave-touched or any of these absurd things you all want to make me." She started toward the log, and he stepped in her path. Her pulse quickened when she looked up into his eyes.

One of his hands rose as if he meant to touch her, then he lowered it again. "Do you honestly believe these unconnected beings—the wave dancers, the Qwilki, and Wavelord Kronach—are all wrong? They see… we all see something in you. Refusing to acknowledge it yourself doesn't mean it isn't there." He stepped out of her way and gestured to the log. "Unless you'd rather lie down. I can spread out the bedroll for you."

She looked away from him, the sting of the emotional distance he maintained stoking a deep hatred in her toward the man who had caused it. "No. It's better if we remain ready to move. We're too close now. I'd rather not take chances."

He stopped her with a touch on her arm when she went to step past him. "I'm sorry, Veyl. I need time to figure out what this is now."

She looked up at him, her frustration manifesting as anger. "This? You mean us." He moved his hand away and held her gaze, his jaw tightening. It was confusing, wanting to kiss him as much as she wanted to hit him, though it wasn't the first time she had felt that way. "Don't you think it's something we should figure out together?"

"Jaysen said you were going to give yourself to him the night my fleet attacked Deepwater? Is that true?"

Her cheeks grew hot. Did this matter? Although, if Jaysen had tormented him with it, it probably did. Was that what she desired from their intimacy that night? Would she have stopped him if his three companions hadn't arrived when they did? It seemed a lifetime ago now. "I don't know."

His expression hardened. "Is that what you wanted?"

"I wanted to be close to him. Our severed tehnaak bond had just reformed. I had my best friend back, if only for a short time. Our roles in life would always keep us from being something else, even if we wished for that, but…" She hesitated. Would it be the wrong choice to admit more? She didn't want to keep secrets from him. "I was also curious. I had never been physically intimate with someone in that way. Because we were tehnaak, and our stations made it impossible for us to be together as a couple, he felt like the safest person in the world to explore that with. I didn't believe he would ever hurt…" Her throat tightened, and she lowered her eyes, that betrayal still a jagged blade in her chest.

How had it gone so wrong? He had become someone else. Abused and rejected by his own people to the point he could trust no one. He had restructured reality to fit the narrative in his head. One in which she had loved him enough to leave her life behind for him, and Kyril had taken that away, using mind-crafters to manipulate her into wanting him instead. What would Jaysen think now, after her escape? Would he still blame Kyril for all of it? Considering she had fled with him, she supposed he would.

Kyril brought his hand up all the way this time, his fingers gently curling under her chin, encouraging her to look up at him. "You deserve better."

"I couldn't care less what I deserve or don't deserve, I want y—"

His hand flipped up from her chin, one finger pressing lightly to her lips to stop her. "I didn't do this to myself. What you and the various fragments of memory suggest we may have had doesn't fit along with the intact memories they left me. I'm trying to make sense of that discordance right now." He lowered his hand.

May have had? His words were a dagger in her chest. "Then Jaysen gets to destroy this, too?" She wiped briskly at a tear, wincing when her hand brushed the healing cut there.

He shifted closer, his eyes sinking to her lips for an instant, as though he wanted to kiss her. Then he shook his head and moved back a step. "When we are safe, and your wound is no longer a threat to your life, we can talk about this more. Until then, I ask you to be patient with me. Someone broke into my mind, took what they wanted, and made a mess of the rest. I am truly sorry, but I need time to come to terms with that."

Veyl nodded, a twisting in her chest. This wasn't his fault. He deserved the patience he was asking for. "I'm sorry too," she murmured before going to sit carefully on the log.

Seyn came trotting in a few minutes later and lay down next to the log, resting her front legs and head on Veyl's feet. Kyril glanced over, raising his brows, his expression clearly stating that he felt this proved him right about the bond. Gannon and Kitria returned soon after with a collection of roots and berries to add to their paltry meal. When they entered camp, Gannon was carrying examples of foliage and showing Kitria how to tell the difference between a specific edible berry and a similar looking poisonous one by the tiny spines along the stem. He was proving he had paid more attention than he let on in classes at the academy in Etrion. Aside from being unexpected in that respect, it was also a pleasant surprise to see him connecting with someone. Considering Kitria had lost her tehnaak in the Devastation, they had that and their shared experience of being abducted by Jaysen and the council to link them.

When he noticed Veyl watching, Gannon tossed the foliage aside and walked over while Kitria turned to working on a meal. Kyril joined his sister, offering to help.

Gannon placed his palm against Veyl's face. "Not feverish yet, but I don't like how that cut was looking earlier. We should check it again before it gets too dark."

Veyl caught his hand when he reached for her side and met his eyes. "If it is worse, what can we do? We need to make it to Vanris. They'll have a healer at the first watchtower we get to who can do more for it than we can here. If we fail, we have far bigger problems."

He nodded, the tension in his jaw exposing his concern without a need for words. "You're right. I'll help Kitria prepare some food."

"Gannon." She didn't release his hand, keeping him there a moment longer. "We wouldn't have made it this far without you. Thank you."

"See, a lifetime spent being a calloch, and now all I have to do to look like a hero is to put forth the minimum effort." He gave her a crooked smile as he withdrew his hand, though the worry never left his eyes.

A few hours later, as dusk blended the colors of the landscape, they struck out again. Veyl rode with Kitria this time on their strongest mount, hoping the gelding would have the constitution to keep up with the other horses with the two lighter women on him if watchtower guards pursued them into the Break. An outcome far more likely than the alternative, though a quiet, trouble-free crossing made for a pleasant daydream. Kyril would keep a connection to all three horses to ensure they remained calm and controlled along the way, assuming they even made it past the border. Seyn trotted out ahead, always staying within visual range, using her keen sense to scout for danger.

A light drizzle gave them an excuse to put their hoods up as they moved out to where the trees were sparser and onto a narrow dirt track heading from someone's homestead. This was where it became tricky.

When they approached the border, someone was going to notice them regardless of where they crossed. The lack of cover, along with the usual patrols and anyone Jaysen might have sent to watch for them, made slipping across unchallenged highly unlikely.

They merged onto a more established dirt road that Veyl recognized as the one her family had taken to Balarus. Her gaze drifted toward Deepwater, the sound of explosions playing back in her head, sending a shudder through her. When she looked away, she found Kyril watching her from his mount alongside them, one brow creeping up a fraction as if to say, "You see my problem?"

Veyl focused forward, adjusting her seat behind Kitria. The group moved into an extended trot, the jarring gait wrenching at the stitches over her ribs. She put her attention to searching for danger and holding on, trying not to let the pain distract her. The more eyes they had watching for problems, the better.

The other helpful aspect of the drizzle was that it added firmness to the sandy soil this close to the coast. They passed a few evening travelers, including a single open wagon hauling vegetables from somewhere to the south. When the road curved more to the west, toward the ocean and Deepwater, they split off into the sandy hills with their thick tufts of cutting grass. The hair and tough skin on the horses' legs appeared to be enough to resist those jagged blades of grass, but guilt still twisted in her chest at making them move at speed through it.

A Sarketi watchtower loomed not far to the west, a towering gray stone building, simple and neutral in architecture for an object that sent the chill of dread through her. Another stood almost directly east of them now, which meant they were about to cross the border into the Break. As she considered the looming structure, a line of mounted guards burst from the stable alongside it, their speed and heading erasing any doubt as to their purpose.

"They're coming," Veyl declared, securing her hold on Kitria as they urged the horses into a full gallop. "Seven, I think, from the east watchtower."

Kyril and Gannon moved their mounts close on either side of the gelding she and Kitria rode. Veyl could do little but try to maintain her balance and avoid making it any more difficult for the horse. Seyn sprinted ahead of them, picking the route out into the Break through low dunes that were now more sand than grass. The shifting surface made it harder for the horses, but if they could get past this area, they would be on firmer ground again. They had hoped to make it that far before being spotted, but luck wasn't with them tonight.

A horn blared from the tower, receiving an answering call seconds later from the one to the west. Veyl didn't bother looking. How many pursuers they had mattered little. They had no choice but to keep running if they wanted to survive.

Where was that crackle of energy? She tried to reach for the fickle ability hidden within herself, but something—fear, infection, exhaustion, or perhaps simple self-doubt—kept it from responding. She clung to Kitria and the horse they shared, a useless piece of baggage slowing them down. Ahead of them, Seyn let out a sharp cry. Looking toward the wave dancer, Veyl spotted figures in the moonlight, standing up from where they had lain in wait beyond the top of a rise. She saw their silhouettes as two raised bows, then the horse on the left, Kyril's mount, let out a squeal and went down, slamming into their gelding as it fell. The animal struggled to stay upright, but Veyl felt the instant it lost its footing and she and Kitria flew from its back as it went down.

Despite her effort to curl into the fall, there was nothing but pain when she hit. Stitches ripped free of flesh in a flash of sharp agony. Blood filled her mouth from her teeth cutting into the inside of her cheek on impact, her body striking the ground with enough force to break something.

Veyl struggled up on one elbow, registering a vague sense of surprise that she could move that much. Gannon had stopped his horse and leapt down near her and Kitria, who lay unmoving a few feet away. Seyn stood growling at the Sarketi soldiers, her hackles up, favoring one front leg. The two horses that had gone down were struggling to get to their feet again, one with a visibly broken leg. She couldn't see Kyril past them.

"Fucking idiots," one man snapped in Sarketi, hurrying down the slope toward them. He pointed at Veyl. "I told you we need that one alive."

She could hear riders from one of the towers coming up behind them, the horses' hooves making a hollow thudding sound on the sandy ground as they slowed their mounts. Her side, where the stitches had pulled out, was on fire with agony, and part of her back and shoulder that had taken most of the impact felt little better.

"Isn't that their princess?" a mounted tower guard asked.

"Are you Vanrian?" another man barked back at him.

"No, sir."

"Then follow your orders." The man raised his voice, shouting to the group that had ambushed them. "Are these the fugitives you were looking for?"

"Yes, we only need that one. The rest can disappear."

Veyl's breath caught. Time slowed. Men on both sides of them raised their bows, nocking arrows and aiming at her companions. They were going to kill them. All of them.

A fire burst to life in Veyl's chest, sending molten agony searing through her to the tips of her fingers and toes. Her vision went white. Screams echoed in her ears, in her own voice and that of many others. Lightning lashed out, and fear swept in. Fear of death; quick and meaningless, or slow and agonizing. Fear of loss; losing loved ones, homes, cherished possessions, purpose.

And she continued to burn, the internal fire blazing hotter with each heartbeat. It blinded her, but somehow, she could see everyone around her falling victim to the storm of flames. The Sarketi soldiers, Kyril, Gannon, Kitria, and Seyn. But it didn't stop there. Everything burned. Her home. Her country. Her family. She watched it all, helpless as the flesh of those she loved melted away along with her own, destroyed by the awful power that had made her its vessel.

Tears ran from her sightless eyes, sliding down her skin as hot as liquid metal. Pain and helpless despair crushed her. Her world died around her. Died because of her.

Then something pushed back against the fire. A soothing presence, cool and bright. Veyl reached for it, barely brushing it with the fingertips of her awareness at first, then grabbing hold and pulling. It swept in like a wave, dousing the fire, easing the pain. The last flickering lightning retreated before it, falling back to the center of her. It lingered there, sullen tendrils lashing out until that cooling wave washed in and smothered even those. She lay in its embrace, floating on the refreshing comfort of it, drifting as her racing heart gradually slowed. Clinging to it, she sailed in a black sea for what seemed an eternity before voices reached her, coming from across a great distance.

"Is she alive?"

"Her eyes are open, and she's got a pulse, but she's unresponsive."

"We can't do much here. Bring her."

She's waking up. Give her something. This journey will be a lot easier for her if she sleeps through it." The voice was unfamiliar and male, but he spoke Vanrian without a Thaelian accent, which brought some small measure of comfort.

"Be a lot safer for us too," a woman somewhere closer muttered under her breath.

Veyl's body hurt. All of it. An intense ache consumed every inch of her. And her eyes refused to respond to her desire to open them, locking her in darkness. The creaking of wooden wheels accompanied the distinctive rocking of a wagon.

Someone slid a hand behind her head, gently lifting.

"Mm…" Veyl tried to speak, but her voice refused to work right. It was as though her body had forgotten how to function. "Mm…"

Something touched her lips. The edge of a cup.

"Drink."

Veyl tried to turn away, but even that effort failed. The most she could do was keep her mouth shut, though she wasn't sure if that was because she didn't want to open it, or because she couldn't. Whoever had her could do as they pleased. She was as helpless as a newborn. At least she could hear, but that was the extent of her functioning faculties for the moment. Even the miserable Frightener ability that landed her in this position had gone as silent as the dead.

"You're lucky to be alive," the woman said, not moving the cup away, "but if the last dose we gave you wears off much more, you won't feel that way about it."

Veyl tried to trust her. She sounded Vanrian, but after everything she had been through, to be blind and helpless in the hands of strangers was almost more than she could bear.

Gentle fingers brushed away a tear that slipped down her cheek. "Drink. You'll feel better when you wake again. I promise."

By the time she convinced her jaw to relax enough to part her lips, she was trembling, and the tears were coming faster. Would she wake up again? If she did, where would she be, and with whom?

"There you go."

The woman tipped the cup enough to pour the liquid slowly into Veyl's mouth. The taste at least was familiar. A common elixir used by Vanrian healers to sedate more seriously injured patients. Once she had swallowed, the hand eased her head back down. She couldn't imagine relaxing on her own, but the sedative would force her to soon enough.

"If you're done there," the man spoke again, "I could use some help with this one."

Dread seized her chest. She yearned to ask who "this one" was, but she couldn't manage more than a desperate moan that they ignored. They lowered their voices, speaking in whispers now as if to avoid her hearing them. She strained to listen, barely breathing, but could make out too few words to put anything together. Meanwhile, the sedative began taking effect, and panic gripped her as it dragged her toward darkness.

Then the presence from before returned. A soothing wave washed over her, calm and reassuring. Desperate to feel something other than fear and pain, Veyl surrendered herself to it, letting it embrace her and ease her descent into forced slumber.

•

When she woke again, it was a slow ascent back to awareness. The movement and sounds of the wagon were gone, replaced by the warmth of a comfortable bed and soft sheets. The all-over agony that tormented her before was also absent, concentrated into a few areas of more severe pain from the cut on her ribs, bruising from the fall, and a sustained throbbing in her head. Other wounds from her fight in the stable—the ones on her arm and cheek—barely hurt. Even the worst one no longer felt hot and angry, just sharply painful.

When she convinced her eyes to open, which they were more willing to do this time, she feared it might be just a dream, though the pain suggested otherwise. The bed she lay in was her own, back in the palace in Etrion. She could hardly believe it was real.

Something moist touched her hand, and she looked over, surprised to see Seyn standing by the bed. The wave dancer licked her fingers a second time, tail wagging tentatively. The beast's presence brought a perhaps unprecedented measure of comfort. She heard voices in the adjacent sitting room and scratched behind Seyn's ears as she turned her attention to listening.

She recognized Feral Ahndhomen Jhanik's voice. "...do with her?"

Her father answered. "She's our daughter. We're going to help her."

"Do you think you can?" Jhanik countered, a demanding edge in his tone that hearkened back to a time when the two men had shared the same rank. "The overflow from what she did out there—just the overflow—scarred the minds of tower guards on both sides of the break. That's an area of several miles. And she broke everyone within half a mile of her."

Everyone?

With her heart in her throat, Veyl sat up, wincing at the pull on the stitches over her ribs, though it was reassuring in a way. Healers had tended the wound, and it had a clean bandage over it. It would mend now. She stood carefully, ignoring the throb of protest in her head and the stiffness of bruised muscles, and went to the wardrobe, selecting a simple, loose-fitting dress. She could still hear them speaking beyond the door as she put it on.

"Why is this happening to her?"

That was her mother. Hearing her parents' voices was nearly enough to break her down into tears, but she couldn't allow herself to indulge those emotions. It was still too hard to believe that she might be safe... and that she might have killed the others.

"Your daughter is an aberration." Nerith spoke now, words that immediately made Veyl feel less confident in her safety than she had a moment ago. "It's not common to have someone manifest an ability so powerful it can break people and wholly defy the wielder's control the way hers does, but given her bloodlines, she is a prime candidate for it. Your father has this problem to a much lesser degree, Kas. In his case, it has proven more manageable. Even your ability is strong enough that, if you were anything other than a Feral, you might have been a Breaker too."

Veyl walked to the door, Seyn at her side, and set her hand on the handle, waiting to hear what else they might say about the situation.

"A Breaker?" her father asked. "That's what we call it?"

Her mother answered him, her voice strained by the tightness of unshed tears. "Instead of doing what its wielder intends, the ability flares out of control, like a violent gust in a windstorm, and breaks the minds of their victims. The damage is irreversible. We don't talk about Breakers often because of how rare they are, but they have occurred now and then throughout our history."

"How have we handled them in the past?"

Silence fell over the room.

Veyl opened the door and walked out. "They put them to death. Mercifully, of course."

In seconds, her parents were on their feet, rushing over to wrap her in a careful group embrace. Her mother kissed her uninjured cheek. Even with how gentle they were, it hurt in places, but she still relished having their arms around her too much to care about the pain. Tears fell from her eyes. For her parents, for herself, for the people she had broken. Had she really broken everyone within half a mile? Did that mean her companions were dead or tucked away somewhere in a catatonic state? She couldn't speak past the agonizing sorrow that clenched her throat.

"No one is putting you to death," her father whispered in a voice ragged with emotion.

Almost as one, they stepped back to look at her. Irith sat beside the couch, watching her intently, but he didn't approach, appearing uncertain what to make of the wave dancer at her side. Veyl held a hand out to the big predator, and he accepted the invitation, padding over to push his cheek into it. He closed his eyes and purred when she scratched behind his ears, snapping them open when Seyn took a step toward him, leaning out to sniff at him and making an odd, querying sound in her throat.

"We were so worried about you," her mother said, drawing Veyl's attention back to them. "The others told us—"

A desperate hope ignited in Veyl's chest. "Others?"

"Gannon, Kyril, and his sister," her father answered.

She could barely breathe. "But I thought… I didn't break them?"

"Not for lack of trying." It was Jhanik who spoke, the tall Feral cutting into her with his sharp words. The shaved sides of his hair were growing out, obscuring the ke'hanoath tattooed there. Down the center, his blond hair hung to the middle of his back. Though he had been a regular presence throughout her life, he regarded her with a stinging wariness now. "Ahnkreth Kyril believes the wave dancer protected them. I don't know if the beast could have done that, but you only scarred their minds instead of breaking them like everyone else in the vicinity, so there might be something to it. They've all seen an Evoker now to erase the incident so they won't suffer the worsening nightmares."

After what the last Evoker did to Kyril, she couldn't imagine that experience sat well with him, but at least he was alive.

"How did we get back here?"

"Jhanik's unit is one of several we've had scouting the western portion of the Crimson Break since we learned of Thrasser's attempt to eliminate Jaysen. They intercepted a couple of Eydarith making their way here who told them…" her father trailed off, nodding to Jhanik.

"They said they spotted a group of Vanrians in northern Sarket heading for the border who looked like they might be in trouble. Bastards couldn't be bothered to help you themselves, but at least they alerted us." He punctuated his words with a low growl, a skill Ferals seemed to pick up from their beasts.

Veyl set a hand on Seyn's head, and the wave dancer sat beside her, no longer trying to sniff at the puzzled cliff cat. "They did help, in their way."

"They clearly could have done more," Jhanik countered, and she couldn't argue the point. "We kept a closer watch on the area after that. When the overflow from your ability hit us, we went searching for you. Fortunately, we were far enough out that you didn't break anyone in my unit, but most required a visit with an Evoker. Arkos protected me, and he's the one who found you. He seemed drawn to that beast." Jhanik gestured to Seyn.

Arkos, his kanodrak. Her father's kanodrak had reacted strongly to the wave dancer as well. They owed Seyn a great deal, especially if the wave dancer truly had protected the others from her ability.

"They feared you were broken when they found you," Nerith added. "Then you started coming back along the way. Kyril believes that was Seyn's doing, too. If that's true, you have quite a remarkable and devoted friend there. She's refused to leave your side beyond allowing him to escort her out to relieve herself."

"He's not injured?"

Her father snorted a laugh. "He is, but he's also strong, stubborn, and carrying a great weight of anger on his shoulders, though he hasn't been willing to talk much about that."

"All of which appear to be common traits among Ferals." Her mother arched a brow at her father, who shared a brief look with Jhanik.

The other feral grinned, apparently happy to be lumped in with the strong, stubborn, and angry set.

Seyn got to her feet, her attention turning to the door a second before someone knocked. The tentative wag of her long tail caused a tightening in Veyl's chest.

As the closest, Jhanik opened the door. Kyril stood there in casual Vanrian attire, which somehow looked more attractive on him than on anyone else she had ever seen dressed similarly. Maybe he just made all clothing look good. He had a brace on one wrist, likely injured when his horse fell, and fresh bruising and scrapes on one side of his face, but he was distinctly alive. His brows rose a fraction, registering a hint of surprise at seeing her standing there. If not for what Jaysen had done, she would have gone to him and thrown her arms around him. She might have even kissed him, regardless of who was watching, but their relationship had changed, so she stayed where she was.

"I'm pleased to see you awake, Khesran." He met her eyes for a heartbeat before his gaze dropped to Seyn. "I was checking in to see if your wave dancer would like to join us for a walk."

Her wave dancer? And who was us?

She could feel everyone watching her, forcing her to hide the dagger twisting in her chest at his formal tone. Then Ceris stuck his head into the doorway alongside Kyril, and her eyes widened at the implications.

She faced her parents. "Grandfather survived?"

Her father nodded. "Arhk arrived a few days ago with three ships from the fleet. The rest had sustained too much damage to make the return voyage. Their crews and soldiers stayed behind to repair them and help handle the situation in Dagony. He told us you disappeared the night the Ukhen'kya attacked, along with the Thaelian council and one of their fleets. He said Jaysen, Gannon, Kyril, and his sister vanished too. Arhk had his suspicions, but we didn't know for certain whether Jaysen was another victim of the council or an accomplice until the four of you showed up."

"Oh, he was most definitely working with them." She couldn't keep the anger and hurt from coming out in her tone. Fury threatened to fill the deep chasm of heartache within her, and she preferred it that way. She could no longer stand the sorrow.

Her father offered a solemn, sympathetic smile.

"I'm sorry. I know what it's like to be betrayed by some-one you trust. After all you've been through, I wish it weren't necessary, but we will need to—"

"You needn't be so tentative. I know how this works." She snapped, cringing inwardly at the sorrow that rose in his eyes in response. "Apologies, Father. I shouldn't have interrupted you. It only makes sense that I should speak to an Evoker. I have information the others don't because Jaysen kept me..." She squeezed her eyes shut for a second, trying to push away memories of his lips on hers, his hands touching her. She shuddered. When she opened her eyes, Kyril and her father wore strikingly similar expressions of rage. "He kept me close to him."

Her mother stepped forward and took her hand. "You don't need to go through all of that yet. Dhomvalen Arhk is resting right now, but he wanted to be there when we spoke to you."

Something in her mother's words caused an un-pleasant squirming in her stomach. "Is he all right?"

"He suffered severe burns in the attack, but they will heal," Nerith answered. "I can check on him, if you like."

Her father shook his head, the scrutinizing look in his eyes making Veyl instantly uneasy. "Let him rest. Do you feel up for a brief walk, Veyl?"

"Kas..." her mother gave a tiny shake of her head. "She only just woke, and she's injured."

"Yes, I do," Veyl answered. Despite her pain, she yearned to feel alive and, more importantly, free to move about at her own discretion.

"Very well. I need to check on Niskenya. We can walk down together." He swept Kyril into their group with his gaze.

Kyril stepped back from the door, misreading his in-tent, perhaps deliberately. "I'll return to my rooms and give you two a chance to catch up."

Her father's gaze didn't waver. "I insist, Ahnkreth."

Despite the tightening of his jaw, Kyril inclined his head a fraction. "As you wish, Khemron."

Her mother gave her a gentle hug before letting her follow her father from the room.

"Be careful with your daughter, Kas," Nerith called after them.

The outing was slow, given that two of them were recovering from injuries, and awkward. Veyl and Seyn walked on Kasiel's left, with Irith, Kyril and Ceris on his right, the Feral ahnkreth staying a respectful half-step behind. The amount of effort he put into not looking in her direction made it worse than if he had glared at her the entire way. When her father broke the silence by asking about whether Seyn had truly protected them from Veyl's ability, Kyril glanced at the wave dancer, keeping his gaze low so he effectively avoided her eyes.

"Wave dancers can shield their bonded companions the same way I understand a kanodrak can," Kyril explained, one hand absently resting on Ceris's shoulders. "They can also form temporary bonds with others that would, in theory, allow them to defend those individuals. Whether they are capable of creating multiple bonds that quickly to use in that way, I don't honestly know, but given how fully the khesran's ability took over out there, I can offer no other explanation."

The khesran. Not Seh'hali. Not Veyl. She wanted to assume that was simply because her father was there, but something in his manner and his voice made it hard to believe that. He seemed more distant now than he had even on their journey from Taro. Had scarring his mind and nearly breaking him been enough to destroy what remained of their connection? If so, she couldn't truly blame him for that.

Veyl drew a deep breath, struggling not to relent

to the desperate urge to excuse herself, so she might return to the privacy of her rooms to cry. Tears threatened to break through her determined resolve, and she clenched her jaw hard enough it made the healing cut on her cheek hurt.

A newly familiar sensation moved through her then. A cool wave of comfort and affection. Veyl looked down to find Seyn gazing up at her, a surprising warmth in her deep sea-foam eyes.

"Veyl, is everything all right?"

She looked up at her father, then at Kyril, who now waited between two tethdrak statues at the entrance to the massive building overlooking the tethdrak canyon. At some point, she had stopped walking, though she didn't recall doing so. They stood looking at her, one with his cliff cat, the other with his wave dancer. She had always envied Ferals for their companions. Now, despite not being a Feral, she appeared to have a companion of her own. One who, as Kyril suspected, had made the choice to bond with her, and saved her and those dear to her more than once. Whether she had permanently lost Kyril, she had gained something priceless in this.

"Apologies, we got distracted."

She walked between them into the towering building with a kanodrak statue at its center. The rear wall stood open to the canyon, with the viewing platform at the back. As they descended on the mechanical lift, she noticed a change of focus in Kyril's eyes that told her he was reaching out to the tethdraks, the novelty of them drawing him in. If her father did the same, he hid it, turning his attention to Kyril instead with a scrutinizing gaze that didn't appear to bother the other man, assuming he noticed it.

When they reached the bottom, Seyn and Ceris bolted from the platform and sprinted around the area between the lift and the bars at the front of the enclosure together, enjoying the opportunity to stretch their legs. Irith watched, leaning forward a fraction as if tempted to join them. When her father gestured toward the two canines in offering, the cliff cat merely shifted closer to him.

Veyl received a little of the wave dancer's joy—a strange but pleasant sensation, like unto the happiness that could sometimes come through a tehnaak bond. It brought a faint smile to her lips. A few tethdraks near the front of the canyon stood and called out to the two in their odd clicks and shrieks.

"How did Ceris end up in Vanris?"

Her father set a hand on her shoulder, a gesture of support and perhaps a desire to reassure himself that she was truly there. "They let him out of the cell the council had locked him in when they found Kyril missing from the prison. Arhk said the beast wouldn't let them leave without him. For whatever reason, he insisted on coming, as if he thought doing so was his best chance at reuniting with his companion. Perhaps he just believed we would help him find Ahnkreth Kyril."

"Kyril is sufficient. My country is in far too shattered a state right now for my title to mean much."

Her father's regard was solemn. "Your title still carries weight in Vanris, regardless. However, I am fine with using your name if you return the favor. Come, let's visit Niskenya. She's impatient to see you," he added with a smile for Veyl, offering her his arm as if he could tell she was already growing weary.

Accepting, she walked with him to the tunnel that would take them through to the kanodraks canyon. Kyril followed with Seyn and Ceris bolting in before the door could shut them out. On the other side, Niskenya was already at the front awaiting her bonded companion, the massive kanodrak pacing restlessly along the bars. The moment they emerged, she dug her deadly claws into the soil and pushed her cheek hard against the bars in a strikingly cat-like gesture, the deep rumble of her purr rolling out to them. The warm, adoring smile that crept across her father's features had once made Veyl jealous of his affection for the kanodrak, but she had long since grown used to the idea that their relationship was something extraordinary.

As her father left her to walk to the bars, she noticed another of the massive beasts lurking nearby. A large male with the same silver-gray scaled hide as all the other kanodraks, but this one had a darker shading on his spine that dipped down his ribs and along the backs of his front legs. His milky white eyes had an unusual outline of bronze around the irises and pupils. The beast watched Kyril with an unnerving intensity that she suspected her father wouldn't appreciate once he let his attention move away from Niskenya. For his part, Kyril returned the kanodrak's scrutiny until it broke the connection to look down at the two wave dancers trotting up to the bars.

After a moment, her father turned to them, his wide-eyed gaze going from Veyl to Seyn and back. "That's no temporary bond."

CHAPTER TWENTY SEVEN

Kyril glanced at Veyl and Seyn, then looked at her father as if he were a recruit who had fallen behind in training. "I told you it wasn't. Their bond is as complete a bond as any we share with our beasts."

That meant he and her father had talked about her before she woke. How much had passed between them in that time? For that matter, how long had it been since they arrived in Etrion? Had the two spoken of anything more than the subject that most interested them—bonds with beasts?

"How is that possible?" her father asked.

"Wave dancers can form a bond with whomever they choose. Most commonly, if they decide to bond with a human at all, it is with a Feral because of the reciprocal nature of the connection. I am aware of only one recorded incident of a wave dancer bonding with someone who was not a Feral in our history on Thaelis. There may be others we weren't aware of. Seyn senses that your daughter is special." Kyril met Veyl's eyes for an instant, then looked away, turning his attention to the male kanodrak that was prowling closer.

Niskenya growled a low warning at the other beast, and her father put his hand through the bars. She quieted, stepping in to press the bone-plating over her forehead into his palm.

"Go ahead," he encouraged. "That one seems curious about you."

Kyril approached the bars, Ceris trotting to his side as if prepared to protect him from the massive beast in the enclosure.

Veyl moved closer to her father, Seyn coming to stand with her now. "You're letting him interact with a kanodrak?" she asked in a low voice.

Her father also spoke quietly, watching the beast approach the bars where Kyril was now standing. "I think it's clear he is choosing to be an ally, and, given the situation in Sarket, we may have need of another kanodrak rider in the future. If he has the potential, it can't hurt to discover it now."

"I assume he'll want to return to Thaelis."

"We'll figure that out later. For now, Vanris must be our priority." He glanced at Seyn. "How does it feel to have a companion of your own?"

"Extraordinary," she answered, though a painful constriction in her chest made it less so as she watched the silent exchange between Kyril and the predator facing him. Seyn pressed against her leg, and Veyl put a hand on the wave dancer's shoulders, accepting the offered comfort. "What else did you see through Niske's eyes?"

"I saw that the bond forming between you and Kyril has retracted some," he answered, easily delving to the heart of what she was asking. "Do you know what caused that?"

"Aside from my nearly breaking him and his sister with my ability? I..." Did she dare tell him more? Did it matter now? "Jaysen convinced himself that I had stopped loving him because Kyril had Nalika and Jinau work together to alter my memories. In retaliation, he had an Evoker strip away many of Kyril's memories of his time around me to try destroying the deeper relationship he believed had formed there."

"That is… nothing less than reprehensible. No wonder he's carrying such a weight of anger."

Silence extended between them. Kyril put a hand through the bars, offering it to the kanodrak. The beast growled, but moved his head closer, the long canines that dipped below his jaw coming within inches of soft human flesh. Veyl's gut squirmed with unease. The mighty predator could tear him apart. And yet, Kyril was magnificent, facing the deadly creature with no sign of fear, his posture straight and confident despite all the abuse he had suffered.

"Had something formed between you?" Her father's question startled her from her observations.

"Yes. You saw it with your own eyes." She tried to keep the frustration from creeping into her voice, but was only partly successful. "Or Niske's eyes, I suppose."

The male kanodrak lowered his head to sniff at the offered hand.

"What Jaysen did is unforgivable, but it might be better this way. Kyril is not a suitable match for you. I am sure you realize that."

She didn't look at her father, but she imagined he would be hard-pressed to miss her bitter smirk. "And how many people insisted you weren't a suitable match for Mother?"

"Veyl, that's not—"

Whatever he was going to say cut off when the kanodrak lunged forward, his jaws snapping shut on Kyril's hand. For a heartbeat, panic burst through Veyl, but Kyril stood perfectly still, facing the beast with no outward sign of pain or fear. The kanodrak's bared teeth had closed on the center of his hand, but they didn't appear to have broken the skin. The beast snarled at the Feral ahnkreth when he didn't pull away. Ceris growled back at it, hackles up, though he also remained still. After a second, the kanodrak huffed and let go, turning to lope off into the canyon.

Veyl saw the faintest tremble in Kyril's hand as he drew it back to his side, and a hint of deflation in the slight dropping of his shoulders. She let out the breath she hadn't realized she was holding. Then she noticed her father was watching her warily rather than the man who had just had his hand in the jaws of a kanodrak.

"Are you all right?"

"I'm not the one who…" She understood suddenly why he was asking. It wasn't fear she saw in his eyes as much as dread. Dread that he might have to hurt his own daughter to prevent her from harming others. She wanted to say he had nothing to fear, that her ability was under control, but that would be a lie. Unless something had changed. There had been no crackle of energy in response to that instant of panic. Why not? What kept it from reacting to her fear for Kyril? Why did it have to be so Break-blasted unpredictable? "I'm fine," she answered curtly.

Her father watched her a moment longer before facing the other Feral, who was striding over to join them. He gestured toward the departing kanodrak with a nod. "He appears to like you."

"It's hard to tell." Kyril glanced at his hand. "He adamantly refused me access to his mind."

Her father smiled fondly at Niskenya. "It will be entirely up to him whether he wants to allow that."

"And would you permit it, Khemron?" Kyril's brow furrowed, something in his shrewd gaze suggesting that he expected a trap.

"Perhaps." Her father gestured toward the tunnel that would take them out and started walking. "We have whispers of war coming from Sarket if the situation continues to deteriorate there. Considering the events in Thaelis, and that Jaysen and the Thaelian council abducted Vanris's heir intending to force her to marry him, there will be conflict regardless of whether he takes the throne from Thrasser." He glanced at Veyl. "In fact, I have the impression that his emerging victorious might be the less desirable outcome at this point."

She looked at him, a spark of unease in her chest. "Did Gannon give you my missive?"

He nodded. "We can discuss that more when we meet with the dhomvalen."

For the rest of the walk back, her father and Kyril talked about what it was like working with the beasts of Vanris and Thaelis, respectively. Veyl tried to appreciate how well the two were getting along. It might have been easier if she didn't know her father was looking for a new soldier to add to his ranks against Sarket rather than simply finding common ground. Easier as well, if her love for Kyril didn't remain the same despite the growing distance between them.

Seyn stayed by her side, ignoring Ceris and Irith, who were curiously venturing closer to one another. The female wave dancer seemed to understand how alone she felt at that moment, despite being around people she cared deeply for. Perhaps more so because she was. Her family feared her power, and the man she loved…

Had Jaysen won? She supposed he wouldn't see it that way, since she had escaped him. From where she was standing, it certainly looked like he had at least inflicted a wound that might never heal, one she had made worse with her erratic ability.

When they reached the palace, Jethan, Gannon, and Kitria met them at the side entrance. Worry pinched Gannon's features as he watched her make her way wearily to them. Pain and exhaustion dragged at her, but she wanted to see her grandfather before she relented to it, not that they were going to give her much choice in that.

Gannon approached her, speaking in a hushed voice. "You look tired."

Veyl nodded, a little surprised he didn't regard her with the same wariness everyone else did, given that he had fallen victim to her ability twice now. "I'm glad to see you well."

His gaze jumped from Kyril to Kitria, who had no visible injuries, though her measured steps were enough to make it clear she was suffering in some way, undoubtedly from their fall from the horse.

"Gannon, could you provide an escort for our Thaelian guests? We must speak with the dhomvalen." Her father drew Jethan into their group with a glance.

"Of course, Khemron." He offered a bow to her father, then looked at her again. "If you're up for it sometime this evening, Iyvalin and Ahrin would like to see you."

It delighted her to discover they were alive and back home, but she couldn't be certain her stamina would hold that long. "I can't promise, but I would like to see them as well."

Gannon nodded and started toward the door.

"Khemron, Khesran." Kyril gave a slight bow to each of them before following him.

Kitria offered an uneasy nod to them before hurrying after him.

Once they were gone, Jethan gave Veyl a gentle hug. "You attract trouble almost more than your father did when he was your age."

She just as carefully returned the embrace, increasingly aware of how much her assortment of injuries hurt. "That's not comforting, given the stories I've heard you tell."

"I'm just glad we have you back," he murmured before releasing her and turning to her father. "The dhomvalen is waiting for us."

"I'm confident we would all prefer to get this part over with." Her father offered her his arm. "You look as if you could use something to hold on to."

She managed a faint, grateful smile as she slid her arm through his, leaning on him a little more than she wanted to as they made their way to Arhk's private chambers. When they entered, she sucked in a breath of surprise, trying not to react outwardly to the change in her grandfather. The skin on the left side of his face, from the corner of his mouth to up around his ear, the pointed tip of which had burned off, was an angry, mottled red, glistening with a recent application of salve. His beautiful white-blond hair was gone on that side of his head and cut shorter elsewhere than she had ever seen it, possibly to remove charred ends.

He stood and walked to her. She noticed burns on the back of his left hand when he embraced her, pulling her into his arms. "I am sorry I failed to protect you."

The contact had to be painful for him. More so than it was for her even, but she couldn't bring herself to pull away. "You didn't fail me," she whispered, her voice cracking. "We were both betrayed."

Veyl rested her head on his shoulder, welcoming the pain in the cut. It helped focus her hatred toward Jaysen for what he had put her through and for what he had done to the people she loved. She felt safe in Arhk's arms, regardless of any notion he had that he had failed her. She didn't see it that way. The others in the room waited quietly. Not just her father and Jethan, but her mother and Keyla were there along with three Evokers. Arhk and her father's Evokers, Ahnvaris Zafyr and Ahnvaris Yserra, and Arhk's romantic partner, Ahndhomen Setera, were all present. Would they ask about the events prior to that night on Thaelis when Jaysen and the council took them? She hoped not, but she would face whatever questions they threw at her. They might fear her now, but she refused to be afraid of the people who raised her.

Finally, Arhk kissed her head and let go of her. A gesture that must have caused him pain. "As distasteful as it may be, there are matters we must discuss, some of which are going to be difficult for you."

She nodded and sank into the chair he gestured to, grateful to be off her feet at least. Once this was done, she would be more than ready for some rest.

Yserra and Zafyr stayed standing behind the couch Arhk sat on. Setera and her parents sat with him, Jethan and Keyla taking chairs to one side. When they had all settled, her parents regarded her with matching expressions of sympathy. Arhk, his eyes glassy with pain he wouldn't put voice to, offered nothing of the sort, and that made him easier to look at somehow.

Before they could start, the door opened, and Tavin entered. He was growing into the very image of their father, though his features had a little of their mother's refined elegance. His hound, Loth, was with him. A short-haired beast with a brindle coat of black on red. He wasn't nearly as tall as Seyn, whose tail swished softly across the floor where she sat next to Veyl's chair, but he was broader through the chest and shoulders.

Tavin glanced around the room and grimaced. "Do we have to make such an interrogation out of this?"

"These are dire matters that affect the future of our country," their mother answered. "Sit."

Tavin gave Veyl a sympathetic look before he sank down beside Jethan. Loth settled on the floor next to him, head tilted to one side as he returned Seyn's scrutiny.

Their father drew a breath and initiated the conversation. "Khesran Veyl, the letter you wrote for Gannon to deliver... was it composed under duress?" He paused, waiting until she nodded. "Prince Jaysen had it in his head to marry you and force an alliance with Vanris. Is that correct?"

"He did."

"And were you planning to go along with it?"

As if Jaysen had given her a choice. How much had her parents figured out from merely reading her words? They knew her too well for her to risk lying about it, and she no longer cared to lie to the people she loved, not knowing that her ability might prove to be a death sentence. Besides, with three Evokers in the room, hiding things would be unusually difficult. "He didn't plan to give me a choice in the matter, though he believed I wanted it and that I merely had yet to remember that. But yes, I considered it. At one point, I thought it might be the only way I could protect Gannon and Kitria and possibly prevent a war."

"But you ultimately chose escape instead. What changed your mind?"

"Aside from the fact that being touched and kissed by Jaysen made me want to kill myself?" The rise of anger in their expressions was mildly gratifying, even if it did nothing to undo the torments she had suffered. Tavin shifted in his seat, lowering his eyes. Knowing the person they had grown up with had treated her this way couldn't sit any better with him than it did with her, though at least Jaysen wasn't his former tehnaak. She took a deep breath, struggling to push away memories of those unwelcome attentions, and glanced toward the door. "I discovered Jaysen had also taken Ahnkreth Kyril and intended to execute him. I might have negotiated freedom for Gannon and Kitria, but nothing I could do would save Kyril short of breaking him free."

Arhk arched a brow, though the habitual gesture elicited a grimace of pain. "And saving this one man was worth going to war?"

She faced him, meeting eyes the same color as her

own. "Would doing otherwise have avoided it?"

"That was not the question."

She held his gaze, trying not to focus on any specific encounters with the current subject of their inquiry in her mind. "Yes."

Her mother spoke into the opening. "And how did you escape a castle full of Thaelian and Sarketi enemies?"

This was where the tale took an unusual turn, in a way that she hoped would distract them from her determination to save Kyril. "The Eydarith hold Taro. They are more of a culture unto themselves than I believe we realized. We had inside help." A few raised brows told her they hadn't dug too deeply into Kitria and Kyril's experiences of the escape yet. Perhaps she had not been unconscious for as long as she feared after reaching the city. She set a hand on Seyn's head, hoping the significance of the animal's devotion wouldn't go unnoticed.

"Wavelord Kronach believes I am something he calls wave-touched, favored by the Tempest, the Eydarith god. He thought that of Kyril as well and admitted that he did not respect Jaysen or feel he was worthy of me. He showed me where they were keeping Kyril and encouraged me to take control of my situation." She could tell by their expressions that the visiting messengers from Kronach also hadn't disclosed these details, assuming they were even aware of them. That they allowed Gannon to stay behind outside Taro and had alerted Jhanik's unit to her group's approach suggested they weren't entirely ignorant of their lord's meddling.

"I…" Veyl lowered her eyes, a flush of shame warming her cheeks. "Seyn allowed me to break her bonded companion—the Feral they had holding my zenyal bond—and my two guards." From there, she related the details of their escape, the interest of her audience growing exponentially when she shared with them the unusual roles of the Eydarith wavelord and his warriors in those events.

Her father and Arhk, upon receiving confirming nods from the Evokers, exchanged a thoughtful look.

Before the others could speak, her mother leaned forward. "Did you get the impression we might find a potential ally in Wavelord Kronach?"

Veyl considered the fierce ruler. He was rude, intimidating, and followed his own moral code, one that proved confusing for anyone outside his head. Yet, for all that, she respected him and was grateful for what he had done for her, even if she might have appreciated a kinder approach. "Wavelord Kronach is fearless and unpredictable. He may not have a high opinion of Jaysen, but he respects Thrasser less for his underhanded efforts to remove the prince. He told me he believes Jaysen has a right to challenge Thrasser for the throne and force a confrontation. I suspect he will support that attempt if Jaysen agrees to acknowledge his sovereignty in Taro. What his intentions are beyond that, I can't pretend to know."

Her father looked thoughtful. "His messengers delivered Jaysen's missive with a distinct air of impartiality, expressly stating that the words within were from Prince Jaysen and their involvement in the delivery was not to be taken as a declaration of any kind from Wavelord Kronach. I don't think we should discount him, nor should we expect him to act on our behalf without considerable incentive."

Her mother placed a hand on his leg. An absent gesture of connection. "As we were getting settled, Kas told me Jaysen had a Thaelian Evoker extract some of Ahnkreth Kyril's memories. Why? What did they take?"

Veyl shifted in her seat.

"We should discuss that later," her father said, taking her mother's hand to soften his dismissal of her query, and Veyl barely held back a look of gratitude. "Khesran, who would you consider the greater threat to us now, King Thrasser or Prince Jaysen?"

Veyl met his eyes, a little surprised by the question and the weight his grave regard put on her response. "We know Thrasser was preparing something. He is clearly a threat to the current peace, but..." She clenched her teeth as the memory of Jaysen's possessive kisses rushed to the front of her mind again. It felt like a betrayal to speak the next words of the man who had once been her dearest friend and spirit sibling, but all that had changed. He had changed. "Jaysen's mind has become dangerously unbalanced. As much as I despise Thrasser, I believe having Jaysen on the throne at this point could prove worse."

Her father glanced around at the others. "We need to collect more information from the other three and consider our next course of action. Do we reach out and offer our support to one of them? Do we wait to see who rises to the top and try negotiating after the dust settles? Or do we take Sarket's future into our hands and move against them while their focus is on each other?"

"There is something else we must address first." Setera's tentative words caught everyone's attention. She gave Veyl an apologetic grimace. "We need to decide how to handle Khesran Veyl's uncontrolled ability before someone else gets hurt. She has the potential power within her to break this entire city."

Veyl's chest constricted, the room crushing in around her, making it hard to breathe. Could she really do that much damage?

Arhk took Setera's hand in a rare public display of affection, his expression free of the distress that showed on the faces of the others. "We do not need to discuss this. Veyl is no longer a Frightener." He stated it with a certainty that defied argument.

"But…" Veyl stared at him, confused. "How is that possible?"

He met her eyes. "I do not understand it, but I can feel that you and I no longer share that bond. My guess is that the wave dancer, when she saved you from breaking yourself out in the desert, may have somehow broken your ability in the process. You are neither a Frightener nor a Breaker anymore."

Veyl stared at him, her emotions oscillating wildly between relief and distress. Despite those extreme fluctuations, not the faintest crackle of power rose within her.

CHAPTER TWENTY EIGHT

I need to rest." Veyl stood abruptly, wincing at the pain the sudden movement caused. "Excuse me."

More than one person got to their feet and called after her, asking if she was all right as she hurried from the room. Seyn conveniently interrupted her parents' efforts to reach out to her when she got up to follow. Every rushed step pulled on the stitches in her side, but she had no intention of slowing. The lack of crackling energy in response to the tempest of her emotions made her want to laugh and weep at once. She heard the door behind her open, a little surprised when it was Tavin with Loth who came jogging up beside her.

"Veyl, hold on."

She quickened her stride, despite the fatigue dragging at her limbs and the soaring agony. A wild sense of panic made her breath come in strained gasps by the time they turned the corner to the hall her rooms were in.

"I would have thought you'd be happy to be rid of it after all of this."

She stopped and faced him so abruptly that Loth's hackles rose, and he growled. Seyn stepped between her and the hound, her membranous black ears folded back and her teeth bared. In a precisely mirrored motion, Veyl and Tavin each placed a calming hand on their respective beasts' shoulders.

"I would be happy, except that I wouldn't have escaped Jaysen when I did if not for my ability, and I couldn't have stopped them from killing the others in the Break. Not to mention that I could not have fought the Unclean in Thaelis or halted the Sarketi naval attack that killed Lorek before they claimed any more lives. I'm helpless to protect the people I care about now." She wiped roughly at a tear that crept down one cheek.

An earnest, gentle smile tugged at the corner of his mouth. "That's not true at all. You weren't helpless before your ability awakened. Why would you be now? I always admired your skill in combat and your courage growing up. I still do. Everything you've gone through this year… I can't imagine facing all that and still being so brave and so willing to put yourself at risk to protect those around you. You are my hero, Veyl. You always have been, and that certainly hasn't changed. The only thing that's different is that you're no longer a danger to the people you care so much about." He smirked down at Seyn. "And I can't even make you jealous of my companion anymore."

Fondness swelled in her chest. "Look at you, being the sensible, supportive one." She gently nudged Seyn out of the way and Loth backed down, likely at an unspoken command from Tavin, allowing her to pull him into a hug. When had her little brother grown so tall?

He chuckled as he returned the embrace. "I was always the sensible one."

A tentative smile curved her lips, and she squeezed him tighter, ignoring her pain. "Thank you, Tav," she murmured.

They stayed that way for several seconds. When they parted, he patted Loth's head. "I'll tell everyone that you went to rest if you need time alone. Loth and I can fend them off for a while."

"I'd appreciate that."

Her intent, when she lay gingerly back on her bed a few minutes later, not bothering to change, was to come up with a plan for going forward from here. Seyn hopped up on the bed, moving with surprising care across the covers, and stretched out beside her, warm and reassuring. In seconds, Veyl was sound asleep.

In that darkness, she returned to the room in Kronach's castle with Jaysen there, mocking her for her inability to break him. Kyril stood in a corner, watching in neutral silence as her former tehnaak drugged her as he had on the ship, then threatened to take advantage of her that way until she bore him a proper heir to his kingdom. No matter how she tried to fight, she could do nothing to stop it when he brought in an Evoker to destroy every wonderful memory she had of being loved by the Feral ahnkreth who now stood passively observing it all.

Then the nightmare changed, and Jaysen came to her in her room in Etrion, his smile vacant, the dagger he had given her in his hand. She lay in her bed, unable to move or speak, as he sauntered over and threw off the covers. He set the blade against her throat with one hand, gathering up her nightdress with the other. Leaning down, he kissed her, then drew away slightly. Her stomach turned as his fingers slid up the inside of her thigh.

"I am sorry, Veyl, but after you ran, I realized you would never remember that I'm the one you love. I can't leave it like that. If you no longer love me, I won't let you love anyone. I'm going to make you mine, and if you still don't love me when I'm through..." He trailed off and dug the edge of the blade into her neck.

Veyl woke with a cry. A hand touched her right arm, and she jerked away, bumping up against someone lying on her left. For an instant, panic threatened to consume her. Then she focused on Gannon, getting up from the chair next to her bed, and Seyn pressed closer to her, leaning over to lick her on the cheek.

"Sorry. I didn't intend to startle you."

Veyl put a hand to her chest, feeling the pounding of her heart as she struggled to catch her breath. The nightmares stuck vividly in her head. "No, it's all right." She forced a few slower breaths, trying to calm herself. "But… what are you doing in here?"

"Tavin told us what happened, and that you were upset. We came to see if you needed anything or any-one. When you didn't answer the door, we were going to leave, but you cried out, so we rushed inside. You must have been having a bad dream. You quieted when Seyn nuzzled closer to you, so we decided not to wake you. After a bit of discussion, we agreed someone should stay close in case you needed anything."

"I assume we includes Ahrin and Iyvy?" She reached out, and he took her hand, helping her sit up. Seyn hopped off the bed and came around to stand next to them.

He nodded. "They're in the sitting room."

It was odd that he was the one they selected to watch over her. Was that because of what they had recently gone through together? Or had he perhaps insisted on it?

"You were having nightmares?"

Veyl nodded.

He stared out the window for a few seconds, and his jaw clenched as if he were fighting some internal battle before he finally looked at her again. "You said Jaysen's name in your sleep, and not in a good way."

To think that less than a year ago, she longed desperately for the chance to be reunited with her tehnaak and childhood friend. Now she still wanted to see Jaysen again, but with a far different purpose in mind. It hurt to think of how dear he had been to her. Of how much she had loved him. Not in the way she loved Kyril, but as someone she trusted implicitly and believed she could rely upon no matter what happened. How wrong she had been. Was it acceptable to mourn him as she had known him, while wanting to destroy the person he had become?

"Do you want to talk about it?"

The concern in his eyes told her he would listen to whatever she had to say. She took his hand. "Thank you truly, but I'm not quite ready to."

"When you are ready, I know I've been a calloch in the past, but I promise you I can be better, and I want to support you."

"I know, and I appreciate it." She found a smile for him, helped along by Seyn's head coming to rest against her thigh, the wave dancer gazing fondly up at her. A latent sorrow lingered in those sea-foam eyes, though, perhaps because of what she had done to her former bonded to help Veyl. "I have something I would like to talk to you all about."

Gannon nodded, keeping hold of her hand long enough to help her up. When they entered the adjacent room, Iyvalin and Ahrin hurried over to give her hugs as Gannon stood by protectively, warning them to be gentle.

When they were through the tearful greetings, the other three sat, but Veyl didn't join them. She clasped her hands and considered them seriously. "I have something to ask you all, and please know I won't be upset if you don't want to do this."

•

A short time later, the four of them stood outside the war room where her parents were holding a small council meeting. Veyl tried not to wonder if they still would have excluded her if she had not been recovering from her injuries. Down that path lay potential for the development of doubts and bitterness.

One guard outside held up a hand to stop them. "This is a restricted meeting."

Veyl stood tall and met his eyes. "And I am your khesran. Open the door."

The other guard, a taller woman who had been working in the palace most of Veyl's life, nodded and knocked. Upon receiving a response from within, she stepped inside, blocking Veyl's view of the proceedings with her broad shoulders.

"Your majesties, Khesran Veyl and her companions have requested permission to enter."

After a moment's pause, she heard her mother's voice. "Let them in."

The guard opened the door the rest of the way and stepped aside to allow them entrance. Her parents, their tehnaaks, and Arhk were at the table, along with Merrin, Avris, Darro, and Kince. Kyril was there as well, and a surge of resentment rose in her. Yet, he had a legitimate place there as the highest-ranking officer from Thaelis present and because of the suffering he had faced at the hands of their current enemies. Besides, her reaction was likely more a product of directionless anger over what Jaysen had taken from them than anything to do with his inclusion here.

"We are pleased to see you feeling well enough to join us," her mother said, gesturing to the table in invitation.

A warm flush infused Veyl's cheeks as her mother's comment confirmed that they only excluded her because of her injuries and need for rest.

Darro arched a brow at his sons when the two of them and Iyvalin followed Veyl into the room, but he said nothing.

Her father waited until they reached the table to speak. "It's good that you arrived now. We just finished sending a messenger off to journey to Thaelis with an update for our people there on recent developments. The next order of business is to open a discussion of options for dealing with Sarket before we retire for the evening meal."

Veyl nodded, appreciating his willingness to include not only her, but the three with her, in the current conversation. "There is something I would like to propose before we proceed, if I may."

Her mother nodded. "Please. The floor is yours, Khesran."

Seyn pressed against Veyl's leg, and a cool, soothing sensation moved through her, bolstering her confidence. "We all know that we face a significant possibility of military engagement with Sarket. As we are preparing our forces for that likely outcome, the four of us," she paused, gesturing to Gannon alongside Seyn on her left and Ahrin and Iyvalin on her right, "would like your leave to join a unit."

Arhk's faint, approving smirk gave her a glimmer of hope.

Her father, however, sat back and shook his head. "The other three aren't a problem, but you are the khesran of Vanris. Heir to the throne. Your country needs you here. Not on the front lines."

Veyl forced herself to stand straighter. "I am one of two khesrans, and I wish to fight alongside my people."

"We've nearly lost you twice already," he countered.

"Yes. Considering such, I imagine you have a plan in place now for dealing with the eventuality of my demise, if there wasn't one before."

Her parents frowned at that.

"Is this an act of solidarity with your people or a

quest for revenge?" her mother asked.

"Can't it be both? This is my fight. With everything I've survived in this last year, I think I have more than earned my place on the front lines." She caught the hint of admiration in Kyril's smile, and her pulse quickened in response. Whatever she had done to win that tiny rekindling of connection, she hoped she could stumble upon it again.

Her parents moved away from the end of the table and fell into a hushed conversation. After a few seconds, Arhk stepped back to join them.

Kyril cleared his throat loudly enough to draw their attention. "Your majesties, before Khesran Veyl and her companions joined us, you asked if I would consider leading a Feral unit in service to Vanris. My answer is yes, but as you pointed out, to form a full unit I will need nine soldiers in addition to the beasts I work with. If you allowed these four to join me, along with my sister Kitria, I imagine that would be enough for us to begin training while the remaining soldiers are being selected."

Her mother gave him a shrewd look. "Why would you want these four?"

Kyril answered without hesitation. "I already know the khesran possesses extraordinary courage and is an excellent fighter with experience around beasts. If the others have half her skill, they will form the foundation of a unit any officer would be proud to lead."

They considered him in silence for a moment, then resumed their quiet discussion away from the table. Darro and Merrin joined them this time. Veyl struggled not to fidget, settling one hand on Seyn's shoulders to keep it still. The hardest part was not looking at Kyril. Was there more to his offering them a place in his unit than simply needing to fill the ranks? Could she work with him without their past and her emotions becoming an obstacle?

After a couple of minutes, the group at the back returned to the table.

As dhomvalen, Arhk was the official head of Vanris's military, so he was the one who addressed them. "We cannot overlook that the four of you were victims of Ahnkreth Kyril's attack on Deepwater. Would you be amenable to serving under him now, despite that?"

Veyl looked to Gannon first, aware that he had lost more than most because of that experience.

He narrowed his eyes at Kyril, then turned to her. "If you are willing, I am, but he'd best not step out of line."

Veyl looked at the other two.

Ahrin nodded.

"We'll follow your lead," Iyvalin added.

Veyl faced her grandfather. "Yes, Dhomvalen."

"Very well, Ahnkreth Kyril. For now, I am assigning these four, and your sister—assuming she will pledge herself to serving Vanris in this capacity—to train with you. At the very least, it will provide you with practice commanding a non-naval force and give them experience working in a unit. Once we have determined our course of action and have a plan in place, we will assess how the unit is performing and make final decisions on who we will send out together."

Kyril inclined his head in a gesture of deference. "Thank you, Dhomvalen. Your Majesties."

"We had planned to adjourn for the evening soon to give everyone time to enjoy their meals. Why don't we do so now and resume discussions when we are fresh tomorrow afternoon?" her mother proposed. "If you are well enough, Ahnkreth, you and the new members of your fledgling unit may join Khemron Kasiel in the morning to learn how Feral units work in Vanris. We shall give allowances to those with recent injuries to observe until they have recovered enough to participate."

"Thank you, Khevarin Velara."

The moment she dismissed them, Iyvalin hurried to Kyril. Veyl glanced at Ahrin in question, but he merely shrugged.

"Pardon me, Ahnkreth," Iyvalin began, "since we will be working together, would you and your sister consider dining with us this evening?"

"I don't…" Kyril started to shake his head, then his eyes met Veyl's. "Perhaps we will join you. Thank you."

After taking time to freshen up and apply numbing salve to her wounds, Veyl met the others in the dining room off the palace gardens where she had dined before with Kyril, Jinau, and Nalika. She and Kyril had kissed in this room. Did he remember that at all? If he did, it didn't show, but she recalled it vividly enough for both of them, the sensation of his lips, his touch, the fire he lit within her. She couldn't look at him without thoughts of it making her cheeks grow warm, so she kept her eyes on anyone else to avoid those heated recollections.

Kyril and Kitria sat on one side of the table, with Ahrin and Iyvalin on the other. Gannon took the seat near the corner, putting himself between Veyl and Kyril. Neither of them remarked upon the placement. Perhaps a little distance would allow them to each find their equilibrium on their own.

Veyl gestured to the food. "Please help yourselves."

Gannon moved some roasted vegetables onto his plate before pinning Kyril with his intense gaze. "Our agreement to serve under you doesn't mean any of us have forgiven you. We just have a common enemy in Sarket now."

"Gannon," Iyvalin snapped.

Kyril waved her off. "It's all right. I earned your hatred."

Gannon shook his head. "I can't speak for the others,

but I no longer hate you. Our journey together from Taro helped with that, but you have a long way to go before I'll say I like or trust you."

Kitria's features pinched with anger. "You don't know—"

Kyril placed a hand on her arm, ending her outburst before it fully started. "I earned this, Kit. If I want to change that, I need to work for it. What I must know is, will you all follow my orders when it matters?"

"As long as those orders are on behalf of Vanris," Ahrin replied.

Veyl focused on serving herself and began picking at a cut of tender meat. She didn't hate Kyril. Not even a little, though perhaps some part of her should. He had committed awful deeds. Deeds that appeared to be most of what he remembered of their relationship now. It was no wonder he couldn't reconcile her affection for him.

Kyril's solemn gaze moved to her then. "You're quiet, Khesran. How do you feel about this arrangement?"

She set down her fork and looked around at them. "If we can put aside the past and focus on what lies before us, we could become as effective a unit as my father's was in their day, but we need to look out for one another. We can't do that if we cling to resentments, deserved or otherwise."

They stared at her in silence for a moment, then Kyril lifted his mug. "I swear I will look out for all of you as my unit and do everything in my power to see that every one of us makes it back from any challenges we face together, from this point forward."

The others raised their mugs to their new commanding officer.

"We will all look out for each other," Iyvalin said.

They drank to that and began digging into the food. Veyl reached for her fork, then paused, noticing that Kyril still wasn't eating.

"What I will not do," he said, "is go easy on you in training out of guilt for what happened before. I will push you to be your best, because that is what will keep us alive if they allow us to deploy together."

"And we expect to give you our best, Ahnkreth," Ahrin answered.

The rest of them voiced their agreement.

They all focused on enjoying the meal then, enjoying the exceptional skill of the palace's cooks. A short time later, Veyl noticed Kyril watching her again.

She looked up, meeting those silver-blue eyes she loved so much, and said, "I, for one, am eager to train together. I believe you and I are due for a rematch. You cheated last time."

Kyril broke the contact, glancing down at his plate, the clenching of his jaw confirming that the Evoker had left that memory intact.

Kitria swallowed a bite and turned to her brother. "Cheated?"

"I used the zenyal bond to subdue her." He looked at Veyl, brows pinched in distress, as if asking why she would mention such a painful memory now.

"This time it shall truly be a test of skill, right, Ahnkreth?" She smiled at him before bringing her mug to her lips, challenging him to move forward.

He lifted his mug to her and smiled back, though the tightness around his eyes exposed the depth of his struggle to do so. "Indeed, it will, Inren Veyl."

Gannon barked a laugh.

Veyl breathed a small laugh, the heavy weight of sorrow in her chest growing a fraction lighter with Kyril's effort at returning her banter. In Vanris, they had never made her an officer, and she forfeited her status as royalty by choosing to serve as a soldier in their unit, at least while on duty. With her ability broken, she was now a basic troop. An inren. Something that brought her relief and dread in equal measure.

They had all been through a great deal, but now they would work as a team to protect Vanris and hopefully gain some satisfaction for the cruelties they had all endured. It was unexpected and strange. An outcome none of them would have predicted several months ago, yet she found the new direction encouraging. Adding this element to their relationships might help them all build something better together. Maybe even rebuild what some of them had lost.

Kitria grinned. "I may actually be looking forward to training now."

The End

<u>**Glossary**</u>
Vanrian and Thaelian Terminology

Calloch

Rank ball of monkey shit. A favored insult in Vanris.

Company (military)

The units and unions under the command of a single dhomen or ahndhomen.

Crack a stone

Popular Vanrian phrase meaning to open and drink a stoneglass bottle of Vanrian Black Mead.

Evalis

Black fruit used to make Vanrian Black Mead. Imported from the original Vanrian homeland.

Ke'hanoath

Each Vanrian's individual story represented in symbols tattooed somewhere on their person.

Mindcraft

Unusual abilities possessed by some Vanrians/Thaelians to manipulate the minds of humans or animals.

Mind-crafter

Someone with a mindcraft ability.

...na sek

Appended to an officer rank when a promotion is temporarily granted for a specific mission.

Sheyvyosk

Stinky smegma.

Stoneglass

A Vanrian light metal alloy that looks like stone and is extremely durable. Primarily used to make bottles for Vanrian Black Mead… naturally.

Tehanyehn

A romantic spirit pairing connected by a Bondmaker (considered a deeper form of the marriage vows practiced in the southern kingdoms).

Tehnaak

Spirit siblings, bound to each other by a Bondmaker and raised together.

Tehsheyn

Spirit family, bound by a Bondmaker.

The Deeps

Vanrian solitary confinement in Etrion.

Union (military)

A grouping of three regular units combined under a third or fourth level ahninveth or inveth.

Unit, Regular (military)

A group of thirty-nine soldiers under a single inveth or ahninveth.

Unit, Feral (military)

A group of nine soldiers and up to twenty beasts under a single Feral ahninveth.

Zenyal	A type of unequal bond formed by a Bondmaker that gives one half of the pairing a measure of control over the other.

RANKS & TITLES:

Khevarin	Ruler of Vanris – the rough equivalent of a king or queen.
Khemron	Spouse of the ruler of Vanris, shares some of the leadership.
Khesran	Child of the khevarin and khemron – basically a prince or princess.
Dhomvalen	Protector or warden. Top Vanrian military leader who answers only to the khevarin.
Ahnvaris	Dedicated elite guard to important personages.
Dhomen	A Vanrian or Thaelian officer – the rough equivalent of a general in the southern kingdoms. There are four levels.
Ahndhomen	A Dhomen who is also a mind-crafter (slightly outranks a dhomen). There are four levels.
Ahnkreth	A Vanrian or Thaelian officer – commander of a naval fleet.

Inveth	A Vanrian or Thaelian officer – the rough equivalent of a captain in the southern kingdoms. There are four levels.
Ahninveth	An Inveth who is also a mind-crafter (slightly outranks an inveth). There are four levels.
Inren	A Vanrian or Thaelian common soldier. There are four levels.
Omren	A Vanrian or Thaelian mind-crafter common soldier. There are four levels.
Idrek	A Vanrian or Thaelian recruit – soldier in training.
Odrek	A Vanrian or Thaelian mind-crafter recruit – soldier in training.

Other terminology

Havaad	A god worshipped in parts of the southern kingdoms, particularly in Sarket.
Pandrean Alliance	An alliance formed between the three southern kingdoms of Delaphine, Sarket, and Fallend to fight Vanris.
Hyeralisk	Qwilki term for a deadly hurricane.
Qwe'pi	Crude Qwilki insult.

Ket'ta

The shell of a crustacean in Thaelis. Often used for making cups and small bowls.

Eydarith

Culture in Sarket that worships the Tempest, god of the sea. They have a unique language and consider themselves separate from the other citizens of Sarket.

Itovanak

Strong alcohol favored by the Eydarith.

Ukhen'kya

The Unclean. A cannibalistic culture in conflict with the residents of the Thaelian islands.

Mindcrafting disciplines

Bondmaker

A mind-crafter who can create bonds between two or more individuals by using the life threads that exist within them.

Breaker

A mind-crafter whose ability is uncontrolled and powerful enough to "break" the minds of their victims to the point that they have no cognitive capabilities or even the ability to respond to their own needs.

Charmer

A mind-crafter who can manipulate an individual or small number of individuals to go along with their suggestions.

Dampener

A mind-crafter who can interfere with the way people's
minds perceive their senses,
effectively taking away the
sight, sound, smell, and/
or touch of individuals or
groups.

Enkindler

A mind-crafter who can
inspire positive or negative
emotions in individuals or
groups.

Evoker

A mind-crafter who can see
and sometimes alter a single
individuals surface thoughts
and memories.

Feral

A mind-crafter who can
connect with, influence, and
control the minds of animals
or groups of animals.

Frightener

A mind-crafter who can access
the fears of individuals or
groups and cause them to see
terrifying visions, sometimes
permanently scarring their
minds.

Heartsmith

A blind mind-crafter who
can tap into people's deepest
thoughts and emotions in an
abstract way to read the story
of who they are in order to
tattoo it upon their skin.

Speaker

A mind-crafter who can speak into the minds of individuals or groups, limited somewhat by range and visibility (less so if their subject is also another Speaker).

Unique Creatures

Cliff Cat

Large wildcats native to the mountains in Vanris. Some Ferals use them in combat. They have a deep blue-gray coat with darker blue stripes down the spine along either side of a ridge of longer hair. Their eyes are sapphire blue, and their tails end in a puff of hair the same blue as its stripes. They tend to be around waist high to a man at the shoulder.

Ji'ikyan

Large ocean serpents with scales a blend of lavender, pink, silver, and pearlescent white, with a translucent dorsal fin running along their substantial length. They have jaws full of teeth designed to tear apart prey that they first paralyze with a toxin injected through a stinger at the end of their tails.

Kanodrak

Impressive Vanrian predators brought to Pandrea from the original Vanrian homeland. Taller than a horse and used as mounts by a few Ferals. Vaguely feline with a silver-grey, scaled hide and milky white eyes. They have bone armor plating that starts at the nose and runs along the spine to the base of their long tail. Their massive front incisors extended well below the lower jaw.

Kednu

Large deer on the Thaelian islands that are sometimes used as pack animals and occasional mounts.

Kel'inuk

Similar in appearance to a salamander, but capable of growing much larger than a horse, these ocean-dwelling amphibians have no teeth. They crush prey repeatedly in their powerful jaws and swallow it whole.

Nightstar Eagle

Large black eagle with gold feathers sweeping back from its eyes and along the lower edge of its wings and tail. Revered by followers of Havaad in the southern kingdoms.

Sandhawk

Desert hawks commonly seen in southern Vanris and around the Crimson Break.

Tethdrak

Vanrian predators brought to Pandrea from the original Vanrian homeland. Some Ferals use them in combat. Built a little like a hound, but reptilian. Adults are mid-rib high to a man at the shoulder. The thickly muscled limbs and torso are covered in light shades of red and brown scaling with spiked plates along the length of the spine and thick tail. Two backswept horns extend from the head and their massive jaws bristle with sharp teeth.

Wave Dancer

Sey'yaluth ayon in Qwilki. Tall, amphibious canines. Narrow built with long slender legs, fishlike, gleaming black scales over the forehead, across the front of the shoulders, and along the back of the hips. They have odd, glossy black fur made up of long, thick strands. The black ears are partially transparent like a bat's wings and have fine ridges at intervals in the membrane, giving them the appearance of fins. They have broad scaled paws, with webbing between the toes designed for swimming. They tend to have eyes of some shade of blue or green.

Places

Andaro   Capital city of the kingdom of Sarket.

Balarus   Large town south of the Break in northeastern Sarket.

Crimson Break   War-devastated, desert region between Vanris and the southern kingdoms.

Crimsondale   Town where the incident that started the war happened. Now part of the Crimson Break.

Dagony   Port city on the main island in Thaelis.

Deepwater   Small integrated town on the western coast of the Crimson Break.

Dekingham   Main capital of Delaphine.

Delaphine   Eastern kingdom on Pandrea. Home to the Delaphinian people.

Doran   The northern capital of Vanris.

Etrion   The southern capital of Vanris.

Fallend

Southern kingdom on Pandrea. Home to the Fallenese people.

Fernwallow

Small village in Fallend.

Hellaris

Town in Sarket.

Kilden Mountains

Mountain range near the coast in Sarket.

Mukyeny

Town on one of the islands in Thaelis.

Pandrea

The continent.

Sarket

Western kingdom on Pandrea. Home to the Sarketi people.

Taro

Coastal city in Sarket, mostly run by the Eydarith.

Thaelis

Island chain about a week west of Pandrea.

Vanris

Northernmost kingdom on Pandrea. New home to the Vanrian people after volcanic activity drove them from their original island home.

Vareyl's Warning

Black crags that create a natural border between northern and southern Vanris. Called Vareyl's Gift before the war.

People

Adnar
Vanrian ahndhomen / Feral kanodrak rider / Nevias's tehnaak)

Ahrin
One of Darro and Tath's twin sons, named after his mother's deceased former tehnaak / Gannon's brother / Iyvalin's tehnaak

Aitan
Vanrian dhomen

Anahela
Qwilki woman

Arhk Cavenos
Dhomvalen of Vanris / Frightener / Veyl's grandfather

Astrid Lodmund
Queen of Sarket / Jaysen's mothert

Avris
Vanrian inveth and combat instructor / Merrin's tehnaak / part of Kasiel's tehsheyn

Cordin
Fish market owner / Quillon's brother

Darith
Thaelian councilor

Darro
Vanrian dhomen / Gannon and Ahrin's father / Kince's tehnaak / part of Kasiel's tehsheyn

Eavara
Thalian Ahnkreth (fleet commander) / Speaker

Ellaris   Jethan and Keyla's second daughter, named after Veyl's deceased grandmother / Tavin's tehnaak

Erkhan   Thaelian Dampener / part of Eavara's crew

Fen   Deck boy / part of Kyril's crew

Ferda   Qwilki woman

Genyith   Former khemron of Vanris / Veyl's grandfather

Halin   Thaelian councilor / Evoker

Heshara   Thaelian ahninveth / Feral

Hila   Qwilki pastry chef

Illis   Thaelian soldier / part of Kyril's crew

Iyvalin   Arin's tehnaak / Veyl's friend

Jaysen Lodmund   Crown prince of Sarket / son of Roald and Astrid / Veyl's best friend

Jethan Markanis   Vanrian ahninveth / Charmer / Kasiel's tehnaak and part of his tehsheyn / father of Ellaris and Veyl's former tehnaak, Minya / Velara's cousin

Jinau   Thaelian Ahndhomen / Charmer

Kasiel Cavanos   Khemron of Vanris / Feral kanodrak rider / Vey's father

Keyla   Velara's tehnaak / mother of Ellaris and Veyl's former tehnaak, Minya

Kince   Vanrian inveth / Darro's tehnaak / part of Kasiel's tehsheyn

Kitria   Kyril's younger sister

Kronach   Wavelord of Taro / Eydarith

Kyril   Thaelian ahnkreth (fleet commander) / Feral

Lanis   Vanrian attendant who helped raise Veyl

Lorek   Gannon's tehnaak / Veyl's friend

Mardi   Thaelian guard

Merrin   Vanrian dhomen and combat instructor / Avris's tehnaak / part of Kasiel's tehsheyn

Meyla   Thalian officer / Kyril's second

Minera   Vanrian ahnvaris / Dampener

Minya   Jethan and Keyla's first daughter who died very young / Veyl's first tehnaak

Nalika   Vanrian subordinate ahnkreth / part of Kyril's crew

Nerith   Vanrian healer / Tath's tehnaak / part of Kasiel's tehsheyn

Nichal   Thaelian soldier / part of Kyril's crew

Nevias   Vanrian dhomen / Adnar's tehnaak

Quillon   Thaelian guard

Rel   Thaelian soldier / part of Kyril's crew

Roald Lodmund   King of Sarket / Jaysen's father

Rysek   Vanrian ahnvaris / Dampener / one of Arhk's elite guards

Setera   Vanrian ahndhomen / Evoker

Seylin Markanis   Former khevarin of Vanris / Enkindler / Veyl's grandmother

Shyall   Thaelian councilor

Tarik   Vanrian city guard

Tavin   A khesran of Vanris / Veyl's younger brother

Tath   Vanrian healer / Gannon and Ahrin's mother / Nerith's tehnaak / part of Kasiel's tehsheyn

Velara Markanis   Khevarin of Vanris / Charmer / Veyl's mother

Veyl   A khesran of Vanris / heir to the Vanrian throne / daughter of Kasiel and Velara

Wilkin Thrasser   King Regent of Sarket

Yserra   Vanrian ahnvaris / Evoker

Zafyr   Vanrian ahnvaris / Evoker

Content Warning: This book contains a plot line involving emotional abuse and sexual assault (unwanted kissing and some touching).

ACKNOWLEDGEMENTS

Whether you started with the Warden's Son series or this is your first adventure in the tales of Vanris, thank you for joining me on this journey. I hope you enjoyed this book and will continue to follow Veyl's story in the third and final book. There are a number of people I would like to offer my appreciation, so I will try to capture them all here.

To my mom, Linda, who has been my alpha reader through so many books and provided so much support and valuable feedback throughout the process. I can't imagine doing this without you.

As always, my best friends and beta readers, Rick and Ann, who somehow continue to stand by me regardless of where my crazy goes. You are now, and always will be, my tehsheyn.

To my additional beta readers, Patrick, Marla, and Lyra, your feedback was invaluable. You are greatly appreciated. And to all the ARC readers who have joined this journey, thank you!

As always, I want to acknowledge the fantastic team who helped me put together the finished book. Robert Crescenzio, my incredibly talented cover artist whose vision helps bring these books to life on the covers. Melissa Nash, the fantastic map designer who helped Kasiel's vision of the land come to life. Alexander Lockwood, my fantastic editor, fellow author, and now friend. Brian Short, my amazing formatter, whom I would also like to thank for your excellent company on many coffeeshop writing days. I love working with you all.

To my other friends and family, know that I love you and value your place in my life even if I don't call you out specifically here.

Last, but certainly not least, to my readers. To me, a book is a collaborative effort between the author and the reader. Without you, this world would only ever come to life in my head. I hope you enjoy experiencing it as much as I did and will continue along the journey as the rest of this series releases into the world.

AUTHOR BIO

Outside of my career as an author, I am a professional technical and creative writer, spider wrangler, animal lover, and devoted cat mom. Writing fantasy and science fiction stories has been a lifelong passion for me. I love to draw upon my myriad life experiences for my books, doing everything from wild cave exploration and horseback endurance riding to practicing iaido and archery.

•

Thank you for taking time to read this novel. Please leave a review if you enjoyed it.

•

For more about me and my work visit me at http://elysiumpalace.com.

OTHER NOVELS by NIKKI McCORMACK

CLOCKWORK ENTERPRISES
The Girl and the Clockwork Cat
The Girl and the Clockwork Conspiracy
The Girl and the Clockwork Crossfire

THE WARDEN'S SON
Child of Vanris
Blood of Vanris
Heart of Vanris
Throne of Vanris

DAUGHTER OF VANRIS
Wave Dancer
Wave-Touched
Wavelord (coming soon)

FORBIDDEN THINGS
Dissident
Exile
Apostate

ELYSIUM'S FALL
Dark Hope of the Dragons
Dark Savior of the Dragons

SILVERBLOOD RAVEN
A Path of Blood and Amber
A Path of Secrets and Dreams
A Path of Storms and Reckonings

STANDALONE WORK
Golden Eyes
The Keeper
Making Monsters (short story)
In Silence Waiting (short story)
And they All Look Just the Same (short story)

WAVELORD

Inren Ahrin," Kyril snapped, pulling the younger man's attention away from a conversation with his brother.

The Thaelian Feral was only a few inches taller than the twins, but something about him demanded immediate respect. Perhaps that long black hair, the early morning light calling out the stained streaks of deep blue in it. An unusual color in Vanris where even Veyl's blood-red hair, like her mother's, was uncommonly dark among her people. Or maybe his silver-blue eyes, bright and piercing within those rugged features. He had gained a few scars since the first time Veyl encountered him on that awful night in Deepwater, but they took nothing away from his predatory allure, as of some powerful, untamable beast.

And yet, none of those things, as much as they pleased the eye, were what drew her to him. Beneath the surface, he possessed a deep sincerity and kindness, along with a desire to help others. Those parts of his nature led him to protect her on that first unfortunate journey to Thaelis and to sail to Vanris at her request to warn her people about Thrasser, despite the risk to himself.

Then there was the connection that had called her to him the night she nearly kissed him on his ship. An inexplicable link that had only grown stronger with time… until now. Did it still exist somewhere beneath the emotional and mental scars from Jaysen's cruel treatment?

She startled when Iyvalin bumped her with her elbow.

"Watching his lips move is not the same as listening to him," her friend whispered, stifling a giggle.

Veyl's cheeks warmed, and she forced herself to focus on what Kyril was saying. Today was their first day of training together as a unit after he had spent most of two weeks with her father and some of the other Ferals learning to handle groups of tethdraks. During that time, the rest of them had worked with some of the other officers on their roles in the unit. To say that she found this chance to spend more time around the Thaelian Feral emotionally challenging would have been understating the issue. Why did her need to be close to him have to remain so intense while he still struggled with the mess Jaysen's Evoker had made of his memories of their relationship?

"What would you consider your strongest combat skill?" Kyril demanded of Ahrin.

"I'm a decent hand at mounted archery," Ahrin answered tentatively, brushing a lock of light auburn hair away from his eyes and looking at Veyl as if seeking confirmation.

Kyril arched a brow at her where she stood leaning against the fence that encircled one of the training rings and, unsure what either of them expected of her, she simply nodded.

"Yours is the light crossbow." He picked out his sister Kitria with his gaze before turning to Gannon and Iyvalin. "What about you two?"

Like Ahrin, their attention drifted to Veyl as they answered.

"Melee with a shortsword, I guess," Iyvalin said, her gaze shifting back to Kyril as she spoke. "Though I'm equally comfortable with a light axe."

"Also melee, but I prefer a longer sword. I can make do with a shortsword or a mace in a pinch," Gannon answered, never looking away from Veyl.

Veyl was standing close enough to hear the deep, frustrated exhale Kyril let out before he spoke. "I get the impression the first point we need to establish is that I am the commanding officer of this unit. When we are training or on duty, Veyl is not your khesran. She is another inren like the rest of you. Are we clear on that?"

The other three glanced at her again as if awaiting her approval of his statement, and she couldn't hold back a small laugh.

Kyril turned a stern gaze her way, though, for an instant before he reined it in, an amused smile tugged at the corners of his mouth, flaring a spark of hope in her. "Are we clear on that, Inren Veyl?"

Forcing a serious expression, she straightened and faced him. Seyn stood up from where she lay beside her and assumed a ready stance, as if attempting to present a unified front with her bonded companion. Veyl set a hand on the wave dancer's shoulders, a gesture that had already become a habit. "We are, Ahninveth."

In Thaelis, Kyril was an ahnkreth, commanding a fleet of ships, but ahnkreths didn't lead ground troops, so her parents had officially made him an ahninveth in Vanris to support the new role they had given him.

The other four echoed Veyl's confirmation. The words came easily enough, but how long would it take them to adjust to the idea of accepting orders from the man who had taken them prisoner aboard his ships not so long ago?

"Then we can proceed." His dubious expression didn't quite match the conviction in his tone. "Today we will focus on archery, since some of us are still recovering from injuries. Kitria and Ahrin, assuming you really are the more skilled archers, you may also provide pointers to the others as needed." He gestured to an array of bows and crossbows laid out for them.

When Veyl moved to join her four companions in selecting a weapon, he stopped her with a hand on her shoulder, the contact making her pulse quicken. How frustrating it was that he could do that even with an impersonal touch.

"Not you."

Irritation subdued the pleasure of the contact. She spun to face him. "I'm as skilled with a bow as anyone else here."

"Drawing a bow requires a strong, stable core. I know how serious the wound over your ribs was. I will wait for the approval of the healers before I allow you to put undue stress on it. For today, you can help me assess their performance."

Under different circumstances, she would have been delighted to do so, but being close to him was unfairly tormenting now, knowing he no longer shared the memories that lit a fire within her whenever he was near. Still, she couldn't argue with him when he was right. Drawing a regular bow would put strain on the healing injury, and the healers hadn't given her permission to do so yet, but there were alternatives.

"A light crossbow won't hurt it."

The long look he gave her made her feel as if she had missed some crucial cue. Then his gaze shifted to the others. "I want to see how each of you works with every type of bow there. Except Veyl," he added with a hint of a sigh in his tone, "who will stick to the latchet crossbow."

Could assigning her to help him have been more than just a way to avoid aggravating her injury? How she wished she could read him better, but he had grown even more guarded around her since losing some of his memories.

Pushing aside her uncertainty, she joined the others to gather their chosen weapons and approach the practice range. Merrin was busy training a couple of newer recruits in one of the nearby sparring rings. Kince, who had been offering occasional feedback throughout the process, abandoned any pretense of being involved and moved closer to watch them. His angular features gave an extra sharpness to his cynical gaze, the stacked dark blue symbols of his ke'hanoath tattoo on one cheek adding a touch of asymmetry.

The interest he took in them wasn't surprising. His tehnaak Darro's sons were out here training to work under the command of the man who had abducted them. He would judge Kyril's skill and leadership ability and report back to Darro whether he felt they were safe with him. The best thing she could do to influence that was to focus on the task their ahninveth had given them. She turned to loading the crossbow and fired her first shot, setting an example for the group that they were quick to follow.

The bolt struck about two inches from the center of her target. Kyril watched as she released another with similar results. Then he walked down the line to observe as each of the others loosed a few arrows. He offered some suggestions before making his way back to her, by which time she had three more bolts in about the same area.

He stopped next to her. "Excellent grouping. Now, let me see you fire it with your dominant hand."

She changed her stance and switched the crossbow to her left hand. It was harder to focus with him standing by her shoulder, but she had grown up learning these skills under some of the best instructors in Vanris. The first ranged weapon her father taught her to wield was a light crossbow. She drew a breath and let it out, allowing the tension from Kyril's presence to depart with it, then fired. The bolt struck the center of the target.

"Not bad," he allowed. "You're wasted as a khesran."

A glance at him caught the faint, teasing smirk that curved his lips.

"I bet she could beat you with any bow here," Gannon boasted.

Though flattered by the pride and confidence in his tone, Veyl shook her head at him and picked up a bolt, passing it and the crossbow over to Kyril when he held out his hands. After loading it, he raised the weapon in one hand and fired in a single smooth motion, not even pausing to aim. The bolt shifted hers as it dug into the center of the target next to it.

Gannon shrugged. "A decent shot."

Kyril handed the crossbow back to her. "My father insisted I learn on a ship at sea before he would allow me to shoot on land. I suspect Veyl might find that more of a challenge than you suggest." He glanced down at her, his expression turning thoughtful. "With a sword, however, I'm not confident she wouldn't win, but we won't be testing that until she's had more time to heal."

Ahrin eyed the distant target. "You must have lost a lot of bolts training that way."

Kyril chuckled. "Anytime an arrow or bolt went overboard, my father made me dive in and try to retrieve it. I became an exceptional swimmer by the time I learned not to miss."

Veyl smiled to herself. "I can't help imagining your father dragging you out to sea in a storm, handing you a crossbow, and telling you to hit the target."

His unreadable gaze drifted back to her. "I don't have to imagine it. It might surprise you to hear how often he did exactly that."

For a few seconds, he considered her, mouth opening slightly, as if he might say something more. His gaze shifted to her lips for a heartbeat, and his brows pinched.

He looked back up. She let those silver-blue eyes draw her in, forgetting that they had an audience. Had he recalled a memory of kissing her that the Evoker failed to strip from his mind? Could some of the passion they had shared still be there, lurking behind that controlled, troubled countenance?

Gannon loosed an arrow, the thunk of it hitting the target snapping them back to the surrounding reality.

Kyril looked away. "Gannon, swap bows with Ahrin. I suspect you'll find that one suits you better."

Veyl turned and fed her frustration into the target, landing a cluster of bolts around the two in the center while she listened to him offering advice to the others and swapping out weapons to check their skills with each. She had made a veritable pincushion out of it by the time he returned to her.

"Whatever it is you're at war with, it looks as though you killed it."

How could he not see that it was him she was at war with?

She drew a deep breath and set down the crossbow. When she glanced over at the practice rings to avoid looking at him, she noticed Kince perk up and start walking toward the palace. Turning farther to see what had caught his attention, she spotted an attendant heading their way.

"There's news," she said.

They stood in silence for a moment, waiting and watching as Kince spoke with the woman. When they finished, he turned and beckoned to them.

"Ahninveth Kyril, Khesran Veyl, you might wish to join me."

Kyril glanced at the other four. "Keep practicing. If I'm not back in an hour, you can leave, but make sure you clean up the targets and put the bows away first."

"Yes, Ahnkreth!" Kitria answered.

The other three echoed her with notably less enthusiasm.

"Ahninveth," he corrected before turning away.

"What's going on?" Veyl asked as they fell into step with Kince behind the attendant heading toward the palace.

"A scout's arrived to report on developments in Sarket. Kasiel summoned the closed council together to hear what news they bring."

The closed council consisted of her father, some members of his tehsheyn, her mother, and her grandfather, Arhk. Limiting attendance made sense, since they would want to see what they were dealing with before bringing it to the larger group. It surprised her a little that she and Kyril were being included in the initial gathering this time.

"Did they ask for us to come?"

"No." Kince glanced back and pointedly met her eyes, making it apparent he was addressing just her. "After what Jaysen put you through, you deserve to be involved."

Ceris nosed her right hand where he walked between her and Kyril, opposite Seyn. "Put both of us through, you mean," Veyl prompted.

A crooked smile curved Kince's lips before he faced forward. "I only asked Ahninveth Kyril along because I enjoy finding opportunities to judge him."

Kyril let out a soft, weary breath, but he held his silence.

"You're a calloch, Uncle," she muttered.

Kince merely chuckled.

They made their way toward the towering, expansive structure of the palace, with the sharp angles of its black stone and metalwork construction presenting an aggressive exterior designed to intimidate enemies. The attendant led them through the main entrance, down halls with black stone walls and dark marble floors.

Instead of stopping at one of the meeting chambers, they turned down another hall and entered a large sitting room. It surprised her to see the soldier reporting in was not a Vanrian scout, but rather a dark-skinned Delaphinian woman with long hair split out into an abundance of tiny braids and bound back out of her face. Her brown eyes widened a fraction when they entered, a hint of awe and curiosity crossing her features as she stared at the two wave dancers.

Her father stood. The rest of his tehsheyn remained seated, the casual bond they shared making it acceptable somehow in this less formal setting. "Captain Annora, this is my daughter, Khesran Veyl, and our new Thaelian ahninveth, Kyril, along with their companions, Seyn and Ceris."

The two wave dancers stood at attention, taking seriously the recognition given them.

Veyl recognized the name. "Annora? The one who acted as a messenger for you back when you ended the war?"

Her father smiled at the woman. "The very one."

Veyl executed a respectful bow. "It's an honor to meet you, Captain Annora."

Annora reciprocated the gesture. "You as well, Khesran Veyl. And you, Ahninveth Kyril." She smiled at the amphibious creatures and offered them each a nod. "And you two remarkable companions."

Ceris and Seyn both cracked broad canine grins, their tails swishing back and forth a few times.

After Kyril returned the greeting, her father had two of his guards bring over chairs set against one wall and bid them join the group. When everyone had settled, he turned his focus back to their guest.

"Our attention is yours, Captain," he said. "What news do you bring?"

"Thank you, Khemron Kasiel. I have been stationed in northeastern Sarket for several months, running a group of scouts to keep track of events there. The Sarketi people have grown angry of late. They've lost faith in King Regent Thrasser now that Crown Prince Jaysen has reemerged and is spreading word of the king's underhanded attempt to remove him so he might keep the throne. They are calling for single combat in the Sarketi tradition. More recent rumors that the crown prince is working with mind-crafters from another country have sparked unease as well. Although many seem to assume they are Vanrian and are less concerned since Vanris hasn't abused Sarket's oath of fealty in the years since the war ended. More importantly perhaps, you should know the king regent has reached out to Delaphine and Fallend in search of allies to support his claim to the throne against the crown prince."

"But not Vanris." Darro dropped the comment as more of an observation than a question.

"He is panicking." Arhk's brow furrowed, the harsh burns on his face still making it uncomfortable to look at him, though they had healed considerably. "He assumes Vanris will support Jaysen, given that we have had close ties with the crown prince in the past. If he cannot find other allies, he knows he will have a difficult time keeping his country if Jaysen has the Thaelians, the Eydarith, and Vanris supporting him."

"Except Vanris isn't supporting him," Veyl remarked, hoping they hadn't made some decision otherwise without her knowledge.

"No," her mother confirmed. "And we are unlikely to after what he did in Thaelis, among other things, though we must keep it on our list of options for now."

Veyl's stomach turned at the thought that they might consider backing Jaysen after all he had done. If the council made that choice, how was she supposed to reconcile herself with it? Would they keep her out of negotiations with him? Would she want them to? Not knowing what he was up to might almost be worse than having to face him again. Yet, could she do so without suffering that nauseating swell of black hatred and fear at the memories of his unwelcome touch, his demanding kisses?

Seyn nosed her hand, pushing calm and reassurance into her. Out of the corner of her eye, Veyl caught Ceris bumping his muzzle up into Kyril's palm too. Was the Feral having a similar reaction to that possibility? The idea of working with Jaysen couldn't sit any better with him than it did with her, not after how Jaysen tortured him and ordered the Thaelian Evoker to tear apart his memories of her. The urge to take his hand was nearly too much to resist, but even if he might welcome it, she didn't dare do so here.

"Our current stance in Delaphine," Annora continued, "according to the most recent missive I received, is one of deference to existing allies while our leadership considers the situation. Jaysen is the rightful heir. As such, they are more inclined to support him, but they are aware of the significant conflict between Vanris and the Thaelians he returned with, so they look to you to take the lead. We have not yet gotten word from Fallend that I know of, but a messenger was sent from Dekingham to advise them of Delaphine's position on the matter."

Her father nodded. "We sent a messenger of our own to Delaphine several days ago. Jaysen and the Thaelian council were behind an attack on the combined Delaphinian and Vanrian fleet we sent to Thaelis. He also took Khesran Veyl prisoner and attempted to coerce her into marriage to force an alliance. She and those taken with her were fortunate enough to escape." Annora's eyes widened as he spoke, and her jaw visibly tightened.

It was possible she knew people in that fleet, or perhaps it simply appalled her that Jaysen would commit such crimes. Either way, the attack on the fleet was an attack against both their countries. "The crown prince would have to provide an extremely compelling argument to gain our support now, but we have not yet decided to grant it to the king regent, as his recent actions suggest intentions to act against Vanris."

"It sounds as if you don't find either option appealing, Majesties." She bowed her head in a gesture that would encourage an appearance of deference, though Veyl caught the edge of burning curiosity in her tone. This was information the Delaphinian king and queen would want to know. "If I may ask, what other possibilities are you exploring?"

Arhk and her mother regarded the woman with the same careful reservation. Her father considered Annora as well, but with a fondness that spoke positively of the brief time she had served under him at the end of the war.

"We could wait to see who emerges victorious and approach them while they are still recovering from that conflict and vulnerable, or..." he paused, an invitation in the glint in his eyes.

"Or you could launch an attack while they are fighting each other and install someone else on the throne," Annora speculated.

Arhk gave his son a look that somehow rode the line between fondness and mild reprimand. He had told Veyl more than once that he thought her father was too trusting. "These are matters we have yet to finish discussing with the full council." He stood. "I will have one of our guards show you to where you can rest and refresh yourself while we deliberate, Captain."

Annora bowed deeply to Veyl's parents, the khemron and khevarin of Vanris, then allowed Arhk's appointed escort to usher her from the room. When she was gone,

Veyl's mother's attention shifted to her, and the skin tightened on the back of her neck before that silver-eyed gaze.

"We would like to revisit the subject of Wavelord Kronach. You spent a little time around him, Veyl."

"You don't... Not as..." She paused, gathering her thoughts, the wavelord leaning in uncomfortably close in her memories, his lips brushing against her ear, his fingertips biting into her jaw. Those moments were nothing compared to the torments Jaysen had seared in her mind, but the man did not respect physical boundaries, and his harsh ways made it hard for her to trust him. She shook her head. "No. Kronach is not someone I would consider putting on the throne. He may have aided me, but I believe it was more for his own amusement than out of any sense of kindness or justice."

"I think he would consider taking the throne if offered it, but he would want more than that," Kyril added. "You would need to offer him something he considered of great value to make it worth his time and effort." His gaze shifted to her, any accompanying emotions well hidden beneath the coolness in his silver-blue eyes. "Something like the hand of a wave-touched khesran."

Anger flared in her so powerfully that the absence of any crackling energy in her chest made her more certain than ever that Arhk was right. Her Frightener ability truly was gone. Why would Kyril suggest such a thing? Not ten minutes ago, in the training area, she thought the connection between them might be rekindling. Apparently, that had been the mere fancy of a desperate imagination.

She wasn't sure who in the room objected most vehemently to his statement, but there was comfort in her parents being foremost among them.

"That is out of the question," her mother snapped.

"The only suggestion more offensive would be to offer her hand to one of the current contenders for the throne. Such an arrangement is not up for consideration." She stood, casting a frosty glance in Kyril's direction. "We should take this conversation to the full council."

Veyl rose, refusing to look at Kyril, and hurried out with her parents, Seyn staying close beside her.

To be continued…